## A Gentleman's Wager

The soft rasp of silk accompanied Lucerne's departure from the *chaise longue*. Bella was sure a silent signal had passed between the two men as Lucerne crossed to the hearthrug. Perhaps they were waiting for her to leave. Well, if they wanted that they would have to be more forthright. Tonight she was determined to stand her ground.

Lucerne took the brandy balloon from Vaughan's hand. He drained the contents then set it firmly on the mantel. Vaughan's expression darkened, and he raised one eyebrow quizzically. He looked at the glass and then at Lucerne. Something was brewing. She knew it.

Lucerne caught a handful of Vaughan's dark hair. Tension seemed to ripple through their bodies. Bella sniffed at the air, suddenly aware that she could make out the musky undercurrent of male arousal. Then the men were hip against hip in the darkness, pressing together, bruising each other with their erections. It was so unlike the previous occasion that she's seen them kiss. They were relaxed, oblivious to their spectator or the effect they were having on her. Bella felt faint: Lucerne and Vaughan were as beautifully matched as sun and moon. She was jealous of their symmetry, and wanted to be a part of it.

**By the same author**

Dark Designs
Phantasmagoria
Broken Angel (In the Novella Collection *Possession*)
Passion of Isis

# A Gentleman's Wager

Madelynne Ellis

BLACK LACE

Black Lace books contain sexual fantasies.
In real life, always practise safe sex.

This edition first published in 2008 by
Black Lace
Thames Wharf Studios
Rainville Rd
London W6 9HA

First published in 2003 by Black Lace



A catalogue record for this book is available from the British Library.

*www.black-lace-books.com*

Typeset by SetSystems Ltd, Saffron Walden, Essex
Printed and bound by CPI Bookmarque Ltd, Croydon. CR0 4TD

The paper used in this book is a natural, recyclable product made from wood grown in sustainable forests. The manufacturing process conforms to the regulations of the country of origin.

ISBN 978 0 352 33800 6 [UK]
ISBN 978 0 352 34173 0 [USA]

Distributed in the USA by Holtzbrinck Publishers, LLC, 175 Fifth Avenue, New York, NY 10010, USA

To Dom
Because it's all your fault.

# 1

'Faster, faster! Come on!'

Bella twisted in the saddle to peer at the distant figure of her groom. Only the low boundary wall and the brook stood between her and victory. She took them at a charge, and cleared them in two easy bounds.

By the old mill pond, she reined in her mare and slipped from the saddle to land among the reeds. Although it was early September, the day was sticky and sweet like honey, drowned with an oppressive heat that made everything damp. It was far too hot to be racing. Her pulse pounded in her head after the short gallop, so that she almost felt that she'd rather be at home, sipping iced tea on the lawn and eating strawberries. But that meant entertaining her neighbours, smiling at their conversation and pretending she cared about their petty gossip.

Bella pulled off her hat and used it to shield her eyes while she waited.

Mark cleared the wall, then slowed his mount to wade the shallow copper-tinted water. He stopped a few feet from her.

'Where were you?' she asked.

Mark's thighs flexed as he dismounted, pulling his homespun breeches tight across his muscular rear. Safely on the ground, he eyed her thoughtfully with one coffee-coloured eye, the second masked by his long fringe.

'Next time you can ride this old nag, then we'll see who wins.'

'Certainly, if you ride side-saddle.'

His brown gaze danced over the bulky, unwieldy saddle, then over Bella's long skirt. 'Fine,' he agreed. 'Let's do it now.'

Bella shook her head. Her chemise was plastered to her back, and her boned stays rubbed more than usual. She wanted to sit by the pond for a while and cool her feet. 'Maybe in a while,' she said dismissively.

'Scared I'll beat you?'

'No.'

Mark rubbed his hand along the edge of his fur-lined jaw, and gave her a crooked, wolfish smile. 'So get in the saddle and we'll race.'

To be called chicken-hearted by her groom was too much. Bella sighed, but hitched up her dress and put her foot in the stirrup.

The warm leather of the unfamiliar saddle felt strange between her thighs; it was nearly sixteen years since she'd sat astride a horse. She'd been eight when her father had given her the vile choice: either ride side-saddle like a lady, or not at all. The threat of losing her pony had won her obedience then. Now she saluted to heaven and her father. No use dwelling in the past when there was a race to be won.

'Where to?' asked Mark, his long legs folded around the uncomfortable side-saddle. To be fair, he looked more at ease than she felt.

Bella peered at the horizon. Grey sheep dotted the North Yorkshire hillsides and in a distant hollow, murky smoke curled from the tall chimneys of the mine that her grandfather had started and her brother now owned – too far. Nearer, across the valley stood Lauwine Hall, its rooftops just visible between the trees. The absent owner had neglected the old house for years, and she thought ahead to how the overgrown gardens would offer some welcome shade.

She nodded her head in that direction. 'Lauwine.'

'All right. Ready?'

Bella dug in with her heels; pushed the horse into a canter down the hillside, determined to prove she was the better rider. She doubted Mark had ever ridden side-saddle before. He was wobbling slightly but, considering how the leather was chafing her bare thighs, that wasn't much of an advantage.

She charged across the footpath at the base of the valley and began the gentle ascent across the fields towards the gates. The beat of hooves sounded muffled in the still air, except for the occasional ring of iron against the patches of bare rock. To her left, Mark was gaining ground. Bella grimaced with determination and swept back her crop, goading the horse to greater exertion. She reached the old gate a fraction behind Mark, sore above her stocking tops and faint from the heat.

'Ouch,' she complained, and pushed her skirts between her thighs to stop them chafing. The saddle had given her friction burns. If she was going to ride astride again she'd have to wear breeches, or at least long fussy underwear.

'Too bad,' Mark offered as he helped her down. He wiped the perspiration from his brow with the back of his hand. 'I still won.'

Bella turned her back on him to peer through the rusted gate: a dried ribbon of earth and rough grasses led through the trees to the house. She gave the wrought iron a push and it creaked open. 'Shall we?'

Leaving the horses tethered by the entrance, they ventured along the overgrown avenue. Bella ran ahead to caress the cracked stone of a beautifully endowed faun. Its silent, pleading expression brought out her coquettish side. As she touched its stone manhood, her eyes locked with Mark's. She'd planned to have him this afternoon; it was just a matter of when. Losing the race meant that she wouldn't have to ask. He'd demand his prize soon enough.

Bella smiled and shot a look at his sweat-streaked shirt. Her groom, like the land around them, was open to her gaze. Judging from his jaunty stride and the smirk on his lips, she knew he was already imagining a tumble with her in the long grass.

At the back of the house the roses bloomed uninhibited, blood red, hard up against the mullioned windows. Wild flowers mingled with the weeds in a flood of colour. Bella stood at the top of the lawn with the grass and the tall yellow buttercups licking her thighs, and watched the summer breeze make ripples through the lawn. She plucked at the ties on her bodice and, once freed from the constriction, breathed a deep lungful of air.

Mark beckoned to her and she joined him by the huge willow tree that dominated the lawn. 'You owe me a prize,' he said. Bella nodded. They scrambled beneath the shady boughs and collapsed against the soft earth, Bella on top.

The fabric of his shirt clung to the contours of his chest. She could smell his body, a musky blend of sweat and horses. His lips moved against hers, nibbling and teasing. Bella tugged the linen from his breeches so that she could lick the perspiration from his skin. The salty taste on her tongue sharpened her hunger for him. Mark's flat, penny-shaped nipples crinkled. Sparing a glance down, she confirmed that his prick was hard too, and already straining towards her touch.

'Have mercy, Bella.' He licked his lips. 'Suck him, just a little ... please,' he added in a voice like warm butter.

Bella shimmied down his body. His cock already lifted the flap fastening of his breeches, tenting the fabric. She kissed him through the cloth, tormenting him with the promise of her mouth.

'How much do you want it?'

Mark's deep-brown eyes glazed. 'You don't need me to answer that.'

She opened his buttons with her teeth, nuzzled into the curls around his root, then let the head press into her mouth. The challenge was to take him all, something she'd never worked out how to do. After the second attempt left her gasping for air, she concentrated her attention on the head, and used her hands on his shaft. His sharp breaths rapidly turned into tiny contented groans. Eager for more, he lifted his hips up to her.

'Shhh! What was that?' Bella hissed.

Mark shook his head, and pushed his cock back towards her lips. Bella merely licked him, then turned her head aside. Along with the birdsong and the rustle of branches, there was another low whisper of movement. Someone or something was wading through the long grass.

'I think someone's coming.'

Mark groaned. A silver bead of dew seeped from the eye of his cock. 'Ignore them. It doesn't matter.'

'I just want to see who it is.'

'Bella!' He grasped her wrist and slid his cock into her palm, then nodded at his straining erection. 'It won't take a minute.'

She frowned and cautiously brushed aside a handful of green twigs to peer out. About twenty feet away, two men stood on the lawn. The man nearest to her was blond, and wore a beautifully cut blue satin frock coat. Bella took her hand away from Mark's cock to rub her eyes, and ignored his moan of complaint. Lauwine infrequently saw visitors. The miners sometimes came here to catch hares, but this pair weren't poachers – they were gentlemen.

Behind her Mark was grumbling, but, surprisingly, he hadn't taken his cudgel in hand.

'It's certainly not the crumbling ruin I've been led to believe.' The man in the blue coat encompassed the house with a gesture, unaware that he'd captured Bella's attention.

'No, but it still needs work. Nature has seen fit to reclaim its own. I'll give you that the walls and timbers are sound, and the furnishings are dated but functional. But you're unlikely to impress anyone.' The other man was plump and dressed like a squire. When he turned, Bella recognised him as Charles Aubury, a local landowner.

'I'm settled on the country, Charles. You may as well accept it. London's lost its charm.'

'Well then, it may as well be here.'

'My thoughts exactly.' He turned towards the house. 'The labourers have been at work for a month and I'm satisfied with the main house, although the east wing isn't fit to be seen. Work on the gardens will commence tomorrow, and I hope to move in by the start of October.'

'Bella!' Mark complained.

Still intrigued, Bella rolled over and presented him with her bottom. She watched the blond man carefully smooth the line of his coat. A flash of sunlight hit the glass in the French doors and briefly dazzled her.

Mark smacked her, half-heartedly. 'What's so damned interesting?'

'You're mad, Marlinscar,' said Aubury. 'You've not spent winter in the country, have you?'

'No, but I'm sure it can't be that bad, and after a bottle of brandy I don't suppose it'll be any worse.' They stepped into the building and swung the door to behind them.

Comprehension dawned. He was the owner, Viscount Marlinscar, Lucerne. She let out a long whisper. Sudden tears prickled in her eyes. Bella blinked slowly to clear them, but they escaped to trickle down her cheeks. It would be wonderful to have the hall inhabited again but, sadly, it would mean the end of the hayfield lawn. Soon a whole flock of servants would move in, and Lauwine would no longer be her own private sanctuary. Certainly sucking off her groom in sight of its windows would be out of the question.

With that thought she remembered Mark, and let the branches fall back into place.

Mark's erection had dwindled. The length was still there, but the rigidity had gone.

'Sorry,' she murmured as she sidled up to him to place an affectionate kiss on his jaw. 'They're gone now.'

'Thank God for that.' He nuzzled against her cheek. Bella dropped a hand to his lap. The shaft of his cock was warm and soft. She stroked it rhythmically, watching his dark eyes cloud with lust as he stiffened. Within seconds, he was hard again.

'Bella,' he murmured, placing his hands on her shoulders and pushing her down. She rubbed her cheek against his chest and stomach, then circled his navel with her tongue, briefly dipping into its hollow. Ignoring his pleading eyes and over-eager cock, she straddled him and pressed her pubis into his face.

'Lick me, just a little,' she said in imitation of his earlier words, and rocked her hips in encouragement. 'Come on, Mark, if you want it, you have to give me something first.'

His groan was muffled, but he obediently thrust his tongue into her. He lapped, twirled and licked at her until he'd coaxed her clitoris from its hood. A couple more strokes and she found herself climbing towards orgasm.

That's it, she thought, as she squirmed over his hot mouth and felt the prickle of his stubble. Her clitoris leapt. Waves of light spirited her skywards. Only his mouth was important. Nothing else mattered: not his needs, or his painful erection – nothing.

Disconnected, panting, floating somewhere close as the afterglow washed through her, Bella was dimly aware of him gently kissing her. His lips softly grazed her swollen mound, almost bringing her back down.

'Do I get a turn now?' he asked, his voice still muffled and slightly hoarse.

Bella lifted her buttocks and wriggled down his body so that she captured his cock between her thighs and the ruddy head nuzzled into her wet quim. The thrill she got from it surprised her; her body wanted to welcome him. It would feel so good just to let him slip inside, but making him wait would be even better.

'Say please,' she demanded, grasping his hands and pinning him down.

Mark struggled unconvincingly. He could easily have broken free, but chose not to. Instead, he lifted himself towards her in a wordless plea.

'Say it or you'll get nothing.'

He clamped his mouth closed and shook his head from side to side. Bella smiled. She rolled her hips so that her outer lips rubbed along the length of his shaft, ready to engulf him. She'd already made him shiny with her dew. Fresh beads of moisture peppered his upper lip. She licked at them and stared down into his eyes.

'Oh, God!' he gasped. 'All right . . . please!'

She took hold of his cock, briefly releasing his hands in order to guide him inside, and then held him down again. Mark panted and struggled. He lifted himself, wanting her, driving into her. On top and in control, Bella rode him hard, taking all the pleasure she could from his stiff cock. Their bodies slapped together; his balls rubbed against her bottom. Her tongue slid into his mouth as their motion became more frenzied.

Bella's sex was all of a tingle. She was climbing again, but she knew she wouldn't get there in time. She'd already put his stamina to the test.

Mark gave a dry gasp. Bella felt his penis twitch, then pulse with life. His spine flexed and he groaned as if he'd been hit. She gripped him tightly with every muscle in her body and willed it to last just one minute more, even as it ended. For a moment, they lay very still. Then he pushed her off, wiped his spent cock on his rumpled shirt, and tucked the linen back into his breeches. When she didn't move, he lifted her hand and kissed her knuckles.

'We should leave, before whoever it was comes back.'

'You go,' said Bella with a heavy heart. Whenever she was eager for more, men always wanted to give up, and frequently they just wanted to roll over and sleep.

Mark frowned. 'We should both go.'

'No, you go. Take the horses. I'll follow on foot.'

It was a half-dozen miles back home to Wyndfell Grange and, although his lips thinned, a sure sign that he was unhappy, he didn't argue. Without another word, he slipped away.

She must have dozed off, Bella realised on waking some time later. The sun was still hot and strong above. She wiped the perspiration from her brow with a grimy hand and listened for voices.

The grounds were quiet. Bella slipped out of the willow cave and headed down the slope of the deserted lawn to the path by the river. As she strolled idly along the leafy track a few moments later, the men had become indefinite, as illusory as her dreams. That was until she almost ran into Lucerne.

Viscount Marlinscar was stooped behind the bushes, rinsing his hands in the stream. The other man was nowhere in sight. Bella dropped to the ground, and scurried into the foliage of the rhododendrons. A reprimand for trespassing was not how she had envisioned her introduction to him. Thankfully, he didn't notice her sudden motion. It seemed her best option was to wait here until he left. In the meantime, she could get a closer look at him.

Bella flattened herself against the damp ground and wriggled forwards. With her cheek pressed to the earth, she had a reasonably clear view of him sitting on the river-bank. He'd hung his coat over a branch and, as she waited, he lifted his loose white shirt over his head, stood and removed his breeches.

Bella blinked then gaped at his bare bottom. A warm glow of desire washed over her as her breath caught. Once she'd recovered from the shock, she realised that not only was he wealthy and fashionable, he was also attractive, something of a rare combination. Mostly, men of any standing or taste seemed unaccountably saddled with gout or else had two chins or none at all. Not so Lucerne Marlinscar: he was by comparison touched with angelic features, though undoubtedly far from angelic by nature.

Lucerne dropped into the river.

While he dipped below the water, Bella wriggled a little closer, eager for a better view. Despite the niggling doubts in her head about invading his privacy, her response was one of rapt fascination. His lack of modesty delighted her. Here was a man who wasn't afraid of his body, who paid no heed to convention.

Deep inside her, the spark of her thwarted orgasm rekindled. Moisture welled between her thighs, and she clamped her legs together. However, instead of reducing her need, the strain only fuelled it. She closed her eyes and could almost feel him beneath her fingertips: hot to the touch, his body heat great enough to evaporate the gleaming beads of moisture left from his swim. His skin was silky smooth, soft against her own. She gasped in anticipation and opened her eyes.

Lucerne looked up, straight ahead to where she lay. A flicker of ice passed through his deep-blue eyes. Convinced she'd been seen, Bella shuffled backwards while her stomach did a triple jump. She lay still for what felt like eternity.

He had seen her, hadn't he?

It was time she went, Bella realised, coming to her senses. He obviously hadn't seen her. Reluctantly, for she was still drawn to him, she stood and began to dust herself off. A few too many twigs and her brother Joshua would ask questions. She was all ready to sneak away and force a path through the rhododendrons when a splash turned her head back to the water.

Lucerne emerged from the stream, glittering like the morning dew on the grass. Upright and completely naked before her, he paused to tilt his head to the sun, and run his hands through his tangled hair.

Oh, yes! Oh, my!

Bella had to fight the crazy urge to undress and join him. All thoughts of departing vanished from her head. Mesmerised, she watched the water trickle down his body. His front was every bit as pleasing as his bottom had been. Long-limbed and lean, lightly muscled across the chest, hairless except for a thin golden line that trailed down from his navel to his groin, he was like the statue of David, and everything Bella admired most.

Her focus narrowed down to one silvered droplet. She followed its winding downward journey as it traversed his abdomen, snaked across his hipbone and finally came to rest on his thigh. Bella stood open-mouthed, frozen like the statues of the fauns, but feeling unbearably hot. She hardly dared look, too terrified she'd be unable to contain a gasp of delight, but she was powerless to stop herself. Her gaze shifted slowly sideways from where the droplet rested to the dangling weight of his manhood, although dangling wasn't quite what it was doing. The contrasting temperatures of the lazy afternoon sun and the cold water had done more than wash the toils of the day away. He stood glowing and half-erect.

Apparently unaware of or unconcerned by his condition, Lucerne waded along the bank through the thick grass. Bella followed behind the treeline, drawn to him by an invisible thread. A few paces on he settled among the rushes and disappeared from sight.

'No! No, no, no!'

Bella looked around in frustration, seeking a vantage point. To her right stood a gnarled yew tree, with comfortable lower branches in which she could perch. She scrambled into its boughs with her skirts hitched to her knees, grazing her shins on the way up.

The view was perfect.

Lucerne lay sprawled out with his eyes closed, letting the sun dry his skin. One hand was combing through his short hair, while the other travelled an erotic, unhesitant path down his body, over his chest and across the flat plane of his stomach to his groin, where a sizeable erection lay. His penis, pale and perfect, splashed with blue veins, curved slightly to the left. The tip, to which he pressed a finger, was flushed deep plum.

Bella's mouth watered. Her body hungered for him. Fascinated by every movement and eager for more revelations, she watched him touch himself. His hand worked while he writhed luxuriously against the grass as if it were soft silk. His handsome face twitched with longing. Soon his movements became more focused.

Bella stifled her desire to go to him by biting her lip. Unconsciously she rocked herself back and forth against the branch. To touch his pale skin, tangle her fingers in the knots of his hair, were her only thoughts. Lucerne was everything. Not even the wren chirping above her head caught her attention. She wanted to come with him, but her balance was too precarious.

Lucerne reached climax with a deep groan, and painted a sticky fountain over the nearby grass. In the afterglow, his hands came back to his head and he relaxed, letting his erection slowly fade. He turned his head to one side and opened his eyes.

'What in hell?' Lucerne jerked upright, his gaze fixed on Bella perched in the tree.

Panicked, Bella came crashing down. Regaining her wits faster than him, she dashed from the underlying bush while he stared after her dumbfounded.

'Jesus! Hellfire and damnation!' she cursed. In a straight race, he would easily catch her, and that could only mean trouble. Her only hope was to weave a path through the tangled web of rhododendrons to the drive. It was unlikely that he knew the grounds as well as her.

Back on the main path, Bella sprinted down the final stretch of canopied pathway, her thighs chafing badly to remind her of the earlier race. Only when she was safely through the gates did she stop running.

She held on to the wrought iron, panting, her breath dry and heavy in her lungs. At the far end of the avenue, having given up his pursuit, Lucerne Marlinscar watched her.

Bella turned her back on him and walked away.

## 2

'Louisa!' Bella screamed and ran towards her friend, her feet crunching noisily on the gravel drive of Wyndfell Grange.

Louisa Stanley dropped her vanity case and opened her arms to greet her. 'Bella,' she said. 'I'm so glad I'm here. The coach was stifling and I had to sit opposite the same gouty reverend the whole way here.'

Bella grimaced sympathetically. 'Oh dear,' she said, then clasped Louisa in a bear hug. It was two years since they'd last seen each other and Bella had been looking forward to having her friend to stay for the winter. Louisa gasped, and her warm breath buffeted Bella's cheek. 'No exciting adventures with ghosts or highwaymen to share, then?' Bella's gaze flickered eagerly over her friend's pale face but Louisa shook her head.

'Um, no. Afraid not.'

Unchecked by the admission, Bella's smile grew wider as Louisa's trunk was lifted from the carriage. 'Never mind. You're here now and I've loads to tell you. Lauwine is occupied again. Can you believe it?' She gave a small laugh. 'Viscount Marlinscar has taken residence and, oh, God –' Her voice dropped to a whisper. '– Joshua's invited him and a friend of his to lunch tomorrow. They called yesterday to formally introduce themselves, but I was out visiting Mrs Castleton.'

'Why the whisper?'

Bella shook her head. 'I'll tell you upstairs. Come on.'

She snatched up Louisa's vanity case and tugged her towards the front door.

In the guest-room, Bella sank into the mattress of the old bed and fingered the heavy embroidered drapes as she watched Louisa unpack. Two years of life in the capital had greatly changed her friend. She'd always been delicate, but London had washed the colour from her cheeks and turned her into a porcelain doll dressed in satin, velvet and lace. Bella wrinkled her nose at the vibrant yellow dress Louisa had lifted from her trunk.

'I know – you hate it,' Louisa said before Bella had a chance to comment. 'But it's the fashion, and my aunt insisted. I suppose you're still living in your riding-habit.'

Bella stroked her hand over her plum velvet outfit. The slightly worn pile was familiar to the touch and becoming a little shabby. She'd had it especially made to resemble a man's frock coat, and it was her favourite even if it was nearly five years old.

'Not all the time.'

'Just most of it.' They shared a smile and two years fell away, as if this was an ordinary conversation on an ordinary day before Louisa's brother had died. After that, she'd been forced to leave Yorkshire to live with her aunt. Bella, who had never been out of the North Riding, sometimes dreamed of seeing the capital.

'So will you tell me why you're at odds about Viscount Marlinscar, or do I have to guess?' asked Louisa. She lifted another dress from her trunk. This one was a more tasteful shade of lilac. Holding both gowns, she opened the closet and sneezed as dust and the smell of mothballs wafted into the room. On the bed, Bella merely wrinkled her nose at the reek of camphor. She leaned across to a drawer and took out a beribboned lavender bag.

'You won't like it,' she said, as she passed Louisa the perfumed sack.

Louisa knotted the ribbon around one of the hangers. 'That doesn't surprise me. Did you meet him at a party?'

A party. Bella hadn't been to one in ages, whereas Lucerne was probably invited to dinner every night. Why hadn't Joshua invited him on an evening when everyone was more relaxed, instead of during the day?

'No, wandering about his garden,' she said.

Louisa pushed the door a little too firmly and it slammed sharply. Tight-lipped, she glanced between Bella and the closet as if unsure what to say.

'It's not that bad. I watched him swimming in the river. That's all.' Bella had to hide her expression in the drapes. Louisa was something of a prude when it came to men. Gracious, Bella wasn't even sure she'd ever kissed one. But just the thought of Lucerne Marlinscar – his creamy flawless skin, his long lean body dipping in and out of the water and his hand working over his beautiful erect cock – plastered a huge grin across her face.

'That's all?' Louisa said stiffly.

'More or less.'

'Somehow, I don't believe you. Even if he were swimming in the buff, you wouldn't fret over meeting him this much. There's obviously something else.'

Bella chewed her bottom lip and clenched her hands to stop them straying towards her thighs. She wondered how much to tell. She'd definitely skip the part with Mark. Louisa wouldn't understand that; servants were just the people who did her bidding. As for Lucerne, she found herself surprisingly reluctant now that Louisa was asking, although all week she'd been itching to tell someone.

'Confession time,' said Louisa. She patted the lid of her trunk, a habit she must have picked up from her aunt. She stared expectantly at Bella, who remained on the bed.

'All right, I watched him masturbate . . . watched him play with himself,' Bella explained, uncertain that her friend would understand the word. She slipped her shoes off, and curled her toes into the cotton sheets of the bed. 'He lay down on the river-bank after his swim, and he looked so peaceful, so . . . anyway, I couldn't help myself. Now you can be shocked.'

Louisa didn't look even slightly shocked. 'Did he see you?' she asked.

Bella frowned, puzzled by Louisa's composure. In the past when Bella had tried to talk about men, her friend had generally turned scarlet and accused her of harlotry. Clearly she'd become used to gossip.

'Well, we didn't exactly get to formal introductions, but yes, he saw me. I think he might recognise me and I don't know how he'll react. Can you imagine the fuss Joshua will make if he finds out? He'll probably try to stop me leaving the house.'

Their parents had died of influenza when Bella was just a girl, and Joshua had inherited the estate, the mine and guardianship of his sister. Barely a man, he'd had trouble controlling her, and she'd driven out one governess after another. Thankfully, these days Joshua trusted her not to get into too much mischief. Consequently Bella enjoyed more freedom than even her married friends did, for she was burdened with neither husband nor chaperone.

Louisa furrowed her brow. 'You should have thought about that earlier.' She picked up her linen and crossed the rug to the chest of drawers. 'As I see it, either you can claim to be ill, which will look suspicious, or you'll just have to brazen it out.'

Bella scowled at her back. 'Thanks for your support.'

Louisa shrugged good-naturedly. 'You do have a knack

of making trouble for yourself,' she said over her shoulder. 'Anyway, you said Lord Marlinscar was bringing a friend. Any idea who it is?'

Bella shook her head. When Joshua had told her, she'd been too overwhelmed to pay much attention to details. 'I think his name's Wakefield.'

'Oh!'

Louisa quickly busied herself with her undergarments. Bella peered curiously at her back for a moment, half-convinced she'd seen Louisa's lips tug into a sly smile, then she slipped her feet back into her shoes and got off the bed.

'I'll go and see how long dinner will be,' she said. 'Come down when you're finished.'

Viscount Marlinscar, six feet two, clothed and with the fire glow warming his pale skin, was every bit as delicious as Bella remembered. Her pulse fluttered in her throat as she stepped over the threshold into the parlour where Joshua was greeting him. Over breakfast, she'd been having doubts about the sense of watching him earlier, but now she didn't regret it one bit.

'Mister Rushdale. Thank you again for inviting us.'

'Lord Marlinscar and Captain Wakefield,' Joshua replied. He turned towards Bella. 'Gentlemen, allow me to introduce my sister, Annabella, and our guest, Miss Louisa Stanley.'

Louisa dropped into a formal curtsey, but Bella was too busy wondering if she was about to be recognised and she barely gave Captain Wakefield a glance. She'd make up for her manners later.

'Miss Stanley, we meet again,' said the Captain softly.

'You are already acquainted?' Joshua asked, and his sharp gaze flickered back and forth between the two.

'Yes, we travelled on the same coach,' Louisa explained. 'Captain Wakefield was kind enough to keep the rogues at bay. Well, the reverend, at least.'

Meanwhile, Bella met Lucerne's eyes and saw an unmistakable flicker of recognition. She watched, temporarily dumbstruck, as he left the chattering group and stepped forwards to meet her.

'Enchanted, madam,' he said before pressing his bow-shaped lips to her fingertips. He studied her along the length of her extended arm, his azure gaze taking in each detail of her face and sparking the first traces of a blush across her cheekbones. 'It is so nice to meet you again, Miss Rushdale,' he said, under his breath so the others wouldn't hear. 'I already feel as though we're acquainted.'

Bella snatched her hand away, but Lucerne's smile didn't waver. He took hold of her elbow instead. 'Shall we sit down?'

Bella reluctantly let him guide her to the window seat; refusing him would draw too much attention. At least on the far side of the room they'd be out of earshot of her brother. She squeezed herself as far into the scuffed upholstery as possible, hoping he would take the hint that she didn't want to discuss her misdemeanour, but Lucerne sat deliberately close.

Bella stared out of the leaded panes at the kitchen garden, presenting him with her profile. His gaze was making the hairs on the nape of her neck stand on end. She wondered if he thought he had a right to stare after she'd blatantly spied on him. She felt very uncomfortable.

'Am I such a monster that you want to hide from me every time we meet?' asked Lucerne.

Bella turned her head in response to his voice. Lucerne opened his eyes wider as if wordlessly repeating the question.

'I don't know. Are you?' she said. Faced with his amused expression, her sense of unease evaporated.

'Lord, I hope not.'

Bella shuffled forwards on the seat so that her skirt covered his knee. She noticed his attention shift briefly to the burgundy cloth, but he didn't brush it off. Instead, he inclined his head towards her face again.

'What were you doing in my tree?' he asked with sudden candour.

Bella couldn't prevent her sudden intake of breath or the nervous smile that immediately tweaked the corners of her mouth. Their eyes locked for a moment. A desire to laugh fluttered in her throat. 'Daydreaming,' she said mischievously.

'Is that so?' Lucerne favoured her with a smile that drove away the last of her fears of exposure. Apparently, their awkward second meeting was going to be a lot easier than she'd envisaged.

Throughout their lunch of soup, grouse and poached salmon, Bella strained to keep her eyes off Lucerne. It was hardly ladylike to stare at the man as he ate, but thankfully the conversation was mostly between Lucerne and her brother, and her interest went unobserved. Also unobserved, at least by Bella, were the intimate looks passing between Louisa and Captain Wakefield. It wasn't until Lucerne pointed them out afterwards, as they strolled around the garden together, that Bella even gave the captain a second glance.

'They seem quite taken with each other,' Lucerne said, indicating the pair who were seated in the wooden arbour, out of the chill breeze that was gently buffeting the empty swing. The weak afternoon sun was streaming into the tiny shelter, flecking the captain's light-brown hair with soft gold highlights and making Louisa seem even more fragile than usual. Bella supposed that they appeared quite interested in each other, but Louisa was always unerringly polite.

'Are you attempting to match-make?' she asked, and peered up at Lucerne. He shook his head.

'Lord no, that would never do. Wakefield can barely afford his own upkeep, let alone set up house.'

'Ah, but Louisa has money of her own. She inherited her brother's estate.'

'Did she,' he mused, and rubbed a finger over his bottom lip and chin as if pondering something. 'Still, society demands.'

Bella wondered if he thought his friend might be after Louisa's money, but she didn't voice the concern; nor did Lucerne, whose expression had become rather serious. Instead, she focused on Wakefield again, trying to see him as a prospective lover for her friend. He was pleasing enough to look at, straight nosed, clean-shaven with smoky-grey eyes. His uniform was rather lovely, though: all scarlet with a silver trim and gleaming silver buttons and gorget. Bella had no idea which regiment it represented, but it must have been very expensive.

'Surely he isn't penniless,' she remarked.

Lucerne stopped walking and rested his hand against the section of trellis work supporting the sweet peas. 'No, but his father left him debts and he has a few of his own, as well as four sisters to support.' He paused for thought and suddenly his expression grew a lot lighter. 'In any case, who said his intentions were honourable? We all know what soldiers are like – not as bad as sailors, but even so . . .'

Bella gave Wakefield a cold hard stare. She hoped he wasn't stringing her friend along. She didn't want to see Louisa married to some decrepit old man because the actions of some idiot soldier had ruined her.

'How do you know he has any intentions?' she asked Lucerne. Switching her attention to Louisa, she noticed that her friend did look rather smitten; there was a hint of colour in her cheeks that hadn't been there at breakfast and clearly wasn't a result of the cold air.

'Because he regaled me with tales of her charms, their meeting and the tedious coach journey all last night.' Lucerne yawned theatrically and brushed his blond hair back from his face. 'No need to worry, though, it's all above board and hopelessly proper. Just one chaste kiss outside the coaching inn, unless she's mentioned something Frederick didn't.'

Bella sucked her tongue, loath to admit that Louisa hadn't confided a thing. 'No,' she said, and her voice sounded reedy and defensive. 'She never even mentioned him.' Instead, she'd let Bella ramble on about Lauwine being occupied when she'd obviously already known, having met Wakefield on the coach.

'How long are you going to stay at Lauwine?' she asked, deliberately changing the subject before her sour thoughts ruined her mood for the afternoon.

Lucerne shrugged his broad shoulders. 'At least until Christmas, I've guests until then, and possibly until spring if I find plenty to entertain myself with.'

'Do you ride? I could show you the best places to go,' offered Bella, thinking of the many desolate stretches of moor where they could be alone together. There was a rocky plateau about three miles away where she'd first seduced Mark, which she thought Lucerne might like to see.

Lucerne tilted his head and moved a fraction closer so that she could feel his warm breath against her ear. 'That could be fun; we'll have to arrange a date.'

A shiver of excitement tingled in Bella's chest and throat. She swallowed as his fingers brushed lightly against her upper arm, stroking gently over the pile fabric of her sleeve. He held her gaze a moment, then broke eye contact and pulled out his pocket watch, an ornate silver affair with a decorated face. 'It's time Wakefield and I were leaving.'

'Already?' Bella said, shocked by his sudden change of demeanour.

'Yes, I'm expecting someone. We'll have to finish our conversation some other time.' He crossed the lawn to where Wakefield was sitting with Louisa, Bella trailing behind him. She wondered if she should mention going riding again. Maybe he was free tomorrow. The possibility made her feel rather panicked. Joshua emerged from the house and walked over to join them.

'Now?' Wakefield asked. Lucerne nodded and Wakefield rose to his feet. 'It's been a delight meeting you all,' he said, sharing a long slow look with Louisa and a very brief nod to Bella.

Lucerne gave the three of them a rather more formal bow. 'Thank you, ladies. Mister Rushdale. You'll have to come to the hall soon.' He touched his lips to Bella's hand, holding her there a fraction too long for decorum.

Bella watched the men ride to where the lane curved out of sight behind the hedgerow, and then turned towards the house with Louisa.

'Your journey obviously wasn't that tedious,' said Bella, trying to keep the accusatory tone from her voice. 'I suppose the gouty reverend had driven the bit about making love to a young army captain out of your head, or doesn't that count as an adventure any more?'

Louisa turned scarlet and bowed her head. 'It wasn't like that,' she said rather quickly, and kicked a pebble so that it rattled on the flagstones by the front door. 'We only met the night before last. I know hardly anything about him, but he mentioned Lauwine, so when you mentioned it as well I put two and two together.'

'And didn't think to tell me.'

Louisa nervously twisted her finger into one of her blonde ringlets. 'What do you want to know?'

'Have you kissed him?'

'Once, outside the coaching inn. But that's all.'

Bella opened her eyes and mouth wide, making a pretence of being shocked. 'Louisa!' she hissed. 'What would your aunt say?'

Louisa didn't take it as a joke. She covered her oval face with one hand, hiding her expression. 'I don't know,' she murmured through her fingers. 'Something horrid, I expect. That she should never have let me come here.'

'You're of age.'

'I know, but you don't know what she's like. She thinks any man under the age of fifty is a libertine and a scoundrel who's only after one thing, so the only men I meet are stuffy, balding, and fawn over me as if I'm some sort of doll. It's maddening. Frederick's six times as good as any of them.'

Bella valiantly resisted the urge to smile. She'd never seen Louisa quite so animated. 'She's not here, Lou. You can do what you want, with whomever you want. I'm not going to tell her, and Joshua's easy to fool.' She clasped her friend's cold hand and drew her indoors. 'Come on, forget it. Tell me more about Wakefield instead. What regiment's he from?'

'The 33rd Regiment of Foot, Yorkshire West Riding,' she recited carefully. 'Under Colonel Wesley. He was fighting in Flanders until last year.'

Later that night, Louisa turned feverishly in bed, tangling her legs in the sweat-soaked sheets. Perspiration ran down her neck and over the pulse point, to pool in the triangular indent by her collarbone. A low, telling moan escaped her lips. She writhed, arched her back and clawed at the cotton beneath her, then with a shudder she awoke.

Within the shrouded four-poster bed, everything was black. Parched and sleepy, she felt for the edge of the curtain, so that she could reach out for the glass of water on the bedside cabinet. Its coolness rolled past her knuckles then, with a horrid clatter, it fell to the floor.

'Blast!' she cursed, and stuck her head below the curtains to see the intact but now empty glass. The liquid formed a slightly darker patch on the carpet, which was cool against her feet once she'd swung her legs free of the bedclothes.

There'd be port – something – in the dining room, and she simply had to have something to drink. Rainwater would do. For the first time she realised it was raining outside. Out on the landing, she heard the muffled patter of large heavy drops bouncing off the tiled roof, streaming into the gutters. Shimmering rivulets ran down the other side of the panes.

The hall clock struck a quarter to two as she espied the tray of decanters, and swallowed a mouthful of the first that came to hand. Fire rippled down her throat, making her eyes water. Brandy, quite coarse. She coughed, and found the port instead.

Across from her, the tell-tale flicker of light spilled from the back parlour. Thinking someone had forgotten to blow out the candles, she delayed her return to bed to investigate. It was hardly likely that anyone was still up this late, yet something stopped her pushing the door fully open. There was barely more than a breath of sound coming from within, so low she strained to hear it, but it made her cautious as she peered around the jamb.

It took a moment for the scene to register. Joshua was

sitting in the old green armchair, facing her, his shirt unbuttoned so his chest hair was on show. To his left, a candelabra cast flickering light over his shoulder, but knelt before him with her plump round bottom on display was Emma, Bella's maid. She was wearing only her stockings and stays. The rest of her clothing was strewn about the floor.

Louisa leaned against the doorframe in mute shock, with her heartbeat sounding like a bass drum in her ears. She shook her head in denial, stunned by what she beheld. Maybe there was some sense to her aunt's warnings. She remembered what Bella had once told her about her grandfather, a notorious roué who'd split from the family, established the mine and built Wyndfell Grange. Evidently Joshua had the same degenerate streak. Anyway, it was disgusting.

Appalled, she took another peek at the lewd pair. From beneath the falls of Joshua's nankeen trousers, a virile column of flesh sprang. Tiny, pearly beads hung from the tip. Louisa blushed self-consciously as she watched Emma lick away the silvered droplets. So that was what a man's pride looked like. She didn't think she'd ever be able to look Joshua in the face again without betraying herself, and she certainly wouldn't let the maid dress her in future. The blushing heat that had started in her cheeks began to spread. When she looked down at herself, she was horrified to find her nipples erect and poking against her lawn nightdress, eager for some attention. Louisa rubbed them in a futile attempt to get them to return to their normal state. Instead, a dart of liquid delight shot through her excited body. It fizzled out between her clenched thighs, but not before it had set a different set of nerves alight, and a deeper need began to make her wet.

'Come up here.' Joshua patted his lap.

Emma obeyed and mounted him. Soon all Louisa could see of him were his limbs, his heavy ball sac and stiff member. He clasped Emma about the buttocks, lifting her up and down while sheathed inside her. She could see everything, every tiny detail, how his shaft flexed, how its colour changed, darkened a more ruddy shade with each thrust, and how it glistened with Emma's juices.

Louisa craved ... something? She remembered that was what she'd been dreaming about. She'd been with Wakefield, somewhere ... but in her mind, the details had been vague, as if seen through a veil. Now everything seemed clearer, more enticing than her fantasy.

She clutched the neck of the port decanter, gripping it as though she could squeeze some life into it. Joshua dug his fingertips into Emma's round cheeks and energetically drove himself deep into her. He gave a strange strangled grunt, then their motion ceased.

A moment later, Emma removed herself from his knee and sought out her clothes. Joshua pressed a crown into her hand once she had dressed. 'Breakfast at seven,' he said, and gave her a wink. 'Now get yourself to bed.'

'Yes, sir.' Emma slipped the coin into the cleft of her ample cleavage for safe-keeping, gave Joshua one last saucy smile, curtseyed, then flounced towards the door.

Louisa's throat closed around her yelp of discovery, stopping the sound before it escaped. Her heart fell into her stomach. Then she fled back up the rickety staircase to the guest room and cowered behind the heavy drapes, still clutching the decanter.

She pulled out the stopper and swallowed two thirsty gulps. The contents calmed her, until the warmth reached her veins and she imagined Frederick Wakefield in the chair, exposed to her, his private parts begging to be touched. Then her blood seemed to boil. She pressed her palm to her brow, frightened by the image.

'Be sensible,' she muttered to herself. 'You barely know him.'

Bella stared solemnly out of the leaded window-panes; the sky was dark and filled with the threat of distant thunder. The glorious summer had come to an abrupt end two days ago, when the morning mist had held until well after noon. 'Perfect!' she said sarcastically, as she watched the wind roll through the ling on the valley floor until the force drove the raindrops so hard against the glass that it was impossible to see out. 'We can't go riding in that.'

She twisted in her seat, turning her back on the dismal weather. She wanted to race across the fields to Lauwine with the wind in her face and her hair whipping around her; storm right up to Lucerne Marlinscar and kiss his Cupid's-bow lips; cover him with tiny love bites to satisfy her craving. She briefly envisaged herself sitting astride his hips, riding his long cock, while his mouth played over her nipples and his fingers were entwined in her pubic hair, massaging her clit. The golden sun was behind them, warming their bare skin, and around them crickets chirped in the grass.

Bella gave a long sigh. Unless he was still here in the spring, that particular fantasy wasn't going to happen. They'd both get pneumonia if they tried it now. Not that she had any certainty that any of her fantasies about Lucerne would happen. Certainly he'd teased her, but it was possible that was as far as it would ever go. She might have to rely on Mark for her fun, except she'd tried that last night when she'd gone to see him in his room above the coach house. It had been a mistake. Tired and in no mood to play her games, he'd been rough with her. Without bothering to kiss her, he'd pushed her over the foot of his narrow bed and entered her sharply from behind. The shock entry of his thick cock had felt good and she'd encouraged him to drive deeper. However, although he had pounded into her powerfully the encounter had only left her feeling more tense.

The door of the back parlour creaked as it opened, and Joshua's shadow fell across the worn carpet.

'I've something to cheer you up,' he said, and waved an envelope under her nose. The faint scent of sealing-wax drifted off the paper. Bella peered up at her brother's hawklike face. He seemed remarkably pleased with himself. His brow had crinkled above his left eye the way it did when he won at billiards or got a good price for the copper ore. She knew he'd recently done neither.

Over by the fire, Louisa put aside her sampler. 'What is it?' she asked Joshua, and Bella noted that, for some inexplicable reason, she blushed furiously when she spoke to him.

'An invitation,' he said candidly. He settled himself into the green armchair and reclined. 'It's from a certain favourite acquaintance of yours, Bella. Would you like me to read it to you?'

'Just tell me what it is,' she snarled. She was too wrapped up in herself to bother to catch his meaning. It was probably a dull proposal for a Halloween dance at the assembly hall. It happened every year with the same dull people attending.

'Very well, if you promise to smile.'

Bella scowled instead.

'It's an invitation from Lucerne. He's holding a ball at Lauwine so he can introduce himself to his neighbours. He asks if we would like to remain as his guests afterwards, possibly until Christmas. Interested?'

Bella clamped her lips together, determined to hide the smile that threatened to give her away. The result was an expression somewhere between sour and stubborn.

'Bella, you've obviously charmed him – poor fellow. You could at least try to look pleased.'

'She is,' Louisa said, clearly delighted by the prospect of being closer to Wakefield. 'She's just being contrary.'

# 3

Bella's heavy riding skirt swished against the stone steps at the entrance to Lauwine Hall, dusting aside the dead leaves as she hurried towards the open door. Two weeks had passed since they'd received the invitation, and those fourteen days had crawled by so slowly that she'd started checking the clocks every half-hour to see if they'd stopped. Captain Wakefield had called twice, much to Louisa's delight, but they'd seen nothing of Lucerne. Bella optimistically assumed he was too busy with the party preparations.

She had been supposed to take the long road by carriage with Joshua and Louisa, but Bella didn't care for the claustrophobic leather interior and had sent her maid, Emma, to travel in her place, while she rode the six straight miles across the moors with Mark. The chill wind and the brisk gallop had put the colour back in her cheeks after too much time stuck indoors, and she felt invigorated and alive.

She paused on the threshold and swept her gaze over the polished marble surfaces beyond as Mark took their horses to the stables. She'd wanted to know what lay beyond this door ever since she'd been old enough to rattle the handle in vain, and she was determined to savour the moment now it had come. The plain chequer-board floor contrasted heavily with the decorative plasterwork ceiling, and the huge oil paintings, coloured predominantly black, orange and brown, created a rather dark atmosphere. She guessed that Lucerne had gone to a lot of trouble making the place habitable again. Lauwine had been neglected for over a decade.

She walked in unchallenged, surprised that nobody came running at the sound of her echoing footfalls, and passed through an archway into a second vast chamber. To her right lamplight flickered around the edge of an open doorway. A smile came to her lips as she crossed to it, picturing herself coming upon Lucerne unaware.

However, the room's sole occupant was not Lucerne, but another man with long dark hair that spilled over his shoulders in loose ringlets. His eyes were closed, and he was cradling a brandy balloon in one palm. Bella removed her kid gloves and yawned to draw his attention.

Bright, violet-coloured eyes settled on her then narrowed under long dark lashes. 'Lord Marlinscar is in the drawing room,' he drawled, then returned to his drink.

Her curiosity roused, Bella rested her head against the doorframe while she watched him sip. Graceful to the point of being languid, he drank so that the smooth liquid only just moistened his lips. He was very beautiful, even more so than Lucerne, but darkly saturnine. And, she suspected, cruel and jealous as a lover. She wondered who he was.

After a few minutes of enduring her gaze, the man turned towards her again. This time he rose from the chair. Bella's eyes lingered on his firm thighs, emphasised by his knee-length boots and black close-fitting pantaloons. As he neared the door she extended her hand for him to take, but instead of accepting it he rudely brushed past her into the hallway. Stunned, she watched him fade into the shadows of the staircase.

'Arrogant bastard,' she swore, more hurt than angry, and turned her attention back to his empty chair. A new light now spilled fresh shadows over the carpet on the far side of the room.

'I see you've met Vaughan,' Lucerne Marlinscar remarked, as he closed the cunningly disguised door behind him, so that it again blended perfectly with the bookcase. He was dressed plainly in cream and beige, and his expression was far more open and welcoming than the other man's had been.

'Evidently,' Bella said, and glanced over her shoulder into the hallway, unable to resist looking for him again. 'Another guest?'

'Yes. Vaughan Peredur Forvasham, Marquis of Pennerley, an old acquaintance. He's recently returned after several years in Italy.'

'Is he always so friendly?'

Lucerne replied with a non-committal shrug of his broad shoulders, leaving her to draw her own conclusions. He lifted her hand and pressed his lips to the soft skin of her wrist in a vexingly intimate manner that had her leaning towards him, eager for closer contact.

'I regret that nobody was here to greet you, Miss Rushdale, but you are rather early.' He cocked an elegantly arched eyebrow. 'I was expecting you to arrive with your brother. I have to wonder what you are so eager for. Not to see me ... I'm sure you've already seen enough?'

Bella bowed her head in response, but she couldn't stop herself smiling at the memory of him, nude and magnificent in the long grass. She glanced slyly at the crotch of his tailored breeches, wondering what he would look like close up, and if she'd ever get the chance to find out. All of his guests would be vying for his attention tonight; she'd better stake her claim now. She just wasn't sure how to make the first move.

'I brought my horse so that we can go riding,' she said,

awkwardly trying to explain her presence. With Mark, things had always been so easy, but then she'd been in charge. Lucerne was an entirely different matter. He was used to fashionable London parties and probably thought her country manners and clothes rather quaint.

She met his gaze again, to find his expression dancing between desire and gentle mockery. Bella parted her lips, inviting him to speak. Instead, he leaned forwards slightly. Her breath caught in her throat as she waited for him to deliver the Rubicon kiss, but he merely pressed his thumb to her lips and smiled.

'I assume your groom's taken your horse.'

Bella nodded. She scrunched up her gloves and shoved them in a pocket.

Lucerne wrinkled his forehead slightly. 'So what now? Would you like to see the house, or shall I introduce you to some of my more, ah, more sociable guests?'

'And Vaughan?' she asked. 'Did I interrupt you?'

Lucerne shook his head and then smiled. 'Don't worry, I'm sure Vaughan will entertain himself.'

Bella headed down the stairs in the direction of music and laughter, and hoped she'd pass for fashionable. Her dress had a high waist in the latest style, but perhaps she'd chosen a more vibrant shade of green than was expected. Lucerne had shown her around the areas that he'd had refurbished, then escorted her to the room which was to be hers for the duration. After that, he'd left her to change.

In the entrance hall, a footman was announcing the arrivals and guiding them towards the grand chamber. Bella followed in behind Dr Garth, the local physician, and his wife. She scanned the sea of faces. It seemed half the county had been invited.

'Bella . . . how lovely.'

Bella checked a frown, then turned to greet the voice. Millicent Hayes usually meant trouble for someone, and she had her prying sister trailing behind. Bella caught her breath – Millicent's dress was a triumph of vulgarity and sensuality. The muslin barely concealed her lavish bust, and she'd clearly dampened the fabric to make it cling. Her dark ringlets had been teased forwards to frame her face and bosom, rather than back as was the style.

'Have you been here long? Miranda and I have just arrived, and we've had a quick look about. Lauwine looks nice. Viscount Marlinscar must have spent a lot of money on it.' She leaned over conspiratorially. 'Tell me, is he very wealthy?'

Bella grunted vaguely. She didn't want to encourage her as a rival. The Hayes sisters were daughters of a wealthy haberdasher and had their eyes on advancement, although Joshua had once expressed the opinion that Millicent would make somebody's husband a wonderful mistress, implying that she'd settle for comfort and luxury over marriage and position. On the face of it, Bella was inclined to agree.

Millicent waved insincerely to someone in the crowd, then turned to her sister. 'Fetch me a drink, and find out who else is here.' She waited until Miranda had left, then turned and linked arms with Bella. 'Let's mingle. But not that way –' she tugged Bella into the thick of the crowd. '– Sir Godric's over there, and he's already drunk and lecherous.'

Louisa hurriedly smoothed rouge over her lips, then stood up straight, pulled her shoulders back and gave a sigh. She was out of time and would have to do as she was. Dressing without the help of Bella's maid had slowed things considerably, but after seeing what the girl got up to with Joshua she was keen to avoid Emma's touch. Perhaps Bella had taken the sensible option when she'd insisted on coming on horseback. The carriage was warmer, but her friend had arrived in plenty of time to dress. However, it was too late to change anything now. She snatched up her fan and skirts, and sprinted along the corridor towards the main stairs.

'Look out.'

A firm hand grasped her shoulder, bringing her to a sudden halt on the landing, and then spun her around. Slightly disoriented, Louisa put her hand out for balance and felt thick soft velvet brush against her palm. She looked up at the darkly clad figure, into the brightest violet-coloured eyes she'd ever seen.

'What's the hurry?' he asked in a low soft voice. His hands slid down her back to her waist and pulled her closer, so that his warm breath brushed her ear. Louisa blinked slowly, conscious of the heat that radiated from beneath his silk waistcoat, and aware also of the taut muscles of his abdomen, and the slight bulge beneath his breeches where his legs pressed against hers.

'I . . .' she recoiled, her breath heavy in her lungs, as her mind recalled the image of Joshua rampant in the green armchair.

'Let her go, Pennerley.'

The sound of Frederick Wakefield's familiar voice made her jump, but the grip around her waist only tightened.

'In a moment, once I've claimed my prize,' said her captor. He tilted her chin so she was looking straight into his handsome face, and lowered his mouth. Louisa instinctively parted her lips.

The sensation of his touch flooded through her already aroused body. His tongue moved between her lips and grazed hers, wakening desires she hardly dared put names to. It was a very sensual kiss, almost dizzying. Nothing like the chaste, nervous kisses she'd shared with Frederick, who gasped behind her.

Pennerley released her and she felt as if she was falling.

'Come along, Wakefield,' he said. 'We're expected downstairs.'

Louisa stood for a moment in mute shock, while Frederick's expression danced between affront and apology. A complete stranger had just stolen a kiss from her without so much as a by-your-leave, and she'd enjoyed it. She rubbed her mouth but could still feel his lips touching hers, and the sensation was strangely delicious. She wondered who he was. Frederick had called him Pennerley.

A shrill laugh from across the hall brought her back to earth. Miranda Hayes, an acquaintance of Bella's, covered her face with her fan. Louisa did her best to ignore both Miranda's childish giggles and the strange rapture she herself felt, and followed the gentlemen downstairs.

Lucerne looked appreciatively at himself in the full-length mirror that stood at the end of the Salon, while Charles Aubury hovered in the reflection. He liked the rotund landowner, but hoped that Aubury's infamous taste for gambling did not spoil anyone's enjoyment of the ball. Behind him the room was set out for cards, two neat rows of baize-topped tables lit by glittering chandeliers. The sound of a string quartet drifted through the open door, accompanied by the chatter of voices.

'Cold but beautiful,' he remarked of his appearance and smiled, remembering to be amused at his own vanity.

'Always,' said Vaughan, and he appeared in the mirror beside Lucerne. 'Your guests are asking for you.'

'Right.'

Lucerne admired their combined reflection for a moment before giving his own outfit a final once-over. He'd dressed in a black velvet coat, cut away at the front in a military style to reveal a band of his satin waistcoat. Silver braiding trailed across the front of the velvet, ran up to the collar and then across the back of the shoulders. His breeches were of cream silk, tight to show his legs and bottom to good effect – a point he hoped wouldn't be wasted on Bella, and that Vaughan seemed to have noted.

Lucerne smiled at their reflection and shook his head slightly, realising his friend was scrutinising him. He swung around to face him, but Vaughan immediately transferred his gaze to the rings on his right hand.

'The guests,' Lucerne said to fill the awkward moment, then swept between the tables with a few graceful strides. 'See that Charles doesn't start gambling immediately, would you?' he said over his shoulder as he neared the door.

Vaughan inclined his head a fraction.

'Humph!' Charles snorted disagreeably, spluttering port over the front of his salmon-pink waistcoat, but Lucerne merely smiled graciously at him and then left the room.

'Perhaps you'd care to join me at the faro table, Lord Pennerley,' suggested Charles, as he brushed the drops of port aside. His main reason for attending tonight was to make the most of the card tables, and to ogle the local maids. He wasn't about to take a blind bit of notice of Lucerne Marlinscar, who had chosen to move to the country while everyone else was heading to town. He peered hopefully up at Vaughan.

'I find faro rather dull.'

'Oh! Whist then, or basset.' He tried not to feel downcast as the marquis feigned boredom. 'Damn it, man, everyone's prepared to bet on something.'

'Perhaps.'

That was more like it. He reached for the decanter and topped up his glass, sure that with a bit more persuasion the marquis would join him.

'Tell me, Aubury. You know these parts. What do you know of Lucerne's guests?'

'Which ones?'

'Joshua Rushdale, his sister and their friend.'

'Nothing very exciting.' He grinned lewdly. 'Not like the tales I could tell you about some of the guests.' The marquis waved him back to the point with an elegant turn of his wrist that sent a spray of Spanish lace over his coat cuff. Charles sighed. He was keen to relate some of the salacious gossip he'd heard about the elder Miss Hayes, and he thought that would be more to Pennerley's taste than anything he had on Squire Rushdale. However, if talking about Joshua, who'd thrice beaten him at billiards, meant they could sit down to some cards, he was willing to go on all night. 'Rushdale's his closest neighbour,' he said.

'For what reason are they his special guests?' Vaughan interrupted.

'As I was saying, they're his close neighbours, and Wakefield pleaded. Apparently, he's set his heart on Miss Stanley.'

'So I observed. Is anyone likely to object?'

Charles irritably scratched the back of his neck where his buckram stock pinched. 'I doubt it. She doesn't have much in the way of family, except some stuffy aunt in London, and Joshua won't be interested. He likes his women warm and willing. If you take my meaning.'

'So he won't stand in the captain's way?'

'No. Why so many questions? You've not taken a fancy to her too, have you?'

The sadistic gleam that lit in Vaughan's eyes at that moment made him wish he hadn't asked. He suspected it heralded trouble.

'Can I tempt you to place a substantial bet?' Vaughan asked. Charles nodded in relief, and picked up the cards ready to deal. 'Ah, no.' Vaughan grasped the back of Charles's chair and leaned over him so that his dark ringlets grazed Aubury's shoulder. 'I had something more diverting in mind. A real bet.'

Charles wriggled uncomfortably against the cushioned seat. 'I'm not sure I follow,' he confessed, and swivelled around to see Vaughan's face. It didn't yield him any clues.

'I'm proposing that we stake sixty guineas that I can seduce Miss Stanley before Wakefield.'

'Sixty guineas on that!' Charles objected. He frowned and shook his head. 'No, damn it, man; Wakefield's far too much of a gentleman for you to fail. Now, if you manage to bed Bella Rushdale before Lucerne does, then I'll be impressed.'

'More work for less reward.'

Charles choked on his port. 'It's got bones in it,' he complained between coughing and topping up his glass. Vaughan offered him a handkerchief, then turned towards the window. Charles mopped his brow with the silk, whilst he tried not to think about how Vaughan intended to attain his goal. He'd heard enough rumours to know the marquis wasn't afraid of taking risks. 'It's a bit *Les Liaisons Dangereuses*, isn't it?' he observed.

Vaughan nonchalantly shrugged his shoulders in response. 'I have no intention of dying, or becoming obsessed, if that's what you think.'

'Yes, but what if people find out?'

'Then I'm the villain.'

Charles opened his pocketbook and scrawled a reminder. 'Very well, sixty guineas it is. But let's make it both.'

Pennerley lifted one of his dark eyebrows. 'If you insist.'

They shook hands on it, just like gentlemen.

Bella was listening patiently while Millicent passed judgement on Lucerne's guests. Her current subject was his tenant, Mrs Virginia Castleton or, more particularly, her usual retinue of young ladies not long out and keen to impress. After Mrs Castleton's husband had died fighting in the American War of Independence, she had taken on the role of matriarch to Reeth and Grinton society, and both Bella and Millicent had served as part of her entourage until they'd outgrown her tutelage and found their own way.

'No competition there,' Millicent remarked. 'And there's certainly a few who'll benefit from Virginia's charm school.'

They paused to admire Lucerne and Marquis Pennerley. 'Of course, old money is more attractive than new money, don't you think?' said Millicent. 'I mean, look at Joshua and Charles. Not that Charles isn't a jolly sort, but . . .' She let her words trail off.

Bella frowned. 'There's not much old money around any more,' she said. 'Most of the old estates are mortgaged or bankrupt. They don't care where the money comes from.' She chose to ignore the veiled insult to her brother. Millicent was never worth rising to. Once she knew the claws were in, she didn't stop digging.

'Who's that?' Millicent asked, as Captain Wakefield joined the two men. 'He's quite smart, and rather manly. What do you think?'

'Captain Wakefield. I believe he's spoken for,' ventured Bella.

'Oh! A soldier. Sounds fun. Well, I'm off to play cards. It's been lovely. I'll see you later.'

Bella smiled, and watched her leave with a mixture of relief and foreboding.

The room had become crowded with card players. Louisa ignored the hand before her and glanced around at the golden interior of the salon, hoping to catch sight of either Bella or Frederick. To her dismay, neither was seated at any of the other card tables.

'Pay attention, miss,' said her partner, a local squire named Charles Aubury, and he tapped her lightly on the back of her hand. Louisa graciously bore the reminder and reluctantly scooped up her cards only to stare unseeing at the pictures. They'd already played several hands and she'd borne his lewd remarks and flattery with goodwill, but there were limits to her endurance. She'd never wanted to play whist in the first place. She wanted to find Frederick and take a turn about the dance-floor, but Charles had refused to let her go until she'd accompanied him for a few games. He'd had at least that.

'I'm not really interested in another round,' she said quietly, placing her cards face up on the felt. There was no other polite way of excusing herself. Surprisingly, he didn't object.

Louisa unwrinkled her forehead, relieved if a little confused. 'Charles?' she said, and turned her head to find his gaze transfixed upon the abundant cleavage of a young woman, whose neckline was so low and rounded that her rouged nipples showed as she leaned forwards to take a seat.

Well, that explained why he wasn't interested in her

any more. She couldn't and wouldn't compete with that display.

'I'm going,' she said, and pushed back her chair so that it grated against the polished floor.

Charles grunted affirmatively. 'All right, Millicent can take your place,' he said, not even giving her a farewell glance as she forced her way through the crowd. Louisa snorted in disgust, not sure who she was more offended by: Charles for his lack of courtesy, or Millicent for her obscene dress.

'Do you always go everywhere in a rush?' a soft male voice asked when she reached the hallway.

Louisa came to a sudden halt. She turned her head curiously, trying to locate the owner of the voice. Beneath the shadowed archway of the stairs stood the man who had stopped her on the landing earlier that evening. She took a moment to look at his clothing – dark-blue velvet and silver-figured silk – before she crossed to where he was leaning against the wall.

'Marquis Pennerley, your servant,' he said, and lifted her hand to briefly press his lips to her skin. The contact was warming. 'I believe I owe you an apology. Taking advantage earlier was rather cruel of me.'

'Yes,' said Louisa, boldly meeting his eyes, only to find herself taking a step backwards, shocked by the intensity of his gaze. He stepped a fraction closer, parting contact with the wall against which he'd been leaning.

'Will you allow me to dance with you later, to make up?'

Louisa fumbled for her dance card, too aware of his gaze on her skin and how he was causing her to flush. He looked at her as if he could see into her head, and hence knew exactly what she'd been thinking and feeling as he'd held her earlier.

'Um, I'm free whenever you wish. Nobody else has asked me yet.'

'Excellent, then I'll book you for those two,' he said, and tapped his index finger to the paper. 'Third and fourth.' Suddenly his shoulders stiffened, and he drew himself up to his full height to peer over her shoulder. Louisa watched his eyes narrow thoughtfully. Suddenly curious, she twisted to see what he was looking at, only to have her attention drawn straight back as he turned abruptly on his heels and strode away.

Louisa frowned in confusion at his retreating figure, and wondered if he still wanted to dance. She hesitantly scribbled in his initials then thrust the paper into her pocket.

'There you are,' said Bella, and tapped her on the shoulder. 'Have you seen Lucerne?'

'No. Have you seen Frederick?'

'He's outside with Joshua, bobbing for apples in the fountain. Are you all right? You seem a bit bewildered.'

Louisa drew her gaze away from the direction in which Marquis Pennerley had gone. 'I'm fine. I've just been asked to dance, but you seem to have scared him off.'

Bella gave her a delighted grin. 'I have? Who was it?'

'Marquis Pennerley?' Louisa replied, and then chewed her lower lip thoughtfully. 'He's quite handsome, but rather intense. I'm not sure what to make of him. I think my aunt would hate him.'

Bella frowned. 'Your aunt hates everyone. Dance with him if you want to, but he was really rude to me earlier and Lucerne acted as if that was normal.'

'He was quite polite to me.'

The admission only made Bella's frown deepen. 'Then I guess Marquis high and mighty Pennerley has heard that you're an heiress, which is why he's speaking to you. I'm obviously too lowly to bother with.'

'Perhaps.' Louisa didn't think he seemed that shallow, although two brief conversations with him had given her little to go on. However, she didn't want to spend the evening discussing him. 'Look, there's Lucerne,' she said, spotting him near the dining room. 'I'm going outside to find Frederick. I'll see you later.'

For a moment, Bella watched Louisa weave her way through the sea of ball-gowns, and then she turned towards the dining room and started after Lucerne. He was trapped between the vicar and three of the five Elliott sisters, and looked as though he'd be grateful if she rescued him from their clutches. The elder Miss Elliott was making big doe eyes at him, while her youngest sister was surreptitiously trying to tug the bodice of her dress down to expose more bust. Bella was only three feet away when Lucerne extricated himself and sneaked into the relative safety of the stag parlour.

'Lucerne,' she called after him, but he didn't hear her over the noise of the guests. 'Damn!' she hissed, reaching the doorway, and slapped her palm against the frame. Stepping over the threshold was out of the question, so she'd just have to wait until he came out. She sank against the wall and impatiently crossed her arms, cursing the Elliott sisters to spinsterhood.

'Come on, Lucerne,' she muttered under her breath every few seconds and glanced hopefully at the exit. 'What are you doing in there?'

It was at least five minutes before the door opened. She managed to get a glimpse into the room over the shoulders of the two men who left. The interior was dingy and full of curling pipe smoke that seemed to hover like low clouds over the heads of the occupants. Even on the threshold, the thick woody taste stuck in her throat, making it dry and ticklish. No wonder they drank so much brandy.

'Do you think you could move over? You're blocking the door.'

Bella turned sharply to find Marquis Pennerley eyeing her suspiciously. If he hadn't brushed past her so rudely earlier, she'd have moved aside, but she didn't feel she owed him that courtesy. At least not until he said please. She stood her ground, returning his haughty stare until she saw his lip curl.

'What are you, captain of the guard?'

'No.'

'Then please move aside.'

Bella lifted her foot as if to acquiesce, but paused mid-step. 'If you'll do something for me.' She glanced over her shoulder, then back at Vaughan, who drew his dark eyebrows together. 'Lucerne's inside; he asked me to meet him here. Would you tell him I'm here?'

'If I must,' he said coldly. Bella stepped aside and let him pass.

'It's hardly a hardship,' she mumbled to his back. 'Annoying prig, strutting about like a peacock.'

Lucerne emerged from the smoke. 'Bella,' he said, throwing a concerned expression in her direction. 'Is something wrong?'

'No, but you promised to spend some time with me this evening.'

The concern faded from his face and was replaced with a smile. 'So I did, but I saw you with Louisa a moment ago and didn't want to intrude.'

'She's gone outside to find Frederick.'

Lucerne pursed his lips again. 'Right,' he said thoughtfully. 'Then I'd best keep my promise. Do you want to dance, or shall we find a quiet corner?'

Louisa followed the narrow path through an archway cut in the hedgerow, towards the sound of voices and splashing water up ahead. She turned a corner to find hanging lanterns spilling warmth over the ground by the fountain, lighting the faces of cheering onlookers and making rainbows on the slippery wet cobblestones. Many of them were soaked; one buxom young lady's dress was so wet it was transparent and drew more competitors than the apple-bobbing. She spotted Frederick and hurried towards him. His hair was wet at the front, and he was drying his face on a towel.

'I won,' he said, and handed her his apple. 'Where did you go? I couldn't find you anywhere.'

'You're the one that vanished.'

'Only into the hall. Someone told me you were outside.' He passed the towel on to another contestant and then drew her further into the shadows. 'Let's go down to the river, we can be alone there.'

Louisa opened her mouth to refuse – this was just the sort of thing her aunt constantly warned her about. Then she remembered nobody was watching her. 'All right,' she agreed as her pulse began to quicken with anticipation. Frederick took her arm and escorted her across the lawn. Louisa stepped warily into the tree line, conscious of him treading patiently behind her. They emerged on to the river-bank just as two swans glided past. Frederick clasped her about the waist and pressed his lips to the nape of her neck.

'At last,' he murmured as she twisted in his arms and looked up expectantly at him for a kiss. 'I've been waiting all week for this chance.'

Louisa met his tongue with a sudden hunger as his

hands moved possessively over her bodice. Beneath the satin her skin felt incredibly sensitive, so that her nipples rasped against her stays, begging to be kissed, just as they had the night she'd watched Joshua and Emma in the old green armchair. But twinned with that thought came the memory of Joshua's rampant phallus dipping mercilessly between Emma's thighs, and suddenly the eager pulse that had started between her thighs seemed like a warning. The apple she held fell to the ground with a soft thump.

Frederick clasped her buttocks in his large hands and pulled her closer. She felt his erection against her abdomen. Its heat branded her, while its pressure frightened and intrigued her.

'Slow down,' she begged.

Frederick sucked in his next breath. 'Louisa,' he sighed. 'I don't want to take advantage. But Jesus, you feel good.'

Louisa looked up and saw that his pupils were wide and dark.

'You don't know what you do to me,' he whispered. He unconsciously brushed his palm against his loins, and Louisa's gaze followed the movement. After seeing Joshua, she thought she had a fair idea what effect she was having. In fact, part of her desperately wanted to touch him, to trace the length of his hard shaft, but she hardly dared. Perhaps he would think her too forward. Instead, she settled for pressing herself hard and fast against him, yearning for something and hoping he'd show her.

'Miss Stanley,' a voice called from the lawn. Louisa jumped and stared at Wakefield. Her heartbeat thundered against her ribcage.

'It's all right, Louisa. Just keep still,' Frederick reassured her.

'Miss Stanley.'

'It's Marquis Pennerley,' whispered Louisa.

Frederick nodded. 'I know. Just keep still, he'll go away.'

'But I promised him a dance. I ought to go.' She pulled away from Frederick's embrace, and shivered as she realised how cold the night air had become. He followed her out from the trees.

'Captain Wakefield was showing me the swans.'

'So I see,' Vaughan replied with a hint of boredom. 'You promised me a dance. I hope you're not going to let me down for a few birds.'

'Oh no, of course not,' she said. She tried not to look embarrassed, despite the high colour in her cheeks and the obvious sparkle in her eyes. Something told her Pennerley knew exactly what they'd been doing. Relinquishing her grip on Wakefield's hands, she accepted his. 'Is it time already?'

Frederick watched them depart in annoyance, then wandered over to the fire that burned on the lawn.

'Never mind, Wakefield. Here,' Joshua soothed, and passed him the port bottle. 'You can't win them all.'

'Tell it to that prize bastard sometime, will you?'

'Certainly. Who is he?'

Frederick spat the cork into the fire. 'Vaughan, the Marquis of Pennerley. She'd promised him a dance,' he said sarcastically.

Joshua smiled politely, none the wiser. 'Bad luck. Next time, eh?' he said, and patted Wakefield's shoulder. Then he turned to Miranda Hayes and asked, 'Shall we join them?'

Wakefield scowled. 'I'll join the card table, then.'

'Yes, do, Milli's there,' purred Miranda. 'She'd love to have you.'

# 4

The dance was a lively gavotte, popular enough to draw a crowd on to the dance-floor. Louisa skipped, stepped and kissed her partner without enthusiasm. She would gladly have changed places with any of the envious ladies around her, if Marquis Pennerley had permitted it. She tried to show an interest in him, but her gaze kept drifting across the room to the card table.

Wakefield and Aubury faced off, watched by a small crowd of friendly hecklers impressively fronted by Millicent Hayes, who had already lost heavily to Charles. They bet on several rubbers while cards changed hands quickly. Charles began to sweat heavily as the game progressed and he frequently stopped to mop his brow. Wakefield was about to strip him of most of his ready cash.

Back on the dance-floor, Louisa and Vaughan completed their solo parts and rejoined the circle. As they danced the final steps, Louisa's gaze again moved to Frederick. Charles, grumbling and red-faced, abruptly quit the table. She watched Frederick scoop up his prize money and hand some of it to the woman at his side, who was leaning close to him. She immediately threw her arms about his neck and kissed him full on the mouth.

Louisa felt a sudden cold jolt. Her perspective narrowed to where he lingered in the woman's embrace, and she muddled the next few dance steps then came to a halt. She looked around in confusion, then fled the floor pursued by a tumult of emotions.

A firm hand caught her wrist; she glanced sideways and met her dance partner's open-faced concern. 'Leave me,' she pleaded. Vaughan shook his head, and wordlessly led her into the deserted drawing room. He found her a chair and she collapsed gratefully into its arms.

'You appear to have had a shock,' Vaughan speculated. 'A drink will help you recover.'

Louisa pressed her palms to her eyelids to seal in the tears, and sighed. She felt slightly sick, almost faint, and wanted to be alone, but she didn't want to rebuke his kindness. She took two sips of the port he brought her, then changed her mind and drained the glass. The sticky sweet liquid numbed her sense of betrayal.

'More?' he enquired.

Louisa followed him to the side-table and watched him refill the glass, which she drained quickly. 'Thank you.' She tried to say more but her voice failed her.

'It's my pleasure. The least I could do.' He smiled faintly, just turning up the corners of his warm red lips.

A strand of his long dark hair fell forwards over his face. Without thinking, Louisa brushed it aside. Vaughan caught her hand and placed a kiss in the centre of her palm, which somehow soothed her wounded pride. She looked up at him, surprised to find him staring back at her intently.

'You remind me of someone,' he said. 'It's your eyes, and your smile. Yes, you have the same smile.'

Louisa found herself smiling despite her feelings over Frederick. 'Someone you're close to?' she asked.

'Reasonably so. Emily was a great love of mine.'

'Is she here with you?'

'Ah, no.' Vaughan's expression grew dark. He turned away from her slightly and bowed his head. 'She's dead.'

Louisa's heart fluttered in her chest; she felt his loss as though it were her own. He was standing so close to her, and his dark eyes glittered with such sorrow that her own anguish over Frederick seemed to melt away. When he tilted her face and touched her honey-blonde curls as if lost in memory, she didn't resist. Not even when his fingers brushed the hot skin of her cheek and traced a line across the soft curve, to her parted lips.

'My lord,' she whispered, and placed a gentle hand on his arm. He shifted his stance, bringing them closer together. An odd sensation trickled down Louisa's spine. Not fright, but something similar: anticipation.

His eyes glinted in the soft light like the jewels on his rings. A gleaming gold hoop earring shone through his hair. The touch of his lips was dizzying. It felt like hot syrup sliding down her throat, enveloping her. Moreover, that same wet heat was soon spreading to the sensitive place between her thighs. Louisa clung to him, opened her mouth to his tongue and returned his darting touches. She felt none of the nervousness she'd experienced with Frederick. Vaughan made her feel totally at ease, so that she felt encouraged to caress him through the fabric of his breeches.

Vaughan felt his cock stir and rise like a charmed snake in response to her hands questing curiously under his shirt.

Really! This was too easy, but then the line about the fictitious Emily normally won them over. Still, her endeavours to find out what lay beneath his clothing surprised him; he'd taken her for an innocent, but she was clearly more knowing than he'd assumed, if not more experienced. No matter, it gave him a chance of some entertainment, and put him a step nearer to securing the wager. He hadn't thought to complete half the task in one night.

He released her lips and traced the curve of her

earlobe with his tongue, then left a trail of feather-light kisses down her neck. With practised ease, he edged the fabric off her shoulder, revealing milky soft skin lightly dusted with powder. 'Hush,' he soothed, as he cupped her tiny breast in his hand. A wrong word would break the spell. Her nipple hardened against the centre of his palm, while her heartbeat hammered against her ribcage, making her breath shallow and quick.

He tongued around her nipple, coaxing it into standing erect, and pulled her against his trapped prick so that she could feel the solid line of his erection through her clothing. A little more patient coaxing and she'd be begging him to slide his pole deep into her cunt. Already her hand was straying across his hip towards his loins. She was still hesitant about touching him, but that wouldn't last.

Vaughan returned his attention to her lips, now quietly aware that they were being observed. Whoever it was had not been subtle in their approach. He suppressed a smile when he caught Captain Wakefield's stunned expression over Louisa's shoulder. Of course, the captain hadn't expected to find his sweet, virtuous Louisa in the arms of another man when he'd finally realised she'd left the dance-floor. It amused Vaughan to see him scowl. He realised that he had the perfect opportunity to pay Wakefield back for an old wound, one that it might even be worth risking sixty guineas for, and this was a safe place to do it.

Vaughan clasped Louisa more tightly to his body, bending her back slightly to reach her hem, and delved beneath her petticoats. Before she realised what he was about his hand was on her upper thigh, pushing between her legs to reach her core. He dipped a finger between her ripe labia, which welcomed his intrusion, and flicked mercilessly at her bud. She stiffened against him. Her eyes flashed open, wild and panicked, but her thighs parted for him.

'No, don't!'

Wakefield predictably bounded across the room. He planted a hand on Vaughan's shoulder. 'The lady asked you to let go.'

'Take your hands off me.' Vaughan deliberately kept his voice soft and low as he spoke, just to lend weight to his implied threat. He sneered slightly when Wakefield failed to take the hint.

'I said, I think you should let her go.'

'And I say, unhand me this instant.'

Vaughan suddenly whipped Louisa around, throwing her off balance. He laughed inwardly at their surprised expressions and at Wakefield's face clouding with thunder as he tipped Louisa's breasts out of her loosened gown. She only trembled slightly at her immodest state, while her rosy nipples perked up in the cool air. Vaughan pinched them encouragingly, so they stood up like two ripe berries. 'Care for a taste?' he enquired, wearing a silky smile.

'My lord!'

Lucerne looked up as the urgent tone of his valet's voice rose above the distant calls and jeers of his guests.

'Sir, I think you should come quickly. Captain Wakefield has challenged the marquis to a duel.'

Lucerne sighed and turned to leave. 'I'm sorry, Bella,' he muttered in a tone of frustration. 'Duty calls.'

She stood aside with a sulky pout, but Lucerne didn't allow himself to be tempted back. It was probably for the best to delay any seductions for a little while, and he understood both Vaughan and Frederick's temperaments too well to leave them to it. Besides, he didn't want the other guests to be upset by those two locking horns.

Damn the pair of them. For once, he thought they'd manage to be civil to each other.

Lucerne struggled towards the drawing room through the crowd of nosy servants and guests who were clustered around the door. He tried the handle but someone was holding it from the other side. 'Open this door,' he demanded, and rattled the handle again.

'Oh, I beg your pardon, my lord. I didn't realise it was you,' Joshua apologised, letting him in. He shut the door behind Lucerne, and stood against it.

Lucerne surveyed the scene furiously. Vaughan stood by the huge fireplace, sipping a glass of port. He looked no different from how he'd appeared twenty minutes ago, stepping gracefully about the dance-floor. He was the incarnation of poise, completely unruffled by the turmoil that was occurring around him. In contrast, Frederick had succumbed to a diabolical rage. He was flushed, stiff-shouldered and aggressive.

'You despicable bastard –' he sniped.

Vaughan cut him off. 'I've accepted your challenge. Surely there's nothing more to discuss. Be sure to let me know who your second is.'

Wakefield lunged at him.

'Frederick!' yelled Lucerne. He caught his friend's arm and jerked him away from Vaughan then, with Joshua's aid, managed to pin him in a chair. 'See reason. I won't have duelling in my house.' He found it unbelievable that they'd even consider it. They both knew his feelings on the subject well enough.

'Ask him about it.'

Lucerne jerked his head towards the mantle. 'Vaughan!'

'The challenge is not mine,' came his laconic reply. 'But Captain Wakefield insists, therefore I feel honour-bound to accept.'

'He's got no honour.'

'Wakefield!' snapped Lucerne. The rapid pulse in his temple warned him that his own temper was about to fray. He hadn't gone to the trouble and expense of a ball to waste it listening to these two squabble. He could do that any time.

'I'll bloody kill him.'

'You will not. Take a hold of yourself.' The combination of his words and icy glare seemed to calm Frederick. Lucerne removed his hands from the other man's shoulders and straightened his back. He glanced at Vaughan then back at Frederick. What he really didn't need was these two at each other's throats from now until Christmas. He'd left London to escape the constant one-upmanship between his friends, and now this . . .

Only then, in that moment of quiet, did he register the heartbroken cries coming from behind the thick curtain over the French windows. He walked across and pulled them back. Louisa gasped in fright, then continued to sob. Lucerne's mouth set into a hard straight line as he cursed himself for tolerating Frederick's infatuation. He knew his friend couldn't afford to marry her, and his flirting was always going to end in tears. 'Stop sobbing, girl,' he said in exasperation.

Stunned by his rebuke she stared at him wide-eyed.

'Joshua, take her to Bella, please.' He gave her his handkerchief for her nose, and waited until he'd heard the door click shut before he turned back to the two adversaries.

'Now,' he said in a voice that he hoped made it clear he didn't want any more trouble. 'What is this about?'

Frederick opened his mouth to speak.

'On second thoughts, I'm not interested,' said Lucerne, as he realised this would take the rest of the night to sort out. 'Freddy, I understand you made the challenge. I'd appreciate it if you'd retract it.' He looked from Vaughan to Frederick, hoping for some sign of reconciliation, but there was none. Vaughan was poking the fire, while Frederick was staring pointedly at the ceiling.

'Look, I don't give a damn why you suddenly feel the need to kill each other. I am not having any fighting, and while you are both guests in my house, you'll obey my rules. Now I suggest you make up like gentlemen and we can get back to the party.'

Neither of them moved. Lucerne turned his glare on Frederick, who stubbornly met his gaze, and began to explain. Lucerne cut him off. 'Freddy,' he implored in a softer tone as he crossed to his side. 'Please do this for me.'

His friend's jaw clenched so that the tendons in his throat stood out.

'Please.'

Frederick dropped his head forwards into his hands, sighed and rubbed his eyes. 'Very well.' He rose and crossed to the fireplace. 'Accept my apologies, Pennerley.'

Lucerne could hear the reluctance in his voice, and resolved to try and find out the cause of their enmity at some point. He watched Frederick extend his hand. Vaughan grasped it warmly, and broke into a triumphant smile. He pulled the glowering Wakefield off balance into his embrace and then planted a kiss on each of his burning cheeks, much to the captain's chagrin. Knowing Vaughan, this was probably the outcome he'd planned all along.

'Now, gentlemen,' Lucerne addressed them before Frederick thought of throwing a punch. 'With our differences settled, let us rejoin our guests.'

The house had become stifling so Bella had taken her frustration outside, but even from her position on the far side of the lawn she could hear Charles Aubury drunkenly extolling the virtues of large breasts to a rapturous audience. From the ribald comments they were making, it sounded like they were using it as an excuse to ogle Millicent's abundant cleavage. She retreated further into the darkened shrubbery, smacking her hand against the foliage as she walked. Even among the waxy leaves, she couldn't escape the irritating blather.

It was all Louisa's fault.

One moment she'd had Lucerne's complete attention and even shared a few discreet caresses. Then suddenly she was playing nursemaid to Louisa, and Lucerne was all ears for whatever Lord Pennerley was saying. Louisa had finally cried herself to sleep, and she'd made her escape.

She struggled on through the bushes, oblivious to the nicks and scratches the branches were leaving on her skin. Maybe if she could reach the gazebo the voices would leave her alone, and maybe she'd find enough solitude to raise her skirts and do something about the itch caused by flirting with Lucerne. Her thoughts turned momentarily to Mark, but her desire for him was superficial and he'd probably already satisfied himself with one of the maids. She stubbed her toe, stumbled and crashed to the ground, jarring her elbow and muddying her hands. 'Damnation!' she snapped and rolled over to sit up, heedless of the damp earth and her new dress. If something didn't go her way tonight, she'd be smashing Lucerne's windows before very much longer.

Bella crawled from the bushes, quite close to the ivy-covered gazebo. She didn't care that her knees were torn, as was the hem of her dress. To her dismay, she found Captain Wakefield sitting on the stone bench inside. He was dressed in cream breeches and a green jacket with gold frogging, less ostentatious than his uniform but still showy. He looked up at her with unfocused eyes as she stepped into the wooden shelter. Bella's triumph of reaching the gazebo felt suddenly bitter. What was he doing here?

'Annabella – were you looking for me? Did Louisa want me?'

Bella glared at him with barely concealed rage. Did he think she had nothing better to do than run about the gardens after him to pass on love notes?

'No.'

'Oh!' He appeared slightly taken aback by her abrupt retort. 'How is she? Do you know?'

'She's in bed and probably asleep by now.'

Wakefield nodded slowly. 'Probably best after the bloody fright Pennerley gave her,' he said, seemingly oblivious to her clipped tone. 'What are you doing out here?'

Trying to escape idiots like you, Bella wanted to say, but she bit her tongue. Insulting him wasn't going to make the evening any better. At least he was showing some interest in her, which was more than Lucerne was doing.

'Escaping an unwelcome admirer, no doubt?' he said, answering on her behalf. 'I expect that makes you rather cross.'

Bella clenched her fists a little tighter. In her chest, a scream of frustration was reverberating, rising quickly upwards towards her throat. He was being so excruciatingly polite she just couldn't hold it in. She shrieked, loud and long, careless of his shocked stare or whether anyone heard. Some of her tension melted away. She turned on him and shoved him to knock him out of his complacency, sending him crashing to the ground.

'Ooof! Hey!'

She couldn't take it any more. If she couldn't have

Lucerne she had to have someone, and Wakefield would do. She straddled him and pushed his back to the ground, ignoring his protest. 'If you really want to know how I feel, let me show you.'

She shimmied back a few inches and brought herself down to straddle him.

'Jesus!'

Bella rocked against him and felt him stiffen. She leaned forwards and snarled through a kiss. Their tongues jousted, the touches making her vulva tingle. His penis was straining against the fabric, eager for release, and she guessed from his reaction that he had his own demons to exorcise. As she moved to unbutton him, he pre-empted her and pushed the flap of his breeches away. Annabella gazed down at his proudly rearing cock. The head was purple, the shaft pale. He slid on her wetness and dipped inside with a satisfied groan.

'You're eager for this,' muttered Frederick.

'Shut up and fuck me!'

'As you say.'

Almost immediately, Bella felt herself climbing. Sensation built between her legs and spread out in waves across her thighs and stomach, making her nipples stiffen so they were visible through her dress. She rode him hard, throwing back her head. Her lower body felt as if it was on fire. All she wanted was him deeper, harder, faster. Whether he was enjoying it was incidental – although he appeared to be, from his eager thrusts.

'Oh, God!'

His body shook as he tried to maintain the pace. Bella knew he was going to come very quickly but the realisation didn't slow her down. She wanted quick satisfaction, and if he couldn't give it to her, she'd find someone else who could. There were plenty of men at the party, and she wasn't feeling fussy.

He gasped wordlessly, as his head whipped back and his orgasm swept through his body. She held herself still until his breathing calmed then began to lift herself from him, but he clamped his hands over her thighs.

'Where are you going?'

'You've finished.'

Wakefield's smile reached his dilated eyes. 'Not properly.' He clenched his muscles and his penis twitched inside her. It was already losing its hardness, but Bella groaned at the stimulation all the same.

'Don't be so eager to run off,' he said.

'I'm not normally encouraged to stay.'

Delving beneath her skirts, he sought out the point where their bodies joined. He circled the base of his prick with one hand and massaged her sensitive nub with the other. Bella felt her whole body leap at his touch as he delivered what Lucerne had only teased her with the promise of. Sensations pure and raw in their intensity flooded her excited body. She flexed her inner muscles around him and ground against his circling thumb, climbing then soaring as her thoughts slipped away. It wasn't until she came back down and the afterglow had washed itself out of her cheeks that she wondered what Louisa would think. Millicent kissing him had already upset her friend, and that was nothing next to what she had just done. It was best Louisa didn't know, she decided immediately, and from the guilty look Captain Wakefield was giving her, she guessed he felt the same way.

# 5

The remote Norman church stood in a hollow, halfway between Lauwine and the source of the copper-tainted stream that flowed down from Hill End, past the Rushdale mine. At first glance the ancient building appeared to be sinking into the earth, for the graveyard that had once been at the same level as the church now came to the sills of the stained-glass windows, and only a narrow channel separated the two.

They had come out to view the tiny building and get some air, amid complaints, mostly from Charles, about having spent several days indoors following the party. Louisa was walking with Captain Wakefield, quite recovered and oblivious to anybody else while Joshua and Vaughan were equally deep in discussion, much to Bella's surprise, with Charles Aubury trailing behind them. Lucerne was admiring the detailed patterns and rich colours of the stained glass. He was immaculately turned out in white breeches and a black coat, square-cut across the front and with a high M-cut collar.

Bella watched the captain cautiously. He hadn't ignored her, but he was definitely keeping his distance. Well, hang it, if he wasn't feeling guilty then she certainly wouldn't, and Louisa's blissful expression made it clear that she hadn't found out. She drifted closer to her brother's party, who were muttering furtively.

'I know a girl who's game for a guinea,' said Joshua.

'I know a lass who's game for a shilling,' grumbled Charles.

'Yes,' retorted Vaughan in a mocking tone, 'but will she pass for a lady? We're after a peach, not Granny Smith.' He glanced sidelong at Louisa, giving Bella the distinct impression that they were plotting something.

'Ahem!' Joshua coughed loudly, and the other two noticed Bella eavesdropping. 'Bella, why don't you show Lucerne around?'

Bella was about to protest, but Lucerne had heard his name mentioned and nodded to signal his pleasure at the idea. They'd had no time alone together since the ball, with the exception of a few odd moments when they passed in the corridors or on the stairs. Very well, she would be bought off this time, but she still wondered what their game was. Lucerne waved to the group, but the only response was a scowl from Vaughan.

'You're rather solemn,' he remarked, turning his attention to her.

Bella inclined her head in acknowledgement. 'The church holds no interest for me. I've seen it a hundred times before.' She surprised herself with her own jaded tone.

'Of course you have. Please accept my apology for inflicting it upon you again.' He smiled winningly as he aped her delivery, and offered her his arm to take. 'Will you indulge me for a hundred and first? I should like to see the inside if it's open.'

'If you like. But there's little enough to see,' she replied, and accepted his arm.

At least it was a chance to be alone with him.

He led her down the broad steps and opened the door to dimness and cool air. Bella pulled her wrap tight around her shoulders as they stepped inside. It was much colder within than out in the bright sun. She wrinkled her nose at the dank earthy smell, then perched on the end of a stone pew to watch Lucerne, who was peering up at the seraphim on the vaulted ceiling. The church always made her think of mouldering corpses and decay, and today was no exception. The gloomy interior made her hunger for the light open spaces beyond the oppressive walls, and the wild hilltops. Lucerne seemed to her more divine than the rapturous painted angels, for all their golden halos and beatific smiles. She hoped he didn't take much longer; the stone pew was beginning to chill her behind.

'Is the church really sinking?' he asked, and his voice echoed slightly off the stone walls.

'I don't think so. Too many corpses in the graveyard, is what I've heard. Joshua used to tell me that the ground would get so waterlogged that they'd float to the top whenever it rained heavily, and that the channel around the outside is to stop them coming into church for the service. He was always trying to frighten me.'

'Truly?' Lucerne responded with a smile. 'That's a pretty horrible story.'

Bella shrugged her shoulders, dislodging her wrap. 'I've read worse,' she admitted as she pulled it tight again.

'You've read *Mysteries of Udolpho*? What about *The Monk*?'

'Uh-huh.' She nodded. 'That too.'

'Scandalous! I had no idea you were fond of such things.' Lucerne shook his head, then crossed to her side and offered her a hand up. The sensation of his soft leather gloves against her skin felt strange. They seemed to lend an air of deception to their wearer, as though the leather were a thick skin he could use to disguise his true nature.

'Shouldn't we rejoin the others?' she asked.

'Why? Are you afraid of me?'

He pulled her close to his chest and slid his hands

down the curve of her back to her bottom, which he unashamedly started to massage. She could feel his gloves even through her dress. They rasped against the satin: determined, sensual and forceful.

'Certainly not.'

'Perhaps you should be.' He swayed his hips against her. The sudden forwardness was surprising, but she wasn't about to discourage him. There was a firm bulge in the front of his breeches, which sent showers of sparks flickering between her pubis and her breasts. Her nipples leaped to attention and stood like two cherries waiting to be plucked. She wanted to feel his lips around them, sucking and playfully nipping. Instead, he kissed the crown of her head and began to tease out the pins holding her hazel locks in place. 'You smell nice, like roses,' he said.

'Lord Marlinscar . . . Lucerne.'

'Yes.'

'Are you trying to seduce me?'

'No.' He brushed his covered fingers across her lips. 'I'm flirting, and so are you. Believe me, if I was attempting a seduction I'd choose somewhere a little warmer, with less company and more wine.'

Bella sucked the end of one of his fingers tantalisingly, tickling the soft leather with the tip of her tongue in the way she hoped to flick it over a rather more sensitive organ. The leather itself tasted a little musky, and she wondered what he'd been doing in those gloves to make them taste that way. Had he touched himself while wearing them? The thought turned her on. She'd enjoyed watching him masturbate.

'Freddy seems keen to avoid you.'

Bella let his finger fall from her lips.

'As if somehow he fears you might embarrass him.'

She stiffened against him and turned her head away, blushing furiously. Although she felt no guilt about what had happened, she felt some regret for Louisa. The captain was the man her best friend loved; she should have restrained herself. Apprehensively, Lucerne's other hand left her bottom and veered upwards to her cheek. He forced her to turn, to meet his eyes again and reveal her secrets.

'Ah! I did wonder.' Lucerne released her, allowing her to turn away. 'Well, I am glad that you enjoyed the party.'

'I'll leave now, shall I?'

He laid a gentle hand on her shoulder. 'Why? Only if you want to.'

Bella's heart fluttered. She didn't know whether it was with promise or grief, but his calm acceptance of the truth was unnerving. She felt like crying. If he'd shouted at her or called her a harlot, she'd have found it easier. At least then she'd have had something to react against.

'Life is too short to fill it with regrets, Bella. I'm not the jealous type, if that's what you're worried about. I'm not interested in your guilt, but Frederick is probably keen on your discretion. I know he won't breathe a word to anyone, and I trust you won't either. Funny, I've shared girls with Vaughan but never with Freddy.'

She considered this, and Lucerne suddenly seemed to realise that he'd been ungallant.

'I mean, I still want you. If you're interested.'

He circled her waist and pulled her back against his warm body. The hard bulge in his breeches was still there, a little softer perhaps, but still warm and urgent. He kissed her by the ear, and then on the cheek. Bella arched against him, lifting her chin so he could reach her lips. He paused an inch from her mouth and a breath passed between them, mingling the potency of their desire, before he descended to kiss her with an aggressive, demanding ferocity.

'You talk too much,' she hissed into his mouth, before their tongues met with equal ardour.

The church door opened with a loud groan.

'How quaint, and in church as well.' Vaughan mocked them from the doorway, bringing their brief moment of passion to an abrupt end. 'Really, Lucerne, I thought you had more finesse.'

Oh, hateful man, thought Bella, as the carriage jogged slowly homewards. Why did he have to spoil everything? Why, when she finally had Lucerne where she wanted him, did Pennerley have to interrupt? And why did he have to look so bloody smug about it? At least she didn't have to tolerate his jibes for the rest of the day, since Joshua had insisted they return to the Grange for the night, so that he could ride off into Richmond on business before sundown.

Joshua sent a note to supper saying he was staying the night in town, and would return tomorrow to take them back to Lauwine in the afternoon. As Louisa didn't appear for supper either, Bella ate in silence, then retired to her bedroom immediately afterwards to read Mrs Radcliffe's new novel: *The Italian*, a romance of the Inquisition. It had arrived from London while they'd been away.

The prose soon filled her head with images of monks in long dark cassocks, who hid their perfectly formed male bodies beneath amorphous robes, until she expected to see them peering around the curtains at the bottom of her bed. Somehow, as her eyelids grew heavy and she began to doze, the story blended with her memories of the visit to the little church earlier that day.

The sinister Schedoni stepped into the aisle of the small church, his black robe swirling around him in the chilling night breeze. Frozen to the spot, Bella watched him approach; he paused just a few feet away and raised a hand to pull back his hood. Her heart lurched into her throat as the visage of Marquis Pennerley was revealed. He offered her a terse smile, before turning his head to draw her attention to a bundle at the far end of the aisle.

Bella crept forwards. The bundle moved. Closer still, and she recognised her lover Vivaldi-Lord Marlinscar. He was bound around the wrists and ankles, and large bruises covered his ribs and upper arms where the inquisitors had tortured secrets from him. She tried to reach him, to comfort him with her body and the light from her candle, but Vaughan-Schedoni held her back, and made the other inquisitors bear Lucerne away. She struggled in his grasp, and somehow managed to shake free, though as she ran through the old dank monastery, she wondered if he had not simply just let her go.

Lucerne was lying slumped over a pew. She touched his pale skin and he drew her into his arms. 'Bella, Bella,' he whispered against her hair, as he sought the welcome of her lips. His kiss was hot and sweet. Like honeyed wine, it made her feel warm inside and eager for more, but there was danger all around them.

'We must flee,' she said, and tilted her head to look up into his eyes. A dark ringlet brushed against her hand where she clutched his robe. 'Vaughan!' She realised. 'No. Lucerne.'

A cold draft blew across her face. Bella drew up the covers the scene having switched to her bedroom. A lone candle flickered before her. It hovered in the air by the foot of her bed. Schedoni leered between the curtains. He tugged at the bedclothes, and a scream froze on Bella's tongue.

'Annabella?'

The images of her dream shattered then resolved into familiar surroundings. It was Louisa.

'Louisa!' Bella sat up in surprise. She hoped Wakefield hadn't been driven to confess after all. 'What is it? Is something wrong?'

'No. It's just that I wanted to talk.'

Relieved, Bella yawned and put her book aside. 'It's late. Can't it wait until tomorrow?'

She turned her head when Louisa didn't reply, and caught the reflective glint of tears. Her apprehension returned.

Louisa began to sob.

Bella decided to offer some comfort, and moved closer to place an arm around Louisa's slender shoulders. 'No need to cry,' she said, then bit her lip. 'Talk to me.' If there was anything to be said, it would be best to get it over with.

The room was cold, the fire having long since died in the grate. Bella tugged back the covers and patted the mattress beside her. 'Come on, no point freezing to death. It's a good thing Joshua's away from home. God knows what he'd think if he saw you wandering the corridors in your shift. Probably mistake you for a ghost and run for his life,' she said, in an attempt at humour.

Louisa's breaths continued to come out as desperate sobs, but she crawled beneath the covers. Bella plumped the pillows for her to rest against, and pulled the bed-spread up to their shoulders. 'Now, what's the problem, dearest Louisa? What's upset you so much?'

'Oh, just everything. Nothing has been right since I left London. Well, since I met Frederick, actually.' She pulled the covers tight up to her chin as her words dried up.

'Is this to do with what happened at the party? I didn't think –'

'Millicent certainly didn't help,' Louisa cut in, preventing Bella from saying too much. She paused and chewed her lip, clearly weighing up the matter. 'Do you think she's a real threat?'

'Don't be silly,' Bella said, and gave a nervous laugh to defray her own feeling of tension. If Louisa was worrying about Millicent, she obviously didn't know what had happened between her and Frederick. 'Millicent has always been a trollop. Any man, any place, anyhow. She probably only did it for a bit of fun.'

Louisa sniffed and Bella found her a handkerchief.

'It's just that I'm so unsure about Frederick's intentions. What he does feels so wonderful, but sometimes it scares me. Especially after what Marquis Pennerley did.'

'Men,' asserted Bella.

'He kept saying it was my fault, that I'd started it. It all happened so fast. I just keep wondering what would have happened if Frederick hadn't come along when he did.'

'I see.'

'Now I know why my aunt keeps me shackled to her side.'

'Don't say that. Not all men are like Vaughan. They don't all pounce at the first opportunity. If you weren't always glued to your aunt, you might be better at telling the difference.'

Louisa tossed the handkerchief onto the bedside cabinet. 'I suppose. Maybe I should compile a list – men to avoid. Approach with extreme caution, all men with a title, long dark hair, too much charm –'

'Arrogant, self-centred bastards,' suggested Bella.

'Good kissers –'

'Is he?'

Louisa smiled so that a dimple appeared in her cheek. 'I've not had much to compare him with, but I'd say so.'

'Damn. What list are we compiling again?'

Louisa dropped her head on to her curled-up knees. She sniggered and shook her head. 'I think he likes you – Vaughan, I mean. He's always staring at you, and today he was the only one even slightly curious about why you'd disappeared into the church with Lucerne. In fact, he looked positively put out.'

The hairs on the back of her neck were standing up. Thinking about Vaughan had brought back the images from her dream and she didn't like them very much. She certainly wasn't interested in hearing about how he was supposedly attracted to her. 'Do you still want some advice about Wakefield?' she asked.

Louisa turned her head to one side. 'I want to know how to keep hold of him, make him interested enough not to wander.'

'Witchcraft.'

'Bella, be serious.'

'Sleep with him, then. It's what I'd do.'

Louisa sat up straight. 'I couldn't, not until we were married. It's not proper. Besides, Frederick's too much of a gentleman; he says he won't because it would be taking advantage.'

Bella coughed into her hand. Gentleman when it suited him, maybe. All right, she'd initiated the encounter in the gazebo, but he hadn't exactly protested. 'Ask Vaughan for another lesson, then,' she snapped, instead of disillusioning her friend. 'I'm sure he'd have no qualms about taking your maidenhead, and then Wakefield wouldn't have to have it on his conscience.'

Louisa winced, but Bella continued regardless.

'Of course, if you don't fancy that, there's Charles, but you're not his type. Lucerne? I don't think deflowering virgins is his forte. Besides, he's shown no interest in you. Or there's Joshua. Yes, you could always try my brother. That would please your aunt.'

Louisa bit her lower lip, draining the colour from it. 'Why are you being so crude?'

'You asked.'

For several seconds they glared at each other, Louisa in affront, Bella in derision. Then Bella began to smirk. 'Alternatively,' she said, 'there's me.'

Louisa's scowl held for several seconds, before it gave way to a confused frown. 'You . . . How?'

Bella gave her a silky grin and pushed back the covers. 'Wait here, I have just the thing.' She hurried across the room, unlocked a small compartment in the bottom of her wardrobe and brought out a box. She returned to the bed before removing the lid. Louisa looked into it and gasped. A highly polished phallus of closely stitched leather lay framed by the delicate tissue paper; it even had balls.

'Of course, Joshua doesn't know I have it. I found it amongst my grandfather's things in the attic,' Bella explained, as she noted her friend's strange fascination. 'Probably used it on the servants after his own vine withered. It'll certainly give you an idea of how a man feels inside you. Tempted?'

'I don't know.'

'It's up to you. It's not as good as the real thing, but it's pretty good.'

Bella watched the rapid rise and fall of Louisa's breasts. Her pert nipples were clearly visible through her white shift, while her eyes were fixed on the dildo. At that moment, Bella could see the appeal Louisa had to men. She was so delicate, so pliable.

'Trust me.'

'All right.'

Louisa tensed for the space of a heartbeat, then breathed eagerly as Bella untied her nightgown. Their lips met and Bella began to explore her friend's delicate mouth. Conceiving herself as Captain Wakefield, she tried to touch as he would, to feel as a man. She imagined that the sudden throb of longing between her thighs intensified and extended into a thick erect cock. With it came a deep desire to touch herself, and to sheath herself inside a warm safe place.

'Close your eyes. Think of Frederick,' said Bella. She crawled on top of Louisa and used her knees to press her friend's legs apart, then sucked and licked at her nipples, sometimes nipping ever so softly, sometimes not being quite so gentle. Her own moisture was gathering thickly between her thighs. She wondered if the same was true for Louisa, who was making only quiet mewls.

The impression of her nails left a red trail across the curve of Louisa's stomach. Bella tangled her fingers in the golden curls over her friend's mound, then dipped her tongue to the velvety folds. She tasted very different to a man, though not unpleasant. However, the crow of joy she received in response to flicking the tip of her tongue across Louisa's clitoris was akin to the response she got from Mark, when she lapped at his shiny cock-head.

'Is that good?'

'Mmm. Nice.'

As she continued to lick and suck, she sought out the leather phallus from where it lay discarded on the sheets. The shaft felt cool and smooth. Bella warmed it between her thighs before worming it into Louisa's honeyed vulva. She continued the tease for several minutes. Each touch, each glancing bump elicited another gasp of desire from Louisa. Suddenly, with a sharp thrust, she gave what was promised.

Louisa jerked up off the mattress at the shock invasion, wide blue eyes lit startlingly bright in the candlelight. Bella began to work her wrist, driving the phallus deep, and using her thumb on Louisa's clitoris. 'Say something, Louisa.'

'More . . . please!'

Bella knew how long she could endure this sort of stimulation herself before reaching climax, and Louisa didn't prove any different. Her delicate nipples puckered, her skin flushed, and she came in a long tremor. Her muscles contracted around the slick baton, almost tugging it from Bella's grasp.

Her eyes opened in wonder.

'Did you enjoy that?' said Bella, and she gave a Harlequin smile.

The November moon was low in the sky as Frederick Wakefield walked over the moors, his pace brisk as he retraced their daytime path. A thick mist had settled just above the heather since their earlier excursion, and now it clouded the valley floor. The distance was lost to vision, and only the lonely granite cross of the church was visible through the shifting haze.

Louisa – he had received a note, a midnight assignation in the graveyard, a *danse macabre*. He could only blame Horace Walpole and Ann Radcliffe for inspiring the setting. Why, like Shakespeare's Juliet, couldn't Louisa have chosen a garden or, better still, a rug in front of a fire? He guessed Bella had something to do with it. Thankfully, she had been discreet; he might have been drunk, but his conscience still plagued him over the night of the ball. He doubted that Louisa was the type to understand or forgive infidelity.

In its hollow, the church was almost swallowed by the choking mists. Would she come? He had his doubts, but he was here now. The grey stone of the boundary wall loomed out of the mist just yards away, fuzzy edged and foreboding.

It had been simple to slip out of the house. The others had retired early after dinner and a few rounds of billiards. They were planning a dawn trek across the moors, and perhaps he would join them. He had not decided; so much depended on tonight. By tomorrow, he might be the happiest man alive.

Vague grey forms spiralled out of the mist as he went down the broad steps to the church door, making him think he was being watched or followed. He shook off his suspicions, rationalising them as phantasms of his own heightened awareness. He wouldn't be put off by a few graveyard spectres.

The mist ended in a wall of grey ether at the door to the little church. From within, the faint rustle of silk against stone caught his attention.

She had come.

'Louisa, is that you?' he hissed.

The church door creaked ominously on its hinges as he opened it. Moonlight spilled, blue, green and rosy through the stained-glass panes. An ethereal figure stood at the far end of the chapel amidst a sea of rose petals that someone had scattered over the floor. The glint of honey-blonde hair spilled out from beneath a hood, as she turned slightly in response to his footsteps.

All around him the still air smelled of church mould, dust, clay, and the faint essence of roses. He felt like he was conducting a love affair with a ghost. If only the location was a little less eerie, he might not feel so nervous. Reaching her, he pulled back the pink hood and pressed a kiss to the nape of her neck. He moved his mouth to her upturned face and tasted the soft comfort of her lips, which were tinged blue from the cold.

All too soon he realised that the woman he held, who peered up at him from beneath delicate, fluttery eyelashes, was not Louisa. This was not his beloved's smooth skin that he brushed his fingers against, and the knowledge hit him like a blow to the chest. Meanwhile, the girl coaxed him with an interminable kiss that sucked the breath from his lungs and made his head spin at its intensity.

'All's well from this end,' Joshua announced, emerging from the fog to startle his friends.

'Do you have to sneak up?' Charles complained. 'This infernal fog is bad enough without you for a bogle.' He fanned the air ineffectually as if to disperse the mist.

'Shhh, Charles,' called Lucerne from behind the hedge where he lay with Vaughan, observing the church door. Charles grunted and scowled at Joshua.

'Everything is fine from this end as well, Josh – he's so smitten, he doesn't suspect a thing. I assume you got the girl.'

'He's going in,' observed Vaughan.

'That's all right. She's already in place. I took her in through the back entrance since we were a trifle late.'

'Why?' asked Charles.

Joshua deliberately ignored his accusatory glances and gave his attention to Lucerne.

'Back entrance? I didn't notice a back entrance, and I went all over the place earlier today.'

'Through the crypt. There's a tunnel set into the bank. You come up in the south-west corner.'

They heard the latch drop on the church door.

'Come on,' Joshua cried, bounding off down the slope. 'We can watch from round the side, peer in the window, eh?'

'Won't we be a bit obvious?' whined Charles.

'No. There are some very convenient gravestones.' He beckoned for them to catch up. 'If you can cope with the grass stains, that is.'

Her body was slight like Louisa's, with small hips. There the similarity ended, apart from the golden hair. Her skin was also honey-gold, tanned by the summer sun. Her bust was ample, soft, and more than he could cup in his hands. 'I think this is some kind of mistake,' Frederick muttered as the girl drew him close. He now knew he was the butt of some joke by his so-called friends, and he tried to push her away. He could picture them spying on him, laughing at his expense. Yet her kisses and skilled touch bewitched his senses, and aroused a cruel longing in his loins.

'Don't you want me?' she murmured.

Frederick focused on the cracked stone floor tiles, engraved with the names of the long-dead, as she traced the line of his crotch with her fingertip. Desire quickened in his balls. It was too much to resist. Helpless, he watched her kneel and nestle her head against his thigh. She released him, exposing his cock to her merciless kisses.

The soft pressure of her lips flickered across his torso as she drew him down onto the pew. The warmth of her body made a stark contrast to the cold bench against his back, while the soft muslin of her chemise grazed his skin, further heightening his sensitivity. He barely touched her.

If he didn't touch her, it wasn't his fault.

She tasted him. She supped on him as if she was tasting the creamy ambrosia of the gods, then gently but firmly guided the head of his cock between her breasts. Vanquished, he gazed up at the rich golds and greens of the angels on the vaulted ceiling, and returned their seraphic smiles.

'Oh yes!' he groaned.

Captive between her breasts, he lost control and instinct took over. He clasped her shoulders and rocked her back and forth along his length. The motion built on the rapture. With sweet anticipation, he focused on the raging waters within his shaft, and ejaculated over her.

Too soon the pleasure faded into memory, receding as rapidly as that tide of emotion had, leaving behind only the echo of his orgasmic cry.

'Louisa!'

From their vantage point, three pairs of eyes watched Frederick and the girl. Charles's were bulging; Joshua's showed amusement; Lucerne's were narrowed but his pupils were dilated. He turned his head away when Charles's excited panting became too distasteful, to find an empty space to his left where Vaughan had been.

Lucerne found him leaning against a tilted gravestone, close to the rough, drystone wall that separated the churchyard from the moors. He was staring up through the branches of a denuded tree at the opaque night sky.

'Vaughan, are you all right?'

Vaughan's gaze shifted sideways and flickered over Lucerne. There was a sad smile upon his parted lips, which made him look ever so slightly fragile. Concerned, Lucerne moved a step closer. 'What is it?'

Vaughan reached out and touched him tenderly with his long fingers. The caress was so soft it barely registered against the skin, but Lucerne felt the undercurrent right through his body. Numbed by it, he watched in a trance as Vaughan leaned forwards and brought his lips to meet Lucerne's own.

Anger, excitement and fear sparked where their lips met. Bewildered, Lucerne simply accepted the kiss. The fierceness of Vaughan's passion burned him and rippled through his tensed body, adding to his confusion. The first stirrings of lust played around his loins. Only when he felt the other man's tongue dart between his lips and flick against his own did he push him away.

'No!'

He stared at the grass.

'Lucerne, remember how it can be.' Vaughan reached out to him again, but this time Lucerne stepped back warily and raised his arms to ward off the intimacy. He set his jaw and met Vaughan's eyes. For an instant, he saw desire and intense pain in the dilated pupils, then the window to Vaughan's soul snapped closed and all that was left was his own cold glare reflected back at him. They regarded each other silently, not quite knowing what to say.

'I . . .'

'No,' said Lucerne.

Vaughan bowed his head, then turned and walked away.

They returned to the hedge where they had all met at the start of the escapade and, after greeting a bashful Wakefield jocularly and bidding Joshua goodnight, began the long walk back to the Hall in silence. Charles, in the hope of drawing forth a few sordid details, attempted to draw Wakefield into conversation, but failed and so enthusiastically recounted the delightful vision of the girl's heaving bosom glistening with pearly dew. He intended to immortalise it in poetry.

Wakefield felt duped and sorely used by people he had considered friends. He was particularly annoyed at Lucerne. The joke was too extreme, being at Louisa's expense as well as his own, though he'd make damn sure that she didn't learn of it. As if what he'd done with Bella wasn't bad enough. Worst of all, he was unable to deny the pleasure he'd experienced that evening, and was still feeling now – of her silky touch and the soft pillowing flesh around his loins.

Lucerne and Vaughan walked apart until they neared the Hall, when Vaughan picked up the pace and broke away from the group to dissolve rapidly into the mist. Lucerne followed him. He knew he'd reacted badly, and that he owed Vaughan an apology, but when he caught up with him on the front steps and tried to speak his words came out halting and cold. Vaughan regarded him with pursed lips and a clenched jaw, and departed without comment at the approach of Charles's droning voice.

Lucerne snapped to attention like a soldier on parade. 'Gentlemen,' he said curtly, with a nod of his head. 'Goodnight.'

Lucerne settled back against the feather pillows of his bed and sighed. The household had retired for the night but he expected the bad moods would still be with them in the morning. At the very least, he knew things would undoubtedly be strained between himself and Vaughan. The others might notice, especially Wakefield who, if he ever forgave Lucerne for his part in tonight's charade, would be overjoyed that they'd fallen out.

Yes, Wakefield would be deliriously happy, but he himself was not. He enjoyed life around Vaughan, and always had. Vaughan made life interesting. He kept everyone on their toes, servants and intimates alike. So how had it come to this?

Lucerne placed his fingertips at his temples.

Ever since he'd arrived, Vaughan had watched him

with those deep dark eyes, and Lucerne had half formed his suspicions, but he'd seen no reason to voice them. He didn't need a man, not when he could have Bella or any other woman who came along, and so he'd brushed those inklings aside. He remembered now Vaughan's expression when he had told him about Bella spying on him, the night they had stayed up late. The scowl that he'd quickly buried behind laughter spoke volumes. They'd watched the dawn break together and Vaughan had grown progressively more moody. Now he understood why. Everything had been going so well as he settled down to life at Lauwine. Until tonight, he'd more or less buried the past . . .

They had not seen each other for three years when they'd become acquainted again in Rome, by chance. Vaughan had been living there for several months, and had greeted Lucerne with his typical reticence, but had taken the viscount under his wing all the same. They had combined their pleasures. At night they gambled, whored and drank, while by day they admired the artistry of their surroundings. Then, one evening as the sun set on the fields outside the city, their relationship had changed.

A night at the card tables had ended with them back at their lodgings surrounded by a dozen or more wine bottles and the remains of a late supper. Lucerne couldn't remember precisely what had happened, or what had sparked off the event that followed. Retrospectively he knew he'd been drunk. At the time, all he was aware of was the soft delicate touch of those long white fingers against his inner thigh, bringing him so much pleasure. Light caresses on the fabric of his breeches, as the moon flowed like liquid silver into the sky. Fingers that had moved with the expertise of a Parisian whore over the shaft of his cock.

He gasped as the memory of that touch burst into the present, and a wave of pleasure stiffened his penis. He pushed his hand beneath the bedspread and tentatively closed it over the shaft.

He remembered the surprise he'd felt afterwards at having been touched by a man, and the confusion at his own arousal. Vaughan hadn't given him the chance to think at the time. He'd pushed him onto the bed and unbuttoned his breeches, releasing his erection. Then he'd kissed his ruddy plum before giving him perhaps the best fellatio he'd ever had. Next morning Lucerne had run away; packed his bags, made his excuses and left Rome. When they met again, enough time had passed and Vaughan had made no comment, so they'd continued to be friends. But now?

Now Lucerne was concerned. His cock was hard in his hand just from the memory of that night. What was he supposed to do if his memories could affect him so powerfully? How could he live around Vaughan? He focused all his senses on his straining prick and blanked Vaughan from his mind. He was already so primed it took very little work for him to come.

Lucerne lifted the towel from the bed stand and wryly mopped his own stomach. It had been a long time ago, he reasoned, and only one night out of a thousand he had spent with Vaughan. He had not forgotten the past, and nor did he deny it, but he wasn't prepared to renew it.

# 6

Bella had first felt a numbing sense of disquiet as the carriage rattled up the avenue of trees the following afternoon. Something had happened in their absence that had made everyone at Lauwine Hall moody, and even the weather seemed to have been affected. Charles was in the upstairs parlour. He looked up from his paper long enough to explain that Lucerne had gone out and that the marquis and the captain were respectively indisposed and tired. Bella didn't care about Vaughan, but she'd been looking forward to seeing Lucerne again. They had some unfinished business to conclude from yesterday, and she was eager for his hands and lips on her face and body. Damn Vaughan for interrupting them. Wakefield's absence also dampened Louisa's mood.

Lucerne didn't return until gone six, when he staggered in out of the wind, blond hair tangled with leaves and his normally alabaster-white skin flushed red from the impact of the gale. His shirt was open to the chest. Icy water dripped from the fabric as he tapped his riding crop impatiently against his thigh while Ivo, his valet, tried to brush clumps of wet grass from his coat. Lucerne quickly lost patience. He barked some orders then pushed Ivo aside and strode up the stairs. Dismayed, Bella gazed at the muddy boot prints on the marble steps and wondered what had happened to the fragile peace. She thought of following him. Perhaps she could change his mood with the promise of a few soft pleasures. She quickly thought better of it; he'd seemed very abrupt, and she didn't want to take a chance on rejection.

She'd laid all her plans around Lucerne, and now she felt at a loss for how to entertain herself until dinner, Joshua and Louisa both having retired for a short rest. She wandered aimlessly through the first-floor rooms. Lucerne had already shown her the vast library, with its row upon row of dusty old books. The dining room was a familiar feature. She stayed only long enough to sneak into the stag parlour. The masculine retreat was choked with paintings, tapestries, and more chairs than was reasonable for such a small room. It led on to the billiards room and, beyond that, the newly refurbished drawing room. Between here and the salon lay several empty rooms and Bella tried the knobs to them all, but only one opened. She cautiously put her head around the door. It was the old morning room.

As she had expected, it was empty. Bella straightened up and went inside. The room smelled of ages past, stale and musty. The walls were covered in faded, mildewed yellow and gold paper, and a large rug covered the centre of the floor. The floorboards groaned and squeaked as she crossed to the window. It was thick with ivy, but she knew it should have overlooked the lawn and the willow tree. She tried the door to the adjoining room but the handle just rattled in her hand.

'It's locked. The east wing isn't suitable for guests.'

The voice startled her. Bella turned sharply, letting go of the brass handle with a guilty start. Vaughan posed languidly with his back to the outer door. He was dressed in tight black trousers and a loose cambric shirt, with thick lace cuffs that covered most of his hands. 'It's not wise to explore alone, nor appropriate without invitation. What were you looking for – Lucerne's room, perhaps?'

Bella stiffened; Vaughan was the last person she

wanted to run into. Although she had hardly spoken to him, she'd decided on the evening of the ball that she didn't like him. He was an arrogant, self-centred, stuck-up dandy, and then there was the small matter of what he'd done to Louisa. Pity, then, that he was so damned attractive. She couldn't help looking at him.

'I thought you were indisposed,' she said.

'Only to certain company. Do you always ignore questions?'

Bella's brows knitted themselves together. His insolence was starting to make her blood boil. 'Only if I don't think it worth answering them. What if I *was* looking for his room?'

His lips twisted into a thin, sardonic smile. 'Then I should engage your services as a whore, for Lucerne will not.'

Colour flooded into Bella's cheeks. She felt her pulse in her temple, while the boned cage of her stays resisted her as she sucked in a deep breath. The arrogant swine was goading her. 'You couldn't afford me, my lord,' she spat.

Vaughan inclined his head to one side; there was a spark of real interest glinting in his pupils. 'Oh, I think I could.' His voice was low, barely more than a whisper. 'I daresay it might even be a pleasant diversion on this dismal afternoon. What do you say, Miss Rushdale: shall we make a bed of this worn rug?'

'I'm no whore,' retorted Bella, lifting her chin. Vaughan crossed the room. The muffled tread of his boots sounded dully on the threadbare rug. He came to a halt before her, on the frayed edge, and regarded her carefully with one eye. His dark hair masked the other.

'Correct. A whore rarely loves her work.'

A low growl burned in Bella's throat. She clenched her fist, whitening her knuckles. 'I should slap you for that.'

'Do, please; be my guest.'

For several seconds Bella glared at him as she restrained the urge to lash out. His patient, mocking expression was what stopped her. She wouldn't be laughed at. Eventually, Vaughan turned his back on her and, with the same soft tread, crossed to the window. Relief flooded through Bella's muscles, releasing the tension in her limbs.

'A pity you haven't the nerve,' he said. 'I think I might have enjoyed it.' He glanced back over his shoulder at her and smiled unguardedly, inviting her to share the joke. Bella felt her anger dissipate as his arrogance briefly receded, leaving only his attractiveness. Unexpectedly, her desire quickened. She stepped closer to him, drawn by the faint musk of his skin and the heat of his hands and thighs.

'If the room isn't suitable for guests, what are you doing here?'

Vaughan brushed the hair away from his eyes and regarded her. 'Sulking,' he said.

'About what?'

'It's none of your business.'

Bella felt the sudden rebuke like a slap in the face, and even felt the sting in her cheeks as blood rushed back to them. She wondered how to trick an answer from him. Perhaps it would explain to her why everyone was behaving so oddly.

'Take some advice, Miss Rushdale. Leave Lucerne alone. He'll do you no good.'

Her nose and brow wrinkled into a frown. Vaughan pressed a cool finger to her parted lips to silence her. His touch was gentle and seductive, and reminded her of last night's muddled dream. Bella slapped his hand away. 'Don't be absurd. I'll do no such thing.'

'That's a shame, else we might have been friends.'

There was a deep melodic note to his voice that hinted at future sorrow and the loss of something far more intimate than friendship. He stared down at her as if he could read her thoughts. A tingle of excitement formed in the pit of her stomach and raced through her breasts and throat. He stepped back and perched on the window ledge. She followed and stood between his parted thighs, drawn by she didn't know what: perhaps the scent of his body, so inadequately masked by his rich aromatic perfume, or perhaps his extraordinary heat.

'Are you trying to trap me?' he asked.

'Of course not.' She took three quick steps back, then looked at the floor in embarrassment.

'Come here.'

'Why?'

'Come here.' He reached out to her. His index finger brushed the centre of her palm, echoing a sweet response at her core. She felt confused. A moment ago, she'd been ready to thump him. He brought her hand up to his lips and kissed each fingertip. The last finger he nipped with his incisors, sending a prick of pleasure-pain through her over-eager body. His arm slipped around her back. She groaned longingly as their tongues danced a heated tango. His heat was so fierce she thought it would consume her.

In the distance, the clock struck the hour.

Bella parted from his embrace reluctantly. She'd never experienced anything quite like that before. His kisses stayed on her lips like the taste of wine.

'Does this mean you'll stay away from Lucerne?' he asked.

'No.'

He drew a finger across her rosy cheek and laughed. 'We'll see.'

* * *

The echo of his laughter still filled her ears when she sat down at the dining table. Lucerne, immaculate once more, sat at the head, while to her right Captain Wakefield was wearing the aura of a thundercloud. He was facing Louisa, but didn't even fake a smile. Opposite Bella sat Charles, whose tiresome anecdotes drew threatening glares from all quarters. Vaughan sat at the far end by Joshua. They ate to the accompaniment of him tapping his nail against the rim of his glass and the low growl of the wind outside. Nobody seemed in any mood to talk.

Bella suffered the oppressive atmosphere until she spotted her brother trying to sneak off furtively during the cheese course. She followed him out into the hall then picked up her long skirts and sprinted across the parquet floor. The clatter of her heels echoed in the alcoves. She arrived at the bottom of the stairs in a swish of fabric. 'Joshua.' The aged timbers creaked as he halted on the landing and turned to meet her.

'What is it, Bella? I'm in a hurry. I told Lucerne I'd only be a moment.'

'What's going on?'

'He's challenged me to billiards.'

'Not that,' she snapped.

Joshua cocked his head nervously. Worry lines creased the shadowed skin around his eyes. 'What, then?'

Tall and hawklike, he stared down at her like a bank clerk, but the austere gaze that worked on his employees at the mine had no effect on Bella, and never had. She knew that her brother would give in to her. She stepped closer to him and met his contracted pupils with a fierce glare. 'Oh, don't pretend to be innocent. Something happened last night, and I'll bet you were privy to it. Why else would you send us home for a night?'

'I went into town.'

'Like hell you did.'

'All right,' he sighed wearily. He knew well enough when to capitulate, and sat down on a nearby stool. 'What is it you want to know?'

'Why has everyone spent the day hiding, and why did Lucerne come home looking like he'd been mud-wrestling with the Brown Man of the Moors?'

The merest flicker of a smile twitched Joshua's lips. His angular features were contemplative. Bella stared at him.

'We played a joke on Captain Wakefield last night. He didn't see the funny side and is still smarting. It's put people at odds with each other.' He blinked slowly, thoughtfully. 'I think Lucerne and Vaughan had a row.'

Bella bit her lower lip. That explained Vaughan skulking about in the morning room. She allowed her brother to stand.

'And no, I don't know what it was about,' he added before she asked. 'Can I go now? Lucerne will be waiting.' He stalked across the landing towards his room.

'Wait a moment, what was the joke?' Bella called after him. She lifted her hem to follow him but heard a footfall on the stairs below her and turned to find Louisa ascending.

'Please, Bella, I need to talk.' Her lip trembled and the glassy sheen of imminent tears glittered in her eyes.

'All right.' Bella stared at the door that had closed behind her brother. 'Let's go to your room.'

Lucerne heard footsteps behind him as he leaned over the billiards table to line up a practice shot. 'About time, Josh,' he remarked, before hitting the ball with a crack. He'd been waiting at least five minutes. As he received no reply, he straightened and glanced over his shoulder. Vaughan glared back. He was standing in the doorway, and his face was a mask. Only his eyes betrayed his smouldering rage, and Lucerne realised that Vaughan wasn't prepared to let what he'd started in the churchyard drop.

'My apologies.' Vaughan's tone was crisp. 'I didn't realise anyone was in here.'

Lucerne took a sip of wine from his glass, and watched his friend. The dusky grey velvet suit worked well against his skin, and showed off the sable ringlets that lay luxuriously across his shoulders. The frosting of crystal beads around the edge of his coat might have appeared excessive on another man, but looked magnificent on Vaughan.

'You'll take a turn at the table with me.'

'I'd rather not.'

'Pardon?' Lucerne deliberately placed his glass on the baize then sent the nearest ball ricocheting around the table. It dropped into the left centre pocket. 'Do I have to remind you that you're a guest in my house?'

Vaughan's back stiffened and his shoulders came up. 'Perhaps my lord would prefer it if I left.'

'Don't be stupid,' snapped Lucerne. He didn't want Vaughan to leave, but he didn't want to deal with his friend's sour feelings either. He'd never asked for this. 'What's your problem, anyway?' he said tightly.

'You know what my problem is, Lucerne. What's yours?'

Lucerne raked his fingers through his hair. Frustration always made him fidgety. 'I don't have one beyond your attitude.'

Vaughan sneered. His expression became vicious and spiteful. 'Of course not. The society darling, Viscount Lucerne Meyrick Aherne Marlinscar, doesn't have any problems. Just don't demand satisfaction from him.'

'That's enough!' Lucerne slammed his fist down on the table. The balls jumped and the white fell into a corner pocket.

'Not yet, it isn't. I haven't finished. Just because Wakefield's content to be your lapdog doesn't mean I am. I remember the night in Rome as vividly as you do. I know what I felt, and you, my lord, are more transparent than you think. I'm tired of your evasiveness and affectations; I'd like to hear the truth from your lips for once.' He brushed aside Lucerne's protests with a wave of his lace-shrouded hand. 'I bid you goodnight,' he snarled, and stalked out of the room.

Lucerne turned back to the billiards table. He tossed aside the remaining dregs in his glass and refilled it with brandy. Vaughan's remarks had cut to the quick. No one else would have dared to provoke him like that, and yet Lucerne didn't want to send him away. He prayed Vaughan wouldn't leave of his own accord, but he had no elegant solution to their dilemma, and the memory of Vaughan's kisses still lingered through the taste of the brandy.

Joshua hurried back to the billiards room with his cues over his shoulder, but pulled up sharply within sight of the door. Vaughan stood just over the threshold with his back to Joshua and, judging by Lucerne's clipped tone from within, he'd caught them mid-argument. After the fiasco at the ball he had no further desire to mediate for anyone, so he quietly stepped into the drawing room to wait it out.

Only a moment later, he heard the door slam. He watched Vaughan storm towards the front door and throw it open, then disappear into the night. Joshua grimaced to himself, waited for the space of a few breaths, then walked briskly into the room. Lucerne was holding a cue in one hand and a glass of spirits in the other. From behind he appeared perfectly at ease but, when their eyes met, it was clear to Joshua that beneath a face of calm Lucerne was furious, and probably well on the way to becoming seriously drunk.

Bella closed Louisa's door quietly behind her, opened her eyes wide and sighed theatrically. She'd spent the better part of an hour calming Louisa's immediate fears. She felt sure that Wakefield's feelings hadn't changed suddenly, despite his frostiness at dinner. As Joshua said, he was probably just brooding over whatever prank they'd played on him last night. She paused at a window to look out on the night. The wind was still howling across the moors, bending the trees, and she could see rain clouds massing to one side of the bright moon. The brewing storm perfectly framed the mood of the household. Perhaps when it broke so would the atmosphere inside.

She let the curtain fall.

Two minutes later she was creeping out of the open front door and heading for the path towards the stables. To the left of the gazebo, a heavy iron gate guarded the entrance to the grotto. She'd never been there – it had always been too overgrown – but she'd heard the gardeners clipping it back on her first morning at Lauwine. A quick examination confirmed that the padlock was missing. Bella brushed the orange flakes of rust from her fingers and gave the gate a shove. It swung open with an eerie creak.

The moonlight barely penetrated the dark avenues. She used the cool brush of waxy leaves against her open palms to guide her as she walked blindly into the unknown. The darkness felt limitless after the closeness of the house. After several turns, the crunch of gravel beneath her feet stopped abruptly and the high hedges gave way to enough moonlight to reveal a small paved courtyard surrounded by tall pines on three sides, and on the fourth by a brick folly. At the centre of the yard lay a pond, like a mirror with verdigris edges, and overhung by a gnarled cherry tree. It was bright enough for her to see how the algae had spread away from the lip to choke the life from the water lilies. The water was brown, and she looked for the ancient carp that was said to swim in its depths, but it was too dark to make out any detail.

The reflection of the folly rippled as a shadow parted from the arched doorway. She looked up. Vaughan stood by the ivy-covered trellis with a half-smile, half-sneer just visible on his lips. Clearly she wasn't the only one who'd come out to escape the house. The breeze that was making gentle waves on the surface of the pond also lifted his sable curls, swirling them about his shoulders. He took a few steps towards her, until he was close enough for her to see the moonlight reflected in his eyes. Suddenly it darkened as the grey clouds scudded across the moon. They were moving in fast. She sniffed at the air and noticed the faint taste of rain for the first time. Vaughan turned away, paused to look reflectively at the pond, then walked back into the folly.

Bella found her thoughts at last.

'Arrogant bastard,' she murmured. Still, she couldn't ignore the obvious invitation. She squared her shoulders, then pursued him into the oak-panelled interior.

He was waiting in the darkness at the far end of the lamp-lit room, half hidden like a ruffian. She measured the distance of mosaic floor between them, then stepped across the cold tiles. Earth and debris scuffed under her feet, and he lifted his gaze at the sound. Mockery danced in his violet eyes.

'Miss Rushdale, what happy circumstance.'

Bella came to his side as her thoughts settled into

composure. He would not have all the upper hand. He had caught her off guard earlier, but this time would be different. She met his dark eyes defiantly, and watched him pout in response.

'What would you have of me?' he asked.

She watched him part his lips and slowly lower his dark lashes over his eyes. The gesture was so deliberate and vain it was astonishing. It was also deeply seductive. She fought down the tide of desire that threatened to upset her poise. Perhaps the power of his self-assurance drew her, or something equally intangible.

'Why did you warn me away from Lucerne?'

For a brief second, rage showed in his eyes like a splinter of diamond. He seemed about to storm past her, out into the tranquil night, but then he mastered himself. His body relaxed and he exhaled his anger.

'Always Lucerne! Is that the only reason you followed me in here, or was there something more?'

He leaned close to her as he spoke, so that she could feel the warmth of his breath and she watched his mouth descend. He grazed her bottom lip and held it. The taste of him released her memory and she answered his kiss, while her arms moved to pull him closer. She clawed at him urgently, then slipped her hands under his coat as he drew her deep into his kiss. Nobody had ever kissed her the way Vaughan did. He made her lips burn with a heat that washed straight to her cunt.

He grasped her shoulders and thrust her against the blackened oak panelling with enough force to make a thump. She didn't notice the pain, feeling only a rush of desire and vertigo, like a foretaste of orgasm. His teeth met her neck and nipped the delicate skin, while he loosened her stays enough for him to slide his fingers between fabric and flesh. Her nipples sprang to attention, then stiffened a little more as he teased her.

Bella hooked her thumbs into his waistband and tugged him closer. All her instincts craved penetration. She was ready for him now, but he was holding himself back. To her surprise, he suddenly sank gracefully to his knees. He lifted the hem of her skirt, bunched up the swathes of velvet and hoisted it to her waist. He brushed his cheek against her stockings, pressed a kiss to the skin above her garter then cupped her buttocks. His hands were hot against her cool cheeks, and warmed the soft skin as he pulled her forwards. She felt his tongue on her labia and the desire for penetration grew stronger. He dabbed at her clitoris with the tip of his tongue, teasing but never quite delivering. Even now, he toyed with her.

'A gentleman should use his tongue fairly in the presence of a lady,' she said.

He snorted, and pulled back long enough to give her a reproving glance.

'A lady has two essential attributes: modesty and underwear.'

Bella almost kneed him on the chin. She'd never known a man who could swing her between desire and anger with such ease, and she wasn't sure she appreciated the ability in him. How dare he! Yet the lapping of his tongue at her sensitive bud sapped the anger from her, taking away all her desire to hurt him.

'Do you like that, my nightingale?'

Bella shook her head, stifling the purrs that rose in her throat. She didn't want him to know how much she was enjoying this. He didn't deserve that.

'You're a harlot,' he said. 'Perhaps I should use you like one. I could throw your skirt over your face, ride you hard against the stone and leave you a crown for you trouble.'

'Bastard,' she hissed. 'Do it, then.'

Vaughan laughed and returned to his feet. 'Maybe I will.'

Bella's heart skittered over several beats. She whimpered as he began to massage her, fingers moving slickly in her wetness. If he entered her now, he would slide into her all at once. She tugged at the buttons on his waistband, then touched the head of his cock. She needed him now, this instant, inside her.

Vaughan stepped back and Bella's eyes snapped open in surprise. 'Vaughan,' she sighed. He turned his back on her and she watched in disbelief as he strode to the door. 'My lord?' In the doorway he stopped and glanced over his shoulder from beneath his dark eyelashes. Bella reached out a hand, desire for him still coursing through her veins. He shook his head, watched her expression change from ecstasy to anguish, then blew her a kiss and left.

Alone and a hair's breadth from orgasm, Bella slumped to the floor, devastated. She couldn't believe he'd walked out on her. Blinking back tears of shame, she reached down with one trembling hand to give herself the relief he had denied her.

Louisa lay in bed for a long while after Annabella left but, although she yawned repeatedly and the quiet darkness made her eyelids heavy, her thoughts raced like the wind outside the window. Eventually the rattling panes drew her from her bed, and once she was up not even the cold could drive her back between the sheets.

She found her dressing gown and slippers and put them on, preoccupied with her thoughts. She had to talk to Frederick. There were so many things unsaid between them, and his moroseness at dinner had frightened her. He'd seemed bitter, and even resentful towards her. From the start he'd behaved like a gentleman, never demanding more of her than she was willing to give, but she knew that her desire to take things slowly and her nervousness about sex were trying him hard. Every time they stole a few minutes together his eagerness showed, and the kisses that at the start had seemed to satisfy him now only caused frustration. She had not told Bella, but the last time they'd been together he'd come in her hands, leaving a sticky cream over her fingers. She'd been too intrigued to be ashamed, but Frederick had seemed grateful and embarrassed at the same time.

The hallway was deserted; the old house groaned in the wind, but there were no voices on the landing or from the upstairs parlour. Either everyone had retired or they were downstairs. Frederick's room was on the other side of the house, but she could cut through the long gallery to reach it. As she crept beneath the portraits, she could almost feel their disapproval. Men with thin cold mouths, Elizabethan forked beards and dark lifeless eyes stared at her, all-knowing. They played on her doubts as she reached his door, making her pause as she contemplated knocking. Suddenly, creeping to his room late at night dressed in a flimsy nightdress seemed rather unwise. She stepped away again in confusion and sat down in the window recess.

Vaughan was returning to his room. His encounter with Bella had improved his mood considerably. He had been laughing to himself all the way back to the house, and now he felt ready to face Lucerne again, confident that his friend would eventually come round. He just needed to give him enough rope to tangle his feet in, and then it would simply be a matter of timing.

So much came down to timing.

He shook his head, still smiling. Charles would be

celebrating if he'd known what had just happened in the folly. He realised he might just have wasted his best chance with Bella, but Vaughan was sure she'd be back for more. Besides, seeing her pleading, almost begging, had given him a far greater thrill than he'd have got from tupping her. Bella Rushdale was rapidly becoming a thorn in his side. Lucerne had become entirely too fond of her over the last week, and he didn't like the competition. He'd considered standing back and watching how things progressed. Perhaps Lucerne's interest would wane once he'd had her but, based on what he knew of his friend, he didn't think so. If Lucerne's only interest had been in bedding her, he'd have fucked her in a haystack by now and moved on.

The key scratched against the brass lock plate as he blindly sought the hole, distracted by the slender figure he saw out of the corner of his eye. He left the key in the lock and walked towards her. Although his arousal had diffused as he'd walked back from the folly, there was still a prickle of lust clawing beneath his skin, and an uncomfortable heaviness to his loins. His erection was gone, but it wouldn't take much to revive it. He knew what Lucerne thought about bedding the servants, but damn it, he was feeling purse-proud and Lucerne wasn't exactly co-operating.

It was only as he got closer that he realised his mistake.

'Louisa?' What was she doing sitting in the corridor at this hour? He followed the line of her vision to Wakefield's door. Well, that would explain it. So, she'd worked up her nerve at last? He'd better act quickly. He was buggered if he'd let her bravery cheat him out of sixty guineas.

'What are you doing creeping about outside my door?' he demanded.

He watched her snap back to reality. She blinked hesitantly, then flushed poppy-pink.

'Nothing.'

Her eyes widened in alarm, bright-blue even in the dim light as he leaned over her to draw a finger across her flaming cheek. He watched her bottom lip quiver. She was so easy to tease. Poor naïve Louisa. 'Are you sure you weren't waiting for someone?'

'No.'

She stood abruptly, cautiously squeezed past him then fled down the corridor. 'Am I so terrible?' Vaughan called after her. He thought of giving chase, but turned on his heels instead and crossed to Wakefield's door. He rapped sharply, then let himself in.

The captain looked up from his book as Vaughan clicked the door to and put his back to the wood. Wakefield was wearing a paisley dressing gown over his shirt and breeches. The pupils of his grey eyes shrank to pinpoints as he met Vaughan's gaze.

'Ah, Wakefield –'

'What do you want?'

'– do forgive the intrusion, but I thought I ought to inform you that you had a visitor lurking outside your door.' Vaughan watched his hostile expression crease into a sceptical frown. Here was another person easy to tease. 'Miss Stanley, in her nightshift, no less. I think she was summoning the courage to knock, unless you think she was looking for my door.'

Wakefield leaped to his feet. His forgotten book fell from his lap and hit the floor with enough of a thump to raise dust from the carpet. 'What have you done to her?' he snapped, as he frantically unknotted his dressing gown.

Vaughan shrugged his shoulders and graced the captain with his most rakish smile.

‘Get out of my way.’

Vaughan stood his ground, while stifling the urge to laugh in Wakefield’s face. He wondered if he could actually incite the captain to punch him. ‘And if I won’t?’

‘Move!’

Wakefield barrelled into his side, winding him slightly. Vaughan righted himself and tensed, ready to hold his ground. He laughed when he saw Wakefield’s jaw clench. When the captain lurched towards him again, Vaughan neatly sidestepped, sending Wakefield hurtling into the solid wood door. He slammed into the oak and reacted with a snarl that bared his teeth, then fumbled for the catch and rattled the knob unsuccessfully, only managing to turn it on the third attempt. As the door finally swung open, he bolted through it.

Precious!

‘Piss!’ muttered Lucerne, as he steadied himself on the doorframe. He glared at the loose piece of carpet, then righted himself. He’d decided to call it a night after finally managing to thrash Joshua at billiards. It had taken six attempts and, although he’d insisted they lay out a seventh, he’d conceded after opening. The balls had become a fuzzy blur and someone was dancing flamenco-style on his skull.

He rocked slightly on his heels, then staggered forwards, keeping his grip on the wooden panelling. Two paces on he froze and watched in horror as a white lady came hurtling towards him. He gulped, then blinked uncertainly. Jesus, he was pickled, and now he was hallucinating. The spirit was closer now, almost on him. ‘Sorry,’ it mumbled as it swerved sharply to avoid running into him.

‘Louisa,’ he hissed. ‘Christ, are you trying to petrify me?’

She stopped dead, then looked back at him with searing blue eyes. 'Sorry.' There were tears on her flushed cheeks.

'Is something wrong?'

'No.' She sniffed. Lucerne held out his hand.

'Has someone upset you?'

She shook her head and bit her lower lip to stop it trembling. Then she threw herself at him, burying her face in his chest. He blinked in surprise, and made sure he had his balance before letting go of the wall to put his arms around her. He guessed Wakefield was responsible, or Vaughan. That name produced a rush of vertigo in Lucerne. He wondered what it did to her.

'Do you think you can make it to your room?' he asked, as he tried to shake the cotton wool fuzz from his head. He really wasn't sober enough to be of much use. She shrugged her shoulders inconsolably. 'Louisa, come on. It's not far.'

She sniffed again, and dried her cheek with her hand. Lucerne's heart turned over. He hated to see anyone cry. He pulled her closer and folded her tightly in his arms, only to become aware of the feel of her lightly clad body pressed against his. When he noticed her stiffen against him, he reined in his instincts to let his hands rove. She was shaking enough already. 'Let's get you to bed where it's warm.'

He bent slightly and swept her up into his arms. It was only a short distance back to her room. The drink had made him clumsy, so it was just as well that she was so light. Still, it was a relief to reach the bed.

'I'll be fine now,' she whispered as he lay her down.

'Are you sure?' He stroked her golden hair where it spilled over the pillow. The mattress was soft and welcoming. He yawned sleepily while wishing he could just put his head down.

‘Certain.’ It took him more effort than it should have to get up. She followed him to the door. ‘Good night, Lord Marlinscar.’

‘Good night,’ he replied, and then bent forwards to kiss her. Her mouth was soft and pliant, hot to the touch, and tasted salty from her tears. He hugged her reassuringly, but she pushed him away.

‘Good night,’ she repeated firmly, then closed the door. Lucerne looked blankly at the wood for a moment, and then turned towards the stairs. His head was buzzing furiously, and he needed to lie down. He thought he might just make it as far as the daybed in his dressing room.

‘You damned whoreson fop!’

The exclamation felt like a plate breaking inside his head. Through half-lidded eyes, he managed to focus on the figure coming towards him like a tempest. ‘Freddy.’ He rubbed his eyes slowly to try to remove the hazy film that was distorting his vision.

‘You utter bastard. Last night you played your stupid joke on me, and tonight you and that mincing dandy just had to tread on my –’ Wakefield’s nostrils flared, and his lip trembled with emotion ‘– my love.’

I’m too tired for this, Lucerne thought to himself, mildly surprised by the passion behind his friend’s words. ‘What are you talking about?’

Wakefield flinched, then recovered and puffed up his chest. ‘You know. Why else would you be making love to her?’

Lucerne wasn’t even certain what they were talking about, but he suspected it might be Louisa. Too drunk for diplomacy, he opted for denial. ‘I wasn’t.’

‘Damn it, I saw you.’

‘You saw me kiss her good night. She was upset.’

Freddy's grey eyes took on the quality of flint. 'That was some goodnight kiss, Lucerne. Did you practice it on your grandmother?' he snarled.

Lucerne shook his head, and the pounding in his skull grew louder. He held up his hand. 'Enough! I wasn't kissing her. And I need to go to bed. Good night.' He pushed past Frederick and lurched onto the landing, feeling rather resentful. What he didn't need right now was another bloody argument; he'd had enough since last night. Wakefield's jealousy was tiresome at any time. Right now, it stood between him and his bed. He'd only kissed her because she'd looked like she needed it. Why didn't he go and yell at her?

'Like hell! I know you too well, Marlinscar.' Lucerne felt a weight on his left shoulder, strong fingers curling into the fabric of his coat. 'What, will you tuck Miss Rushdale in as well?'

'Get off.' Lucerne jerked aside to try and shrug off the restraint, but Wakefield moved with him and shifted his grip, boxing him in against the wall.

'You'll apologise.'

'For what? You're the one who's been free with your favours.'

Lucerne clawed at Wakefield's hands, trying to bend his fingers back, but to no avail. The stitching of his coat began to give under the strain. Lucerne yanked at Wakefield's arm and the fabric tore. Wakefield held up a piece of the cloth and Lucerne shoved him backwards. Rage filled Lucerne's eyes like a bloody film, making him conscious of the brooding anger he'd muddied with drink. It loosened his tongue. 'Might I add that after tupping her best friend you've no right to be jealous.'

'You told me you weren't interested.'

'I'm not.'

'So what's this, *primae noctis*?'

Lucerne's patience broke. He'd swallowed his anger and tried to be fair for too long. 'Cur!' he snarled. 'Which of her accomplishments are you interested in? Her painting and singing, or her money and her muff?'

Wakefield swung at him; Lucerne blinked uncertainly as he saw the fist coming towards him. He put up his arm to block the punch, somehow deflecting it so that it only caught him slightly on the chin, but he felt the dull explosion in his ear. In retaliation he lashed out wildly with his right fist, followed by a sharp uppercut to Wakefield's jaw with his left. His opponent swayed backwards, slightly disoriented. Lucerne hit him squarely in the midriff and sent him sprawling to the floor. He choked down the urge to continue, feeling that his point had been made. He staggered past the downed captain, wheezing slightly, wondering if he'd taken more hits than he remembered. As he turned to cross the lower landing to the east wing, he saw Wakefield grab the banister and haul himself to his feet. He glared at Lucerne then charged at him.

Lucerne's shoes skittered on the stone as he was thrown forwards by the impact. He threw his arms out to save himself and saw the marble stairs rise towards him. Everything slowed around him and he tasted bile in his throat.

He hit the bottom surprisingly intact but, by the time he'd recovered, Wakefield was on top of him.

Lucerne tried to roll, but a shooting pain in his ribs stopped him. He gasped and spat out the metallic-tasting saliva in his mouth as Wakefield hit him in the stomach. Still coughing, he made a grab for Wakefield's head, caught a handful of thick brown hair, and twisted. It earned him a howl of outrage, bringing a grim smile of determination to his bloodied lips. They both fought for advantage, grappling and pummelling. Lucerne felt a thumb digging into his throat, and reacted by driving his elbow into Wakefield's eye socket. The hand gripped harder and he kicked away, gasping for air.

'Gentlemen ... please.' Vaughan's voice echoed down the stairwell, accompanied by his descending footsteps. Lucerne breathed hard. After a moment he felt a hand on his shoulder pulling him away from Frederick, who had fallen against the bottom of the stairs.

'Lucerne!' Vaughan squeezed his shoulder, and put a restraining hand to his arm. 'Calm down.'

'What's this infernal racket?' bellowed Charles gruffly. Lucerne looked up the stairs to see him tiptoeing around the blood-spotted marble in his nightcap and gown, just above where Frederick had collapsed.

'It appears they're trying to kill each other,' explained Vaughan. He glanced at Lucerne, then at Wakefield. 'Perhaps you'd prefer pistols at dawn, gentlemen? Brawling is for the rabble.'

Lucerne shook his head, having suddenly lost his will to fight. 'That won't be necessary,' he said. He watched Wakefield nod in agreement, then accept Vaughan's handkerchief for his bleeding nose. Vaughan returned to Lucerne's side and offered him a hand up. Lucerne pushed him away. He was no greenhorn; he could get up on his own. No matter that his legs protested. He grimaced with determination, and managed to stand.

'What were you fighting over?' asked Charles

'Nothing,' he mumbled, and tried not to think of how he was going to feel once the numbing effect of the brandy wore off. A sliver of ice seemed to have embedded itself in his left side. He thought he might have to resort to laudanum just to sleep.

'Louisa,' admitted Frederick.

Charles snorted derisively. 'What the hell for? The maids are more comely. Got more meat on 'em.'

Lucerne frowned. He saw Frederick's jaw harden and his eyes narrow. He wanted to warn Charles not to make light of it, but was distracted by Vaughan sniggering behind him.

# 7

'You're leaving?'

Lucerne met Joshua's cheery face with a troubled frown. They were standing in Lauwine's marble entrance hall, not far from the bloodstained steps which a pair of maids were busy scrubbing. The smell of scouring powder assailed his nostrils, mingled with the cleaner odour of the rain beyond the open door.

Joshua shrugged on his greatcoat. 'Yes. I've business in Richmond, and a few days in town should give Frederick's temper a chance to cool. Plus, it will give us some time to sort out this nonsense with Louisa.

'It'll do you both good,' he continued, as he patted Lucerne's shoulder. 'The bruises will be gone by the time we're back, and heads will be clearer too.'

'I suppose so.' Lucerne rubbed his aching jaw and peered out of the door at Frederick, who was already seated in the carriage. He'd hoped for a chance to sort out last night's muddle and retract some of his remarks, but the other man showed no inclination to talk.

'You've a nasty gash there,' remarked Joshua, and Lucerne came back to the present. He had one cut on his cheekbone that he was hoping wouldn't scar.

'Quite. How's Freddy?'

'Some nice bumps, and a beautiful black eye,' Joshua replied tactfully. 'I trust honour is satisfied?'

Lucerne broke eye contact.

'Now, Lucerne –' Joshua's expression became unusually serious '– I'm going to have to leave Louisa and my sister under your protection. I could send them home to the Grange, but I know Bella; she'd be back before nightfall. Can I trust you to make sure that decorum is observed?'

'Of course. You have my word,' replied Lucerne, surprised and flattered by his request. He wondered what had built such an understanding between brother and sister. In the city, it was virtually unheard of for an unmarried lady to be left in the care of a man to whom she wasn't related. Of course, now that he'd given his word he'd have to behave himself, at least until Joshua returned.

'Come back soon,' he called as he watched Joshua sprint down the steps to the carriage.

He shut the door against the weather and looked around. For the first time, he noticed Bella on the balcony and Vaughan waiting in the shadows by the library door. He turned his back on them both, and strode away towards the east wing.

'Ah, Aubury. You've finally made it,' Lucerne congratulated Charles as the portly landowner reached the top of the hill, puffing like one of James Watts's steam engines. 'Do sit down awhile. Only another three miles to go.' Too out of breath for a more eloquent reply, Charles resorted to a glare, before he collapsed wheezing against a flat stone.

Vaughan allowed himself a smile. He was perched beside Lucerne on the top of a dry stone wall, listening to the wind whip around them. The sky had mostly cleared after lunch and only a few clouds remained. It had been Lucerne's idea to come out on a long walk; he probably thought it would clear the air. Vaughan supposed it was working quite well, given the fact that the exercise was likely to kill Charles; for his own part, fresh air wasn't going to change his mind. Eventually, he mused, Lucerne was going to have to face the facts about himself.

He leaned across to Lucerne and pulled a stray fern from his friend's hair. He saw a nervous smile twitch about the viscount's lips.

'Begad, Lucerne, there was no need for that mountain,' gasped Charles.

Lucerne stopped drumming his fingers on the moss-streaked wall and turned away from Vaughan. 'It's a hill,' he remarked dryly.

Vaughan released the fern, letting it sail off on the wind.

Charles blew out a long breath and propped himself on his elbows, face glowing beetroot red. 'Aye, for sheep and goats, maybe. How is it you two aren't out of breath?'

'We have less of a load to bear,' said Vaughan. He dropped to his feet, feeling the springy turf give beneath him. The spray of droplets splashed Charles.

'Hey, watch out,' he complained.

'You should spend less time at the card table swigging port and get out more,' said Lucerne.

'Get out more!' exclaimed Charles as he shook out his spotted cotton handkerchief. He mopped the sweat from his brow. 'Damn your eyes, Marlinscar. I often ride out with the hounds. What would you know? You've spent your life idling in London.'

'I'm not the one panting.'

'Clearly your chosen sport isn't taxing you enough,' remarked Vaughan.

Charles made a throaty grumble. 'You stay out of this, Pennerley.'

'I was merely going to suggest that you take up steeplechasing.'

'What an excellent idea!' Lucerne sprang to his feet. 'Let's race.'

'No,' groaned Charles.

Vaughan met Lucerne's twinkly blue eyes and saw laughter in them, and then they were both running.

'Last to the steeple pays the tab at the Golden Cock,' Lucerne called over his shoulder.

'Marlinscar, you confounded popinjay!' Charles yelled as he staggered after them, all red face and brown corduroy.

Giggling like boys, they ran down the grassy slope. It was half a mile of rugged pasture to the village of Reeth. At the end of the gorge, Vaughan leaped the stream and heard Lucerne splash through just behind him. He picked up the pace as he ploughed through the thick wet grass; it was hard work since the ground was still boggy after the rain, and there was no clear path. His soles squelched in the mud with each step. By the time they emerged on the grazing field that bordered the church, they were neck and neck.

Lucerne was racing him for the kissing gate. They'd only be able to go through one at a time. Vaughan veered right, pushed off on the top of the church wall and cleared it. He landed heavily on the far side, ducked to avoid laying himself out on a huge granite cross, and saw Lucerne sprint past him. Kicking out with his last reserve of energy, Vaughan chased him the remaining hundred yards to the church door. Lucerne won by a fraction of a second.

They staggered into the leafy porch, bent and panting. 'Lucerne.' Vaughan rubbed the sweat from his palm on his trouser leg, and offered his hand. They shook warmly.

'I'd never have won but for that wall,' confessed Lucerne. He straightened his back and coughed the phlegm from his throat as he smiled. 'That was hard work.'

'I daresay Charles will think so as well.'

Lucerne shielded his eyes and turned to look for him. A blurry figure was moving slowly towards them in the distance. 'I believe that's him coming.'

'Quick!' Vaughan grasped Lucerne's sleeve and tugged him along the uneven path around the side of the church. They scrambled between the blackberry bush and the vestry steps and fell on to the grass snickering behind a high, boxy sepulchre.

The sun was warm against Vaughan's chest. He lay still for a moment, listening to the birdsong and the sound of his own breathing. Lucerne was kneeling beside him, peeping cautiously around the edge of the tomb. Vaughan tugged at his coat. 'Get down. He'll see you.'

Lucerne allowed himself to be pulled back. He fell on to the grass beside Vaughan, stifling his laughter. Charles's voice drifted towards them on a breeze that smelled of ripe berries. Vaughan looked down into his friend's bright cornflower-blue eyes and sighed. He watched all the humour vanish from Lucerne's face, as the viscount's lips thinned and the light in his eyes dimmed.

'Vaughan, we have to talk,' he whispered.

There was a heavy silence. Vaughan shook his head almost imperceptibly. 'What's to be said?' He shifted his gaze to Lucerne's gently rising and falling chest to hide the pain of rejection in his eyes. He thought that, after all this, Lucerne's defences might have shown at least an appreciable crack.

'I'm sorry, Vaughan.' Lucerne touched his ringlets, unintentionally brushing the skin of his cheek. Vaughan flinched; the well-meant caress hurt more than a slap. He didn't need Lucerne's sympathy.

'Don't pity me.'

Lucerne shifted uncomfortably, drawing back his hand and laying it palm up on the grass. It looked like a gesture of surrender. Vaughan pounced, pinning his wrist, and felt the viscount's startled exhalation against his cheek as he lowered his mouth to kiss him. He'd prove his point yet.

'Ho, found you.' Charles leaned over the top of the sepulchre, just as their lips were about to brush. Vaughan jerked away sharply and rolled on to his side. Beside him, Lucerne sat bolt upright.

'What were you doing?' asked Charles.

'Nothing.' Lucerne's voice was gratingly sharp. Vaughan watched him pull himself to his feet, and brush down his breeches. 'Let's go for that drink.'

'Of course, of course, though I suppose you still want me to pay. Still, the Golden Cock has the finest ales, porters and small beers around, so I shan't complain. I expect such beverages will be wasted on your lordships. You'll be wanting sherry or Madeira,' he finished dubiously.

Vaughan caught Charles eyeing them suspiciously. Aubury wasn't as simple as he made out. At the very least, he was now wondering how far their friendship went. Let him wonder, he thought. Vaughan had never been afraid of his own sexuality, and he wasn't the only man among the nobility that played both sides. He graced Charles with a lecherous grin, and enjoyed the startled-rabbit response. They might have to have a talk later about ill-timed intrusions.

Lucerne offered Vaughan a hand up and he accepted it graciously. Their eyes met for the briefest moment before Lucerne turned away and led them into the lane. Anything left unsaid would have to wait, for the moment.

Lucerne watched as Charles swigged noisily from his second tankard of ale and pushed aside the remains of a dish of Yorkshire pudding and gravy. Vaughan idly dipped a fingertip into his mulled wine and sucked the sweet red liquid away: a sure sign that he was bored.

'We ought to head home,' Lucerne reminded them. 'I do have other guests.'

'What? We haven't had our pudding yet!' Charles sounded close to panic. Lucerne shook his head in exasperation. He and Vaughan hadn't eaten anything.

'How much pudding can one man eat?' sniped Vaughan, but Charles ignored them both and called over the buxom serving girl to order stewed plums. His eyes followed her plump breasts as she approached.

'B'gad, I'd love to pour cream over those dumplings,' he muttered.

Lucerne glanced across the table at Vaughan and they exchanged a mutual look of distaste. 'Lucerne, about that matter we discussed ...' Vaughan said, and he stood abruptly.

Lucerne thought of deferring the issue, but he realised Vaughan would never let it go, and in some ways the bustling inn was preferable to the intimacy of Lauwine. He rose warily. 'There's a private room at the back. You don't mind, do you, Charles?'

Charles glared disapprovingly at them, but just then the girl returned and leaned across the table to set a dish before him. Lucerne made use of the distraction to steer Vaughan towards the rear of the inn.

They found a small, comfortable room. Lucerne crossed to the fireplace and watched as Vaughan dropped the latch on the door, cast himself into the snug and lifted his elegantly heeled boots onto a chair. He'd been aloof and sullen since they'd come in, but he'd kept his remarks neutral in front of Charles. Lucerne had been thankful for that, but now he was clearly building to a confrontation. He wondered if they could keep this amicable, because the thought of Vaughan as an enemy didn't rest well with him. If it came out at Court, the bucks would make a scandal into a tragedy.

'This is already boring. Why don't you speak your mind?' Vaughan taunted as he returned his feet to the floor. Lucerne bowed his head and sighed to signal his intent. There was no avoiding it any longer.

'You ask too much.' Vaughan watched him expectantly. Lucerne pressed his fingertips to his temples. He'd never expected this to be easy. 'Can't you accept things as they are?'

'No. I was spoiled as a child. I always have to have my own way.' Vaughan left his seat and came to stand at Lucerne's side, then gently touched his arm. Contrary to his words, his eyes held tenderness and devotion. 'Please, Lucerne.'

Lucerne stared at the door and set his mouth. 'It's not what I want.'

'Do you deny the temptation?'

'No.' He plucked hesitantly at his cuffs. 'But I'm afraid of what it will mean.'

'You're damned stubborn,' Vaughan growled softly.

'So are you,' countered Lucerne.

'Agreed. I'm also persistent, so I ask you to surrender for the sake of my dignity.'

'Never,' hissed Lucerne, recognising Vaughan's humour.

Vaughan drew himself up straight, and gave Lucerne a challenging stare. 'So be it,' he said, then grasped Lucerne by the shoulders and kissed him, quickly and fiercely. Lucerne opened his mouth to protest and found his words silenced by Vaughan's tongue. Instead of struggling, he froze. Vaughan's mouth tasted warm and spiced from the mulled wine they'd drunk. Vaughan's hips pressed against his loins and the marquis's strong hands caressed him through the seat of his breeches. Vaughan's scent was all around him, male and very sexual. He trembled with fear and longing, growing fiercely and helplessly erect. Vaughan reached down and stroked him from the base of his cock to the tip, making him gasp despite himself. He felt a sudden terror that someone would enter the room, but the danger seemed to add to the thrill.

'That's damned unfair,' he protested.

'I know.'

Lucerne closed his eyes and offered no resistance to Vaughan's intimate caress. So it had all come down to this. He could sometimes deny his attraction to the other man, but he didn't have the willpower to force him away. The muscles of his stomach tightened and his mouth opened, but he didn't make a sound. Vaughan's thrilling attention was worth the risk of weathering discovery here or gossip at Court. He reached out to Vaughan and met his friend's desire with an urgency of his own. Outside, the muted hubbub of the inn went on. He hoped the latch was firm.

They clawed at each other's clothing and ground their pricks together, rubbing and kissing, while Lucerne tried not to think too hard about what he was doing. He slipped his hand inside the waistband of Vaughan's figure-hugging pantaloons, touched his friend's sensitive glans and heard him gasp. The sound gave Lucerne a surprising sense of satisfaction, and he allowed Vaughan to pull away long enough for the marquis to pull his black cambric shirt over his head.

Vaughan's body was lean but muscular and tapered neatly at the waist. His arms and shoulders were strong from his love of fencing, the same sport that had given him his oft-admired thighs. However, the most striking feature of his near-nakedness was the pale silvery line across his left side that marred the surface of his skin.

Lucerne traced its length curiously with his fingertips, and then with his tongue. It appeared to be a duelling scar.

'An unpleasant scrape,' elucidated Vaughan, as he tilted his head forwards to watch Lucerne. A fiery gleam showed through the shadow of his dark lashes, while his lips curled into an aggressive smile. 'Deuced Italians. I swear they've fire for blood.'

Lucerne smiled and pressed himself against Vaughan's warm body, glad that whatever implement had caused the wound hadn't done more damage. He felt Vaughan's arms snake around him and pluck at his coat. Lucerne shrugged it off, for once letting it fall to the floor. Then he unknotted his cravat, while Vaughan drew the curtain across the small, grimy window.

They fell upon each other again, as if mere closeness was not enough. Lucerne sank to his knees, then felt Vaughan about to follow suit and stopped him. He eyed the erect penis before him uncertainly. This would be a first. He cautiously closed his mouth over the head. It tasted salty against his tongue.

Vaughan inhaled sharply and sagged against the panelled wall for support, holding Lucerne's head to his cock as he moved. He didn't speak, but Lucerne didn't need him to. He knew how this felt, knew exactly how incredible such focused attention was. What surprised him was the pleasure he was deriving from the friction against his lips, and the addictiveness of having his mouth repeatedly filled.

Vaughan's fingers tangled in his hair. His hips rocked slowly. Lucerne knew he was resisting the urge to thrust deeper. He tried to take a little more, but felt the tip brush the back of his throat and had to fight back the instinctive cough that threatened to explode. He circled his fingers over Vaughan's arse, and then moved one hand to cup his friend's balls. Vaughan stiffened. He gave a deep emotive sigh and his whole body flexed as he came, shooting his seed into Lucerne's waiting mouth.

Lucerne released his hold and kissed him once, intimately. He watched Vaughan's prick continue to twitch as the afterglow of his orgasm washed over his body, and saw a contented smile spread over his face. Vaughan's eyes flicked open as Lucerne stood; they were dilated and unnaturally bright. They fastened on the trickle of come at the corner of Lucerne's mouth.

'Come to me,' he beckoned.

'No.' Lucerne wiped away the evidence of their encounter. 'Later,' he soothed, when he saw anxiety cloud the joy in Vaughan's eyes. 'Somewhere more private.' The risk of discovery suddenly felt very real.

Vaughan smiled and nodded. He rose to his feet and dressed quickly. There was a fresh glow to his skin now, and he positively radiated sexuality. Once he'd buttoned himself, he turned to Lucerne and caught his wrist, then forced a kiss on him. This time Lucerne accepted it without question, then they went out to collect Charles.

Bella closed the door to her room and sauntered towards the stairs. She felt listless with nobody around to spar with. The men were out walking, and Louisa was moping over Wakefield's departure. This left Mark as her only viable option, and one she didn't particularly relish. Compared with the breathless excitement she felt in Lucerne's company, Mark left her feeling unaroused and vaguely bored.

She paused at the top of the stairs, above the freshly scrubbed marble. She'd missed the fight, having come through the front door just as everyone was sloping off to bed. Nobody had noticed her. She'd been surprised by Joshua's news this morning: that the affray had been between Wakefield and Lucerne, not Vaughan, and that her brother was taking Captain Wakefield into town. She'd seen Lucerne only briefly after lunch; he had a long crimson scratch over one cheek, and was slightly yellow about the jaw. According to Joshua, the fight had brewed over the joke they'd played the night before. He flatly refused to relate any details and had changed the subject, extracting her promise to behave herself in return for permission to stay at Lauwine.

Bella put her back to the banister and stared across the hall. If she was at home she'd have gone riding or sneaked into the kitchen and got her hands dirty kneading pastry, taking out her frustrations on the dough. She couldn't very well do that here.

The door to Charles's bedroom was ajar. On impulse she strode across the landing and peered into the room. His possessions covered all the surfaces in a higgledy-piggledy fashion. Combs and shaving brushes lay alongside tatty books, while half burned candles made hangers for discarded neckcloths. She turned over a few of the volumes and scanned the cracked spines – military texts and poems, which summed up Charles perfectly.

She tried the door of Lucerne's room, keen to see how it differed from Charles's comfortable disorder. An ancient four-poster dominated his surprisingly sparse bedchamber. All his accoutrements were laid out on the dresser. She picked out his shaving brush and tested it against her neck. The soft bristles tickled, reminding her of the butterfly kisses she'd exchanged with her father as a child. The razor she left untouched. She didn't know how he could bear it near his throat, even in the trusted hands of Ivo.

The closet was packed tight. She searched through the garments by touch, and found the black velvet coat he'd worn on the night of the ball. The pile was thick and silky against her cheek as she pressed against his absent shoulder. They'd come so close to an understanding that night, and then she'd ended up astride the captain instead. The memory made her frown. She replaced the coat and took out another familiar garment: the blue silk he'd put aside that day in September to take a swim. The light in the chamber gave it a deeper hue than she remembered. From the hem, she removed a dried blade of grass that still held the faint but tantalising sweetness of the riverbank. She pushed her arms through the sleeves, and turned before the mirror to admire herself. It didn't work with her chemise dress, and it was not cut for a feminine figure: too broad across the shoulders, and too tight around the bust. But it did have a certain daring appeal. She wondered if he'd be prepared to let her borrow it.

Finally, she let herself into Vaughan's room, expecting to find implements of torture or a girl tied to the bed, but it was meticulously plain and masculine. She slumped onto his big soft bed and swung her legs petulantly.

'Trust ... Vaughan ... to keep ... all ... his ... secrets ... to himself,' she intoned as her heels drummed an accompaniment to her words on a solid object beneath the bed.

Bella paused.

She experimentally tapped her heel against the wood again and heard the hollow echo.

The metal corners of the trunk grated loudly against the floorboards as she dragged it from beneath the frame. It was a sea-chest, slightly wormy, and stamped in gold with Vaughan's initials.

'Bugger, padlocked,' she grumbled, as she lifted the weighty metal clasp. Where could he have hidden the key?

For someone of such refined tastes there was precious little in the way of filigreed snuff boxes in which to hide his treasures, and the drawers revealed only practical, if expensive, underwear. 'Damn him,' she cursed, returning to the bed. Trust Vaughan to be selfish. He probably carried the key with him just in case anyone dared enter his room to snoop.

Bella raised her head from the fluffy top pillow and puffed a stray eider feather from her fringe. The bed linen smelled of him. An image of his dark hair cascading over the pillow beside her swam in her mind. There was no use denying the attraction, but she owed him a reckoning for last night. A title didn't give him the right to treat anyone like that. These weren't feudal times, and she was nobody's whore.

She smashed her fist into the pillow, fracturing his image, and let her breath out slowly. Only then did she notice the gold chain dislodged by the impact. Bella drew it out. At the end was a small ornate locket. It held a lock of blonde hair, and was engraved with a date from three years earlier – 15 June 1794. 'How curious!'

She turned it speculatively in her palm. It seemed certain that she held something she could use to get back at him, but without knowing the full history of the item she'd be relying on heavy guesswork. Knowing there was a woman in his past was hardly a revelation; there were probably hundreds. Nevertheless, knowing he held enough affection towards one of them to sleep with a memento under his pillow might come in useful. She doubted he'd want anyone to know.

Her ears pricked at the sound of voices in the courtyard below. 'Hellfire!' If Vaughan's room wasn't the worst place to get caught ... She rubbed the locket on her dress to remove her fingermarks, pushed it back beneath the pillow, and then frantically smoothed the coverlet. Thankfully, the corridor was still clear when she poked her head around the door, so she dashed across the carpet into the long gallery. Skirts flapping wildly, she sprinted the length of it, then stopped to compose herself at the far end. Finally she walked calmly into the upstairs parlour and sat down as if she'd been there all afternoon.

A little later, Lucerne and Vaughan were both sitting in the bay window of Lauwine's long gallery, overlooking the gardens. The two ladies were taking a stroll along the gravel walkway below the window, deep in conversation, unaware that they were being watched. Bella was dressed in cream muslin with a broad claret-coloured sash at the waist, Louisa in an open robe of pale coral-coloured wool.

'What did you do to Louisa?' Lucerne asked, turning to Vaughan, who was still looking slightly flushed across the cheekbones from the walk home. It was some time since the ball, but somehow he'd never found the time to discover the details of Vaughan and Frederick's quarrel. It had been an awkward topic to raise before, while both of them were still in the house.

Vaughan turned away from the glass. 'What did *you* do to her?'

'Nothing.'

'Then there's your answer.'

'Come on, Vaughan, Freddy wouldn't have called you out for nothing. You must have done something to upset him that much.'

'If you recall, I found you and Captain Wakefield at the bottom of the stairs beating the hell out of each other. Isn't that a strange sort of nothing as well?'

Lucerne frowned. Vaughan did seem to have a point. 'Perhaps,' he murmured. He glanced down at Louisa. For someone so mild mannered and petite she caused an awful lot of discord. 'But I know why Freddy lost his temper with me. He was sore over the joke and then he caught me kissing her goodnight.'

'Really?' mocked Vaughan.

'I was drunk!' He bit his tongue at Vaughan's tone. There was no need to explain further. 'So what happened in the drawing room?'

'I gave her a drink to calm her nerves. The dear captain had upset her by pushing his tongue down Miss Hayes' throat.'

'And the rest.'

Vaughan gave a nonchalant shrug. 'I offered her a little comfort.'

'I see. A genuine interest, or were you just provoking Wakefield? I can't believe Louisa's much to your taste.'

'You'd be surprised. I've always had a thing about blondes.' Vaughan smiled knowingly and reached out with his bejewelled fingers to smooth Lucerne's ruffled hair.

'Vaughan!' Lucerne warned, and pushed his hand away. 'I thought Bella would be more your thing.'

'Why, because she's yours?'

'I've never denied that.'

Lucerne noticed Vaughan's eyes narrow as the marquis focused on Bella. He hoped the pale flicker of jealousy wouldn't mean more trouble to come. Still, he couldn't resist teasing. 'Pleasing, is she not? Dare I say she was even quite taken with you at first. I could almost be jealous of the effect you had.'

Vaughan turned sharply towards Lucerne, and stared unblinkingly at him. 'You still mean to pursue her.'

Lucerne rose from the window seat and took a few thoughtful paces. 'I think so,' he confessed. 'Though I have to say I don't generally follow where Freddy has led.' He turned back to Vaughan in time to see his eyes widen in genuine surprise.

'When was that?'

'The night of the ball.'

Vaughan cocked an eyebrow. 'My, my, the captain does seem to put it about. Three women in one night, and he accuses me of salacity. However, it begs the question: who jumped who?'

Two days had passed since Joshua and Frederick had left, Bella reflected as she put her book aside. Lauwine was quiet without them, especially in the evenings when the early sunset forced everyone indoors to huddle around the fire. A draft from the window made the candle at her elbow sputter. She blew it out. Louisa and Charles had both retired for the night; she might as well do the same, unless she could find Lucerne to talk to. He'd been strangely formal with her since her brother's departure. Perhaps she could convince him to relax a bit.

Vaughan and Lucerne were playing billiards; their laughter echoed through the quiet hall. Bella paced along the edge of the hall, staying close to the wall to avoid the squeaking floorboards. It was rare to catch them unawares. She peered jealously into the billiards room, and saw them offering crude encouragement to each other as they played. A half-drained decanter of brandy stood open on the mantle, and as she watched Lucerne topped then drained his glass. He was in shirtsleeves, his coat and waistcoat lying discarded over the back of a gilt chair. He exuded an air of careless sensuality, in no way diminished by the yellowing bruises on his lower arms from where he had fallen down the stairs.

Vaughan was equally appealing, like a libertine on the way to someone else's bed. He was lining up a shot at the table when his cravat got in the way and he missed the pocket.

'Damn, foiled by my own Daventry knot,' he cursed in good humour. Lucerne laughed, and patted him affectionately on the back.

Vaughan loosened the knot and tossed the scarf aside before he noticed her in the doorway. 'Well, well . . .' he muttered, holding her gaze as he unfastened the neck of his starched shirt to reveal his throat. 'Do you feel like trying your luck?'

Bella decided to brazen it out, encouraged by the amiable smile Lucerne gave her. Vaughan bowed formally and offered her his hand to cross the threshold. She wasn't sure if she was welcome, but the overwhelming maleness in the room drew her in.

'Your turn, Vaughan,' said Lucerne, after missing his own shot. He held out a cue for Vaughan to take, but the marquis shook his head.

'Miss Rushdale's going to take it for me.'

Bella opened her mouth to protest as Lucerne thrust the cue into her hands. She'd never played billiards before, and hadn't the faintest idea about the rules, despite Joshua's occasional attempts to teach her.

Help!

She stared blankly at the table and tried not to frown at their ribald encouragement. 'I don't know how to play,' she confessed.

'No problem. You soon will.' Vaughan guided her to the edge of the table.

'I'll make you lose.'

'Not if you've the same aptitude as your brother. Take the shot.'

Bella brushed her long hair back over her shoulders then leaned over the table to reach the cue ball. His instructions were confusing, while Lucerne distracted her by grinning as he stared pointedly down her dress. At least she had his attention again. She tried to block them both out only to feel Vaughan's hand on her bottom. 'Hands off,' she hissed, as she turned her head to meet his eyes.

He lifted his hand in surrender, a gesture that made her nervous. The win felt too easy. She returned her attention to the table and drew her elbow back to take the shot. As the cue connected with the white ball, Vaughan nudged his loins against her out-thrust bottom. The shock threw off her aim and sent the ball bouncing ineffectually against the cushion. Aroused and humiliated, she turned on him with the stick.

'Perhaps we should try that again,' he offered innocently in response to her threatening clasp of the cue.

'I think not.'

'A pity,' he remarked in a patronisingly offhand fashion, and took back the cue.

Bella watched them resume the game, assuming a fixed smile while she attempted to hex Vaughan's attempts. To her joy and Vaughan's disgust, Lucerne eventually won.

'What shall I claim as my prize?' asked Lucerne, as the pair joined her by the fire. His blue eyes were merry and alert as they met hers, full of impish good humour. 'A kiss?'

Bella purposefully put her glass aside. She remembered Vaughan's warning about staying away from Lucerne and felt her pulse quicken at the chance to defy him while he watched. To her astonishment, Lucerne turned to kiss not her but Vaughan. He caught the other man completely offguard and stole a deep passionate kiss.

Bella's mouth fell open in astonishment. She'd never

seen two men kiss – she'd never even heard of such a thing – but a warming prickle between her thighs told her she wholeheartedly approved. How far did their relationship go? she wondered, recalling the blond hair in the locket. Was it Lucerne's? The colour matched. Was jealousy Vaughan's motive in warning her off?

The two men parted, and Bella thought Vaughan looked riled, though he was clearly trying to disguise it. She guessed he hadn't wanted her to witness such intimacy between them. He drank deeply for several seconds, while re-establishing his typical hauteur. The ticking of the clock grew louder. He caught her looking at him and smiled wickedly, then grasped her about the waist.

She wanted to resist him but the instant his lips touched hers she was aroused and ready for him. His mouth was soft and he seemed to breathe a kind of carnal fire into her that cranked her desire up three or four notches. The touch of Lucerne's lips against her neck cranked it even higher.

'I think it's your bedtime,' Lucerne whispered into her ear and, for a brief moment, she imagined herself a game-piece between the two men – both pressing into her, front and behind, both pleasuring her and raising her to a zenith that she'd never achieve with only one man. Lucerne had let slip that day in church that he'd shared women with Vaughan before. Then she realised that there had been no trace of innuendo in his voice just now, and that he had meant exactly what he said.

It was her bedtime. And hers alone.

Lucerne sipped his cognac slowly, aware of Vaughan observing him from beneath his long dark eyelashes. He felt uneasy now that Bella was gone, as if something profound was about to happen. There were butterflies in his stomach and his breathing was quick and shallow despite his attempts to slow it. When he'd given in to Vaughan's advances two days ago, he'd not expected patience from his new lover, but patience and understanding were what he'd got. Contrary to all his expectations, Vaughan had not insisted on resuming where they'd left off, in either of their rooms that first night or the following one. If he intended to do so tonight, he seemed in no hurry.

'Dreaming of your next religious experience with Bella?'

Lucerne was suddenly reminded of Vaughan disturbing them in the little church, and how he'd mocked them. At the time he'd put Vaughan's scathing remark down to his desire to appear witty. Of course, now he knew better.

'What if I was?'

'Oh, nothing. I just thought your radiant glow that day was a result of your sanctity, not your sins.'

'And I suppose your little diversion in the drawing room was a lesson in country manners, not just an excuse to grope Frederick.'

Vaughan smiled pleasantly. 'Well, there must be a reason for your close association, and it clearly isn't his wit or his wealth.'

Lucerne bit down the urge to defend his friend. He knew Vaughan was just goading him. 'Speaking of wealth,' he began, 'I've heard you left a lot of yours behind in Italy. Did you work your passage, or did you let the sailors do that for you?'

The corners of Vaughan's mouth twitched at the comeback. He put his glass aside. 'You heard wrong. The voyage was tedious in the extreme, which is why I intend to make up for it now.' He pounced at Lucerne, who had luckily already noticed him tensing, ready to spring, and had kicked into motion himself, so that Vaughan's fingers closed on air.

Vaughan pouted.

Lucerne laughed, and then ran from the room. He sprinted into the corridor, aware of Vaughan's footsteps giving chase behind him, and slid on the polish, but somehow managed to right himself before Vaughan got close enough to catch him. He had several options when he reached the other end of the passage: either he could double back and return to the billiards room from across the bottom landing, take the chase upstairs, or head into the dingy east wing. The dark emptiness of the latter appealed most. By the time he reached it through the old morning room, the game had developed into cat and mouse.

Lucerne dived through a set of double doors. Inside, the furniture was shrouded and shapeless beneath the white dustsheets. A huge tattered cobweb hung from a stack of paintings, and the smell of old linen filled the air. He slipped behind a tall draped object to the left of the door, and waited.

A moment later, Vaughan stepped into the room. He pulled the doors to behind him and Lucerne watched him cast his eye carefully over the furniture for places to hide. Lucerne held his breath. However, Vaughan stepped forwards and tore the cloth from the object he was standing behind, to reveal an ancient giltwood harp. They stared at each other through the strings, then Lucerne feinted left and stepped right, straight into Vaughan, his move perfectly predicted.

They wrestled briefly, Lucerne trying to escape as Vaughan snaked his arms about him, trying to pull him into an embrace. Lucerne's heart was beating wildly against his ribs, and the closeness of the other man washed desire across his loins. Unsurprisingly, when he stopped struggling and their lips and hips met, they were both erect.

They swayed and staggered backwards through the inner chamber door. The moon shone pale through the bare windows, painting the room in shades of blue. Vaughan steered Lucerne across the bare floorboards and pushed him between the silk drapes, onto the high canopied bed. Lucerne relaxed into the mattress. He caught a glimpse of himself in the half-covered dressing table mirror, as Vaughan's fingers worked open the tiny pearl buttons of his waistcoat. His eyes were flecked with sapphire and wide as a china doll's.

'Is this private enough for you?' Vaughan asked as he reached the last button. Lucerne swallowed and nodded. He stared apprehensively at the man who was undressing him: now unfastening the neck of his shirt, now pulling the fabric away from his skin to run his agile fingers down the centre of Lucerne's torso to his waistband. Lucerne felt trepidation tighten in his stomach as Vaughan's fingertips brushed lightly over his erection. Then urgency overcame him, and he allowed his member to be uncaged.

He wriggled out of his breeches and helped Vaughan do the same. Lucerne hid his face in the dark ringlets, which smelled of a rich herbal perfume. Vaughan's fingers moved down Lucerne's stomach and tangled themselves in his golden thatch of pubic hair, as his erection pulsed and reared eagerly towards Vaughan's hand. Lucerne kissed his neck, tasting salt and scent. He gazed dreamily at the canopy then closed his eyes. Vaughan's lips brushed at his inner thighs. His cock was throbbing with need. He felt light-headed. Vaughan closed his lips over the head of his cock before releasing him, only to swallow him again to the root. Lucerne stroked his hands through Vaughan's dark curls and wondered if any woman had ever been so skilful.

'Turn over,' Vaughan urged.

Lucerne rolled on to his stomach as well as his erection would allow. Vaughan began to massage his back; starting at the shoulders, he worked down Lucerne's spine in increasingly tight circles, which soothed the tension that had knotted the viscount's muscles. He repeated the movements twice, once with his hands and once with his lips, stopping at the base of the spine. He pressed his cheek against the warm skin of Lucerne's bottom and then ran the very tip of his tongue into the cleft between the soft globes. Vaughan licked a firmer trail along the channel and his tongue brushed the surface of Lucerne's anus.

Lucerne gasped in shock. He felt the blood rush to his face as his muscles contracted, and a dark ripple of excitement crept through him. His erection brushed the sheets, leaving a spot of pre-come on the linen. He felt the tickle of Vaughan's warm tongue again, and then the sigh of the mattress as Vaughan reached over to his waistcoat and retrieved a small vial of liquid, which he unstoppered. He poured a few drops into his open hand, and then a few more between Lucerne's buttocks.

'What is that?'

'Almond oil.'

'Almond oil? Oh!'

Vaughan's thumb pressed against Lucerne's anus, then a cheeky finger nudged its way inside.

'Vaughan!'

The finger entered him up to the knuckle and stroked him inside. Lucerne wriggled at the intrusion, shocked and wary but also surprised at the sweet intensity. Vaughan withdrew his finger but poured more oil into his hand. Afraid, Lucerne watched him lubricate himself and then Vaughn rubbed more oil into Lucerne's behind.

'Vaughan,' Lucerne said apprehensively. He wasn't at all sure this was where he wanted to go. The butterflies in his stomach began to flap wildly.

Vaughan leaned forward and kissed his shoulder. 'Relax,' he said reassuringly. 'I won't do anything you don't want me to.' His hands slid smoothly over Lucerne's hot skin, adding to the ache of arousal the viscount felt in his loins. 'Just tell me to stop, and I will.'

'I . . .'

'We'll take it slowly,' Vaughan promised. He kissed his way down Lucerne's spine and then gently pulled his buttocks apart to press his glans against the muscular ring. Lucerne tensed as the heavy, insistent pressure swamped him. A blaze ran through his loins and into his balls, adding another inch to his already enormous erection. He tried to relax, curious as to how it would feel to have another man penetrate him. He felt so well lubricated that he was sure Vaughan would slide in easily. However, despite Vaughan's insistent pushing, he did not make the breach.

Vaughan moved away and Lucerne groaned loudly at the loss. 'What's wrong?' he asked.

'Nothing.' He felt Vaughan's finger penetrate him again, and more oil being spread over his skin. Vaughan returned to his former position. He pressed firmly and the muscles relaxed. Slick and hot, he slid in part of the way.

'Oh God!'

Vaughan was barely inside him and it felt like he was being torn apart. Vaughan gradually pushed until his cock was halfway in. Lucerne felt every moment magnified with incredible intensity, as if every inch were a yard. Yet, despite the overwhelming sense of fullness and the combined feeling of pleasure and pain, Lucerne craved complete penetration. He tried to push backwards but Vaughan held him still.

'Ready for more?' he asked.

'Yes!'

Lucerne bit his bottom lip, then exhaled hard as Vaughan pressed forwards until his hips nudged against the viscount's bottom. They moved in short rhythmic strokes that seemed to bring them closer than Lucerne had ever thought possible. He groaned ecstatically and clutched the bedspread as Vaughan's prick hit his prostate. Hot, dark pleasure ran through him like an opium dream. The soft sheets felt rough as his painfully sensitive erection rubbed against them. Suddenly, his world seemed to explode around him. He continued to feel the thrusts as his anus contracted around the intrusion and he shot warm semen over the old linen.

Lucerne gasped. He felt he could no longer breathe. The sensation was, unexpectedly, suddenly too raw.

'Stop, please,' he begged.

Vaughan withdrew without question and brought himself to climax with a few quick strokes. He came with a gasp over Lucerne's thighs.

Lucerne rolled over and looked up at him. Vaughan's eyes were virtually black in the dim light and glittered like diamonds. His skin shone with perspiration and his mouth was red and hungry. He looked incredibly sensual. Lucerne kissed him with a mixture of passion and tenderness he dared not qualify.

Vaughan rested his head on Lucerne's chest and closed his eyes. 'Thank you,' he whispered. 'You don't know how long I've waited to do that.'

'I think I've some idea,' Lucerne replied. He held him affectionately, and listened to the combined sounds of their heartbeats as they drifted off to sleep.

# 8

Bella paused at the stable door and set her jaw in an expression of grim determination, but the attempt to muster some self-control fell flat. After a fitful night spent dreaming of Lucerne and Vaughan crushing her between them, kneading the soft round fullness of her bottom and sucking her nipples, willpower alone wasn't going to quell the craving. She needed something physical, and Mark could always be relied on.

He was in the end stall.

Bella tapped him on the shoulder. He gave a guilty start and grinned shamefacedly. His thick woollen breeches were partially unbuttoned and the coarse fabric strained over an obvious bulge. It appeared that she'd arrived at an opportune moment.

'You're riding out today?' he said. The weather was still miserable. Bella had ventured out during a brief respite in the rain. No, she thought, but I came for a ride anyway.

'I just came to check on the horses.'

The taut skin of his stomach showed clearly through the gap in the fabric. Instinctively drawn to the glimpse of nakedness, she reached out and traced the muscle tone.

'Here?' he said, and the skin around his warm brown eyes crinkled into a nervous frown.

'Who's going to come out in this weather?'

The worry lines transformed into a broad smile. Bella slipped a gloved hand through one of his galluses and tugged him towards the ladder to the hayloft. The low ceiling of the upper storey smelled strongly of hay and horses. It reminded Bella of the summer afternoons she'd spent rolling in the long grass with Mark, before Lucerne had returned to Lauwine. Mark followed her through the hatch and strode casually over to the hay-covered boards to sit down on a bail.

'So you want me to stud for you again, do you?'

'Am I that obvious?'

'Always.'

He placed one of his big hands behind her neck and pulled her close, then kissed her roughly so that his stubble grazed her chin. A smile played at her lips as she ran her hands over his broad shoulders and felt the muscles working beneath his shirt. Lucerne and Vaughan, even Frederick Wakefield, were in a different league to Mark, but when it came down to raw sex appeal his earthiness had its own charm. Mark was attractive without trying; he didn't need a starched collar, perfume or any other finery to persuade her of his appeal.

'Are the fine gentlemen drunk or spent?' he asked as he guided her hand through the vent of his breeches. 'Or did you just fancy a tumble in the hay?'

'This is what I fancy,' she said. Mark gave an affirmative growl as she closed her fist around his plum. He nibbled her earlobe then reclined, sinking into the hay. Bella lowered her head and flicked her tongue across his cock-head. Something about this act, about having a man's cock between her lips, really turned her on. She'd quite happily suck him to climax, but none of the men she slept with ever let her do that. At the tip, she pressed her tongue into the sensitive spot beneath the eye.

'Stop it. Stop it, Bella.' Mark pushed at her shoulders, and reluctantly she let him fall from her lips. Instead, she bunched up her skirts and lifted herself over his prick. A thread of fire licked around her clitoris and her vulva felt hot and wanting. The dark thatches of their pubic hair kissed as she watched herself slide over his cock, until he virtually disappeared inside her. She mewled sluttishly at the sight, and then released her skirts so that their bodies were hidden beneath the blanket of cloth.

Mark grasped her legs beneath the skirts and began a slow, cautious rhythm that made her smile. She fought against him. 'Too slow,' she muttered. He would come before she did – he always did – so what was the point of delaying the inevitable? As if performing a rising trot, she began to take her pleasure as she pleased.

'Bella!' He dug his fingertips into her thighs in a desperate attempt to slow her down, but Bella increased the pace instead. She flexed her inner muscles around him as she rode him, watching as he grunted and his expression changed from bliss to exhaustion. When she felt his penis soften, she lifted herself from him. The dull ache of arousal clawed at her nipples as she sat down in the hay. Frustration, thrice what she'd felt when she'd come here, knotted her insides and pricked at her skin. It seemed whatever relief she was going to find would have to come from her own fingers.

'Minx!' Mark groaned, though he smiled at her from beneath the dark line of his eyelashes.

'I'm obviously just too much for you,' she said. Her eyes fixed on his limp penis as Mark leaned back on his elbows.

'We'll see about that.'

Who was he fooling? He'd never yet brought her to orgasm, and Wakefield had managed that at one attempt. Besides, in his present state he'd be useless for at least half an hour.

Mark tugged off his breeches, a wolfish grin plastered on his face. He lurched towards her and wrestled her into the sweet smelling hay with a manoeuvre he usually reserved for the village fair.

'Get off me, Mark.' Bella tugged ineffectually at his shirt. She already felt uncomfortably aroused without him tormenting her any further. The weight of his body above her and the sense of helplessness made her ache to be filled.

'Not a chance. You're going to get a good swiving, my lady, so you know what a real stallion's like. Not like the jessamies you've been with.'

Bella laughed. 'Jealous, Mark?'

'No.'

He pinned her arms and straddled her. Bella wriggled, but he just gripped her harder and pulled up her skirts. The hay prickled against her legs and caught in her stockings. Mark pressed his cock to her stomach. To her surprise, he was already partially hard again. He kissed her neck and face as she began to whimper in lust.

Bella felt herself open for him. The flush of full arousal she'd previously felt became intolerable. She wanted him so desperately she was ready to beg. But Mark wasn't Vaughan: there was no artifice in him, and he gave what he promised. There was no resistance to his entry; she was open, wet and completely ready for him. Bella groaned as he possessed her. She felt overwhelmed and ravished. It was delicious.

'Is this what you came looking for?' he growled.

'I'll tell you when you've finished,' she hissed into his ear.

She wondered briefly, as he penetrated her with hard quick strokes, at how he'd improved since the last time. Then again, maybe it had always been this good with him, and she'd just never realised or appreciated it.

Whichever way, she was soaring now. She kissed his shoulder as ripples spread out across her body in waves. He briefly tweaked a nipple, and the rush grew to an explosive crescendo, about to engulf her.

Suddenly, Mark released her hands and stopped moving. Bella's eyes flickered open. She knew he hadn't come. His eyes were wide with alarm. She recognised the long black leather boots moments before he winced as Vaughan's riding crop came down across his flanks.

Mark cursed. He lifted his hips to withdraw but found Vaughan's heeled boot planted firmly on his buttocks.

'Continue,' Vaughan said, and pushed him down into Bella.

Bella gasped as she felt Mark slide deep inside her. His forced action aroused her more acutely than any previous act. She was balanced on a precarious pinnacle. The smallest movement might either make her come or topple her from ecstasy into unbearable frustration: something she was sure Vaughan was aware of.

'Get to it, boy.'

Bella listened to the angry growl roll at the back of Mark's throat. His face had flushed the colour of ripe blackberries. Within her, the acute arousal she'd thought couldn't possibly get any more demanding seemed to flare. She almost felt drunk on lust.

'Do hurry, or you'll have a queue waiting to throw up the skirts of this tuppeny whore.'

It was Bella's turn to flush with anger. She clenched her fists, but her retort escaped as a purr as Mark found exactly the right angle, driven a little deeper by Vaughan's boot.

The tail of his crop whistled through the air and hit Mark's bottom with a sharp crack. A line of fire rose across Bella's abdomen. It felt as though he'd hit her. Mark snarled as a second crack scored his flesh. Within

Bella, his erection thickened and lengthened. 'More,' Bella whimpered silently.

'Consider this a reprimand for fucking above your station.'

Mark moved with dizzying fervour as the crop goaded him on, his motion both instinctive and spasmodic. His brown eyes grew glazed and shone with liquid light. Bella gripped his upper arms, the bite of the crop lighting every nerve as it fell. She threw her arms out wide, soaring, breathless, almost there.

Vaughan reversed the crop in his hand. He coated the supple plaited leather with oil, then prodded the handle purposefully between Mark's cheeks and past the tight ring of his anus, which elicited a growl of protest. Mercilessly, Vaughan twisted the crop. Mark whimpered as it hit his prostate. His eyelids dropped as his eyes seemed to roll back into his head. He froze.

'No!' Bella's cry filled the hayloft as Mark came. 'No, oh!' she sobbed, digging her nails into his skin. But her howls were to no avail. Mark was finished, his short, hard orgasm over before he even thought of restraining himself. He gave a final groan as the crop was pulled from his anus. Bella banged her fist against the wooden boards, while Mark turned his head slowly to look at Vaughan.

'Get out.' Vaughan's voice was barely above a whisper.

Unsteadily, Mark got to his feet.

'Get out now.' Vaughan raised the crop and, when Mark hesitated, struck him across the cheek. Mark blinked in confusion, putting his fingers to the wound in shock. Then he grabbed his breeches and fled through the open hatch. The crop flew over his head as he dropped to the stall below.

'Alone at last.' Vaughan turned back to face Bella, and gazed down at her glistening pubis. 'Delightful, disordered and certainly wanton.' He smiled thinly, then took her hand and pulled her to her feet. 'I wonder what Lucerne would think of this little tableau. Do you know, he has some interesting thoughts on guests copulating with the servants.'

'What do you want?' Bella asked. Now that it was clear he wasn't about to give her what she wanted, she was losing patience with him.

'We have a small matter to discuss.'

'Why don't you just get on with it, then, instead of boring me with your pathetic power games?'

Vaughan shook his head and laughed at her. 'What! Hungry for more?' He tweaked her nipple through the cloth and Bella only just stopped herself from swooning. She grasped his coat for support, but the tickle of the thick fabric only made her more wanton.

'Actually, I'd rather have sex with Charles.'

'My dear, that can be arranged, but I don't believe you would. He may have the heart of a poet but he lacks the brilliance of a true bard.'

'Don't overrate yourself.'

Vaughan's lips twitched with a smile. A cold chill tickled over Bella's bottom as he raised her skirts and pulled her against his leg. Bella held on to him and rubbed her pubis against his chamois breeches. The friction relieved some of the tetchiness she felt towards him, but not much. She still owed him for what he'd done in the folly, and now he'd compounded that with what he'd just done to Mark.

Vaughan grabbed the low neckline of her dress, pulling her back from her thoughts. 'Before, I asked you to stay away from Lucerne,' he said. 'Now I'm telling you.' He tugged the fabric sharply and snapped the ribbon that criss-crossed up the front. The sections fell apart, exposing her chemise and breasts. Bella cried out inarticulately in protest but he just bent his head and flicked his tongue across one nipple. The wash of sensation made her shake.

'I don't appreciate competition,' he said.

He pulled her hair, forcing her to tilt her head back and thrust her breasts towards him.

'Ow!'

His lips closed over a teat and he sucked firmly, while he grasped her bottom in his still-gloved hands. Bella's heart leaped into her throat. She almost sobbed as she felt the nip of his teeth against her neck, but she wouldn't let him get the better of her again. His words had just confirmed her suspicions about the locket – the hair was almost certainly Lucerne's, and that made Vaughan her rival.

'You're a monster,' she said, and tried to push him away.

'If I was a monster I would fetch Lucerne to queue behind your stable-boy.' He pulled off his right glove and cast it on to one of the hay bales. Bella struggled as he sucked his thumb, but he easily stopped her half-hearted attempt at escape. 'You know you want it. Why pretend?'

Bella clawed at him as he kissed her. Fine! If he was going to use her, she would damn well use him too. She knew he was aroused. The outline of his prick was pressed against her thigh. She wondered how he'd like it, to be left a single touch away from orgasm.

The hand on her bottom pulled her more firmly against his thigh. His wetted fingers slid into the valley between her cheeks and his thumb pressed against her anus. No, she thought, not that, but her resistance was weak. Pleasure fluttered through her chest at his touch. Despite her desire to repel his overtures, she whimpered softly and failed to pull back when he put his other hand to the back of her neck, and pressed his thumb inside her.

A burst of heat exploded between her thighs. Her legs felt wobbly, he was making her so dizzy with desire. She felt light-headed, as though she were drunk.

'I'm prepared to barter with you,' he said. 'Ask and you shall have.'

'No.' Pressing firmly against his chest, she shook her head. Lucerne was too high a price, even when satisfaction was only one word away.

Vaughan removed his other glove with his teeth. He dropped it to the floor behind her, then made no further move. Bella closed her eyes, but the air between them was charged with possibility, and she couldn't convince herself she didn't want him. The warmth of his breath against her neck and the heat of his loins against her thighs were too much. Also, there was the matter of his thumb tormenting her in a place she'd never imagined had so many nerve endings.

Recklessly, she pulled at the fastenings to his breeches. 'Damn you. Make love to me.' There was nothing to stop her breaking the agreement later. They were enemies, after all; she didn't owe him anything, and he was extracting her word under pressure.

'Here?'

He pushed his thumb deeper, shocking her to the core. The very thought of him entering her in that sensitive place made her recoil in disgust, and yet the caress brought such sweet agony.

'No!' she whimpered, although in her mind's eye she pictured him doing just that.

'No?' He met her eyes, wearing a deliberately confused expression. 'How, then?'

'Like a normal man would.'

He inclined his head slightly, frowning almost imperceptibly. 'Would you care to clarify that, Annabella?'

'In my quaint,' she said, burning with shame. She couldn't believe he'd forced her into being so crude.

'Aah. Thank you.'

He slid two fingers between her thighs, releasing a flood of fresh arousal. Bella wrenched at his waistband and a button sprang away. He had kept her waiting long enough. His cock reared proudly just out of reach, and he held her back with the twin penetrations of fingers and thumb while he settled on the bale at his back. Then he used his thumb to pull her gently into his lap. Bella squatted over him. Her skin was flushed and her breathing was shallow as she tried to find her balance.

'No tricks this time? No false promises?' she pleaded.

'Not this time. This time you get what you deserve.' His cock nudged at her labia, and he entered her fully.

Bella rocked between the two penetrations, trying to find her pleasure. He throbbed inside her and his breath was scalding against her ear. All her insides felt liquid, as if she were filled with molten sugar. Her climax built to an unbearable intensity until she came, her muscles clenching around his thumb and cock as he reached his own release.

They sobbed and laughed at the glow in each other's cheeks and he kissed her once, passionately.

Vaughan wiped the fine shadow of perspiration from above his lip, then dug into his pocket and produced half a guinea. He took her hand and placed the coins in the centre of her palm. Bella dropped them as if they had burned her.

'Damn you!' After what they'd just shared, she was stunned by his viciousness. 'I'll have Lucerne when and where I like, and you won't stop me.'

Vaughan pushed her from his lap. 'Don't be so sure. Or do you really care so little for your friends?'

'Leave them out of this.'

'Stay away from Lucerne.'

'I won't.' She stamped her foot in frustration. How was it that he always seemed to come out on top?

Vaughan mounted the ladder. 'That's your choice. *Vale*, Miss Rushdale; until next time.' He blew her a kiss.

'But where have you been?' Louisa asked for the third time in quick succession. Bella gave her a noncommittal shrug.

'I told you, just for a walk in the gardens.'

'But it's been pouring with rain, and we saw lightning. What were you thinking of? Look at you, you're soaking wet.'

It wasn't strictly true; she was merely clammy. Bella sighed, but held her tongue and allowed Louisa to push her closer to the fire. She ran her hands through her loose curls. Her hair was still damp and tangled from rolling around in the hayloft. She pulled a piece of straw from it and cast it into the fire. After Vaughan had gone she'd wandered around the gardens aimlessly, trying to justify her actions to herself. Finally, she'd taken refuge in the gazebo when the thunderstorm set in. It had been dry inside and the air had been warm, providing a comfortable backdrop for her to reflect. If Vaughan made good his threats it would result in Mark's immediate dismissal without references, and her own disgrace, but she didn't think he would. Vaughan was sadistic and vengeful, but she didn't think he was that petty. He was more likely to attack the subject of his wrath than he was a bystander, and she feared far less for herself than for Mark or Louisa.

'Lucerne was concerned about you,' Louisa said.

Bella turned her back to the fire and looked at her

friend. Louisa was working on her embroidery: a waistcoat with a motif of delicate flowers. She smiled impishly, clearly bursting with knowledge she wanted to share.

'He was very concerned,' she reiterated.

The corners of Bella's mouth twitched upwards and she broke into a girlish smile. She joined Louisa on the sofa and linked arms.

'He was pacing about, and kept staring out of the window. Vaughan scolded him for being tiresome but Lucerne just rebuked him for an unfeeling wretch if he didn't care that you were out in the rain.'

'What did Vaughan say to that?'

'He said, "She's probably in the stables with the other horse."'

Bella thumped the cushion. 'How dare he!'

'That's exactly what Lucerne said. He told him to get out of his sight with his vile slanders. He was very angry.'

'What happened then?'

'Vaughan disappeared with Charles, and Lucerne wandered off. I haven't seen any of them since. Why is Vaughan being so nasty about you?'

'I don't know,' Bella lied. That comment was something else she owed him for, she thought, as she mentally chalked it up alongside the other slights.

'He's a venomous, spiteful man,' said Louisa. 'I wonder that Lucerne likes him so much. They are very different.'

'Perhaps he sees a side of him we don't.'

'Ahem!'

They both looked around to find Lucerne's valet observing them.

'Yes, Ivo, what is it?' asked Bella.

'Milord wishes to speak with you,' he said, his voice liquorice thick with his Italian accent.

* * *

Bella stood outside Lucerne's quarters, with a candelabra clutched tight within her whitened fist. Through the closed door, she could hear Ivo's low voice. He was announcing her presence. She shivered. It was cold away from the fire, and this part of the house smelled musty and old. She wondered why Lucerne had chosen to sleep here, so far away from his guests.

He had his back to her when she entered the room. He fastened the window latch and then turned around and met her bedraggled appearance with a neutral expression. Bella tried to read his eyes. Had Vaughan already been called upon to explain his remarks and, if so, what had he said? Lucerne wasn't giving anything away. She prepared herself for a reprimand, or worse.

'You're shivering. Please sit by the fire,' Lucerne said.

She obeyed and sat down on the sofa, grateful for the warmth of the fierce blaze. She felt chilled. Lucerne produced a glass from a cabinet and poured out a large measure of brandy.

'Here, drink this; it'll warm you.' He knelt before her and closed her hands around the balloon. His touch excited her, but his scrutiny made her feel clumsy and unkempt. The faint smell of damp fabric wafted over her. Self-consciously, she sipped the fiery liquid, unable to meet Lucerne's serious expression. This was the first time they'd been alone together since the brief incident in the chapel, and she looked and felt abominable. She stared over his shoulder at the hand-painted Chinese wallpaper; it was mildewed in one corner near the picture rail. Clearly Lucerne hadn't been able to undo all the damage to the property from it standing empty so long, at least not yet.

'Are you warm enough?' He pressed the back of his hand to her brow. 'I'd hate for you to become ill.'

Bella swallowed the lump of self-pity in her throat. His tenderness made her feel far more wretched than her knotted hair or her damp clothes. She guessed he was oblivious to what had happened in the stables, and that was how she preferred it to stay. However, thoughts of how she must have appeared, first straddling Mark then beneath him, and finally with Vaughan, kindled a sudden heat between her thighs. She stared at Lucerne – his eyes, his mouth, and his hands. He had large hands, with soft skin and rounded fingertips. What would they feel like against her skin? She couldn't stop herself wondering, or imagining how his cock would feel in her hands – thick, large and hard. She pushed her promise to Joshua to the back of her mind and unconsciously licked her lips.

'I nearly sent a search party out for you,' he said. 'I feared you were lost on the hillside.'

His comment tempered her lustful thoughts. 'I was in the garden,' she explained.

'You should have let someone know. Your brother entrusted you to my care.'

'I'm sorry.'

Lucerne placed a reassuring hand on her shoulder and sat down. The fresh tang of his eau-de-Cologne made her long to bury her face in his clothing. 'I trust you would tell me if anyone had offended you,' he said. 'Have Vaughan or Charles said anything?'

Bella stiffened slightly under his touch, still on edge and battling with her rising desire. 'No, I just lost track of time,' she lied, and hoped Lucerne couldn't read the deceit in her eyes. Vaughan had been offending her since they'd met, but that wasn't why she'd gone out, and she didn't want to discuss either matter with Lucerne. Meanwhile, he gazed uncritically at the soiled hem of her dress. She stared at his covered crotch. What's the matter with you? she thought to herself. You've already had two men today. When did you become so cock-starved?

'What made you come to Lauwine?' she asked, determined to master her thoughts. She'd always thought Lucerne somewhat out of place here. Maybe at the height of summer he'd fit in, but in the winter?

His shoulders came up at the question. 'I remembered I had it, I suppose.' Unaware that Bella was staring at his mouth, he twitched his lips into a brief ironic smile. 'London has a strange effect on people. It makes sensible young men do irrational things. Too many of my associates ruined themselves by mistaking an obviously ridiculous idea for adventure. I nearly lost Lauwine without ever having seen it, and several other things besides.'

Bella focused on the imperfect Cupid's bow of his lips as she considered his impact on her little world, and that of the trials and tragedies of Wakefield and Louisa and even the alluring malice of Vaughan, against her dull and tedious alternate future rutting with stable-hands. Did you break any hearts when you left London? she wanted to ask him. Did you frustrate them with your poise as much as you frustrate me? Did they also wait too long for a kiss?

He turned away from her and stared unseeing into the fire. Hellfire, she thought, realising that she'd unintentionally dredged up melancholy thoughts for him. Afraid of seeing their conversation end in miserable silence, she placed her glass upon the floor and touched his arm. 'Lucerne.' He looked so sad, so fragile when he turned back to her, with his bright ocean-blue eyes filled with unshared memories. She leaned into him and pressed her lips to his, mindful only of taking away whatever unhappiness she had reminded him of.

For a long, awful moment Lucerne's mouth remained

closed. Panic washed over Bella like icy waves. She had meant to comfort, but her own arousal was not forgotten, and his cold response came as a shock. She pulled back, but as she did Lucerne's arms came around her, and his tongue flicked against her lips.

'I don't like taking advantage,' he whispered into her mouth.

'Don't you? Then it looks like it's up to me.'

'But I made your brother a promise.'

'So did I,' she said dismissively, as she drew him down onto the thick Persian rug. Still gazing into his dilated eyes, she was aware of the irresistible magnetism between their bodies and knew without a doubt that he wanted her. She didn't need to confirm it by brushing her palm across the hummock in the front of his breeches, though she did it all the same.

'Not too forward, am I?' she asked.

'Do you fear for your reputation?'

'No, but Joshua does. Black sheep run in the family.'

Lucerne held himself poised above her. His fingertips traced her collar-bone, and then the lace neckline of her gown down to her breast. He hesitantly plucked at the knotted ribbon fastening, unaware that Vaughan had broken it earlier. Then, giving in to his desire, he trailed his lips into the hollow of her neck as he pushed one sleeve from her shoulder. Bella struggled to free her other arm in the same way, eager to feel his skin against her own. She'd waited for this long enough; now she wanted him as fast as possible. There'd be time to savour his every delight later. Now she just wanted his cock in her cunt.

Lucerne casually threw her stays aside. 'Mmmm!' he remarked, pausing to admire her liberated bosom and to cup her into fullness. On his knees between her thighs he tugged loose his cravat and waistband, and pulled his buttoned shirt and waistcoat off in one energetic movement.

'Stop a moment,' she said. 'You're beautiful. Let me look at you.'

Lucerne waited with obvious pleasure and embarrassment while Bella gazed at the flawless skin of his chest. She traced the golden line of hairs across his abdomen. 'I've always liked watching you, ever since . . .'

'Ever since you caught me tossing by the river,' he finished for her. They laughed at each other.

As she gazed up at him, the pressure of arousal in Bella's stomach grew, rearing and flicking over her skin like the firelight that lit the smooth musculature of his chest. 'Let's get you out of this,' said Lucerne.

Bella glimpsed his erection, long and thick, before he lifted the muddy hem of her chemise and swept it over her head. She freed her wrists from the tangled linen and pushed it away from her.

'Much better,' he coaxed. Lucerne knelt between her parted thighs, his hand curved over her pubis as his tongue lapped into the wetness between her legs. Hot needles of tingling, fluttering arousal crept out over her limbs, spreading upwards into her breasts. Heat stronger than that of the fierce blaze coloured her skin and had her reaching for him. 'Lucerne,' she gasped. She opened her legs wide as his pelvis descended and the crown of his prick dipped firmly into her.

He paused.

Their eyes locked as if to underline the moment. A part of Bella wanted to savour that instant but, with startling suddenness, the initial thrill of penetration was over and their bodies were linked.

Being with Lucerne was very different from sex with Vaughan. It wasn't a constant battle of wills, and he gave as well as took.

'Slow down,' he hissed against her cheek, and took charge of their frenzied motion, moderating it. 'It's not a race, Bella.' At the same time, his middle finger found her clit, then rubbed and teased it from its hood. Intense pleasure coiled tight around her navel and shuddered through her legs, sapping her strength. She fell limp except for the rocking of her pelvis. Lucerne sucked at her nipples, making the sensitive peaks stand tall. He covered her in sensation, shivers racing between her clitoris and breasts. Before she realised it, her orgasm was almost upon her.

'Please, Lucerne,' she begged, tugging on his upper arms to bring his lips to her waiting mouth. 'Hard.' Her voice was pleading, urgent. He drove his penis deep. Their pace quickened, becoming almost frantic. Lucerne bucked out of time as he came, roaring out his orgasm. Somehow, he managed to keep his erection, pulsing within her until her own climax shook her and her muscles clenched around him. As the intense shock waves faded into a warm glow, they collapsed breathless and exultant upon one another.

Presently, his penis slipped from her. He kissed her tenderly before rolling onto his back. Bella snuggled up to his warmth and lay her head on his torso with a self-satisfied grin on her face. She listened blissfully to the muffled rhythm of his heart, and allowed herself to mewl softly as he brushed his fingers through her hair. 'Joshua did tell you to look after me,' she said, her head tilted so her chin pressed against his warm stomach as she peered up at his face.

Lucerne's relaxed expression immediately contorted into a grimace. 'I don't think this is what he meant.'

'Did you intend for me to wait forever, then?'

'Perhaps. I hope your brother isn't as proficient with his fists as he is at billiards.'

Bella straddled his stomach and looked down into Lucerne's unguarded face. He was frowning, and there was a shadow of doubt in his blue eyes. 'My brother never thumped anyone in his life. Besides, there's no reason for you to fight.'

'Honour's a strange thing.'

'Lucerne! How can you say that?' She kissed him where the yellow bruises were fading from his ribs. 'You worry too much.'

'I don't like abusing my authority.'

'Don't be so bloody arrogant. I started it.' She shimmied down his chest, and began to fish around for her clothes. 'You can't be responsible for everyone. I knew exactly what I was doing.'

Lucerne propped himself up on his elbows, watching her sort through the jumble of linen. 'I suppose so. In London, I couldn't even be responsible for myself.'

'Is that why you came here, to run away from yourself?'

'No, not exactly.' He helped her into her chemise dress. 'Urgh!' he said as he released the wet muddy hem. He rubbed his thumb across his palm to remove the wet mark.

'Urgh!' Bella agreed as the damp cloth stuck to her skin. 'I didn't realise it was this bad.'

'Never mind, it's time you changed for dinner anyway.' Lucerne rose to his feet. Still naked, he made a game of relacing her stays. When she was clothed, he walked her to the door. 'We'll have to do this again sometime,' he said facetiously. Bella gave him a coquettish pout. Obviously he wasn't feeling too guilty or threatened over breaking his promise to Joshua. Lucerne bowed gracefully and gave her a final dizzying kiss before he shooed her out into the dark corridor so that he could re-dress in privacy.

* * *

Bella made her way back along the dark gallery to her own room. She had only fifteen minutes to tidy herself and get dressed for dinner. As soon as she'd moved away from the fire, her damp clothes had made her limbs feel heavy and tired. After more sex than most men claimed to have in a week, she had only one final craving – sleep. To her utter dismay, Vaughan came through the door to the wing as she neared it. He was already dressed for dinner, and his excessive finery made him look like he was expected at Court. She wondered whom he was trying to impress. Not her, she was sure. Lucerne, perhaps.

Deciding that the best way to deal with him was to ignore him, she attempted to walk straight past, but he stepped in front of her and blocked the way.

'Excuse me.' Bella tried to make her voice sound commanding. Vaughan merely smirked at her discomfort.

'Why, what have you done wrong?' he asked.

Bella snorted to hide her nervousness. She tried to slip under his arm, but he closed his fingers around her upper arm in a vicelike grip. Her struggles only prompted him to pin her against the wall. 'Don't you think you could spare me a moment?' His dark eyes flashed demonically in the dim light. 'After all, we are on intimate terms.'

His lips brushed against the sensitive pulse point on her neck. The kiss was sharp and sweet, tinged with dark threat and erotic promise, but the memory of being held safe and loved in Lucerne's arms was too fresh. 'Intimacy implies trust,' she snapped, and thrust her hands against his chest.

Vaughan responded by playfully nipping her ear. Bella kicked him on the shin.

'Bitch!' He gripped her by the chin and squeezed her cheeks. Her temper rose dramatically at the indignity. 'I warned you to stay away from Lucerne.' His eyes flashed with hatred.

'You don't scare me,' she blurted. Her heartbeat sounded loud in her ears. She hoped Vaughan couldn't hear it, and wouldn't realise how much he frightened her. 'Let go or I'll scream.'

'Don't think you can keep him.'

He released her ungraciously. Bella sealed her lips to stifle the angry retort that echoed in her skull. He was trying to trick her into revealing what had happened in Lucerne's room and she wasn't about to rise to the bait, as satisfying as it would be to hurt him with the truth. 'Go hang yourself!' she snarled.

His dark eyes narrowed with malice. Bella held her breath as she waited for him to retaliate, but instead he turned on his heels and strode off in the direction of Lucerne's room. She watched him disappear while she rubbed her neck, as if she could wipe away both the intimacy and the aggression. 'Evil bastard,' she swore under her breath, before making a quick escape to her own room.

Bella retired immediately after the tense, uncomfortable dinner. Exhaustion had set in and she needed to sleep, to release her body of exertion and her mind of the horrid situation that was building around her. It seemed inevitable that she and Vaughan would eventually go to war; he'd scowled at her throughout dinner. She was still dwelling on his threats when there was a gentle knock at the door. At first she feared it was Lucerne, come to renew their earlier lovemaking. She longed for him but she was so tired she doubted she could move a muscle and she didn't want him to get the wrong impression. To her relief, it turned out to be Louisa.

'I came to make sure you're all right. You're not ill after today, are you?'

'I'm fine. Just very tired.' Bella snuggled deeper into

the eiderdown. 'And before you ask, it has nothing to do with getting wet.'

'Oh!' Louisa stared at her with wide judgmental eyes.

'Don't look at me like that. I don't pass judgement on you . . .'

'Yes you do,' Louisa cut her off. 'You do it all the time. Just because I don't throw up my skirts for every man that passes, doesn't mean that I don't . . . don't desire Frederick as a man.' She bit her lip. 'And you snicker at my embroidery.' She looked both accusatory and defensive.

Bella wriggled into a half-seated position, with her weight on one elbow. 'I've never laughed at your accomplishments. They're just not for me. What's this about?'

Louisa shrugged her narrow shoulders.

'Is it because I can climb another pole if I can't have Lucerne?' She was too tired for niceties.

'No!'

'Then what is it?' Bella tempered her voice and started again in a softer tone. She didn't really want to argue with Louisa. 'Talk to me, Lou. It's what you came here for.'

Louisa's gaze dropped to the eiderdown. She shook her head as if oppressed by some evil thought. 'I went to his room. That's why he left.'

Bella sat up in shock. 'You went to his room! Alone?'

'I thought I'd try to be more like you, but then when I got to the door I lost my nerve, and Vaughan scared me off. After that Lucerne put me to bed, and he kissed me, Bella – quite passionately. I think he was drunk. Anyway, Vaughan must have told Frederick because he hit Lucerne and they had a fight, and it's all my fault.' She looked utterly miserable. A slow, fat tear rolled down her cheek.

'Oh, Louisa,' Bella soothed. She placed an arm around

her friend. 'Don't fret. Wakefield will come back. He probably just needed to calm down. They've been friends for years.'

'No he won't.'

Bella forgave the obvious plea for sympathy. 'He will. In the meantime, if you miss him so much, why don't we pay him a visit? I'm sure Lucerne will allow us the use of the carriage to go into Richmond for a few things. We can see Frederick and my brother while we are there.'

'I'd like that.' She pressed a palm to her cheek.

Bella gave her a friendly pat. 'I'll ask him in the morning and sort it out, but now can I please get some sleep? I'm exhausted.'

# 9

By mid-morning the next day the sky had cleared enough to risk the carriage journey into town. They had explained to Lucerne that they wished to look for new outfits in Richmond. It was a dreary cobbled street that they found themselves in when they stepped down from Lucerne's carriage, but nothing could dent Louisa's exuberant mood, not even the drab little hat-maker's shop or the uninspiring array of bonnets and caps within. At the milliner's they fared little better, except for a cream satin sash and five yards of sarcenet.

The White Boar Inn was a white-faced, low-fronted building, with a bowed roof and dusty lattice windows. Bella bullied the room numbers from the landlady over a bottle of mouldy claret, and she and Louisa eventually parted company on the stairs.

'Annabella!' Joshua exclaimed when he opened the door to find his sister on the other side. 'I thought you were safe at Lauwine trying to steal Lucerne's heart or something. What are you doing here?'

'Shopping, and paying you a visit.' She hefted her purchases at him, and smiled at his frown. Good old predictable Joshua, only bothered about how far she stretched his finances. This was just as well, since she preferred not to lie to him.

'Oh lord! I hope you haven't spent too much.'

'Don't worry. I haven't.' She chuckled. 'I couldn't find anything I really liked.'

The clouds vanished from his eyes and his expression

became more welcoming, though he still eyed her packages suspiciously. 'Well, I guess you'd better come in.' He held the door open for her. The room was boxy, with lime-washed walls that were yellowing near the ceiling and around the low-set window. It held a dresser with a cracked washing jug set on top of it, a table, two armchairs and an uncomfortable-looking bed with a patchwork coverlet. Joshua's greatcoat was hanging from a hook on the back of the door.

'You're not on your own, surely, are you? Isn't Lucerne with you?'

'No. Louisa.'

'Then where is she?'

Bella dropped her purse on the chair. There was a spider's web stretched across one of the window-panes, she noted with amusement as she tugged open the ribbon fastening her cloak. 'She went to find Captain Wakefield.'

'Oh!'

Bella turned sharply to face him, fabric flapping about her shoulders. 'What's wrong with that?' she demanded. Surely he wasn't going to make a fuss over her going in to see him alone. 'It's not as if they don't know each other.'

Joshua closed his hands over his face. 'It's not that,' he said in a low, almost plaintive voice.

'Then what?'

'He's with bloody Millicent Hayes, isn't he.'

Bella let her cloak drop to the hardwood floor. Oh God, she thought, feeling slightly sick. She met her brother's hazel eyes. Perhaps there was still time to stop her.

Louisa stood before the door with her heart pounding. Once again she was poised outside Frederick Wakefield's room, summoning her courage and beating down her self-doubt, but this time Vaughan wasn't around to frighten her off. She tapped lightly twice, but there was no reply.

Perhaps he was out.

She thought she ought to rejoin Bella but, instead, she lifted the latch. It made a tiny click and the door swung inwards an inch. Cautiously, she peered around the edge. The room was dark, the heavy curtains still drawn against the daylight, and it smelled odd: overtly raw and masculine.

She stepped in and let her eyes adjust to the light. Discarded clothes littered the floor, and she stepped over an empty wine bottle to reach the curtained bed. Was this really his room? She found its squalor hard to equate with him; he was always turned out so smartly. Perhaps he was ill. She tiptoed to the bottom end of the bed and peeped through a slight gap in the fabric. Frederick was indeed still in bed. His head lay upon the pillow; he looked sleepy and dark around the chin. Louisa started to say his name, but then the blankets moved and a thin arm snaked across his torso, stopping the sound in her throat.

He was with another woman.

Less than seven days apart and he'd forgotten her. She nearly retched as her bile rose. Meanwhile, Millicent Hayes rolled over and propped her head on his chest.

Louisa had managed to stumble out into the corridor when Joshua and Bella found her. She felt drained and cold, but allowed herself to be steered into Joshua's sparse chamber.

'Don't worry, Louisa. It'll be fine,' lied Bella.

Louisa slumped into the only comfortable chair, content to let Bella fuss over her. It meant she didn't have to think. Instead she clutched Bella's lace kerchief, too numb to cry, and watched Joshua order tea in a bid to make himself feel less superfluous. When it arrived, she reluctantly accepted a cup. The scalding liquid made her swollen lips tingle with pain, but at least it made her feel something.

Five minutes after the tea arrived, a second loud rap at the door broke the stiff silence. It was Captain Wakefield. He seemed to sense all eyes on him, but he was clearly unaware of the tension in the room, or the fact that he was the cause.

After the most uncomfortable five minutes of her life, Louisa caught Bella's eye and they stood in unison. 'We ought to get back before it gets dark,' Bella explained as she swung her cloak about her shoulders.

Frederick Wakefield stood in the street and watched the carriage roll away. He was surprised nobody had come to find him, although he conceded that it hadn't been the best-timed visit ever, and Joshua had known full well he was busy. Jesus! Only a few moments either way and they'd have met Millicent on the stairs – then all hell would have broken loose. 'Did you know they were coming to town?' he asked Joshua.

'I had no idea,' the other man replied weakly. He was staring at the dirty cobblestones with a rather moody, downcast expression etched into his brow.

'What's wrong? Is something the matter with your sister?'

Joshua shook his head. 'She saw you,' he said.

Wakefield blinked. 'Excuse me?'

'She saw you.'

'Who? When?'

'Louisa. She saw you with Millicent. I'm sorry, there was nothing I could do.'

Wakefield shook his head in disbelief. 'Impossible. I was in my room! She couldn't possibly have seen me.'

'She let herself in. Clearly your attention was diverted.' Joshua thrust his hands into his pockets. There was no sympathy in his voice. His comments were just neutral statements of fact. 'You're bloody lucky, you know. Bella would have emptied the chamber-pot over the pair of you.'

Wakefield's shoulders sagged. Leaving Louisa behind at Lauwine had been hard and he hadn't wanted to go, but the fight with Lucerne, and Vaughan's constant tormenting, had forced him out. Of course, nobody had forced him into Millicent's arms, but her abundant charms had been a welcome comfort. That tumble had probably just cost him what little chance he had with Louisa. He couldn't chase after her, and he doubted she'd read a letter. In short, he had no way to undo the damage. His only hope was to pray for a miracle.

'Lou, open the door,' called Bella as she pounded the wood with her fist. Only the muffled scrape of wood on wood answered her, as though a heavy object were being dragged across the room. Bella tried the latch again. It rattled ineffectually; the bolt had been pulled across on the other side. A loud thump came from within the room, followed by a tearful curse, and then the scraping resumed.

What was the stupid girl doing?

Pulling the beech blanket box in front of the door, Bella realised. 'Louisa, don't be stupid. Open up.'

She slumped against the frame. It was no use. Louisa hadn't said a word all the way back to Lauwine. Why would she choose to talk now, when locking herself away was a far easier option? She cursed Vaughan for causing the fight in the first place, and cursed herself for suggesting they go to town. This whole stay at Lauwine was a nightmare. They should have stayed at the Grange, dreaming of possibilities instead of trying to live them.

'Louisa, open the door!'

Her cry was met with silence.

Louisa hid in the bottom of her closet with the hems of her long skirts swaying around her. The sound of Bella hammering on the outer door was muffled here. She closed her eyes and saw Millicent coiled like ivy around Wakefield, their limbs entwined and their skin exposed to the cool air.

He was naked. She'd never seen him naked. He had dark hair around his nipples and a darker bush about his rearing cock. Even in the gloom, she could see how eager he was. All this time she'd thought that he cared for her, but now he'd thrown her over for this trollop.

His body had moulded to Millicent's as he moved to kiss her. Revolted and fascinated, Louisa had continued to stare as he rolled over onto her belly. When it became clear he was about to enter her, she'd turned away, unable to watch any more.

In the darkness of the closet, she swallowed her rising bile, and finally her tears began to fall.

Bella stirred, roused by the noise of Lucerne stoking the fire, and stretched out her stiff joints. He'd also laid on more coal, and she guessed he'd probably come straight from the stables. His hair was windswept, and wisps of steam were rising from his damp clothing. She wondered where Vaughan was; the two men had ridden out together.

'When did you get back?' she asked.

'A few minutes ago.' Lucerne came over to her. He

took up one of her cold hands affectionately. 'You're freezing. Come closer to the fire.' He began to rub some life back into her fingers. 'How long have you been sitting there?'

Bella shrugged her shoulders; her fingers were tingling as the circulation returned. 'I came up after dinner. I must have dozed off.'

'Have Charles and Louisa turned in?'

'Louisa has. I don't know about Charles.'

'He's winding the clock with your between-maid,' announced Vaughan as he entered the room. 'And he's making enough noise about it. You can hear him grunting from the landing.'

Lucerne frowned.

The corner of Vaughan's lip curled up as he noticed Lucerne's solicitous attention to Bella. He shoved a hand into the pocket of his wine satin robe and glowered sullenly. Bella self-consciously pulled her hand away from Lucerne. 'Thanks,' she mumbled.

'Where's Louisa?'

'I was just about to explain to Lucerne; Louisa isn't feeling too well. She went to bed right after we got back.'

'Oh.' Vaughan licked his lips slyly.

'Nothing serious, I hope,' said Lucerne. His blue eyes flickered with concern.

'No, she's just tired from the trip. I expect she'll be fine tomorrow.' Bella realised that at some point she would have to explain to Lucerne what had happened. She hated lying to him now, but what choice was there? She wasn't about to tell him in front of Vaughan.

'Do you want a drink, Lucerne?' asked Vaughan. Lucerne inclined his head. 'Bella?'

'Yes, thank you.'

Vaughan pushed a strand of hair behind his ear. His hair was wet, like Lucerne's, but had recently been brushed and fell about his shoulders in tight damp ringlets. He walked to the sideboard and returned after a moment.

'My lord. Miss Rushdale.' He handed them both balloons of cognac. Lucerne settled on the *chaise longue* and beckoned for Bella to join him. She sat down at the opposite end, but Lucerne moved along and put his hand on her knee. He'd obviously decided that, having already broken his promise to Joshua, there was no point in being hypocritical. Vaughan shot them an odd glance but made no comment, so Bella relaxed. She watched him throw a cushion onto the floor and stretch out before the fire like a sleek black cat. He rolled onto his back and clasped his hands behind his head.

'How was town?' he asked.

'Quiet.'

'But Louisa's tired.'

'She tires easily. You know that.'

'Of course.' He closed his eyes and yawned languorously. Lucerne pressed his thumb into Bella's palm, but his reassurance didn't stop her wondering why Vaughan was curious about their trip. He didn't normally inquire after Louisa, so she found his sudden interest faintly disturbing.

Vaughan yawned again. The fire gave out a shower of sparks. He rolled over to avoid them and sat up to rest his back against the *chaise longue*. He was right beside them now, but that didn't stop Bella snuggling closer to Lucerne. She rubbed her cheek against his chest and let a contented smile spread across her face as he began to stroke her hair, comforted by his closeness. He dropped a kiss on to her forehead. Bella craned upwards and he kissed her again, this time on the lips. Their duplicity made her feel a little smug. It was a rare pleasure to put one over on Vaughan, especially when he sat so close.

However, Lucerne wasn't playing favourites; no sooner had he kissed her than he reached out to Vaughan and brushed a solitary caress across the nape of his neck. Vaughan sighed affirmatively, while Bella found herself grinning, unaccustomed to hearing him make such a revealing response.

Lucerne kissed her hand and then guided it to the back of Vaughan's neck. Her fingertips pressed softly against the sensitive skin. Vaughan tilted his head forwards and Bella drew a line upwards through his hair. She wondered if he could tell the difference between her touch and Lucerne's. Her fingers darted back to his spine then bravely edged forwards around his collar-bone. She wished she really had him as completely under her power as he seemed at that moment. He'd teased her so often that she was desperate to see him at her mercy for a change.

Vaughan tilted his head to one side. Bella slid her hand into the open neck of his shirt and ran her palm over his chest. He sighed, resting his head on Lucerne's lap. Then his eyes opened and he looked up at them.

Suddenly the atmosphere in the room changed. Vaughan's eyes narrowed alarmingly. They seemed to smoulder with the realisation that it wasn't Lucerne touching him. Bella unrelentingly tweaked his right nipple. Angry he might be, but there was no denying that he was also aroused, and she owed him. Vaughan clapped his hand over hers, preventing any further action on her part. Bella reluctantly started to pull away, but he held her fast.

Uncertain of what to make of this she turned to Lucerne for answers, but his eyes gave her no clues. Vaughan's grip on her wrist slackened and his hand slid up along her inner arm, tightening again below her shoulder. He jerked her forwards so that she was looking down at him, her mouth poised just above his. He flicked his tongue across her bottom lip, making the sensitive nerves there sing. She could see his erection; his tight form-fitting trousers hid nothing.

Bella whimpered as his tongue drove deep, and he pulled her further from Lucerne. Was this some new power game, or real desire? Lucerne was growing restless; she could feel him shifting uneasily beside her. He wrapped his arms around her waist, tried to pull her away from Vaughan, but the marquis wasn't about to relinquish her that easily. His grip tightened. Bella's whimper became a moan. If one of them didn't back down soon she was going to have some bruises.

'Let go,' said Lucerne.

'You let go,' Vaughan hissed into Bella's mouth, never breaking lip contact. Lucerne's shoulders stiffened.

'No.'

Vaughan curled his free arm around Lucerne's leg and caressed his inner thigh. Lucerne's hold on her waist slackened. She was stunned that he'd been conquered so easily. Vaughan's action had completely overcome his resistance. Vaughan broke off the kiss and she pulled back, eager for air. She looked straight down into his eyes. They were dilated and liquid, so open she thought she would fall into them. She gasped and escaped back into Lucerne's arms.

Lucerne immediately cupped her face in his hands. 'Bella,' he mouthed, ready to kiss her. Then suddenly he released her. She turned her head, following the line of his gaze to find that Vaughan was pacing towards the door. Lucerne's sigh of relief when Vaughan only closed it was audible. Bella was less relieved. She wasn't entirely certain how she felt about Vaughan. He'd done nothing to ingratiate himself with her. The only thing he was useful for was a damn good lay.

The beeswax scent of snuffed candles filled the air as Vaughan moved about the room extinguishing them. Soon the only light came from the flickering coal fire. Bella watched him pour another cognac and position himself before the hearth to sip it. The orange fire glow lit his prominent features, his high cheekbones and angular chin. There was no denying he was a physically attractive man, but he was also cruel, and he was her rival.

The soft rasp of silk accompanied Lucerne's departure from the *chaise longue*. Bella was sure a silent signal had passed between the two men as Lucerne crossed to the hearthrug. Perhaps they were waiting for her to leave. Well, if they wanted that they would have to be more forthright. Tonight she was determined to stand her ground.

Lucerne took the brandy balloon from Vaughan's hand. He drained the contents then set it firmly on the mantel. Vaughan's expression darkened, and he raised one eyebrow quizzically. He looked at the glass and then at Lucerne. Something was brewing. She knew it.

Lucerne caught a handful of Vaughan's dark hair. Tension seemed to ripple through their bodies. Bella sniffed at the air, suddenly aware that she could make out the musky undercurrent of male arousal. Then the men were hip against hip in the darkness, pressing together, bruising each other with their erections. It was so unlike the previous occasion that she'd seen them kiss. They were relaxed, oblivious to their spectator or the effect they were having on her. Bella felt faint, and sucked down a deep breath to compose herself. Lucerne and Vaughan were as beautifully matched as sun and moon. She was jealous of their symmetry, and wanted to be part of it.

Lucerne held out his hand to her.

With eyes wide and bright she stared at his outstretched palm, uncertain whether she was more frightened of accepting it, or of missing out. Lucerne beckoned her again, and this time she rose as if mesmerised. She crossed the short distance with tiny nervous steps, weighed down by the lodestone of excitement around her neck. There was something about watching the two men kiss that seemed dark and forbidden. Was she joining them on the path to damnation? If so, it was already too late for her. She was beside them. Lucerne grasped her hand and they trapped her between them in a crushing embrace.

The soft cotton of Vaughan's shirt pressed against Bella's forehead. Her cheeks were flaming. She felt vulnerable, but deliciously wicked.

'Brave, adorable Bella,' Lucerne whispered as his kisses plucked at the nape of her neck.

'Hmmm,' murmured Vaughan approvingly, but Bella had a flash of him calling her a whore. She risked a quick glance at him, sure he was thinking the same thing. His expression was distinctly sybaritic. You think of me as a toy, to play with or discard at will, she thought. As if to confirm this, he smiled and nudged her playfully with his loins. He was fully aroused, and his cock pressed relentlessly against her pelvis. There was no easy way to escape him – they were both holding her, caressing her. Lucerne's erection nudged against her bottom. Two sets of eyes regarded her wolfishly, awaiting a decision. Play along or go to bed alone.

'Let us make love to you,' Lucerne urged. His hands ran up her taut body and found her nipples, which leaped to attention under his touch. Her breasts felt heavy, and a dull ache of longing filled them. She wanted to feel his warm mouth around the teat. Instead, he began unfastening the back of her dress. The loose fabric chafed against her stays and chemise, while Lucerne's breath tickled against her exposed skin and Vaughan's lips grazed her throat. There was an understated bite to his action, as if he was letting her know that things weren't as simple as they seemed. They were doing this because it pleased Lucerne, but that didn't mean they weren't enemies. Still, his lips trailed downwards, his hands cupping her into fullness as he buried his face in her cleavage.

Her dress slid to the floor.

'I never said yes,' Bella reminded them.

'You never said no, either,' said Vaughan. He rolled her pert nipples between fingers and thumbs, and the melting between her thighs grew thicker.

'Which is it to be, yes or no?' asked Lucerne.

'Yes, of course,' mouthed Vaughan.

'Yes,' said Bella.

Lucerne moved to kiss her, but she turned her head and offered him her neck instead; she wanted to watch Vaughan. Her rival had sunk to his knees and was pulling the cord from her boned stays with startling precision. When he reached the last hole, he pressed a kiss to her stomach that made her tingle inside. His lips felt warm and soft even through her chemise. He lifted the hem and passed the bunched fabric to Lucerne. Being naked between them seemed to magnify every sensation; she could feel the air around her moving to Vaughan's slow, deep inhalations and Lucerne's sharper ones. Vaughan nuzzled her inner thigh. He inhaled her scent as though he were about to taste wine, and licked firmly at her clitoris. Her heart began to hammer; the brush of Lucerne's clothing against her bare skin made the hairs on her arms stand up. She felt fully exposed, but her doubts had fled, pushed away by the men's attentiveness. The past was done, finished with; they were writing a new page together.

Vaughan took a step back from her and removed his robe. He allowed her to pull his shirt from his trousers and over his head. Infused with confidence, Bella also unbuttoned him. His erection reared and jutted towards her accusingly. She circled his navel, resisting the urge to go down on him, and then traced his scar in fascination. She wondered who had given him the silvery gift, and what for.

While Vaughan stepped out of his remaining clothes, Bella turned to Lucerne. She realised immediately that he felt uncomfortable from the rather fixed expression on his handsome face. They had been leaving him out. She plucked at his clothing, frustrated by the many fastenings. He was hot to the touch and his body was firm beneath her fingertips, but the immediate goal was to get him naked. She wanted to rake her nails across his skin.

Vaughan wrapped his arms around her waist from behind, again demanding her attention and getting it. Bella could only watch as Lucerne undressed. Frustrated by his nearness and the gulf between them, she pushed back against Vaughan's hardness and his penis pressed into the channel between her buttocks.

'Changed your mind about a certain point of entry, have you?' Vaughan whispered.

'No.'

'Mmm, too bad.' He thrust against her anus.

'Stop pushing your luck,' she hissed, too distracted now to pay more than passing attention to Lucerne, the man she really wanted. Vaughan mercilessly nudged her again. 'Vaughan!'

'I think you want me to –'

'I don't.'

'– you just won't admit it. Deny that it feels good, that you're not tempted.' The pressure of his cock became insistent.

'Vaughan, stop it.'

He relented and entered her vagina, leaving her gasping at the sudden entry.

Lucerne stood nude and magnificent before her, his clear skin shining a seductive ivory in the firelight. He had a curiously beatific smile playing about his lips that Bella couldn't fathom, but there was no mistaking his arousal or the interest he was paying Vaughan's leisurely penetration. Did Lucerne suspect, she wondered? She must have seemed to give herself far too easily to her rival.

Lucerne moved forwards to join them. With a single caress, he massaged Vaughan's shaft and her clitoris. Vaughan immediately withdrew, as if the touch had been a signal. The two men sank to their knees either side of her, pulling her down to the carpet between them.

The sensation of being handled by the two men quickly became almost unbearable. Lucerne's prick felt like a burning brand against her stomach, while Vaughan returned to his earlier position and slid his cock eagerly between her ripe cheeks. They were nipping, kissing and caressing her.

'Vaughan!' Again the reprimand was ignored, but now Lucerne was smiling. He stroked down her spine to the base then clasped her round bottom and pulled her cheeks apart to slide his fingers into the valley. Bella tensed as he touched her anus.

'Relax,' he whispered, and she did. He wetted his finger and slipped it past the ring of muscle, making her gasp into his shoulder. He was stretching her, stroking her inside, preparing her. She'd said no to Vaughan, but what about Lucerne? She trusted him – he was so much gentler than Vaughan was – but she still wasn't sure she was ready to see herself impaled on his thick cock in that tender area.

Then the scent of almonds filled the warm air and some viscous liquid ran slowly between the cleft of her cheeks to pool around her dilated anus. Vaughan pressed in close. She felt his cock nudge her again, taking the position of Lucerne's fingers.

'Please ... I ...' she managed to gasp. Lucerne's smile was reassuring, his kisses intense, white-hot, distracting. As she fought for breath, she felt Vaughan's cock hard against her. She clutched Lucerne and screwed her eyes shut. The crown went in. She bit Lucerne's lip. Jesus, it hurt.

'A little more,' Vaughan urged.

'No. I can't, it's too much.' Tears prickled her eyes, ready to spill.

'Try to relax, it'll be worth it.'

'Try,' Lucerne repeated.

Relaxing was not easy; she was too aware of how stretched Vaughan already made her feel, and all her instincts were screaming at her to push him out.

'Please, Bella.' The urgency in his voice made her heart quicken. He really wanted this – really wanted her. She tilted her hips to ease his entry, and felt him push.

His full penetration was quite painful. She couldn't bear him to move. She felt too full, as if the slightest thrust would tear her apart. 'Please, gently,' she gasped. Vaughan kept still. Lucerne supported her, while kissing her gently. Gradually her muscles stopped fighting, and she rocked herself gently against his loins.

Vaughan impatiently clasped her hips and thrust. He slid in deep and somehow seemed to strike a lance straight to her clitoris. Her rear throbbed under the onslaught, but the heavy sweet pleasure outweighed the pain tenfold, and the twin sensations made her feel light-headed. The experience was all-consuming; animal grunts quickly replaced her gasps. Vaughan's thrusts drove her roughly against Lucerne's lips. Her rectal muscles contracted around him, clasping him and making his sighs as voluble as hers. He was being more aggressive than she was ready for but Bella revelled in the moment, pushing back eagerly against his hips.

'That's right, move for me,' Vaughan encouraged.

'Make me come, make me come. Please.' She grasped Lucerne's hand and pushed his fingers to her clit. He touched her in all the right places, and in just the right way. Her body was liquid. Sensation rippled through her. She couldn't get enough. She wanted more. Her cunt felt empty. 'Lucerne,' she cried, hardly able to express herself.

'I think she wants you to fuck her,' said Vaughan, characteristically blunt. By now she was past caring about his tone, concentrating instead on the way their bodies were moulded together and his breath was coming as fast as hers.

'Speak, Bella. Do you want us both?' asked Lucerne, ever the gentleman.

'Yes, yes ...'

He stopped massaging her and moved between her thighs while his penis bobbed beneath her, waiting for a pause in Vaughan's thrusts so that he could nudge his way in. Bella briefly wondered if she could accommodate both men or if she would faint with the effort. Neither of them was small, and Vaughan's thick member already filled her to distraction.

Lucerne was careful not to upset their precarious balance as he entered her, slowly pressing deep until he was inside her up to the hilt alongside Vaughan. As they began to move in unison Bella's sense of reality vanished.

Vaughan's laboured breathing was sharp against her neck. Lucerne's eyes were glazed. She mewled into his shoulder and clutched him tightly as they ground into her, front and back. Vaughan's hand snaked forwards from her hip to her pubis and encircled Lucerne's prick at the base. He pulsed strongly within her at Vaughan's touch and she heard the harsh rasp of his indrawn breath. The edges between the two men blurred and they became as indistinguishable as the sources of her pleasure. Her mind was filled by their rhythm as she struggled to meet both sets of thrusts. Then her vagina contracted sharply and she screamed as her orgasm enveloped her in a waterfall of light, pulsing through her anus and clitoris with equal force. Tears wet her cheeks and fell like scalding raindrops onto her breasts. She cried out again and her thoughts cleared enough to hear Vaughan groaning her name as he bucked wildly. He swore through clenched teeth and pressed his mouth hard against her shoulder to stifle himself.

Lucerne withdrew carefully, while Bella sighed. His whole body trembled as she languorously masturbated his shaft, causing the thick seed to erupt over her stomach and thighs. Vaughan lifted her buttocks from his spent cock and she fell forwards onto her hands. Lucerne clearly relished the sight of her, spent and soiled on the rug, before he thought to find a kerchief with which to mop her gently.

'Well, was that enough, or more than enough?' asked Vaughan.

Bella curled up on her side. Too dazed to be catty after her orgasm, she admitted, 'It was ecstasy. It was almost too much. What else do you want me to say?'

Vaughan smiled thoughtfully. 'That I understand your needs better than you.'

'Leave her be,' warned Lucerne. He kissed Bella by the ear. 'I'm glad you enjoyed it; I know I did. Vaughan is just jealous because he wasn't in the middle.'

'Kiss my arse, Lucerne.'

'Think I hit a sore point.'

Vaughan smirked and reached over to the table for the bowl of crystallised ginger. He swallowed a piece and fed one to Bella. Lucerne laughed. 'Now he's just feigning indifference.'

'Who's goading people now? Give it a rest. I'm going to bed.'

# 10

When Bella went down to breakfast she found Lucerne with his plate pushed aside, blowing steam from a cup of tea.

'You're up early today,' he commented as she peered under the lids of the silverware.

'No, I'm always up at this time. You're the one who normally has breakfast at ten with Louisa.' She selected two rashers of bacon and heaped a spoonful of scrambled eggs on to her plate. An amused smile was playing around Lucerne's lips when she joined him at the table.

'I sense a criticism of my habits,' he said from beneath half-lidded eyes.

'Only a minor one.'

You wouldn't have guessed he was up half the night rolling around the parlour floor, Bella thought as she gazed at Lucerne. He looked remarkably healthy and handsome this morning, and the early sunlight was streaking his blond hair with flecks of gold. She felt buoyant in his proximity. The intimacy they had shared last night had brought them closer.

Lucerne continued to swallow tea as she ate, observing her discreetly.

'Why are you up so early?' she asked.

'I flattered myself you'd enjoy my company.'

Bella pursed her lips and flicked a glance at him. He was smiling from the depths of his seductive blue eyes. She hoped it was at least a partial truth; it certainly made her happy to think it was.

Lucerne returned his cup to his saucer. 'The barn roof by the west lodge has blown off, and I'm expected to go and look at it. I could use your brother's practical bent, since I know nothing at all about roofing. Gentleman's prerogative.'

'That barn was always rickety,' she mumbled between mouthfuls. 'It's the wind on that hill. Goodness, everyone's up with the larks, I see. Good morning, Vaughan.'

'Morning,' echoed Lucerne.

Vaughan blinked at the brightness of the room but didn't respond to their greetings. He walked over to Lucerne and ran long, quick fingers through his hair. Lucerne gazed at him, bemused then puzzled as Vaughan's grip tightened and pulled his head back, tilting his lips upwards. His mouth hovered above Lucerne's, but he did not make contact. Bella observed them, diverted by their interplay.

'Still hungry, my lord? Tarts are for supper, not breakfast,' said Vaughan.

Bella's jaw clenched and her thoughts swung to anger. She believed that something special had happened last night, but now Vaughan was implying that they had merely shared her as they would a whore, and Lucerne was gazing up at him as if she didn't exist, waiting for a kiss.

Vaughan released Lucerne unsatisfied, and settled opposite Bella. He poured himself tea, and regarded her rigid expression over the rim of his cup. 'Pass the butter, Annabella, and save a little for yourself.'

Bella contemplated bouncing the silver butter dish off his conceited head, but managed to restrain herself. She was as taut as a bowstring and ready for a fight, if that was what he wanted. She looked to Lucerne for reassurance but his attention was still on Vaughan, which gave her no comfort.

'I shouldn't make breakfast a habit if I were you; daylight really shows up your defects,' she snarled.

'On the contrary, it merely chases away fancy and self-deception.'

'If that were true, your own shadow would reach up and take you,' she spat, now really angry. Vaughan glowered at her, then brushed off her icy remark with a forced laugh.

'Could you at least try to get on today?' asked Lucerne. He frowned when neither of them replied. Lucerne pushed away the dregs of his tea impatiently and left them to it. They stared blackly at one another until Vaughan turned away with his cup and left for the library. Bella dashed her knife and fork to the plate with a clatter. She knew that last night had been intimate and special. Vaughan was just trying to reassert himself, but knowing this didn't take the sting out of his remarks.

Louisa had left her room out of hunger and boredom by the time Lucerne returned to the house. He found her huddled before the fire, busily ignoring the book in her lap. 'Are you well?' he asked, as he shielded his face from the heat. He wondered how she could stand it.

'Yes, thank you.'

Her response sounded a little too eager, even before he noticed her very red eyes. She was obviously withholding some personal tragedy, but he didn't expect her to confide in him; she hardly knew him. He guessed that Bella would know.

He found her in the bay window of the gallery, looking out across the gardens. She seemed relieved rather than pleased to see him, and he suspected that she and Vaughan had continued to bicker in his absence. Lucerne sighed. He cared for them both, and wished they wouldn't fight.

'What happened yesterday?' he asked. 'I've just seen Louisa and she's obviously been crying.' He sat beside Bella on the cushioned window-seat.

'We saw my brother and the captain.' Bella paused, and gave a deep sigh. Lucerne remained silent. He missed Frederick, and was sorry he hadn't returned yet.

'It was a dreadful mistake,' Bella continued. 'She walked in on him with Millicent Hayes, and I think it has broken her heart. I should never have suggested it.'

Freddy, you fool, he thought. 'You couldn't have known,' he reassured Bella, and took up her hand. He gave it a comforting squeeze when he realised that she was staring at their entwined fingers.

'I meant to tell you last night, but Vaughan was there.'

'I understand.' Lucerne nodded. He'd felt all along that their relationship was doomed. Frederick's debts and Louisa's vulnerable reputation had always been a volatile combination, but Vaughan's comments would turn a tragedy into a pantomime. 'Have you seen much of him today?' he asked.

'No, and I'm glad. I think he's locked himself in the library.' She pulled her hand away irritably. Lucerne pursed his lips, slightly angered by her hostility. It was too personal, and threatened to sour his relationship with them both. He moved so that he was facing her.

'Please ignore what he said at breakfast, Bella. He's just trying to provoke you. Last night was precious.'

'Couldn't you have said that, then?'

'I didn't think you'd taken him so seriously.'

She stiffened, then slumped, but avoided meeting his eyes. Lucerne gently stroked her temples while he listened to her shallow breathing. It grieved him to see her upset, but last night had made him realise how much he wanted them both, and preferably together. There had to be a way of reconciling them to each other.

After dinner, Bella's mood was lighter. Lucerne had made her the main object of his attentions and had settled opposite her at the hexagonal gaming table for several hands of cards. They weren't alone; Vaughan sat reading only a few yards away, but Louisa's relentless hammering at the piano meant their conversation couldn't be overheard.

'I'd like to teach him some manners,' Bella grumbled, while she glowered tigerishly at Vaughan. Lucerne smiled broadly, showing off his white teeth, but he refused to be drawn. His gaze rested on Bella's low-cut dress and the shadowed valley between her breasts.

'And I should like to bend you over a chair and give you a swift hard ride,' he said. 'What do you say?'

'Lucerne! I was being serious.'

'So was I.' His voice was husky, and he met her gaze with a roguish smile. 'Forget Vaughan,' he said. Bella shifted the focus of her attention and reached out to caress Lucerne's wrist, where the cuff of his shirt peeked from beneath his coat. Lust coiled in her abdomen like a serpent.

Lucerne turned over another card.

'My hand!' she claimed.

'Also your game, I believe.' He counted his cards. 'What underhand tactics you play by.' His eyes moved from her cleavage to where her hand lay upon his. He turned his hand palm up and stroked her, while he pushed his last crown across the table. 'Shall we take a stroll now?'

The serpent coiled itself tighter, sending a lick of colour to her cheeks. Bella nodded. Unless she was very much mistaken, walking was not the only thing he had in mind, and she had to rein in the urge to drag him from the room to embrace him all the quicker. Instead, she stood before Vaughan and pulled her wool wrap around her shoulders with deliberate care, so that he noticed. He scowled over the top of his book at her. Bella glared back in a manner she hoped left no doubts about her intentions. Vaughan merely stuck his thumb up between his index and middle fingers.

Twenty paces along the corridor Lucerne pushed her into a recess. 'You were marvellous last night, very brave,' he commented as he leaned over her.

'You weren't bad either.'

'So, do you fancy an encore?'

'I'd prefer it without Vaughan.'

'Would you?' He fumbled with the fastening of her dress. 'Do you think I'll manage to satisfy you all alone?'

'I'm sure of it.'

She gripped his flanks and drew him closer, until she could feel his breath upon her face. When he kissed her again his tongue parted her lips. Bella fought to get her hands into his trousers, but they were well fitted and didn't allow much room for her fingertips. She struggled with them until he came to her aid and snapped the fastening open himself. Bella's hands immediately fell to his loins. One crept under the edge of his lawn shirt and closed around the soft base of his rising shaft.

Lucerne looked her deep in the eyes, breathing hard as his prick slid through her curled fingers. 'Oh, Bella, that's so good.'

He trembled. Bella ran her free hand through his thick blond hair and watched pleasure light up his face. She pushed her fingers into his mouth, and he began to suck and nip at them with growing excitement.

'I thought I was supposed to be pleasuring you,' he managed to gasp. His cock still drove through the ring of her finger and thumb, a solid erection now that pressed into the palm of her hand and left it slick with his seed.

'You are.'

How could she explain? Would he ever understand that with her hand around his cock she felt invincible? When she drove him to the edge with her touch, nothing else mattered – not Vaughan, nor all the promises to her brother. Not anybody.

Her thoughts of conquest dissolved as Lucerne began to tease her ear with his tongue.

'Lucerne,' she said hoarsely.

'Mmm, *mon amour*.'

'Should we find somewhere more comfortable?'

'Why, what's wrong with the corridor?'

Bella gasped. 'You're incorrigible.'

'No. Just hungry.'

He nuzzled against her neck, pretending to devour her. Bella squealed and held his arms, uncertain whether to hold him closer or push him away. Lucerne closed his hands around her wrists to trap her. He put all of his attention into kissing her throat. Bella whimpered and became still, overcome by the sensation. She wanted him to kiss her like that for eternity.

She was furious when she looked up and found Charles heading towards them but, as he drew closer, he looked so staggered by what he saw that her frown transformed into a smirk. 'Oh, I'm sorry!' he blustered, and lurched away towards the salon, setting Bella off into fits of laughter against Lucerne's shoulder. He was also sniggering; she could feel him shaking. Vaughan glanced out into the corridor, caught her eye and scowled before he turned his back in disgust. Bella laughed all the harder.

'It's getting a little crowded,' Lucerne observed. 'We'd best rejoin the others.'

Bella stifled her mirth with her handkerchief, while Lucerne forced his erection back into his clothing. He pulled his waistcoat straight and adjusted his collar, but all his adjustments couldn't hide the long, mouth-watering bulge beneath his breeches. The sight of that would surely turn Louisa scarlet.

'A little bit obvious, isn't it?' she commented, and drew a finger along its length.

'Behave yourself.' Lucerne clasped her hand and tugged her out of the alcove.

They had been back in the salon for less than five minutes before Lucerne whispered something into Vaughan's ear and then excused himself. Bella watched him go with some surprise. When, moments later, Vaughan also got up to leave, she became suspicious.

Convinced they had arranged a tryst, she followed at a distance. She wasn't about to sit by and let him have the joy of Lucerne's erection, which had still been straining the fabric when he'd left.

It proved difficult to pursue Vaughan discreetly. Several stretches of corridor had no hiding places, and when he entered the east wing, the darkness meant she had to stay closer to keep track of where he was going. He passed through many rooms she'd never seen before.

She took a tentative step around a particularly dark corner where Vaughan had vanished. Something brushed her ear, then a hand closed over her mouth with deadly strength and she was dragged backwards through a concealed door. Bella shrieked as a second arm clasped her waist. She tried to bite the hand that covered her mouth but couldn't get a hold on the flesh.

'Why are you following me, Miss Rushdale?' Vaughan asked. His sable curls tickled her cheek. He continued to restrain her as he pulled the door closed. They were in a small room, scarcely bigger than a cupboard, with no furnishings. A tiny square window let in a thin beam of moonlight. She struggled and he released her. 'Well?'

Bella flashed him a look of defiance. 'Rot in hell!'

He smiled briefly. 'Exactly what did you plan to do? Lock me away? Club me over the back of the head? We both know I can make you talk, Bella.'

You can't, she thought, but his commanding presence reminded her exactly what he was capable of. He'd made her beg before now and, as strong as she was, she couldn't deny that his proximity and the threat of punishment excited her.

Vaughan smiled again and swivelled his hips. Bella guessed that he knew her thoughts, but his arrogance knew no bounds if he thought his power over her was absolute. She decided to play along with him, to teach him a lesson.

'I want you,' she said in the most seductive voice she could manage. Vaughan's gaze dropped to her prominent breasts, then flicked back up to her face.

'I know.'

'I mean to have you.'

'By force or seduction?'

Bella placed her open hand on his thigh. 'By catching you offguard, of course.' He felt warm and desirable to the touch. Between her thighs she was melting. Playing games with him was exciting.

'I see,' he replied, as if intellectually fascinated by the idea. 'Is that why you followed me?'

'Perhaps,' she replied.

Vaughan regarded her evenly. 'You'd probably have to drug me, which would give you no satisfaction. Perhaps I should let you arouse me with your tongue?'

Bella's pulse quickened. Rarely was she offered that pleasure with such boldness and candour. The opportunity to hold him powerless in her mouth was heady wine; he'd never before allowed her to taste him. 'Show me how much you want it,' she said, determined to make him work for his reward. Vaughan swept forwards and descended on her for a kiss. He sealed his lips over hers and invaded her mouth with a fiery, hungry penetration. Bella's head swam. To her disappointment, he soon drew back, his ardour temporarily dimmed.

'Tell me why you were following me, and then maybe we can continue.'

It would take more than a kiss to make her talk. She laughed at him to emphasise this.

'Bella,' he murmured, and forced another kiss.

Her laughter died. She pushed him away, sick of the game, and snapped, 'I thought you were going to meet Lucerne.'

Given any number of tries, she could never have predicted his response. 'I see,' he said, and his voice was ice-cold. He grabbed her wrist so that his grip bit into her flesh, and dragged her out of the door on the other side of the small chamber. They raced along several dusty passages until they burst into Lucerne's sitting room.

Lucerne stood up in mild surprise, lips parted to ask for an explanation.

'There! Go to him.' Vaughan shoved her across the room. Bella put her arms out to save herself when she stumbled under the impact, but Lucerne caught her and only one knee hit the floor. The graze stung, but no worse than his words.

'Vaughan?' Lucerne said, as he helped Bella regain her balance. 'What's this about?'

A vision of high colour, Vaughan glared back furiously. His jaw tightened as Lucerne crossed the room and attempted to embrace him. 'No,' he said, and stepped backwards. Lucerne repeated his entreaty. He forced Vaughan to look at him, and rubbed his thumb over the other man's lips.

Bella stared in shock as tears of anger welled from Vaughan's eyes. He had never seemed so vulnerable before. She thought he was hard and cruel, but she saw that when it came to Lucerne all that fell away. Her concept of Vaughan being dominant in the relationship was obviously incorrect. Lucerne seemed to be in control as she watched him force a kiss.

Vaughan shoved him away and tried to leave, but Lucerne grabbed his arms and grappled with him. They fought amid snarls and curses, before finally ploughing into a chair which overturned, throwing them both to the floor. The thump made Bella wince. Lucerne trapped Vaughan beneath him.

'Leave me be,' he pleaded, but Lucerne shook his head and began to caress Vaughan's tense body with aggressive excitement. As Vaughan struggled to prevent his own inevitable response, Bella felt herself becoming aroused. She'd never seen two men fight for sexual dominance. She'd wondered what they did beyond touching and kissing. Their responses seemed magnified and inappropriate as they veered from tenderness to violence.

Vaughan's tortured eyes met Bella's gaze and his features contorted into an image of pure hatred. 'I won't perform for her amusement,' he snarled.

Lucerne's hold slackened and Vaughan easily extracted an arm. He lashed out and caught his lover hard across the jaw. Lucerne reeled aside, shocked and hurt but, as Vaughan got to his feet, Lucerne gently touched his thigh as if seeking an explanation. However, Vaughan only clenched his fist again, ready to strike.

'No!' Bella darted forwards. Vaughan looked up and

spat at her in his rage. She stumbled over her feet to back away. Only when she'd reached the relative safety of the bedpost did she dare look back at Vaughan. He hadn't moved. His eyes were closed and he breathed deeply as if to control his anger. Stunned by his inexplicable violence, she realised that she actually regretted the rift she'd caused, and wondered how to calm the situation. Before she could reach an answer, Vaughan's eyes snapped open. He gave her a vicious stare, then stormed from the room. The sudden slamming of the door shook the soft furnishings, then an eerie silence settled.

Bella quickly collected herself and then helped Lucerne get to his knees. Although he rubbed his jaw, he didn't appear too hurt. He ran his hand through his thick hair and looked thoughtfully at the door. For an awful moment, she thought he would leave her and go after Vaughan. 'What did you say to him?' he asked.

Bella shook her head. Vaughan's fury had been sudden and fearsome. She wondered if it would abate just as rapidly, or if he would stew for days.

'Are you all right?' Lucerne asked. He got to his feet. Bella buried her head against his chest. As his warmth seeped into her she realised that she was shaking, and craved comfort.

'Kiss me, Lucerne.'

'Just a kiss, *ma chère*?' he said, and he pressed his lips to her brow. 'That's uncommonly reserved of you.'

'I didn't say that.'

'Ah, only an aperitif.' He seemed determined to make light of the situation. He took hold of her as if he meant them to dance, and then kissed the tip of her nose. Bella tilted her head so that he could more easily reach her lips. Instead, he pecked each cheek, and then her chin.

'Lucerne, please.'

'I was getting around to it, but perhaps I'll kiss you everywhere else instead.' He continued the tease, and pressed the next kiss to her inner wrist.

'You're as bad as Vaughan.'

'Am I, indeed?' he averred, raising his eyebrow an eloquent quarter-inch. 'And since when were you so well acquainted?'

The words, 'We're not', stuck on her tongue. It was a lie she couldn't speak. Thankfully, Lucerne seemed to have already forgotten the question. He walked her to the bed and stopped just before it. 'Are you staying the night?' he asked coyly.

Bella gave the oak bed an appraising look. God knows, she'd dreamed about it often enough, and the opportunity was just too good to miss. She'd have to find a way to thank Vaughan for his intervention later, although she still wondered at his reaction.

'If you'll have me,' she remembered to respond when Lucerne raised an eyebrow questioningly.

'I certainly intend to.'

Lucerne undressed. Naked, he blew out all but two of the candles lighting the room, then sat down on the edge of the bed. Mesmerised, Bella watched, suddenly shy of him. She removed her lace fichu from around her neck and knelt between his legs. The eager stalk of his penis rose to greet her. She dipped her head to draw her tongue across the tip. His eagerness was salty on her tongue. 'Too soon, too soon,' he gasped as her mouth closed over him. He pulled away and pressed her down onto the bed to recline alongside him. 'You're always in a rush. Let me look at you.' Bella hesitated, but let him undress her, garment by garment.

His eyes roamed over her entire body in a way that made her feel like she was being caressed. His fingertips followed and traced every peak, curve and hollow. As his hands moved across her thighs, she whimpered with need. Unhurried, Lucerne traced a luxurious path from her navel to her breasts, before lowering himself so that his face was level with her hips. 'Kiss me,' she begged. Lucerne nuzzled into the dark curls of her mound, before lifting her thighs to lap at her cunt and flick the little nubbin with steady sideward strokes.

'Not there, up here.' She pressed a finger to her lips.

His body covered hers and she rubbed against him lasciviously as he moved in for the kiss Bella had longed for. She did not open her lips but allowed him to part them with a seductive foray. He kissed her softly but deeply, so that she tasted herself on his tongue.

Lucerne rolled onto his back, and pulled her on top. 'Touch me – and take your time,' he added as she headed straight for his cock. Bella reluctantly obeyed. She wanted him inside her but, as her hands moved over his body, she became absorbed with the texture of his skin. He wasn't overly muscular, but he was well made. She sat astride him and gripped his waist with her thighs. His penis brushed against her bottom, anointing the crease between her cheeks.

'I want you,' she whispered. 'Lucerne.'

'And only me?'

'Only you.'

Lucerne pulled her forwards and down, so that her pubis pressed on his loins and his penis pulsed against her. 'Ready?'

Bella raised her hips and his impatient prick reared towards her. He slid into her easily. 'Not too fast,' he said, but let her set the rhythm. Bella pushed down hard to enclose him completely before taking charge. Steadily she rose to a climax, rocking on his hard prick, her hands clasped upon his shoulders, his thumb on her clit. When he finally bucked inside her she knew that, for that moment at least, he was entirely hers.

'Vaughan.'

He didn't even turn his head as Lucerne walked the length of the gallery towards him. Vaughan was still sulking. Lucerne stopped three feet away from him and addressed his back. 'You weren't at breakfast.'

'I had no stomach for it, my lord.'

Lucerne bit his tongue in response to the acid in Vaughan's voice, and wondered what to say. Portraits of ancient Marlinscars stared down from the walls, offering neither wisdom nor comfort. Their faces were stern and guarded, never allowing emotion to betray them. Lucerne knew that giving in to Vaughan would cause problems, aside from courting public disgrace, but he had not counted on the marquis being so possessive.

'Did you want me for something?' Vaughan asked.

'I wish we hadn't fought last night. I didn't want you to leave. Bella didn't tell me . . .'

Vaughan shifted uncomfortably.

'Vaughan,' Lucerne said insistently. He stepped closer, and tried to avert some of Vaughan's anger with a caress.

'Get off me.' Vaughan shook himself free, then side-stepped out of Lucerne's immediate reach. Lucerne followed him, and placed his hands on Vaughan's hips.

'Don't be like this.'

'I told you to leave me alone.'

Lucerne took a few steps back, determined to maintain the dialogue. He felt frustrated. He knew what they both wanted, and his direct nature demanded a quick resolution. He couldn't understand why Vaughan had to poison things with his resentment. Couldn't he live in the moment, and let the past become history? In agitation, he ran his hand through his short hair, and reached the conclusion that, no matter what, he wouldn't get Vaughan to face him; he'd have to try a different tack.

He glanced over his shoulder to the open doorway at the far end of the gallery, and considered closing it for privacy. It would mean leaving Vaughan, and he wasn't sure that the other man wouldn't just disappear through the near exit. He'd rather risk intrusion. For the third time, he closed the gap between them. This time he pressed his cheek to Vaughan's shoulder. 'I'm sorry,' he said. 'Don't be cross.'

Vaughan turned his head away.

'You're jealous!' Lucerne moved his hands to Vaughan's waist. 'I don't believe it, you're actually jealous. What did you suppose would happen? Did you honestly expect me to give up women?'

'That woman is in love with you.'

Lucerne considered himself fortunate that Vaughan still faced the window. 'Should that matter to us?'

Vaughan shivered. 'She matters to you.'

Lucerne nuzzled against Vaughan's neck and slid his hands forwards over Vaughan's hipbones to his loins, in an attempt to pacify him. Although Vaughan's back immediately stiffened, another part of him also hardened. With a light but insistent touch, Lucerne traced the erection. One button on Vaughan's waistband fell undone, followed by a second. Soon Vaughan's buttocks were bared, and Lucerne began to prepare himself for entry.

'I'm going to fuck you,' said Lucerne. 'You know you like that.'

He heard Vaughan's heart hammering. 'Let me be,' Vaughan said without conviction. Lucerne bit into the muscle of his shoulder through the fabric of his shirt. When he moved himself against Vaughan's bottom, his penis prodded between the downy cheeks.

'Stop it!' Vaughan lashed out with his elbow, but Lucerne held on, unswayed by the attack. 'Get off me, Lucerne.'

Lucerne pinned Vaughan's upper body against the polished surface, pulled his arms into the small of his back and gripped his wrists in one hand, while he explored Vaughan's puckered whorl with the fingers of the other, seeking entrance. 'Remember Italy ... *il mio amore* ... Vaughan,' he soothed. From Vaughan's waistcoat pocket, he retrieved the stowed vial of oil. 'Don't fight so; let me give you what you want.'

The cabinet rocked against the uneven floorboards as Lucerne slid his oiled cock in. Bright sparks kindled in his loins, beating a pathway of fire to his brain. All that mattered was the sensation he felt in his cock, and the pleasure he derived from repeatedly plunging himself into another man's arse. Not so long ago that idea would have disgusted him, that now he could hardly imagine why he'd lived twenty-seven years without doing it. It seemed, at this moment, such a sensual act.

He was distantly aware of Vaughan's bitter swearing and cursing, but there was no resistance to his penetration. Vaughan wasn't fighting, and he wouldn't be able to deny the pleasure he derived from being taken thus, even if he did protest to the end.

'Admit it, you just hate being at somebody else's mercy. You're too conceited. But you don't fool me.' Lucerne knew exactly how much of a melting-pot of emotions Vaughan was – just how passionate, jealous and vengeful he could be, but also how sensitive and kind.

‘Mercy!’ spat Vaughan in return. ‘You’ll be the one begging for mercy before I’m done with you!’

Lucerne continued to penetrate him with hard, unrelenting strokes. He knew that later Vaughan might make him pay dearly for this, but he didn’t care. He was getting far too much selfish pleasure from overwhelming him. Orgasm came upon him, and his whole body arched as he soared. Vaughan’s muscles contracted around him. When he opened his eyes it was in time to see Vaughan, with a reluctant groan of pleasure, peak and fount semen over the polished surface of the bureau.

Exhausted, Lucerne released his partner and stepped back. He wanted to kiss him, but Vaughan pushed him away with a snarl, then pulled up his breeches and stormed out. With an outstretched arm supporting him against the cabinet, Lucerne watched him go, too tired to pursue. His body awash with the afterglow, he turned to the mullioned window and drew a deep breath. Eventually, Vaughan and Bella were going to force him to take sides, something he was desperate to avoid. But if he couldn’t reconcile them, then he’d have to choose one over the other.

He was still catching his breath when he heard footsteps behind him. Lucerne fastened the flap of his breeches and turned around, expecting to see Vaughan. Instead, he met Charles’s florid face.

‘I’ve just seen Pennerley storm off down the corridor,’ he said. ‘Looked like the devil had bitten his arse.’

Lucerne blinked, but managed half a smile. Charles gave him such an odd look in return that it wiped away his attempted raillery.

‘I was hoping to discuss that ditty of mine you said you’d give me an opinion on. If it’s not too much trouble.’ Charles tugged at the bottom button of his waistcoat, and it came off. 'Well, I'll just wait downstairs, shall I.' He gave Lucerne a hard stare, then left.

He knows ... no ... suspects too much, Lucerne thought. It was only by pure luck that he hadn't arrived any earlier. Eyes closed, he shook his head. Anyone could have walked in on them. Their argument had made them indiscreet, and it mustn't happen again. Once he'd seen that Charles was safely through the door, Lucerne turned back to the bureau. The puddle on the surface made him grimace. With his silk handkerchief, he mopped the evidence of their passion away.

Louisa's embroidery lay untouched in her lap. It was mid-afternoon, already dark outside, and the wind whistled in the chimney while the flames danced in the grid. Bella had been watching her with hawk eyes for the last five minutes, ready to swoop the moment she looked up. She probably wanted to drag out the drama of Wednesday afternoon, but Louisa no longer had anything to say on the subject. Her infatuation with Frederick Wakefield was over. She'd seen him for the rogue he was; no different to Vaughan when it came down to it. Except that at least Vaughan was honest. Still, it wasn't easy; almost every room held a memory of him, a shared moment or a secret smile.

The fierce wind rattled the latches and managed to lift the heavy Jacquard curtains. Louisa turned to find Lucerne peering out of the window at the rain-sodden lawn. He smiled wanly at her reflection in the dark glass and she smiled back.

'It's very stormy,' she said.

'Yes, it is.'

There was a distant, almost haunted look in his eyes, which the reflection only emphasised. He pulled the thick drapes across, obscuring her view. Louisa balanced her sampler on the arm of the settee, suddenly aware that not all the troubles in the house were her own. She studied him as he poured himself a drink and went to sit by Bella. Although he appeared at a passing glance to be his normal immaculate self, once she looked beyond his fine clothing and outward geniality, she noticed the dark smudges beneath his eyes and the worry lines criss-crossing his brow. She wondered what was bothering him. His voice was too low for her to hear what he was saying to Bella, but they appeared to be disagreeing on a matter of importance.

The conversation stopped dead as Vaughan entered the room.

'Don't let me stop you,' he said, and gave an insouciant wave, although his gaze remained fixed upon the settle where Bella and Lucerne they sat, as he stalked across the room like a sleek black panther.

Despite his presence and persistent stare, they began to talk again, albeit on a different topic. Louisa sat back to find Vaughan resting against her chair. He leaned forwards over her shoulder and his hair brushed her sleeve. 'It's very pretty,' he said of her embroidery.

Surprised and delighted, she smiled at him, although her joy quickly changed to alarm as his mouth hovered just above her exposed skin.

'Don't worry, I don't always bite,' he said close to her ear. She flushed crimson, but relief quickly cooled her skin, for Vaughan moved in front of the fire, and then to a seat.

'Some port, I think, Lucerne.'

Lucerne immediately rose to serve him. Louisa watched as he placed the glass in Vaughan's hand. Their eyes locked.

'Have you forgiven me?' asked Lucerne.

'Forgiven, but not forgotten.'

* * *

‘What did he say to you?’ Bella hissed to Louisa. Her friend only shook her head in reply, and continued to affect a smile for the two men. Forgetful of Louisa’s own misery, Bella inwardly cursed her silence. She had issues with Vaughan, and what she didn’t need was her best friend freezing up on her.

‘Not chasing rain clouds today, Bella?’ Vaughan’s voice was full of crisp mockery. Bella shifted to the edge of her seat and sat with a stiff back.

‘No, my lord.’

‘No doubt your groom is finding his sport elsewhere.’

‘No doubt,’ Bella said through pursed lips, struggling to conceal her fury. The bastard had deliberately said that so that Lucerne would hear. He hadn’t told Lucerne what had happened in the stables, and he wasn’t going to. Nevertheless, he’d use the knowledge to get at her.

Vaughan gave her a silky grin while he idly toyed with his crystal goblet. To his right, Lucerne reclined against the edge of the *chaise longue*. He made a low comment to Vaughan that Bella couldn’t hear, and they both laughed. Their amusement jarred. She could tell from Vaughan’s expression that he was taunting her, but she was uncertain whether Lucerne was an accessory or a cat’s paw. Vaughan peered at her through slitted eyes and ran his index finger around the rim of his glass, dipped it into the sticky sweet liquid, and then sucked the tip of his stained finger suggestively. He seemed delighted at the joke, which only made her mood worse. She watched stiffly as he slipped his arm around Lucerne’s shoulder on the side away from Louisa, and stroked the smooth line of the viscount’s jaw.

Apparently unaware of Vaughan’s game of one-upmanship, Lucerne smiled at the affectionate touch. Rage began to bubble in Bella’s blood. His subtlety might mean that Lucerne and Louisa missed his declaration, but she knew what he was saying as clearly as though he'd stood on the table and proclaimed it.

Lucerne is mine; your victory is not complete, and don't forget it.

Lucerne flashed her a smile as he tilted his glass to his lips, but the acknowledgement did nothing to reassure her. As long as Vaughan's hand was on him, Lucerne would never belong to her. He shared something with Vaughan she couldn't compete with, and all she could do was watch.

She turned away.

'You look like you've lost something,' said Vaughan. 'Perhaps you should retire.'

Even in victory, he had to mock. Bella jolted to her feet, gave him a wounded look, and then dashed from the room.

'Was it something I said?' he called after her, but she didn't look back. She ran blindly with no destination in mind, startled Charles in the corridor and fled into the next room, very nearly crashing into a suit of mail in her flight. The wolfhounds stirred by the fireplace. One looked up at her with its big brown doggy eyes before it lay its head back on its paws. Only once she'd reached the back stairs did she slow, and she finally slumped against the bare stone wall.

Her pulse beat loudly in her temple and, as much as she tried, she could not stop shaking. The subtext of Vaughan's conversation had driven her from the room, but she wouldn't let his presence drive her from the house.

She wouldn't.

Lucerne appeared on the steps below. He reached up and laid a gentle hand upon her arm. 'Are you all right?'

'Lucerne,' she said in a husky voice. 'Do you love me?'

The space around them went so quiet that she heard

his indrawn breath. He opened his mouth, then closed it again.

'I suppose not,' she said, and hoped her disappointment didn't ring too clearly in her words.

'Don't say that. You rather took me by surprise.' He coughed into his hand. 'You look pale; are you sure you are all right?'

Bella sighed, stricken but not surprised. All she wanted was some reassurance that she wasn't just a diversion for Lucerne and Vaughan, but she'd asked the wrong question. She doubted Lucerne was even capable of bringing the words to his lips. Tears stung her eyes, but she refused to let them spill. Lucerne would not take that weakness back to Vaughan.

'You're precious to me – is that enough?'

Bella looked down into his deep-cornflower eyes and sensed that he meant it.

'Don't let him get to you,' he said, and opened his arms to her. 'I want you here. That's all that matters.'

# 11

The miserable weather had cleared by mid-November, giving way to the cold starry nights of winter. A week after she'd discovered Wakefield in the arms of a trollop, Louisa awoke to find the ground frozen and the grass crisp with white frost. Louisa sat painting by the window, mirroring the clean white beauty of the courtyard on her canvas. She watched a lone figure cross the cobblestones and duplicated the light impressions of his passing in her picture.

The stranger peered through the glass, revealing himself as Vaughan, then let himself in by the French window. An icy blast chilled the room and made Louisa shiver in her flimsy muslin gown. She paused to rub some warmth back into her bare arms. Meanwhile, Vaughan shrugged off his heavy greatcoat and removed his gloves with his teeth. He cast them with careless grace over a chair, then turned back to the fire to warm up. Louisa watched him warily from her position across the room. She liked to look at him – he was an attractive man – but as a rule she still avoided being alone with him. Overcautious, perhaps, but she knew from experience that he was dangerous and unpredictable. Nevertheless, she craved any kind of company to divert her from brooding over Frederick and that tart Millicent.

'Good morning,' she said.

'It's a bitter morning.' He turned sharply to face her, and Louisa recognised a hint of cold humour in his expression. 'Whether it is also a good one remains to be seen.'

She immediately regretted having drawn his attention. Vaughan licked his lips, a gesture that was entirely vulpine. He crossed to the giltwood mirror and stood before it, smoothing his curls over his shoulders.

'You needn't look so frosty,' he said as he watched her countenance in the glass. 'Even rogues and scoundrels have off days. I'm not set upon robbing you, it's much too cold.'

Louisa turned her back to him in reply. She cautiously daubed paint onto her picture, unconvinced of her safety. She heard his light footsteps, then stiffened as he rested against her back, his groin level with her shoulder blades. The musky scent of him wafted over her.

'Quite an impressive piece,' he commented, while she forced herself to relax. 'You never cease to amaze me, Louisa. I wonder what other accomplishments you might yet reveal beyond embroidery, piano, and painting.'

'None, unless you include a smattering of French.'

Where was this leading? she wondered. Maybe she should leave. She couldn't see his face properly to read his expression without turning, and in any case she didn't trust herself to keep her reaction neutral. After a moment or two he picked up an unused brush and began to toy with it. Louisa watched out of the corner of her eye as he tested the bristles against his skin, then used it to caress the back of her hand.

She bit her lower lip. All her instincts told her to pull away from him, but she guessed that was just the sort of encouragement he was looking for. Instead, she kept her hand still and concentrated hard on her painting. Vaughan brushed her hair to one side, so that she could feel his breath on the side of her neck, and then he very gently ran the tip of the brush along the edge of her ear. Louisa shivered at the odd fluttery sensation it awoke in her breast.

'You're ignoring me,' he said. 'Don't you think that's a little rude?'

'If I am, it's your own fault.'

'Oh? And why would that be?'

'You know why!' she snapped as she stood abruptly. Two hot flashes of colour rose across her cheekbones. Vaughan coolly drew himself up to his full stature.

'Are you inferring that I was responsible for the departure of that lapdog Wakefield, or is it some other matter? I can assure you that if it is the former, he left entirely of his own accord.'

'That's of no consequence. I refer to the night of the ball.'

'What of it?'

'You forced me.'

'Strange, I remember it differently,' Vaughan mused. 'I had an inkling that you were enjoying it, until we were rudely interrupted.'

Louisa swallowed hard as vivid images of the ball flickered before her eyes. It had been in this room. Her mouth suddenly felt very dry, and her balance unsteady. Vaughan laid a hand on her shoulder, and she sat down again.

'Perhaps I might tempt you again sometime, now that we would have less chance of being disturbed,' he whispered into her ear. 'I could show you what you're missing.'

Louisa shuddered, unable to prevent the reaction. She lowered her gaze to the carpet to avoid facing the cruel smile playing about his lips. He brushed her neck with the paintbrush, then circled her protruding nipple. 'It must be hard work always being so nervous. You should learn to relax, Louisa. You'd enjoy everything so much more.'

Louisa closed her eyes and tried to steady herself. If

she kept her nerve and didn't react to him, he would grow bored and leave. The brush continued to tease her through the light fabric. She felt his hair graze against her neck and expected to feel his lips, but the kiss never came. She opened her eyes and found to her surprise that he was gone.

The remainder of the day passed without incident, but Louisa awoke the next morning to find wild heather on her pillow, tied up together with a soft-bristled paint-brush. Consequently, she was still in bed and deeply confused at midday, when Bella knocked to enquire if she was all right and collect her for lunch.

It was shocking enough to think he'd been in the room while she was asleep, particularly since he must have passed through a door that was bolted on the inside, without contemplating what he might do next time.

'Are there any secret passages in the house?' she asked Lucerne as they left the dining room after lunch. Lucerne paused a moment and thought.

'Not as such. There are a few dusty corridors in the east wing, and a couple of doors in odd places, but none of the windy mysterious passages our novelists are so fond of. Why do you ask?'

'Oh, no reason.'

Lucerne gave her an odd, quizzical look.

'I just thought I heard something behind the wall in my room,' she added, and his look softened. He smiled beneficently.

'Probably mice. I'll get someone to take a look for you.'

'Thank you.' Louisa waited until he'd moved away, then frowned. If he hadn't used a secret passage, how on earth had he got in? There were no other doors to the room, and even a spare key from one of the servants wouldn't slide the bolt.

'What was all that about secret passages?' asked Bella as she came up behind Louisa.

Louisa bowed her head in dismay. She didn't really want to explain to Bella, but she was her only real ally in the house.

Bella gently touched her arm. 'Lou, what is it?'

'He's been in my room.' Louisa stared at the wall, and hoped for a little sympathy.

'He?'

'Vaughan.'

Bella immediately checked over her shoulder. 'What did he do? Did he hurt you?'

'No. He left a bunch of heather on my pillow. I just don't understand how he got in when I had the door bolted all night.'

Bella pulled her into the alcove below the stairs. 'Are you sure it was from him? Couldn't it be from someone else?'

'Such as?' Louisa shook her head. 'No, it's definitely him. Besides, it was tied up with the paintbrush he was teasing me with yesterday.'

A strange gleam appeared in Bella's green eyes. Louisa imagined she was thinking of the marquis sneaking about her room at night as she lay dreaming beneath the sheets. Despite Bella taking every opportunity to criticise Vaughan, her friend did seem to have a soft spot for him.

'And you're definite the bolt was drawn?' she said. Louisa nodded. 'What about the window?'

'My room is on the first floor, Bella. Have you seen any ladders? Anyway, it was shut tight.'

'Then it certainly is a puzzle.' Bella frowned. She sucked in her cheeks as she thought. Louisa looked past her to the walls of the vast second entrance hall and wondered whether it hid passages Lucerne was not aware of, but that Vaughan had somehow discovered.

Perhaps the secret lay behind a tapestry or in the cellar, where it wouldn't easily be found. She stared at the oil painting to the right of the door, expecting to see roving eyes watching her.

'Oh Louisa, you ninny,' Bella suddenly cried, and dragged her across the hall to the front door. The wind was bitter outside and the porch steps were slippery beneath their flimsy pumps.

'Look!'

Bella pointed towards Louisa's room, just above the brow of the porch. 'He must have climbed out of the parlour window, there –' she indicated to the right '– and scrambled across the roof. The drop to the lintel isn't far. I don't suppose it's so difficult if you've a mind to try.'

'I suppose not.'

Louisa hugged herself. Bella, immune or oblivious to the cold, continued to stare up at the icy plinth as if she expected to see him climb out of the window at any minute. 'I imagine he's had lots of practice climbing in and out of bedroom windows,' she said. 'Lecherous rake that he is.' She lay a reassuring arm around Louisa's shoulders. 'Don't fret, you can easily fasten it down.'

That night Louisa sat upright in bed with her legs bent before her, hugging her pillow for comfort. The door was bolted and she had done her best to lash the window down with a piece of brown string, but she still didn't feel safe. During the afternoon, she had nearly asked Bella if she could share her bed, but had dismissed the idea. After all, if ravishment was his intention, why hadn't he taken her last night instead of leaving tokens on her pillow?

Vaughan the rakehell who emerged from the shadows carrying the threat of erotic promise, she understood, but Vaughan the sensitive gallant she did not. Again, she considered the possibility that it might have been somebody else.

'No,' she said aloud, and retrieved the soft blue paintbrush from the quilt. It was definitely Vaughan. She ran the bristles over the back of her hand thoughtfully, stopped, then blew out the lone candle on the bedside and snuggled beneath the covers. Her eyes fell shut and she yawned, pushing her hand and the paintbrush under the pillow. Let him come if he must; she could always scream.

Unbidden fantasies came to her. Vaughan crept into her dreams and draped something dark over her eyes. He slipped between the sheets to lie naked beside her, and the heat of his body warmed and excited her. Fingertips danced over her curves and hollows, and a thumb traced the outline of her lips. Kisses fell as rain on her face, neck and breasts. Firm hands parted her thighs, and a thrilling hardness stood poised to claim her maidenhead.

He pressed into her, and she opened to receive him.

She gasped and awoke with a start. Her pulse raced and her skin was bathed with sweat. It was past midday and she was alone. She sighed with relief, or perhaps regret, thrust back the quilt and got out of bed.

'We should have asked Louisa to join us,' Bella said as she climbed into Lucerne's carriage. 'We used to ride over to Meyrick Lodge to see Mrs Castleton together before she went to live with her aunt.' She thought back to the days when Mrs Castleton had arranged introductions to young gentlemen for the two of them. Some had been tolerable, at least, but none had had the dark, heady appeal of Lucerne or Vaughan.

Lucerne closed the carriage door, tapped the side wall to signal the driver to move on, and finally reclined on the upholstered leather seat. 'I didn't realise you liked sharing so much.' Bella's eyes widened as he parted his thighs and stretched his palms over them. His uncharacteristic directness was just as exciting as the thrilling bulge in his tight-fitting breeches. So this was what the impromptu social call was about; not so much a necessity as a chance to have her alone without Vaughan for three or four hours.

'Come here.'

'Not scared of my brother any more?' asked Bella.

'What's done is done. *Carpe florem*.'

Bella knelt on the carriage floor between his knees. Expectation prickled through her body as she watched him slowly unbutton his breeches. His cock sprang to attention, almost leaping into her open mouth. Unable to restrain herself, she pushed out her tongue and gave it a sly lick.

As the carriage rumbled over the rough track, she gazed up at Lucerne. As he dipped his head to kiss her, she slid her hands around his neck and into his thick blond hair. 'A gallop was too obvious,' he said.

His prick rubbed between her breasts. A compulsion to handle it, to pleasure him, shot down her throat to her nipples, and they sprang to attention. She wanted him to cup her breasts, tease them, and then fill her up.

'Let me breathe, you vixen,' Lucerne gasped. He held her back as he regained his breath and some of his poise. Meanwhile, Bella contemplated his shaft. Her hands crept beneath the hem of his shirt and into the golden hair that grew in a thin line from his navel to his prick. He watched her with lustrous eyes. 'Suck me.'

'What!' Surprised by his crudity, she sat back on her haunches. 'What happened to the well-mannered libertine I thought I was with?'

'Lovelace.'

Bella frowned in incomprehension.

'The word you're looking for is Lovelace.'

'Never mind,' Bella said, still a mite stunned, though she curled her fingers around the base of his shaft.

'I was after your mouth, not your hand,' Lucerne drawled.

Bella laughed. This would be a rare pleasure. She leaned forwards. His musky scent tingled in her nostrils, sending anticipatory shivers down her back. He tasted somewhat musky, too, as she put her tongue to work on his plum.

'Ah,' he sighed. His fingers worked urgently at the back of her neck, caressing that sensitive area of skin as she rhythmically sucked him, swallowing as much of his shaft as she could.

Bella's jaw ached but she was enjoying herself far too much to stop. Having his cock in her mouth was making her wet. She rucked up her skirt to reach her aching clit, and flicked her middle finger across the pearly bead a few times before dipping the tip into the pool of dew. Her head spinning with wicked thoughts, she then lifted her slippery finger and stroked it along his perineum. Finally, she circled his anus impishly.

'Don't you dare,' he warned her.

Pretending she hadn't heard, she continued the circling motion. The low gasps from his lips became progressively louder. Bella slid the tip inside up to the first joint and waggled it gently.

'Bella!'

Between her lips, he was as stiff as a broom handle. She squeezed her index finger into him beside the first, whilst her tongue lapped at the eye of his cock. Lucerne gasped as if all the air had been knocked out of him. His whole body tensed, and then his hot seed pumped into her hungry mouth.

Bella held him between her lips until the last drop

had leaked from his cock, and his erection was all but gone. Only then did she sit back on the carriage floor with a contented sigh. Lucerne remained with his eyes closed for several long moments, while his body continued to spasm with the echoes of orgasm. When he finally opened his eyes and reached for her, it was with a beaming smile plastered across his lips.

'You've a wicked tongue,' he said against her hair.

'And wicked fingers.'

'Hmm.'

Bella twisted to see his expression. It was unfathomable. 'Does he do that to you?' she asked without forethought, and immediately regretted the question. It put an end to their embrace.

Lucerne frowned. 'He may do,' he said evasively.

Bella straightened her clothing. There was a damp patch on the front of her gown where his pre-come had leaked. She hid it beneath her fichu then glanced anxiously at Lucerne, who turned away. The carriage soon rumbled to a halt. Bella railed against herself; she'd spoiled everything with one stupid ill-considered remark. However, as the footman opened the door and lowered the steps she felt Lucerne's breath on her neck. A quick glance back at him told her that she need not have worried. A mischievous twinkle danced in his eyes and he nipped her earlobe.

'Your turn on the journey home,' he said as he led her from the carriage.

Louisa paused at the library door. Behind her in the hall, the familiar sound of the clock striking the hour reverberated. Across the room she could see Vaughan's forearm, draped over the edge of a leather armchair facing away from her. She knew it was Vaughan's arm from the spill of lace at the wrist, and the jewellery. She guessed he was reading, an occupation he favoured when not engaged in some debauchery. Clearly Lucerne's collection of cracked leather volumes and exotic texts held greater appeal than a quick glance at their spines had suggested to her. Her book lay on the table to the right of the door. If she was lucky, she'd be able to get it without disturbing him. Carefully, she stepped into the room.

'Annabella has accompanied Lucerne on a visit to Mrs Castleton, so you won't find her in here,' Vaughan said, before she'd completed three paces.

Louisa turned to him. 'I only came in for my book.' He waved her towards the table.

She quickly crossed the remainder of the carpet to retrieve it, and yelped as Vaughan's arm snaked in front of her. He picked up the book and read the title. '*Novella Justine*. An interesting choice,' he commented. 'Doubtless recommended by the delightful Miss Rushdale. I trust you find it informative.' He handed her the slim volume.

Louisa snatched it from him and took a hasty step away. Vaughan arched a single eyebrow and then took a deliberate step towards her. When she retreated again, she found herself pressed against the bookcase.

'Ooops, trapped,' he said.

Louisa quaked. The shelves dug into her back. He was very close to her and she could feel his breath on her face. She wondered if he could smell her fear.

'Put aside your book, Louisa dear, and let me educate you.'

'No,' she said, and her voice sounded rather shrill.

'Don't you trust me?' he chided. Louisa began to say something, then changed her mind and stared at his chest. Vaughan tilted her chin up with his fingertips. 'You look worn out,' he observed, gazing at the dark circles below her eyes.

'Do I?'

'Yes, you do.' He caressed her cheek and brushed a stray wisp of hair behind her ear. Louisa felt numb, as if all her strength had seeped out of her toes into the carpet. Yet again he had switched from wicked intent to tender concern, and it muddled her thinking. In his eyes she read hurt, but he still had her pinned.

'This will not do,' he said in exasperation. 'I really think things would be more pleasant if you didn't try so very hard to despise me.' He took a large step back and turned away from her.

'You frighten me,' Louisa said, as if she owed him an explanation. Vaughan glanced over his shoulder at her, and gave her a half-mocking predatory smile, which faded the moment she stiffened.

'Only because you're afraid of the unknown. If you would just let me . . .' He stopped, holding the pause. 'Well,' he continued at last. 'Perhaps we won't go into that.'

Louisa tried to read his expression. She moved forwards an inch or two, which eased the pressure of the wood against her back.

'Did you sit up much of last night?' he asked.

Louisa bit her lip. 'How did you know?'

'Just a guess. Did you dream of me? Of what might have happened to you if your window had not been tied?'

She didn't reply, but was sure her expression must have told him everything.

'B'gad, madam! I won't deny I've been a scoundrel before now but, as a rule, I prefer my lovers to be willing. Do you think I'd force you?'

'You did before,' she snapped, finding her tongue at last.

'Hmm – I believe we discussed that once already.' He turned on his heels. The skirt of his coat swirled out around him, glinting with azure and sapphire. When he faced her next, he favoured her with a dazzling smile. 'Indulge me. What did you have me do in those dreams of yours?'

She flushed at his words, trying desperately not to think of her nocturnal fancies.

'Did I caress you with my hands, or did my tongue tease your nipples? Did I wet your chemise until it stuck to the ripe flesh beneath and became transparent? Did I fuck you?'

A scandalised gasp escaped her. Vaughan walked towards her until his hands brushed against her waist. False memories awoke at his touch. She held on to his wrist and the lace prickled her fingers. He lifted his arm to kiss each of her fingertips in turn.

'I could scream,' she warned.

'No one will hear.'

'Charles.'

'Snores louder than I suspect you scream. Which is fortunate.' He laid his hands on her shoulders.

'What are you going to do to me?'

Vaughan smiled. 'Nothing I can't make you beg for.'

She thumped her fists against his chest. He looked down at her patiently. 'I won't be thwarted by such a feeble gesture, Louisa. I'm sure you can fight harder than that.'

A knot of anger rose in her at his smugness. She lashed out, delivering a smarting blow to his cheek. Vaughan laughed. 'I shall have a bruise because of that,' he said, then easily grasped both her wrists. Louisa struggled against him, but he easily overpowered her, sealing her mouth with a kiss. For a moment she fought for air, then he simply overwhelmed her. She moaned. Vaughan pressed her hand over his prick. It pulsed with life, hard as a ferule but soft as velvet. A brief shadow swam before her eyes.

'I do hope you've not been deceiving me,' he said as he dropped elegantly to his knees. 'Tell me, am I your first?' Her underwear fell away beneath his practised hand.

The warm, rough surface of his tongue snaked through the blonde curls covering her mound. He made a V with his fingers and parted the swollen lips of her delta. His tongue-tip delved into her, gently lapping at her clitoris, and sent honey-sweet darts through her body. She cried out once for shame, and then all embarrassment left her. She no longer cared that she meant nothing to him, or that she sometimes hated him, or even that briefly she wished it was Frederick; her only concern became the tongue palpating her bud.

Vaughan sat back on his haunches. He held her on the brink of climax, lost in her need, and making only small mewling sounds. Her pleading gratified him. He derived perverse satisfaction from knowing that he could arouse her to this extent despite her hatred of him, and further that he could walk away at any moment and deny her fulfilment. However, there was a wager to win.

'Don't stop,' she pleaded when his tongue left her bud. Her eyes flicked open, pupils dilated so that only a thin rim of blue iris remained. 'Why have you stopped?'

Vaughan disguised a smirk by drawing his brows into a contemplative frown. 'Alas, I bore easily,' he sighed, and watched her shoulders slump.

'But you can't ... I want ...' she gasped with shock and hurt. It was too much. The thrill of sadism brought a welcome throb to his balls, and his penis stiffened a fraction more. She was a pretty piece, with her eyes sparkling with lust, and her innocence added spice. But he wouldn't be hurried with this treat.

'And what do you want, Louisa? Tell me. Spell it out.'

Her delicate mouth opened but no words came out. Vaughan gave her at most five minutes before he could get her to say something unspeakably crude.

'You want me to . . .' he prompted.

She shook her head so that all her blonde ringlets bounced and quivered. Vaughan trailed his tongue over her clitoris again. 'Why do you tease me?' she asked.

'I assure you 'tis no tease. You've merely to ask.'

She writhed against his fingers, trying to manoeuvre them to where it gave her most pleasure. Her attempts to foil him, and her silence, greatly amused him. He realised that he had slighted her before now. She had more spirit that she let on; perhaps Bella had been giving her lessons. He didn't suppose Wakefield would much thank her for it.

Vaughan took away his hand and licked the honeyed musk from his fingers. The look she gave him with those wide luminous eyes was one of lust and outrage. He sucked the last of her dew from his thumb.

'Ask.'

Her lips trembled. The tight lacing around her bust pulled taut as she took a deep breath. 'Very well,' she said at last. 'Since you make me. I want you to . . . to make love to me.'

'To fuck you.'

The shot of distaste that leaped through her face, flaring in her cheeks as a rosy hue, made his cock buck in his breeches. Silly how that one word could make her blush when her quim was on display. He was only glad that she couldn't tell how much all this delay was costing him; his own needs were overpowering. He wanted to push himself inside her immediately, but he also wanted to milk this situation for all it was worth.

'To make love to me,' she repeated steadily, and even managed to meet his eyes while she spoke.

'In that case, you'll have to tempt me a little more. *Quid pro quo*, Louisa, for only then shall you have what you desire.'

'How?'

Vaughan rose, and let her skirt drop. 'We will consider that dilemma in your bedchamber.'

Louisa shivered as the excitement and boldness she had previously felt ebbed from her. Vaughan turned the key in the lock and then faced her. They were alone in her room; it was final; there was no turning back. At any moment he was sure to lose patience, to push her onto the bed and ravish her. All she could hear was the sound of her own heart. It beat simultaneously in her chest, her throat, her stomach and her ears. Vaughan, however, showed no signs of impatience as he carefully removed his coat and cravat and placed them neatly over a chair. Nor did he seem overeager as he stripped off his rings, and then removed her necklet and earrings and left them on the dressing-table.

'Relax, I'm not going to devour you,' he reassured her, when she jumped as his shadow fell over her.

Louisa closed her eyes and trembled as he pressed a long suggestive kiss to her lips, though she no longer knew whether she felt fear or lust. She could feel his trapped erection hard and firm against her body and was overcome with the sudden desire to look at him. Vaughan watched her with a mixture of amusement and desire in his eyes as she slowly unfastened his waistband and pushed his shirt aside. His cock reared proudly, silky smooth and long, but curved like a sabre and with a plum tip.

'Later, maybe I'll let you taste it,' he said with a lewd grin.

'Put it in my mouth,' Louisa blurted, shocked at herself, but overcome with curiosity.

He laughed, genuinely amused. 'Then again, maybe you'd like to do that now,' he suggested, and ran his thumbs over her taut nipples. He pinched harder, and made her groan. 'Hmm, yes,' he drawled. 'I think so.'

Louisa sighed. Vaughan's head rested against her milky thigh, while his gaze lingered over her body. Now, in the afterglow, she was growing wary of him again. Even stroking his hair felt like petting an alligator. One wrong move and his present gentleness would result in a vicious bite. She felt no regrets at having lain with him, and knew she'd do it again given the chance, though she didn't expect to have it. He had shown her her only pleasure of recent days, though doubtless his motive was selfish. He had also taught her a lesson in irony. She probably still loved Frederick, but she'd slept with his enemy for a fleeting pleasure, and deep down she knew she'd done it to hurt him.

Vaughan kissed his way up her body to her mouth. His lips were still soft and warm against her skin. A faint feeling of arousal stirred at the tease. He propped himself on one arm and regarded her meditatively. 'Beautiful Louisa,' he said of her dishevelled appearance. 'How exquisite you look with your hair loose and your skirts thrown awry.'

She thought perhaps he was being sarcastic, but a glimpse at herself in the mirror only resulted in her agreement with him. She was flushed with the aftermath of sex and wet with salty perspiration, but had never looked or felt so alive.

Vaughan leaned over the edge of the bed and retrieved his rumpled shirt from the floor. He shook out the worst of the creases and pulled it over his head whilst grinning to himself.

'What are you smiling about?' she asked.

He stood and fastened his breeches over his shirt. 'Quite simply, my dear Louisa, that you have just won me sixty guineas.'

'What?' Her brows crinkled in confusion.

'Sixty guineas,' he repeated slowly. 'I had a bet with Aubury. Miss Rushdale and yourself before Lucerne and the captain, which I've now achieved.'

Louisa rolled over and tugged a sheet over herself. Somehow, his revelation didn't shock her. 'Is that all I am to you – a few coins?' she asked calmly.

'And one less virgin. Good night.' He bowed mockingly.

Louisa waited until she heard the door close, then collapsed into the pillows with a sigh.

'We have returned!' said Lucerne.

Bella grinned as she watched Charles sit up abruptly, startled from his repose. He was ensconced before the fire with a glass of port at his elbow and a roughly scribbled text open on his lap.

'More interruptions,' he grumbled as he arranged his plump figure more comfortably in the chair. 'So, you're home. How exciting for me.'

'What are you writing?' Bella asked, curious about the manuscript.

'Nothing at the moment . . . Well, poetry actually, but the atmosphere is ruined. It's impossible to write about strange happenings and deserted rooms with you lot scaring the ghosts away.' He gave a throaty sigh and looked mournfully at his notes.

Bella wondered if his gruff moans weren't just for display. He didn't seem to be concentrating very hard on the words before him, and the ink had dried on the nib of his pen. 'We've only just arrived back. Surely you've been alone all afternoon to work,' she said.

'I believe he is taking issue with my presence, not yours,' said Vaughan, as he emerged from the shadows with a theatrical flourish.

'Yes, you,' said Charles. 'Can't you languish someplace else? And don't hover so close.' He pulled a boorish expression as Vaughan leaned over the arm of his chair.

'Sixty guineas, Charles, by the weekend if you please.'

'It's no good,' he howled, while he mopped the beads of sweat that rapidly appeared on his brow. 'I can't get it by then.'

'Saturday afternoon.'

Vaughan pulled himself up to his full stature, then nodded politely to them all, and left. Lucerne shook his head in obvious disbelief.

'You should know better than to incur debts with Vaughan, Charles,' he said sagely. 'I would start digging deep into your pockets. He's not the sort of person one likes to owe money to. I'm sure you've heard the stories.'

Charles turned away, ashamed. Bella empathised. She knew exactly what it was like to have Vaughan constantly on your back. 'Pay him,' she advised, but if Charles heard her, he didn't respond.

'Bella, let's have some tea,' said Lucerne. 'We'll leave you for the ghosts to find, Charles.'

The following evening Louisa stood in the minstrel gallery which overlooked the dusty splendour of the great hall. Once, she imagined, it would have lived up to its grand name, but few furnishings had survived the ages. The only piece that was free of cobwebs was the armchair that Charles had artfully positioned before the central fireplace.

They were surveying the room prior to its refurbishment. At least, that's what Lucerne was doing. Bella was too busy flirting, Charles too drunk, and Vaughan – what could one say about Vaughan? That, surprisingly, he was at the top of a ladder, currently examining the last of four vast windows on the east side of the room; each stood above five feet of blackened oak panelling and behind thick mildewed drapes, which she suspected might once have been red.

She no longer knew what to think of him. Not hatred any more, but certainly not intimacy either. For a brief time they had connected, but then she recalled how chillingly callous he'd been when he left her room, as if he were deliberately re-establishing his distance. Marquis Pennerley was definitely confusing – infuriating, but at least interesting.

He must have noticed her watching him, for he blew her a discreet kiss. Louisa tried hard not to smile. Twenty-four hours had changed her almost beyond recognition. Yesterday, she'd probably have reacted by shaking for an hour. Now it reminded her of something entirely different. As she watched him descend from the ladder to exchange notes with Lucerne, yesterday afternoon came clear and sharp to her mind . . .

'What are you dreaming about?' Bella asked as she emerged from the narrow arched entrance to the gallery. 'You're flushed.'

Louisa turned her head slowly, trying unsuccessfully to shake off the powerful, lewd memories before she faced her friend. She only just managed to veil her expression.

The scent of beeswax candles drifted up to them from below, where Lucerne was raising the iron cartwheel candelabra back to the rafters.

'Vaughan has Charles in fear of his life,' Bella said.

Disinterestedly, Louisa resumed her former position and rested her chin on her folded arms. She could guess why.

'I can't work out what it's about. Charles refused to say, and I didn't think it was worth asking Vaughan.'

'You wouldn't have liked his answer anyway,' she mumbled into her clothing. Apprehensively, she bit the cotton sleeve of her gown. Bella would have to be told. She'd hoped she wouldn't have to be the one to break the news, but if Bella discovered that Louisa had known and not said anything, her reaction would only be worse. Beside her, Bella put her back to the railing.

'What have you found out?' she asked. 'And how did you find it out?'

'It's about a gambling debt. Charles owes Vaughan.' Louisa was pleased to find the strain didn't show in her voice.

'I didn't think Vaughan played cards,' Bella said.

'It wasn't cards.'

Her expression clouded, though her voice retained its light-hearted note. 'What else have they found to bet on? There's not exactly much going on here.'

There was no escaping it. 'Us,' she admitted.

'What do you mean, us?'

'Exactly what I said,' Louisa replied. She drew herself up to her full four feet eleven inches. 'Bella, try to stay calm,' she hesitated, tense, and ready for the explosion. 'They wagered sixty guineas that Vaughan couldn't bed you before Lucerne and me before Wakefield. He's after payment.'

'But you haven't . . . Christ, Louisa! When?'

'Does it matter?'

'My God!' The colour drained from Bella's face, leaving her ashen. She recovered quickly. 'Sixty guineas. That's less than he spends on a tie pin,' she bellowed.

Louisa tugged at her sleeve and pulled her away from the edge of the balcony. 'Bella, keep your voice down.'

'How can you be so calm? And let go of me.' She pulled herself free.

'It doesn't really bother me.'

'What?' Bella cut her off. 'You're not making sense.' She leaned over the railing. 'You bastard,' she screamed, then fled.

'Bella . . . Bella,' Louisa cried as she pursued her down the narrow stairs. Bella had already disappeared through the door when Louisa reached the bottom and found herself face to face with Lucerne.

'What was that about?' he asked.

'Nothing.' Louisa shook her head, aware of Vaughan in the background. He looked unaffected by the outburst. Lucerne's expression was sour, but she refused to be the bearer of any more bad tidings. They could sort it out amongst themselves. 'I'd better find her,' she said, and excused herself.

As she darted into the corridor she heard Lucerne ask, 'Which one of us do you suppose that was aimed at?' The closing door muffled any replies.

Louisa perched on the corner of Bella's rumpled bed, regarding her friend with genuine concern. Bella lay sprawled across the covers. She was cursing incoherently between heart-wrenching sobs, and Louisa didn't entirely understand why. What Vaughan and Charles had done was brutish and unkind, but Bella seemed to be taking it rather to heart. It wasn't as if she were in love with either of them, or even cared much for their opinions.

'Damned worthless whoreson!' Bella thumped the mattress and then flung her pillow to the floor.

'Bella!' Louisa had never heard language so coarse. It

seemed pointless to get upset by callous and unthinking behaviour and, although she wasn't happy with recent events, next to Bella her annoyance was barely significant. Perhaps it was down to clarity. Louisa suspected that there was more to this than just an idle wager: Vaughan's intention had probably been to humiliate Frederick. She didn't understand why, but it didn't take a genius to work out that there was no love lost between them. Charles was just a compulsive gambler. To Vaughan, the money was unimportant. He'd done it out of spite – but then, so had she.

She quietly rose and left Bella to her cursing.

'Bella.'

Bella froze at the sound of her name. Slowly she turned about to greet Lucerne with a fixed smile. She had no argument with him, since he probably didn't even know about the bet, but she'd been avoiding everyone since her outburst and was eating early. To her relief, he had come down to breakfast alone, relaxed and informal.

'There's a letter for you,' he said, lifting a sealed package from the pile of correspondence to wave at her. 'It's Joshua's handwriting, I believe.'

'Thank you,' she replied, and took the letter from his outstretched hand. He pressed his thumb into her palm before allowing her to withdraw. The reassurance gave her the strength to endure his searching gaze. He was clearly worried about her.

'Is there anything I can do?' he asked. 'Should I have someone flogged?'

'No. It was just a silly outburst. I apologise for my behaviour. It wasn't very ladylike.'

Lucerne frowned. She realised that he knew she was holding something back. 'You can confide in me,' he said. 'But it's your choice.'

Bella shook her head. If he didn't know already, she didn't want to humiliate herself by explaining.

Up in her room, facing the dressing-table mirror, Bella wondered if she had hurt his feelings, but she doubted he'd be pleased with her admission. A threesome with him and Vaughan was one thing, but confessing to sex with Vaughan as well as Wakefield before she'd ever lain with him was quite another.

To take her thoughts away from Lucerne's possible jealousy, she broke the seal on the letter. He was right. It was from her brother, but the contents were unexpected. Bella scanned the sentences again; her hands shook so much she could hardly hold the paper still enough to read.

*My dear sister*

*Aubury informs me all is not well between himself and the marquis. If all I hear is true, then Charles is right to fear for his life and therefore I find myself tasked with the role of peacemaker once more, though it irks me to undertake it. I understand the sum is some sixty guineas, lost at the cardtable. I can not yet return to Lauwine in person, since Frederick is too unstable to leave. I must therefore task you with settling the debt. I have sent word to Haggard at the mine, and he should have the sum ready for you to collect out of the reserve fund. The wages are not due until the end of the month, and I hope to have roused Wakefield from his sullenness by then, and so be able to replace the shortfall myself. I hope all is well with you and Louisa. Wakefield sends his deepest regards.*

*Your ever devoted brother,*

*Joshua Rushdale.*

Annabella read the letter three times, then folded it carefully and placed it at the back of a drawer.

# 12

Emma watched her mistress smile for the first time in two days as they stood together outside Charles's door. She hoisted the heavy jug of water, knocked and then let herself in. She didn't understand what Bella Rushdale had against Mr Aubury, but she'd been promised a new dress and a day off with money for a visit to the coffee shop in Reeth Village, in return for her help. Never one to refuse a gift or a bribe, Emma had agreed immediately.

It was only mid-afternoon but the curtains were drawn inside Charles' room, and the only light came from flickering candles. He lay in the great steel bath-tub which had been hauled up from the kitchens, with one arm draped over the edge and the other below the water line. If he had heard her enter, he showed no visible sign of it, but then he was expecting a servant with more water. He just wasn't expecting her.

Emma put down the large jug and stepped out of her clothes with one eye on Charles. Slow ripples were spreading from the region of his crotch. There was no mistaking what he was about. She wondered what he was imagining: filling a girl's mouth with his seed, perhaps, or soiling her breasts or buttocks.

After she peeled off her stockings, she padded over to the bath. 'I see you've picked up your cudgel for the one-man Morris dance,' she commented as she poured the hot water into the tub. Charles virtually leaped clear of the water. He gurgled at her, and tried to hide his thick stubby erection.

'No need to be shy, sir, it's a fine pole.'

It seemed to dawn on him that she was nude. His cock reared eagerly from behind the shield of his hands. Emma deliberately turned her back on him and bent over to put the jug on the floor. She'd been told before that her plump bottom was her best asset, and she knew how to use it to her advantage. She wriggled, then glanced coyly back to find him gawping at her.

When she returned to the side of the tub, she cupped her breasts, gave him a lewd grin and licked her own nipple. He made a strangled noise. Emma purposefully picked up the soap. 'Let me give you a hand,' she said ambiguously, and dropped the fragrant bar into the water.

Her hands dived after it. Charles drew a careful breath as her dusky nipples bobbed three inches from his face. Emma brushed his thigh, then closed her palm around his erection.

'Jesus!' he swore.

As stiff as the iron poker she used to stoke the fires, and twice as thick, his cock jerked eagerly against her lathered hands. He was so hard she knew he wouldn't last long.

'I could join you in the tub, sir, if you like,' she offered, knowing he was unlikely to find the words for a refusal. That wasn't part of the plan, but it couldn't do any harm and she saw no reason not to exploit the situation for her own purposes. Once succumbed, eager for more, was her experience of gentlemen, and she wasn't averse to a few more gifts.

'Err,' said Charles.

Emma translated this as a yes, and straddled him. Although he whimpered, he somehow managed to restrain himself as she swung into a rhythm. She let him build to a crescendo, encouraging him with her inner muscles and tempted him with her swinging breasts, and then just when his eyes were really starting to glaze over she banged twice on the side of the bath.

True to the plan, the door flew open and Bella stormed into the room.

Bella stood just over the threshold until Emma scurried past her, arms laden with her discarded clothes. She'd obeyed Joshua to the letter so far, and had returned from the mine with the sixty guineas. Each one Haggard had counted into her palm had felt like a slap, and now she was going to have her revenge.

Charles had slumped back with his eyes rolled heavenwards. Another minute, she suspected, and he wouldn't have cared if Robespierre's ghost had burst in, but that was exactly the point.

She walked slowly but purposefully over to the bath and looked down with disdain. 'I hear you are a little short of cash,' she said, while he blushed and his rampant phallus wilted away from her scornful gaze.

Bella wanted to laugh, but she forced a neutral countenance and absently pretended to consult Joshua's note. 'Well, my brother has seen fit to come to your rescue.' She produced a heavy pouch. 'Do, please, have these.'

Charles flinched as she upended the drawstring pouch, and the coins it held fell with a clatter over his unprotected body and into the bath.

'Sixty shillings in total,' Bella explained as he stared up at her, stupefied. 'You can tell him from me, that was all he was worth.' She dropped the empty purse on the floor and left the room, leaving Charles to wallow in self-pity and enjoy what remained of his bath.

Four hours later, Bella hid herself carefully among the shadows at the back of the coachhouse, where an open space had been cleared for stage two of her revenge plan. The air was heavy with the smell of lamp oil, and straw prickled her through the thick fabric of her gown. She took a deep breath to reassure herself. There was no reason why her plan shouldn't work perfectly. Mark and the other grooms were already in position, and Vaughan had taken the bait.

The stable door opened and the night's chill cut through the thick air. Vaughan's slim outline appeared in silhouette. He scanned the empty-looking building. 'Lucerne?'

There was no reply. The wind caught the door and slammed it closed behind him, forcing him further into the trap as he took a step forwards. Bella muttered a silent prayer. She watched, fingers crossed as two shadows parted clumsily from the walls to either side of their target, joined by another three from deeper inside. They moved in and surrounded Vaughan.

'Lose your way?' he said, clearly unperturbed by a few stocky stable-hands.

They replied by lunging for him.

Vaughan stepped quickly to his right, kicked and connected a well aimed blow with a burly assailant's groin. The man doubled in agony while giving a yelp of pain. Next, it was the turn of the men to either side of him. Vaughan banged their heads together.

Bella watched in dismay. The incompetent fools were going to let him escape. But finally, they piled onto him. There were a few muffled thumps and curses before they managed to overpower him through force of numbers and bind his mouth with an old rag.

The scuffle had made more noise than Bella had anticipated. She hoped no one was close enough to hear, since any interference would completely wreck her plans. She watched nervously as two of the men manhandled

Vaughan into position and stripped the shirt from his back, her gaze darting between them and the stable door. Only as Mark snapped the last shackle around Vaughan's ankle did she give them her full attention. There was a smug grin on Mark's face as he pulled Vaughan's black pantaloons down to his knees. She couldn't help thinking that was unwise of him, but then he was probably thinking this just revenge for the rough handling he'd received from Vaughan.

Their work done, the grooms beat a hasty retreat. Bella waited a few moments, watching and anticipating, while Vaughan pulled at the chains. He managed to spit the rag loose from his mouth and an oath followed its trajectory to the floor.

'What in hell is going on?' he said as he heaved against the heavy chains.

Bella announced her presence by cracking her riding crop across his bared buttocks. He snarled but managed to twist around enough to glimpse her. Then, to her horror, he laughed and relaxed in his bonds.

'Annabella, it appears that you have me.' He lifted his wrists and jangled the chains. Bella gave him another taste of the crop, but this time he didn't flinch.

'How can I be of service to you?'

Bella ground her teeth. 'I thought sixty lashes might suffice.'

'Really. I'd have doubled it. After all, I have been extremely badly behaved. But I doubt you have the strength for that.'

Bella swapped her crop for the horsewhip and lifted it, ready to strike. She'd soon show him what she was capable of, and she doubted he'd be quite so cocksure at the end of it. Vaughan merely turned his eyes to the front and set his jaw. After a moment, when she still hadn't landed a blow, he sighed as if bored.

'You bastard,' Bella snarled. It appeared that this wasn't going to be as easy as she'd hoped. How could he take this so lightly? She knew the crop hurt; she'd tested it against her own leg and had the bruise to prove it. Mark had warned her to go easy with the whip, unless she really wanted to flay him. 'You utter, despicable bastard.'

'Do I have to endure a verbal lashing, or do you plan to use the whip in your hand?'

Provoked, Bella struck. The whip slapped against his lower back, raising a thick red weal. Vaughan laughed through his teeth.

'Is that the best you can do? Here, give me it, I'll do it myself.'

Again, she flicked the whip across his flanks.

'Come on, Bella. I'm at your mercy. If you want an apology, you can just beat it out of me.'

'Sixty guineas,' she cursed.

'Considerably more than you were worth.'

'You'll take that back.'

'Make me.'

Bella raised the lash again and again, until his buttocks were crossed with welts. 'Whoreson. Fraud. Lecherous, mean-spirited cad,' she yelled.

'Money-grabbing trollop,' spat Vaughan. 'Aren't you supposed to count?

He hissed as the next stroke landed, but Bella only stamped her foot in frustration. He wasn't supposed to be enjoying this. 'You're nothing but Lucerne's catamite,' she said.

'And you're nothing but his doxy.'

Bella yelped in outrage.

'Except, of course, he hasn't paid you yet. I did warn you about that, did I not?'

Blinded with rage, Bella growled and put considerably

more strength into the next blow. The tail of the whip snaked between his parted legs and caught him at the base of his testicles. Vaughan lurched forwards in the chains, unable to bend double. He gave a cry and then bit his lip in pain. Silence followed.

The horsewhip hit the floor with a thump.

'Oh my God. I'm sorry,' Bella said. 'I'm sorry. I'm so sorry.'

'Please just release me.'

She scurried forwards and unclasped the shackles from his wrists, then bent to do the same for his ankles. Bella felt tears spill from her eyes and then she was sobbing uncontrollably. Vaughan took her gently by the shoulders, but with enough force to pull her into his arms. She pressed her wet cheek against his chest.

'What are you crying for, you silly fool?' he asked. 'It's supposed to hurt.'

'I know.' She gulped. 'I feel stupid. I wanted you to apologise.' She expected him to push her away, but instead he sighed and ran his hand through her loose hair.

'Bella, Bella, everything's fine. No harm done, but your choice of punishment leaves a lot to be desired. Don't cry.' As he spoke, he stroked her neck with agile fingers. She tilted her head to look up at him and a salty tear ran over her lips. Vaughan cupped her face and brushed the moisture from her cheeks with his thumbs. She stared up at his long dark eyelashes and his beautiful violet eyes, and remembered looking down into them, being frightened by their openness when he'd held her hand trapped against his chest. She felt as if she were falling into them now as he bore down on her, kissing her bee-stung lips open.

It was a gentle, passionate kiss, devoid of the bite she'd grown to expect from him. She imagined this was how, in tender moments, he kissed Lucerne. When he moved away, she stood with her tear-streaked face turned upwards, waiting for another. It came, more intense than the first and with more of a sharp edge. Her unhappiness and confusion retreated a little as he kissed the tears from her eyelashes before returning to her mouth, this time kissing her hard.

'Aren't you hurt?' she asked. She thought she'd near unmanned him.

'Believe me, I've had worse, and from a more experienced hand. Benefit of a classical education,' he reassured her.

Fresh arousal washed through her as his fingertips met with the stiffened buckram of her stays and began to blindly pull open the ties. In the haze of sensation she realised he was guiding her towards the pile of sweet-smelling hay. His lips travelled to her neck. One hand captured a nipple. Desire so intense she almost swooned drew her to him. She didn't understand why this was happening now; they hated each other, didn't they? And he had already won his bet. Which meant it could only be an apology.

They lay down together on the bed of straw, and Vaughan covered her like a blanket. His lips and fingers worked over her skin, eliciting sweeping rushes of excitement. She felt his penis nudge against her labia, trying to find a way in, but he didn't push inside. He only licked her nipples instead, until her dark areolae crinkled into hard points. Whatever happened from now on, she wanted to keep this memory of him being gentle.

'Vaughan,' she whispered, concerned that he would transform into the same man who had left her frustrated too many times. After the bitterness and shame of the previous few days, she desperately needed the tenderness he offered her.

'Yes, Annabella.'

'I want you.'

'I know.' She felt his smile against her breast, and just for a second she feared the worst, but then his cock found the entrance it was looking for. The first few thrusts were effortless, but he couldn't hold the extremely gentle pace for long. Bella soon felt him shaking with determination as he restrained his instincts to selfishly take his own pleasure.

'It's all right. I just need you,' she confessed.

He held the pace, breathing hard and deep, but gradually she felt the urgency of his motion increase. Still, right until the end he was gentle, even affectionate. When he came, it was with a soft groan. Bella watched the ecstasy in his expression and realised that for once it hadn't mattered that with him, she hadn't come.

Vaughan rolled to her side and reclined in the hay. His dark curls stuck to his damp skin and the scar on his torso showed like a silver river in the lamplight. Bella watched him. They would be enemies again tomorrow, but at least they were lovers tonight. She touched his arm but he didn't respond.

'Vaughan, I'm going back to the house now,' she said quietly.

'As you wish.'

'Goodnight, Vaughan,' she whispered as she stepped from the coachhouse into the night breeze, and left him to brood.

'Bastard!' Lucerne growled.

'Possibly. One never can tell. What am I supposed to have done now?' Vaughan asked as he fed coals to the fire, where he was warming up after his encounter with Bella in the stables. Lucerne joined him.

'You know full well what you've done.'

'Oh, that.' Vaughan shrugged his shoulders insouciantly. 'Did Charles tell you?'

'Yes, while he was begging for money. You could at least be sorry.'

'What, for giving them what they asked for?' He put down the tongs meaningfully and then twisted the signet ring on his middle finger so that it lay straight. Lucerne frowned, suddenly unsure of his ground. Had Vaughan really only given them what they wanted? Somehow, he doubted it. Even after six years abroad Vaughan had a reputation in London three times as damning as the worst rakehell. It was just far too unlikely.

'Are you angry?'

'Considering your attitude, I could be, especially about the wager with Aubury. As for the rest–' Lucerne waved his hand indifferently '– it hardly seems worth fretting over. I'm not so much of a hypocrite as to expect fidelity from you or Bella, when I don't claim to offer it myself. But did you have to involve Louisa?'

Vaughan responded with a sneer. Lucerne put his fingertips to his temples and briefly closed his eyes. At times, he really wondered why he tolerated Vaughan, but when he reopened his eyes, he remembered why. Vaughan stood before him with one hand resting on the mantel and a sly, sultry smile upon his lips. His dark hair curled elegantly over his shoulders, adding to his brooding mien. He was too exquisite, too rare, to hate for more than a fleeting moment.

One of the shaggy wolfhounds padded over to the fire and settled down. 'Just what did Freddy do to you?' Lucerne asked, coming to a sudden realisation. He noticed Vaughan's frown, but continued regardless. 'That is what this is about, isn't it?'

Stubborn to the point of absurdity, Vaughan shook his

head. 'No. It's nothing to do with Wakefield. It's to do with boredom and reputation.'

'Twaddle!'

'Believe what you will.' Vaughan ignored Lucerne's pained expression and set about examining his fingernails for traces of coal dust.

'I intend to. And besides, I can always ask him.'

'Assuming he comes back before he has to rejoin his regiment abroad.'

'He'll come if I send for him. Maybe I'll write to him this evening.' Vaughan's devlish scowl set Lucerne off laughing. 'So are you going to tell me what the reason is or not?' he asked.

'No.'

'Vaughan,' coaxed Lucerne. He moved a step closer into Vaughan's personal space, and gently kissed his neck. 'Tell me.'

'It's really not that exciting.'

Lucerne snaked his arms around Vaughan's waist, and gently nipped his earlobe. 'Tell me anyway.'

Roused to sudden anger, Vaughan shook Lucerne off. His expression clouded with real resentment, his eyes narrowing to dark slits while his lips twisted into a scowl. 'The bastard had me imprisoned for a night. He told the magistrate in Vienna that my papers were stolen. Damn near had me hanged as a spy.'

'Freddy did that? Well, I'll be damned! When was this?'

Vaughan took several uneasy breaths through his nose, and seemed to regain some of his humour. 'About four years ago, at the start of the coalition, before Flanders. I was in Austria for a month.'

Lucerne nodded. He remembered the political and military wranglings of the time. Things hadn't improved all that much since then. 'So, why did he have you arrested?' he asked.

For once Vaughan looked embarrassed. 'I don't know.'

'I think you do.'

Vaughan picked up the poker again and prodded at the glowing coals. 'I commandeered his date at some poxy military ball I was invited to. She was the only attractive woman there, and he'd left her stranded with some withered old stick so he could discuss tactics with his superiors.'

Lucerne shook his head in dismay, and wondered why none of this particularly surprised him. 'So, who was she?'

'Miss Phillipa Faringdon, if I remember correctly. It has been a while. Anyway, I suppose he didn't take too kindly to losing his companion, but he had no right to expect anything else. She was a beauty, and every eligible bachelor in Vienna was there. It was hardly necessary to have me arrested.'

'You think he overreacted?'

'I only asked her to dance.'

Lucerne sighed. 'No ... no. I doubt that very much. I know you too well, Vaughan. I expect you gave him plenty of incentive to act as he did. All right, having you locked up seems a tad extreme, but he was pretty smitten. You see, I remember Miss Faringdon from before she went to Austria with her father. Remember her quite well. She was very similar to Louisa in temperament if not colouring.'

Lucerne watched Vaughan's tight expression. He could very well imagine what had gone on away from the other guests at the ball; something similar to the incident with Louisa here at Lauwine. Without any interruption the scene would have turned out very differently. No surprise, then, that Frederick had seemed distracted when Vaughan had arrived at Lauwine. He was probably thinking his luck couldn't get any worse.

'I saw Phillipa in London last autumn with her husband,' he said. 'She'd changed quite dramatically from how I remembered her. I have to say she even appealed to me, until I discovered she had at least four gallants on the go.'

Vaughan snorted. He sipped his port. 'Very like Louisa, then.'

Lucerne frowned to make it clear he wasn't impressed, but his warning expression only induced Vaughan to shrug his shoulders.

'He thinks I'm the great corrupter. Really, I only show them what they're missing.'

Lucerne bit his lip. 'Can't you just let it go?'

'Why should I?'

'Because I'm asking you to. You've had your revenge and you've probably made him far more miserable than you were during your night in a cell.'

'Possibly, though the cell was deuced unpleasant. I'll consider your request but, whatever I decide, you won't make us into friends, Lucerne. He's dull and I'm immoral.'

Lucerne cautiously nodded, glad that Vaughan was at least prepared to consider a truce. It was a start. 'At least I can hope that you won't constantly be at war with each other.' He walked out of the room and returned with the port decanter. Vaughan held out his glass for a refill.

'So, can we forget this vulgar bet with Charles as well?' Lucerne asked as he poured.

'Hardly. Aubury still hasn't paid up and, although the wager was primarily designed to annoy Wakefield, the outcome is about money. Incidentally, the bit about you and Bella was Charles's idea. He didn't think Louisa would prove much of a challenge.'

'Just how much does he owe you?'

Vaughan tapped his index finger to his full red lips.

'That's hardly your concern, however, the sum is a mere sixty guineas.'

'Which I know he doesn't have.'

'Also not your concern.'

'It is while he's my house guest. And it's not as if you need the money.'

'That's hardly the point. So you need not appeal to my better nature.'

'Are you sure it won't work?' asked Lucerne, as he ran an enticing hand down Vaughan's stomach. Vaughan caught hold of his wrist and swatted the hand away, before it got any lower than his navel.

'The matter is settled, Lucerne, and you won't dissuade me. If Master Aubury doesn't pay up by Saturday, he's going to have a painful meeting with the sharp end of my sword.'

'Vaughan, you know the law!'

'And if he's lucky,' Vaughan continued, cutting off any further remarks, 'I won't blow off his balls afterward, for fun.'

Lucerne bit down on his retort. Vaughan was smiling, and Lucerne realised his friend was probably just pulling his leg. Yet he could see how things were likely to develop, and all he could do was hope that Charles would find the money in time, so that Vaughan wouldn't feel obliged to keep his promise.

'If you won't dismiss the wager, do you think you could possibly apologise to Bella and Louisa?'

Vaughan's smile faltered briefly then returned. 'I've already tried, but I don't think that Miss Rushdale knows how to forgive me, and besides, she's too enamoured of having me as an enemy. As for Louisa, I'll try to think of something to endear myself in your eyes, for I don't believe she herself has a problem with me.'

* * *

Louisa peered through the denuded trees towards the river-bank. Eleven days had passed since the disastrous trip into Richmond, and she needed air and space to clear her head and sort out her thoughts. All her efforts to try to forget Frederick Wakefield and his infidelity had failed. She wondered what he was doing at that moment, whether he ever thought of her, and if she should write or try to see him. If she hadn't tried to talk to him that night, then he would never have argued with Lucerne and left Lauwine, and none of what had followed would have happened either. She didn't blame herself, but neither did she claim innocence.

On reaching the old moss-covered stone bench that had become her favourite retreat over the last few days, she was dismayed to find it already occupied. Vaughan sat with his legs drawn up and his head resting on his knees, staring out across the rushing water of the river. For the first time since she'd met him he looked vulnerable. As she stepped towards him, a twig snapped beneath her feet, and he turned his head. The moment he saw her his demeanour changed. He instantly became the epitome of the libertine. Louisa sat down beside him, not fooled.

'What do you want?' he said disagreeably.

'Nothing. I came outside for some air.' She raised a hand to stroke his shoulder, then thought better of it. 'You look unhappy.'

'I don't require comfort from you.'

Louisa sat on her hands; the stone was cold beneath her bottom. 'Who said I intended to give it?' Unafraid, she met his eyes. The lick of lavender in his irises made her realise the depth of his emotions at that moment. That he could be so fragile gave her strength. 'Have you fallen out with Lucerne?' she asked.

'What makes you think that?'

'Have you?'

Vaughan gave her an innocuous smile. 'No, we just disagree on a few points. He thinks I'm a rogue and I think he lacks perspective.'

'You're probably both right,' Louisa said diplomatically. 'Perhaps you should make an effort to meet halfway.'

'Who made you a makepeace?'

Louisa pulled her hands from under her bottom and smoothed her dress over her knees. 'I didn't expect you to listen, but, personally, I'm sick of arguments. Friends shouldn't fight.'

Vaughan sat up a little straighter. He cocked his head towards her. 'What about lovers?'

'They shouldn't fight either,' she said, without comprehending his meaning. To her surprise, he began to laugh.

'I suppose you're right,' he said as the smile slowly faded from his eyes. 'Though an argument can be an aphrodisiac. Perhaps you should take your own advice. Where is the delightful Captain Wakefield these days?'

It was Louisa's turn to glower. 'I don't require Frederick Wakefield for my happiness,' she snapped.

His smile became condescending. 'Drop the pretence, Louisa; I'm not a fool. You still love him; if you didn't you'd never have taken me to your room. You forget, I know an awful lot about bitterness, resentment and revenge. What did he do to upset you that day you and Bella went to town? Did you surprise him while he was with a strumpet?'

'Yes!' she blurted, turning scarlet.

Vaughan looked neither shocked nor surprised by the revelation, though he pretended not to notice her blush.

'I thought so. Wakefield is that sort of man. He just can't help himself. Something to do with being a soldier,' he mused.

Louisa's embarrassment turned to horror. Her mouth

fell open, but Vaughan pressed two fingers to his lips then transferred the kiss to her, thus stopping her making any remarks.

'There are worse vices to have, Louisa, and I'm sure that if you married he'd be tediously faithful.'

'Unlike you, when you marry.'

'Something I never intend to do, so 'tis unlikely to be an issue.'

Louisa clenched her fists. For a moment she considered spitting in his face, but he turned his attention back to the choppy water. The recent stretches of rain had flooded the river to capacity, and any more heavy rainfall would cause it to burst its banks. Still maddened, Louisa rose to her feet. Vaughan caught her wrist in an iron grip.

'You can be as angry as you like with me, but I've never deceived you, Louisa.'

He let go.

Louisa gazed blankly at the dappled leaves on the ground before her. Her anger twisted itself tighter then began to disperse. She knew it was pointless; the world would go on despite her feelings.

Vaughan idly brushed a faded leaf from his arm. 'Who was he with?' he asked.

'Millicent Hayes. The witch from the party in the obscene dress.'

'Ah, the aspiring courtesan. You've nothing to fear from her.'

Louisa sat back down. Her skin had returned to its typical pallid hue except for two bright spots on her cheeks, but her eyes were still hot and fierce. 'It was awful,' she confessed. 'She was in his bed. They were doing it.'

A tear trickled down her cheek. Vaughan brushed it away. 'You lay with me. Is that any different to what he did?'

'You're not a common whore.'

He smiled. 'Thank you. Although I fear many would disagree, including your captain. Now listen to me. Unless I'm greatly mistaken he's never made you any promises, but I'll wager he would if given the opportunity. But first you have to forgive him.'

'How can I?' she snarled peevishly.

'Don't be such a prude. This is the Age of Enlightenment, Louisa; your morals are out of date.'

Sighing under her breath, she shook her head. 'What's the point? Even if I can forgive him, he's miles away, and short of a miracle he'll never forgive me.'

'Yes he will.' Vaughan's sharp gaze seemed to blur a little, as if he were turning his thoughts inwards. 'If he doesn't, tell him I forced you. I'm sure that he'd be only too happy to champion your honour.'

'What use is that? All that will happen is he'll call you out again.'

'And, as before, Lucerne will stop him. He lost both his brothers to duels. He'd have us both arrested before the pistols were even out of the case.'

Louisa sniffed and Vaughan handed her his handkerchief.

'He still wouldn't marry me,' she said. 'He's convinced I'm too wealthy, and that everyone would think he was just doing it for my money.'

'Then he's an idiot and you're better off without him.'

'That's not a helpful comment.'

'No, nor was it intended to be.' Vaughan got to his feet and brushed down his coat. 'Keep praying, eh? Oh, and tell Lucerne I'll be back in a day or two.'

'Why, where are you going?' She grabbed the edge of his coat.

Vaughan pulled the fabric out of her fingers. 'To settle a few accounts.'

# 13

A loud rumbling woke Christopher Denning from his repose. He carefully opened one bleary eye and then a second, and squinted at the canopy over his bed. He noted with some small concern that his left arm was dead, trapped beneath Francis Lambton's accursed head. Looking down, he realised that his friend was naked apart from the sheet. He slumped back with a groan. He had no recollection of offering to share his bed with Lambton, who was infamous for his infernal snoring. More confusing yet was the fact that Denning was still fully clothed apart from his coat and shoes. He rescued his arm with some difficulty, drawing only a grunt from Lambton.

Somebody began to rattle the bedchamber door from the other side, and Denning looked towards it with interest. It was probably Joseph, his man, and damned if he was going to let a hangover put him off his breakfast. The door came unstuck and opened. Denning quickly shut both eyes and feigned sleep. The tyrant, as he was affectionately known, strode purposefully across the tiled floor to the window and threw back the long drapes; bright stinging light flooded the room and was greeted by anguished groans from the bed.

'Damn it, Joe, have a little mercy in the morning.'

'It's two o'clock, and mercy is a quality we are both supposed to lack,' said a voice not at all like Joseph's.

'Hell's teeth!' Denning exclaimed, sitting up abruptly. 'Pennerley, what the devil are you doing here?'

Lambton grumbled in response to the loud noise and pulled the sheet over his head. Vaughan perched on the end of the disarrayed bed and nonchalantly picked up a roll from the breakfast tray that he had just set down. Denning watched transfixed as he slit it in half, buttered it and then carefully replaced the knife.

'I thought I might come and pay my respects,' he said, as he tossed Denning the roll.

'Did you send a card? I haven't seen it; thought you were still abroad. Joe!' he called. 'Damned fiend, did you lose the marquis' card?'

'I never sent one.'

Denning settled his back against Lambton and chewed the buttered roll. 'What do you want? Not a social call at this hour.'

'Business,' replied Vaughan. He glanced at the figure next to Denning with a mixture of appraisal and disdain. Lambton still bore the ravages of last night's drinking, and appeared to be asleep. Denning well understood Vaughan's circumspection.

'Lambton's safe to talk in front of.'

Denning smiled avariciously. Men only came to him for one sort of business, and Pennerley was the last man he'd ever expected to get a hold of. Denning was a moneylender. A clergyman's son, he had started lending small sums to his friends, but those amounts had gradually grown and, by learning to apply pressure at critical moments in his debtors' lives, he had made himself a very wealthy man. However, unlike most of his kind, Denning was still accepted in society. He was a regular dinner guest at the most exclusive houses and frequently gambled with the fashionable and the gentry. He always listened to polite gossip and paid strict attention to who was doing well and, more specifically, to who was not.

'A small sum to tide you over,' he said, looking Vaughan up and down. The marquis had always had expensive tastes; it would be a pleasure doing business with him.

'Hardly. I do not require your services. I came to dispose of a debt, not obtain one.'

'I don't accept payments on behalf of another man unless he is present,' Denning replied, vexed that he wouldn't have a grip on Vaughan after all.

'Of course not; why would you. However, I wish to buy this particular debt from you, not depreciate its value.'

'Buy it! What for?'

Vaughan yawned theatrically as though bored, and offered no further explanation. Denning gave him a hard stare. Generally, he tried to stay out of personal quarrels. 'Who are we talking about?' he asked.

'Captain Frederick Wakefield.'

'A friend of yours?'

'No.'

'His debts amount to one thousand and seventy-four pounds and six shillings.'

Vaughan pursed his lips. 'So little? I'm surprised. I wonder why his friends wouldn't lend him the money.' He looked at Denning. 'Perhaps they tried and he refused to involve them ... You'll have it within the hour, in exchange for the bonds.'

'I haven't agreed to sell.'

'Shall we make it a round eleven hundred pounds?'

Denning gulped; he couldn't really refuse. The truth was he doubted he'd ever recover his money from Wakefield in the normal way, because the man didn't have any money; he never had, and nobody got rich on a captain's salary. This was ridiculous. He was briefly tempted to push for more money, but Pennerley didn't appear to be in the mood for haggling. 'I'll fetch them for you now,' he said.

Garret Pryce hunched over the single fat candle on his desk. It was well past supper but Pryce was lost in his books and unaware of the passage of time. Balancing columns of figures was an obsession to him, in a way that his late partner William Watson had approved, but never understood. His ageing tabby cat slunk around the bottom of the door and leaped on his desk.

'What is it, Milo, puss?' he asked as he brushed the cat away from his ledger. Milo mewed loudly and Pryce glanced up from the cramped figures. He took a moment to refocus over his spectacles on the tall masked stranger staning on the opposite side of the desk.

'What do you want?'

The man arched an elegant eyebrow so that it appeared above the upper edge of his mask, and levelled an expensive pistol at him.

'A small service.'

Pryce mastered himself; he wondered if he should run or shout for help. But this poised young man looked rather agile and unafraid of shooting, while he was pushing seventy and had a few too many creaky joints to be fleeing down the stairs two at a time. Pragmatism quickly overcame fear. Besides, he decided, this man was no ordinary thief; he wore a fine lawn shirt beneath a shabby coat, and his hands were clean and neat.

'If you'd care to explain what you want, I'll do my best to help,' he said in his best attempt at a reasonably steady voice.

'Pen and ink: a letter to Miss Louisa Stanley.'

Pryce squinted at the man. Miss Stanley was one of his most favoured clients. He handled all her accounts, as he had done for her brother before her and their parents and grandparents before that.

'Tell her that she is ruined; that the investments you made for her have gone awry. Arson in one instance, a workers' revolt, and the war with France – make it plausible.'

'Why?' he asked, bewildered by the request. 'Miss Stanley's finances have never been better.'

'Do it.' The young man cocked the pistol. Pryce picked up his quill but hesitated before putting it to the paper. 'Start writing. You will also explain that you have been forced to close her accounts here, until she makes sufficient funds over to you to cover her losses. Unfortunately, you are unable to discuss the matter with her in person, as you are making a long-overdue visit to relatives in Scotland for the foreseeable future. That should suffice.'

'But . . . but . . .'

'Do as you are told, old man.'

Pryce hurriedly scribbled down the letter in his distinctive spidery scrawl, turned it for the other man to read and then reluctantly added his signature to the bottom, feeling rather sickened with himself. The Stanleys had always been good to him. They had kept their money with him even when the larger banks had tried to force him and his partner out of business. The man folded the letter and commanded him to address it to Miss Stanley at Lauwine Hall.

'Now, Mr Pryce, since I cannot rely on you to take yourself to Scotland for a month or so, you will kindly accompany me.'

'Yes, Charles, what can I do for you?' Lucerne's tone was clipped and disapproving. Charles had burst into his study without any invitation. He was scruffy and unshaven, and stood trembling as if from drink or fever. 'Speak up, man!'

'Pennerley! He's going to kill me,' spluttered Charles in one breath. He peered anxiously at Lucerne, who was watching him in the mirror while he smoothed his hair.

'I'm sure he won't.'

'Lucerne,' pleaded Charles. He ran around the desk and stood between Lucerne and the mirror. 'Please, I just need some money; about twenty pounds will do.'

'Sorry, Charles, I can't give it to you. We've already been through this.' Lucerne watched the other man's face drain of colour and had to admit he appeared to be on the verge of collapse. 'It's no use begging. I don't approve of what you've done, and I hope that in future you'll consider your actions more carefully. For my part, I refuse to become involved.'

'Then you'll see him murder me.'

'If there is one thing I have learned from years of friendship with Vaughan, it's that his bark is considerably more vicious than his bite. He may have threatened you, but I very much doubt he'll go so far as to kill you over sixty guineas. I suggest you brazen it out.'

'Begad, Lucerne, have a heart.'

'That's my final word on the subject. I'll talk to him again when he returns but, beyond that, I'm not prepared to help. The ladies are my guests and I've been a bad enough host already for allowing this disgrace.'

'Lucerne, please.'

'The door is behind you, Charles. Now, for God's sake, go and shave.'

Charles stumbled blindly into the corridor. The last rays of daylight were filtering through the windows of the gallery. Vaughan had disappeared from Lauwine two days ago, and Charles expected him back at any moment to collect on his wager. He had scraped together every available bit of cash he had, including the shillings Bella had poured into the bath, and yet he was still woefully short. Vaughan put the fear of God into him. He'd heard the stories – how Vaughan had reputedly once repaid a slight by calling the fellow out and deliberately shooting him in the kneecap. He wished he'd never shaken on the bet. Lucerne had been his last hope, and he'd refused. Not that he was surprised – there was something distinctly odd about the relationship between those two – but his fate made him utterly miserable.

'Charles,' said Bella. She hurried down the corridor towards him. 'Lucerne refused to loan you the money.' Charles bowed his head. Bella linked arms with him and walked him along the gallery. 'I might be able to help.'

'You?' He goggled at her, unable to hide his surprise.

'I don't mean with the money. You would only give that straight to him. But I could help in other ways, with your escape, for example.'

Charles grimaced. 'Why would you do that?' He pressed his handkerchief to his fevered brow.

Bella's eyes flashed. 'Some measure of revenge against him.'

'I don't know.' He didn't trust her motive, regarding either himself or Vaughan. He wasn't the mumphead they all took him for, and he was aware of Bella's war of debauch with Pennerley. 'Where would I go to, and how will you stop him following?'

'You could go to the Grange for the night, and head into the village or home tomorrow.'

'I could, but what's to stop you sending him straight after me?'

'Nothing. You'll just have to trust me.'

'And they'd let me in at the Grange?' He feared Vaughan but also loathed the idea of spending the night in a bush.

'I'll send Mark with you.'

Charles hesitated; he still didn't trust her, but what choice did he have? Stay here and face Pennerley, or risk taking her at her word.

'Aubury!' Vaughan's voice echoed threateningly through the house. Charles came to a snap decision.

'I'll just get my things,' he blurted.

'Too late for that. Quick, Charles, this way.' Bella grasped the ruff of his sleeve and dragged him along the corridor towards the stairs to the kitchens.

'Charles!'

'Vaughan, please.' Lucerne blocked the entrance to the gallery. It had been two days since they'd seen each other and this was not the sort of welcome he'd planned to give him. When Lucerne had heard from Louisa that Vaughan had left Lauwine abruptly and without a farewell, he'd been rather concerned. Now that Vaughan was back, Lucerne's relief was cut short by the fact that he was only interested in hunting Charles down.

'Where is he?'

'Vaughan,' Lucerne said firmly.

'Where is he?' He pushed Lucerne aside so that he could move into the corridor.

'He's not here,' Lucerne explained, in a vain attempt to stall Vaughan for a few more moments. After refusing to aid Charles, he'd immediately regretted his decision. As host, it was his duty to aid an agreeable solution, no matter how the dispute arose. He'd been about to pursue Charles into the corridor when he'd overheard Bella's voice. Then the pair had fled down the scullery steps.

Vaughan's face darkened with rage. 'You sent him away.'

'He went of his own accord.'

'When?'

Lucerne didn't reply, and he tried to keep his expression neutral as Vaughan searched his face for clues.

'I see. Then he won't have got far.'

Vaughan turned on his heels and headed towards the stairs up to his room. Lucerne kept up with him at a discreet distance. He followed Vaughan into the marquis's room and watched apprehensively as he pulled a trunk from beneath the bed, then unlocked it and drew out a gilt-handled rapier.

'Vaughan, please reconsider.'

Vaughan paused and looked at him with dark eyes. He pursed his lips into a satirical smile, buckled on the sword and strode past him out of the room.

'You, lad! A horse now, and quick about it,' Vaughan bellowed at the startled young stable-boy lounging in the yard. The sun had dipped below the edge of the horizon and the stars were just beginning to appear in the heavens. It would be a clear, cold night; there wasn't a cloud in sight. Perfect for night hunting. Vaughan mounted and galloped from the stable yard out on to the still and quiet moors.

He checked his horse and looked about at the vast expanse of land that surrounded him. It offered little cover to a fugitive on foot. Only in the sudden ditches or hungry fog would Charles find a hiding place, and both were evils best avoided by a man who hoped to live to see the dawn. He headed north, following the pole star to a rocky stretch of land beyond the boundary of

Lucerne's estate. The distant lights of Reeth were ahead now, advertising their promise of shelter. It was the last place Vaughan would go if he feared pursuit, but Charles was a different case. He would head to a place where comfort could be bought, where he could cower beneath the blankets in a private room in the coaching inn. Vaughan was looking forward to it; he could already imagine the startled look on Charles's face when he pulled back the bedcovers. He'd make him sweat for a while, teach him a lesson, and then – and then he'd probably buy him a drink and come back to Lauwine and Lucerne.

Vaughan spurred the horse and, as he did so, a black shape slid between the cover of two outcroppings. He smiled grimly to himself and, with the firm pressure of his thighs guided the mare towards his quarry, with the intention of flushing it out into open ground. Apparently, Charles hadn't got as far as the village.

The shadowy figure began to run, then stumbled over a tussock and almost fell. Vaughan pushed the mare into a canter and began closing the gap. They slid down the side of a deep wet ditch and pressed on through the pools of foetid water. He was amazed Charles could run so well; fear was obviously inspiring him to greater effort. Twenty yards on he coaxed his steed up the slippery bank, while Charles scrambled up and crawled the last foot, clawing at the grass for leverage. At the top, it was a straight race across open fields and, even if Aubury ran as if the devil were after him, he was no match for a horse.

Vaughan drew up nearly even and sprang, knocking his quarry to the springy turf. Charles had the breath driven from him, but struggled violently enough that Vaughan was forced to restrain both wrists and put a knee to his back to still him. Only when he was recovering his own breath did he notice that Charles's tricorne hat had been dislodged in the struggle, and a long stream of brown curls spilled out from underneath it.

'Bella!' he exclaimed, though he didn't slacken his grasp. 'By God, Charles has sent a wench to settle his debts!'

'I've a score to settle but it's not for Charles. Besides, he's escaped.'

Vaughan looked both left and right across the twilit moors. If Aubury was still out there, he was not close by. 'So it would appear,' he admitted. 'However, that's of little concern to me. It was merely to see him run that I pursued him this far.' He gripped her wrists more tightly and removed his knee from her back. 'But now I have you, my dear, a prettier prospect by far. It would be churlish to complain about the loss of Charles.'

He straddled her thighs and transferred his hold to one hand so that he could give her a friendly squeeze. He didn't understand why Bella had helped Charles escape, unless it was to provoke him. She'd already had her revenge; now she was just addicted to sparring with him.

She struggled to lift her face from the damp grass. 'Let go of me, you unspeakable rogue.'

'Certainly not.'

'Get off me.'

Vaughan bound her wrists with the ribbon from her hair, then let go. Bella scrambled forwards, but he easily recaptured her by grasping the thick leather belt about her waist. 'Madam, you will stay still unless told otherwise.'

'I'll do as I please.'

'Will you, indeed.' He reached beneath her and unbuckled the belt that held up Charles's over-large breeches, then pulled it free of her clothing. Bella stared at it in horror, clearly afraid of his intentions. They both knew he had every reason to use it on her, as retribution for whipping him or for helping Charles escape. Vaughan enjoyed the uncertainty in her eyes, and held it meaningfully for a moment before laying it aside and pulling the breeches down over her hips. He intended to use her, but not like that.

With her bottom exposed to the chill night air, her hands securely tied and nobody else for miles around, Bella began to wonder if helping Charles had been such a bright plan after all. She struggled against her bonds as Vaughan sat back and observed her, only reaching out to prevent her escape when she was almost free. He retied the ribbon and then smacked her rump with his hand, forcing an indignant squeal from her lips.

'You will do as you are told unless you want every man, woman and child in the next post coach to see your glowing behind.'

'You wouldn't dare.'

'Don't tempt me. I could easily canter to the road with you over the back of the horse.'

Bella fell silent. Damn Charles, she should have let him fend for himself.

'Why are you here?' Vaughan asked.

'To help Charles.'

He spanked her behind again, and Bella yelped in protest. 'The real reason.'

'That is the real reason.'

Vaughan spanked her again.

'Well, I certainly didn't come out to be humiliated by you.'

'Though you appear to be enjoying it.' He gently pressed his thumb to her swollen labia and they parted for him. Bella whimpered as he moved in her wetness and fingered her roughly in that infuriatingly overconfident manner of his. She hated the fact that he turned her on so easily, and stubbornly set her jaw in a bid of defiance. She wouldn't react. Not this time.

Vaughan brought his thumb to his mouth and sucked it clean. 'For a wonder, you don't taste of Lucerne,' he said. 'Perhaps your appetite for him wanes.'

'That's because last time he came in my mouth,' Bella snarled. 'Which part of you tastes of him?'

'Not the sort of charming phrase you expect to hear from a lady,' said an approaching figure.

'Lucerne!' Bella gasped. They both watched him dismount. He stepped up to them wearing a rather serious frown.

'Where is Charles?' he asked.

'Damned if I know.'

'Safe,' said Bella.

'Good, then we can return home.' Lucerne reached out a hand to untie the ribbon that bound Bella, but Vaughan blocked him. Their hands met above hers and their eyes locked in a silent contest. Bella whimpered, overwhelmed by a sudden fear that they would fight, as they were both wearing swords.

'You've made your point,' said Lucerne.

To her surprise, Vaughan relinquished and took a step back. Lucerne loosened the knot. 'Are you all right?'

Bella nodded. She hitched up her oversized breeches and accepted the leather belt from Lucerne to fasten around her waist. She stared out across the Pennines as she tucked in her shirt, resisting the urge to look at the two men standing only a few feet away from her, who shared a tense, uncomfortable silence. It was as if, after several days apart, they couldn't work out what to say to each other: whether to argue or apologise, or just to kiss and make up.

To her relief, they did the latter.

Vaughan eventually broke off the embrace and led the short ride home to Lauwine.

Warily, they parted company in the hall. Bella stole a careful glance backwards at the two men before she left to change out of Charles's clothes. They were speaking in low voices and, from the tilt of Lucerne's head, she guessed that not everything was fine, although he also seemed eager for contact. When she returned there was no sign of either of them, but the fire in the salon had been lit. She crossed the polished floor to the doorway and found Vaughan standing to the right of the mantel, looking down into the dancing blaze.

'Where's Lucerne?' she asked.

'How should I know?' The dark cascade of his ringlets ebbed against his shoulders, while ebony glints sparkled against his equally dark coat. Bella felt a surge of jealousy, though whether it was over Lucerne or the man before her, she wasn't sure. Either way, she suspected he knew exactly where Lucerne was. Vaughan was probably hoping to persuade her to leave so he could have him to himself.

She moved to the other side of the fire, as far from him as possible without straying from the source of heat. In the soft red and orange light of the fire, he was both primal and beautiful. She wondered how many past lovers had been mocked and humiliated by him and yet still desired his affection. For a fleeting moment, she rather hoped that he would finish what he had started out on the cold moors. He offered her a predatory smile.

Bella began to pace nervously. Lucerne always managed to defuse these tense moments: where was he now? Vaughan was following her movements. She could feel his gaze like a caress against her skin. She stopped pacing, looked up to face him and found herself toe to toe with him, her own reflection drowning in his fire-lit pupils.

She was caught.

His mouth bore down on her, his kiss both savage and unmerciful as he tilted her off balance with his hold. Wild and ferocious, he sucked hungrily on her tongue and then moved to her throat, where he nipped the skin. Bella protested at his intention to mark her. He was a terrible and beautiful man, but she wouldn't let him possess her.

However, he was stronger.

All too soon he had her undressed and rolling on the floor like a cheap whore, while she raked at his skin, craving any contact at all. He pressed into her back, kissing the nape of her neck and the space between her shoulder blades while his erection probed her thighs. He drew a wetted fingertip along the crease of her bottom, and then across her perineum and into her vulva.

'Mmmm – madam is apparently still eager for me, despite her derision of my talents,' he said. He entered her suddenly, and forced a groan of delight from her. The sensations he roused in her were beyond description. He filled her in a way unlike anyone else, for she had never hated and yet desired another so much. Eagerly, she pushed back to meet his thrusts. She shook her head in joy as his fingernails dug into her hips.

Then abruptly he withdrew, leaving her empty, as if he had taken away something unbearably precious. 'Vaughan,' she whimpered. His reply was to hold her writhing against the tiled floor with him straddled across her thighs, his thumb drawing dew from her cleft to her anus. 'No,' she gasped, but he only snorted and swapped the digit for his cock.

Her tight muscles yielded too easily, and he slid inside

in a rush while releasing a gasp of glee against her neck. 'You're mine, little bird,' he hissed.

'No, Vaughan. You're hurting me.'

Once she had permitted this, when Lucerne had been present to protect her, but now she was alone with the fiend, and she didn't trust him not to hurt her. The only movement she could make was with her hips, but her wriggled attempts at escape only succeeded in impaling her further, and intensifying the sweet, burning sensations in her behind that struck similar chords in her quim. His hand covered her mound and his middle finger sought out her clitoris. He ground the sensitive nub against her pubic bone, and an intense buzz fizzled through her pelvis from two points.

'Not all pain, I see,' he said, and stopped rubbing. Bella pushed herself down against the floor on top of his hand but, even trapped, he refused to renew the stimulation.

'You will beg, Annabella.'

'No,' she snarled.

He bucked, withdrew, thrust again, drawing her hips back to meet him, then repeated the action, using her bottom entirely for his pleasure. Bella whimpered. The taboo, the deep heavy penetration, and her own feelings of helplessness as she was buggered, all left her in a heady state of arousal. However, she knew he would finish before she reached orgasm, and that he would leave her frustrated, with self-stimulation her only solace. 'Please, Vaughan,' she begged.

'Please what?'

'Give me what you give Lucerne,' she managed to blurt between the throbs of pleasure caused by his rough thrusts.

He laughed aloud. 'I thought I already was.'

Two fingers brushed her clitoris, then formed a V around it to tease it from its hood as they rocked together. Bella soared under his caress, her first orgasm breaking like the day, here then gone. The second was deeper and pulsed through her body as intense waves of prickling light, while his cock jerked and spasmed inside her.

He lay on top of her in a state of brief exhaustion, his loins still captured between her buttocks as he held her lightly, almost as if temporarily unaware of her. Soon his penis softened and slipped out of her bottom-hole. She felt the loss keenly and nuzzled back against him. Vaughan sighed and got to his feet, denying her the contact. He picked up a decanter and poured himself a cognac, then began to drink.

Bella felt the rebuke throughout her sated body. Suddenly she was overcome with shame, since again he had used her. She gathered her clothes and left the room. Back in the lonely comfort of the entrance hall, she felt cold angry tears roll down her cheeks onto her torn gown. She wasn't ashamed of the act, but of the way she let him treat her. His callous disdain made her feel sordid and hollow; time and again he had proved himself an unfeeling wretch, but always she hoped for better treatment. Her heart told her that there had to be something else; a better person for Lucerne to love.

Lucerne was at the top of the stairs.

Bella pulled the ties on her gown a little tighter to hide the marks Vaughan had made. Lucerne had changed out of his day clothes and now wore a beautifully embroidered dressing gown of black and red satin. The smile he found for her vanished when he saw her tears.

'Bella, what's wrong? Has he upset you again?' His voice rang with care. Bella couldn't face him. She lowered her head and tried to move around him to the sanctuary of her room, but he refused to let her pass. He pulled her into his arms and looked into her tear-filled eyes with open concern. His affection almost broke her heart.

'I'm all right, Lucerne,' she admitted some moments later. 'I just feel a bit fragile, that's all.' He nodded, accepting her explanation without question, until his eyes came to rest on the fresh bruises around her neck. Self-consciously, she tried to tug her dress across them.

'Vaughan?' he said very quietly.

'Yes.'

Bella felt sick and dizzy. All the light drained from his angelic face as the significance of her reply sank in. Dear God, how had the fine prospect of a few weeks ago developed into this mess? The floor seemed to rise up to meet her.

Lucerne caught her, and held her in both arms. 'I never thought I'd see you faint,' he said.

'I'm tired. So desperately tired.'

He nodded. 'Maybe I can give you something to help you sleep better.'

She clung to him and felt the strain in his muscles as he carried her along the corridor. Bella closed her eyes, concentrating on the motion of his walk, and tried to ignore all the bad thoughts in her head. He stopped and balanced her body as he turned a door handle. To her astonishment, she realised it was his room he'd taken her to, not her own. On the four-poster bed he removed her dress and unpinned her hair so that her curls fell across her bare shoulders and all down her back. Then he stood, statuesque, just looking at her.

Vaughan appeared in the doorway. The enquiring look he directed at Lucerne was responded to with an eloquent shrug. Bella guessed that they had planned to spend the night together, but the bite marks around her neck had changed that. Lucerne let his gown slip down his arms to the floor. He was naked underneath. Sure of the reaction he'd provoke, he joined her on the bed.

Without a word, Vaughan turned his back on them and shut the door.

Lucerne left Bella sprawled out, asleep between the sheets with a satisfied smile on her face. His sitting room was dark, lit only by the fire, but welcoming and warm. By the hearth, Vaughan sat turning a glass of port nervously in his hands. He turned his head as Lucerne closed the bedroom door.

'She's asleep,' said Lucerne. He gave Vaughan a weak smile. His lover was pale, and his lips were drawn. He looked tired and fragile, probably as a consequence of hearing them making love in the next room. Obviously he had something important to say, to keep him here.

Lucerne curled up on the rug and lay his head upon Vaughan's lap. He shivered at the gentle touch against the nape of his neck. Vaughan brushed his long fingers through the thick blond locks. There was tension in his grip, and sometimes he twisted a little too hard, but Lucerne bore the slight discomfort, and eventually the hold slackened and softened into a gentle massage.

'Things can't go on as they are,' he said.

He peered up at Vaughan, who nodded. 'I know. I've been thinking the last few days, and while I waited here. Perhaps it will be best if I leave. My estate almost certainly needs putting in order and it would give you time to decide how you feel about Bella. We could meet again in the spring.'

'Don't do that. I know exactly how I feel about Bella, and about you.' Lucerne curled his fingers around Vaughan's arm. He knew his skin was flushed, and that his feelings were too near the surface to hide, but for once he didn't care. He wanted Vaughan to know how he felt.

By comparison, Vaughan's visage was a mask. He broke eye contact after a few seconds and bit his thumbnail. 'What are you suggesting?' he said.

'That you stop fooling yourself and accept her as part of the equation. I'm not blind. Nor am I stupid. If the only interest you had in her was as part of a wager, why are you still tormenting her?'

Vaughan stared into the blaze and didn't reply for a long while. Eventually, he raised his head and spoke. 'I need time to think about it.'

Lucerne shook his head.

'Really, I mean it. It would be easy to say yes to your *jolie ménage à trois*, but I don't know if I can reconcile myself to the thought of sharing. I have to have things my way, Lucerne. You wanted me to be honest, so I have been. Now you're going to have to give me some time to think things over.'

Vaughan rose and pressed a kiss to Lucerne's brow. He crossed to the door and paused just over the threshold. 'Go and sleep with her, Lucerne. It's what you want.'

# 14

Frederick Wakefield sat in the front parlour at Christopher Denning's house, praying for a brief, painless interview. For the second month running he was short on his payments, and his debt to Denning was steadily increasing. He would have avoided coming here, but he already owed Joshua a month's rent for their lodgings.

'What can I do for you, Captain Wakefield?' asked Denning in his customary brisk tone. Wakefield seethed inwardly. He hated Denning for his smugness, his mockery and outward geniality; hated him for his success. 'I'm a bit short this month,' he began, although he sounded lame to himself.

'What, you want another loan already? I've just got rid of you, man.' He picked up the morning paper and used it to swat at a fly. Wakefield stared at him blankly. 'You don't know,' Denning realised. There was a cautious undertone to his voice. 'I don't own the debts any more; they've been sold.'

It took a moment for the statement to sink in. 'To whom?'

Denning paced across to the window then returned to his seat, and shook out the creases in the newspaper. 'Sorry, I can't say. I'm sure they'll make themselves known to you soon enough. But to be honest, I'm surprised. I assumed it was a friend of yours, since he paid over the odds for them.'

'What did he look like?'

The only person Frederick knew who would consider

meeting that sort of expense to help a friend was Lucerne, and they hadn't spoken since the fight on the stairs. Perhaps it was an attempt to persuade him back to Lauwine. Strange that he hadn't said anything, though.

Denning shook his head. 'It was part of the agreement. I can't say. Good day, captain.' Frederick found himself escorted out into the street.

It had to be Lucerne, he reasoned, as he sat in his room at the inn. Had to be. There wasn't anyone else.

At that point, Joshua bounded through the door. 'Have you seen this?' he said as he thrust a grubby broadsheet at Wakefield. 'Garret Pryce is missing. Disappeared from his office with half the bank's notes and a number of their records. They believe he's absconded with it all, run off to France. Damn stupid place to run to but he's gone all the same. I suspect he's lost his reason; the old weasel's done nothing but look at ledgers for years.'

'I take it you're not worried by this.'

'I bank elsewhere. Watson and Pryce were fairly small, but it'll be a blow to the families that do use them.' His words petered out, and he suddenly looked anxious. 'We have to get this to Lauwine.'

'Why?' Frederick sat forwards in the chair, surprised by Joshua's change of mood. 'Lucerne doesn't bank there, his accounts are still managed from London.'

'Yes, but Louisa does.'

Frederick felt his heart jolt as Joshua spoke her name. The thought of facing up to Louisa was the reason why he hadn't immediately hired a horse and galloped over to Lauwine to thank Lucerne. He was terrified of seeing her, and now, today, when he felt happy for the first time in days, Joshua was telling him she was ruined and they would have to go and break the news to her.

* * *

'She already knows,' said Lucerne, forestalling Wakefield's jumbled explanation for their sudden return. They were standing in the marble entrance to Lauwine as Joshua paid off the coachman. It was lunchtime and Lucerne had come out onto the steps to meet them. 'A letter arrived from Garret Pryce this morning that explained what had happened.'

'I don't suppose he put it like this.' Wakefield thrust the broadsheet into Lucerne's hands.

'No,' replied Lucerne after he'd read the headline. He scanned through the remainder of the page.

'Is she all right?' asked Joshua as he joined them.

'To be honest, I'm not certain she's taken it on board yet. I think this will really upset her. The letter suggested it was just her investments that had gone bad, but it seems more than likely that the old man's run off with her money.'

'Where is she?' asked Frederick.

'She's in the music room, I think. Please don't make her miserable, she's enough to think about already.'

'I'll try. Oh, and thank you, Lucerne, thank you most sincerely.' Frederick dashed off towards the music room, leaving Lucerne and Joshua puzzling over his words.

'For what?' said Lucerne, looking questioningly at Joshua, who shrugged his shoulders.

Frederick stood at the door to the music room, while he wondered how to approach Louisa. She was sitting at the piano with her back to him, picking out a concerto. He couldn't just blunder in and ask how she was coping; he had a difficult apology to make to her, one he felt deeply embarrassed about. He wished he could just tell her how beautiful she was, how much he'd missed her and just how sorry he really was, but he feared her reaction.

He shifted his weight from one foot to the other, and she must have heard him, for she stopped playing immediately and peered over her shoulder. Frederick did his best to give her an apologetic smile, but only managed a sheepish grin. Her response was to snatch up her music file and slam the piano lid shut. Without saying a word, she hurried towards the other door.

Frederick was shocked. He'd never expected such an abrupt response from her. He had envisioned tears, cold anger even, but he had always presumed she would allow him to say his piece. 'Louisa,' he pleaded as he raced to intercept her by the other doorway. When he tried to grab her, she slipped and put her arms out to save herself, which sent music scores skidding across the polished wood floor. Her balance recovered, she glanced disdainfully at the sea of paper littered around them. Frederick bent to retrieve the sheets, but the moment he was on his knees she shot past him.

Too stunned to react, he watched dumbly for a moment, then his body seemed to respond of its own volition and the muscles of his legs pumped hard as he sprinted after her. He caught up as she disappeared through the doorway of her room. Only just in time, he managed to get a foot across the threshold. The door slammed into him, bringing a brief explosion of agony which turned his next breath into a hiss of pain. Undeterred, he put his weight to the wood and inched it open. It swung suddenly inwards as she retreated towards the bed.

Frederick closed the door and faced her awkwardly. He wondered how he appeared to her. Did she notice that he was thinner? That some of his muscle tone was gone? Did she see him as a rakehell, a reprobate? Was he even still attractive to her, or had he destroyed that forever? Even with her eyes red from crying he was still moved by her delicate beauty. She was everything he found most attractive: fine boned, fine featured, petite and extremely blonde. He felt the familiar twinge of desire he always got just from looking at her, despite all the tension between them.

How could he make this work? What should he say?

'I'm sorry.'

Louisa glared at him with hard eyes. 'You're sorry,' she threw back at him. 'You come charging back from town and chase me to my room to say you're sorry. Is that it?' She paused, but didn't allow him time for a reply. 'I'm ruined, Frederick; what little money I have left is barely enough to pay off the servants and keep a roof over my aunt's head, and all you can say is you're sorry. Sorry for what, exactly? That I'm destitute or for sleeping with a harlot?'

Wakefield felt himself blush scarlet to the roots of his hair. He felt clumsy and stupid. 'For both,' he mumbled, as much to himself as to her. Her breath was coming in deep, heavy gasps, and her knuckles had whitened from clenching her fists so hard. 'I don't have an explanation for my behaviour. It was unforgivable. I don't expect forgiveness.' He stumbled for the right words. 'I do care about you, Louisa. I wondered if there was anything I could do to help.'

She stepped forwards and paused uncertainly, then swung her fist in an arc, which connected solidly with his jaw. 'You can't, so you may as well give up and go back to your tart.'

Well, now, thought Frederick as he straightened his face, it can't get any worse. She turned her back on him while she surreptitiously massaged her wrist, and he felt a surge of obstinacy.

'I'm a soldier,' he announced forcefully enough to make her turn back. 'I won't run from any fight, and I'm prepared to dig in for a siege. I love you, Louisa. I want you more than anyone else alive. Please listen to me. I'm begging you.' He grasped her hand and dropped to his knees, holding on tight as she tried to pull free. 'I never meant to hurt you. I was an idiot and I should have known better. I realise you can never forgive me after what I did, but I am sorry and I never stopped loving you.'

He watched a lonely tear roll down her cheek. It dropped on to his hand, from which it trickled into his shirt cuff.

'Don't cry,' he said, and rose to embrace her in his arms. 'Please don't cry.'

He was overcome with relief that the worst seemed to be over, but her tears were nearly breaking his heart. She muttered something into his chest he didn't quite catch between the breathless sobs, but it sounded important. 'What did you say?' he asked.

She looked up at him, her eyes strangely luminous but also serious. 'It could have been you,' she repeated.

Wakefield shook his head very slightly. 'I don't understand.'

'Vaughan. I slept with him.'

Scalding anger licked at his skin, turned his face red and set the pulse at his temple racing. His back stiffened as all his muscles tensed. 'Why?' He forced the question out with his next breath.

'You pleasured yourself with a whore. I wanted to hurt you back,' she explained as the salt tears dried on her face.

'So you slept with one yourself. You're right, it does hurt,' he said, pleased to find he sounded calm despite the fact that his mind whirled.

Vaughan! It was always bloody Vaughan. Why did it have to be him? He hated him. He'd never forgiven him for Austria. Anyone else, anybody at all, and it would have been better.

No, he realised. It wouldn't. He'd have hated them just as much.

Louisa sniffed and tried to dry her face with her hands. He didn't know whether to yell at her for being so stupid or to embrace her again. He looked at her for a long moment, debating the issue, then gave into his body's whim and kissed her savagely.

She whimpered as his lips crushed hers, and dug her fingers into his arms. Wakefield pulled her firmly against his body and began to caress her. Her whimpers softened into tiny mewls from the back of her throat. He felt flushed and light-headed, painfully erect, but he couldn't let his urgency spoil everything. He paused for breath and tried to steady himself.

'I hated you, but I couldn't make myself forget you.' Louisa gazed at him.

'Forget it. Forget them. You're all that matters.'

Her eyes were deep azure rims around wide black pupils. Even over his own panting, he could hear her ragged breathing. He kissed her again, this time gently, though no less passionately, and her arms crept beneath the layers of his clothes until her fingernails dug into his skin. Then her hands were at his hips – at the fastening to his breeches – and over his cock. Without further ado, he pushed her onto the bed, pulled all the layers of cloth aside and entered her.

'Louisa.' Saying her name made it real.

He felt both joy and relief as her hands clawed at his buttocks and pulled him deeper. How different to voluptuous Millicent: tupping a plump tart was like sliding into a pool of water. Making love to petite Louisa felt like putting on a glove. He withdrew several inches and then penetrated her again, to relive the sensation.

Louisa's eyes flickered open. 'Hold me down,' she begged, surprising him. Still, he pinned her down, his hands clamped around her wrists, then bucked into her. She writhed beneath him. Wakefield felt the thunderbolt of his orgasm start at the tip of his cock and forgot to breathe as it spread through him until he jerked suddenly, consumed by its power. White flashes filled his brain, and for a fraction of a second, he blacked out.

'Will you give me away?' Louisa asked Joshua a few hours later.

'Of course,' he replied with a smile. 'It will be an honour.'

Lucerne shook hands with Frederick and congratulated him. Their argument was now long forgotten and they both seemed genuinely pleased to see each other.

Louisa tensed as Vaughan entered the room. She feared Frederick would make a scene, or Vaughan would provoke one. The room fell silent. Left with little choice, she took charge. 'Will you wish us well?' she asked as she gazed boldly into his fathomless dark eyes. 'Frederick and I are to be married.'

The corners of Vaughan's lips turned up into a smile. It spread to his eyes, and she realised that he was genuinely happy for her. 'I've always wished you well, but congratulations all the same,' he said amiably, then caught her by surprise and leaned forward to kiss her full on the lips. Louisa blushed. Frederick growled, and Vaughan let her go. 'I told you so,' he whispered.

He turned to the captain. 'Wakefield, I hope you make her happy.' He offered his hand and Frederick accepted it, after Louisa begged him wordlessly with her eyes. However, as she sighed with relief, Vaughan pulled Frederick into his arms and kissed him in the same way he'd kissed her. Only Lucerne's laughter stopped another fight.

Outside, the breeze was cold and crisp; it nipped at their clothing. Two weeks had passed uneventfully since Wakefield's return to Lauwine with news of Louisa's financial ruin. Winter had reached the top field, and the wind whipped up a storm around them as Bella and Louisa walked arm in arm up the bank of grass. Louisa had been chattering continuously about wedding preparations and her husband-to-be, but finally she stopped for breath and took a good look at her friend. Bella's face was drawn and weary. She had dark circles below her eyes and was still nodding dumbly, as if she hadn't even realised that Louisa had stopped talking. Her green eyes were glazed and held a faraway look. Louisa realised that Bella was deep inside herself with some problem her friend had no idea about.

'I'm sorry,' she apologised, and gave Bella's hand a squeeze. 'I have been going on rather a lot. Is there anything you want to talk about? You seem troubled.'

'No,' sighed Bella, coming out of her trance. She forced a smile and seemed to try to shake off her glum mood, but her faked smile rapidly lost its hold. 'I think it's just the change of season. Let's go down to the grove. I'm freezing up here in this wind.'

They carefully descended the slope while exchanging few words, since Louisa now found the conversation hard going. She was certain Bella was bottling something up, and felt awkward because she was so wrapped up in her own happiness that she'd forgotten everyone else. Being ruined was the most marvellous thing that had ever happened to her. Although she still got the odd twinge of worry about her aunt and the outstanding bills, she wouldn't change her situation for anything. Frederick made her far happier than any inheritance. However, that didn't help Bella.

She guessed the source of the problem: she knew her friend was a frequent visitor to Lucerne's bed, but often he seemed preoccupied with Vaughan, and since Bella went out of her way to provoke the marquis it was clear that she was jealous.

They reached the sheltered valley on the other side of the hill and Bella turned to watch two dark spots in the distance. The sound of galloping filled the air and grew louder until Lucerne appeared and swept past them on his chestnut stallion. He saluted them with what attention he could spare. Moments later, Vaughan also thundered by. He swerved at the last moment and only just avoided running them down. Both men disappeared from sight around the edge of the wood.

Bella's face lit with sudden interest. 'Come on, let's see what they're up to.' She tugged Louisa's sleeve. They ran quietly up to the edge of the lake and hid behind the rhododendrons. For a moment, Bella seemed like her old adventurous self. In the copse of trees opposite, in the spot where Frederick had taken Louisa to see the swans and had first kissed her, Lucerne had Vaughan pinned against a tree.

'What are they doing?' Louisa asked, uncomfortable with the idea of spying on them.

'Shhh!' hissed Bella, not taking her eyes off them for a second.

Louisa reluctantly returned her attention to the men across the water. Lucerne leaned forward and appeared to whisper something to Vaughan. She didn't understand why they were being so secretive when they must have believed they were unobserved, and they seemed to share an uncommon intimacy, which did nothing to quell her misgivings about intruding. Poor Bella, she thought. Her friend probably saw Vaughan as competition, and he wasn't a rival anyone would want.

On the opposite side of the lake, the men had begun to wrestle. Lucerne was astride Vaughan, who was squirming as though he were being tickled. Louisa considered it an odd day to choose to wrestle, but each to their own. Frankly, she was more concerned about Bella, whose expression showed such a raw depiction of excitement and longing that it was blatantly clear that, if she could have, she'd have thrown herself between the two men just to be part of their rough games.

In the end, Louisa threw a rock into the lake. It made a large splash that Vaughan and Lucerne obviously heard, for they both rose hastily and slipped out of view, into the bushes.

Bella turned on her crossly. 'What did you do that for?' she snapped.

'Because we shouldn't be here –'

'Why not? We're guests here, we can walk wherever we wish.'

Louisa formed her thoughts before replying. She didn't fancy a battle of wills with Bella. 'We don't have permission to pry. It isn't right to spy on people when they think they're alone. You wouldn't like it.'

Much to her amazement, Bella nodded in reluctant agreement. 'You're right, I suppose,' she mumbled.

They started back towards the house. The wind had changed direction and now held the distinct smell of coming snow. It whipped about their skirts and sent the fallen, decaying leaves scuttling over the cobblestones of the courtyard like gangly spiders.

'They're very close,' commented Louisa of the two men as they neared the French doors. 'I suppose you realise you'll never have one without the other. Not that I suppose you'd want them any other way.'

Bella turned sharply and gave her a threatening glare. 'What's that supposed to mean?' she demanded.

Somewhat cowed, Louisa took a pace back. 'Nothing. I was just saying that I don't think you'll ever be satisfied with just Lucerne –'

'Don't be ridiculous. I just never get him to myself. I'd be perfectly happy with just Lucerne.'

'Whatever you say, Bella,' said Louisa, backing down. 'I don't believe you, though; I think you want both, and you're going to end up with neither if you don't accept it,' she added, under her breath but loud enough for her friend to hear.

Was Louisa right? Bella asked herself later as she sat alone in the upstairs parlour. Did she want Vaughan as well? If she was honest with herself, she missed his attention. She liked fighting with him. Since the night that Charles had fled and Lucerne had carried her to his room, Vaughan had never come near her. They still argued frequently, but these days he rarely started it and he never touched her, however much she provoked him. She assumed it was because she was no longer a challenge to him. After all, he had won his wager with Charles, he spent most nights with Lucerne, and she was just some passing fancy of Lucerne's that he no longer considered a threat.

Louisa was right. She did want them both. She wanted Lucerne's care and gentleness, and Vaughan's sexual dominance. The problem was that Vaughan had lost interest in her, and she didn't know how to rekindle the flame.

# 15

Bella nuzzled into the warmth of Lucerne's shoulder as they sat roasting chestnuts over the drawing room fire. He was wearing a thick wool coat, the pile of which was soft against her cheek. The heavy brocade curtains were drawn to keep out the cold white light, and it could have passed for late evening. It was a pleasant diversion, away from the others. Vaughan had confessed to hating the taste the night before and had consequentially been responsible for planting the idea in Bella's head.

'I don't think we're doing this right,' Lucerne confessed as he handed her the charred remains of one shell. The nut inside had been reduced to ash.

'Doesn't matter,' mumbled Bella. 'I wasn't hungry anyway. It's only an hour since breakfast.'

'Shocking. That's rather late for you.'

Bella snorted. She now had a rather clearer idea of why Lucerne rose so late. He had a rather flattering affliction in the mornings that seemed to demand immediate attention, and she certainly hadn't refused. 'I'll be able to pass for a city dweller before long,' she said.

Lucerne thoughtfully prodded the fire with the poker. 'How would you like practical experience?' Bella craned her neck up to meet his eyes, unsure she'd heard him right. 'Come to London with me for the rest of the winter. I'll take you to all the best parties, and buy you a whole new wardrobe if you want it.'

Bella's heart did a peculiar fluttery dance. 'I thought you were sick of the debauchery.'

His face creased into an easy smile that went straight to his blue eyes. 'I'm also sick of the cold. Say yes.'

'Yes.'

Lucerne hugged her tighter, and placed a kiss in the centre of her forehead. 'That's settled, then,' he said as his lips grazed her skin. 'You, me and Vaughan.'

'Wait a minute.' Bella pushed him away, a feeling of betrayal building inside her chest. 'You never mentioned Vaughan. I never agreed to that. I suppose you've already invited him.'

Lucerne shook his head. 'I haven't, actually. I was hoping you'd do it.'

Incensed, Bella felt the colour drain from her lips. 'I will not,' she snarled. Why did they need Vaughan, anyway? Things were far calmer without him.

Lucerne's elegant brow furrowed. 'And why is that?'

'You need to ask?'

'He's the best person to have around in the city.'

'He's also a son of a bitch. In case you've forgotten, he gambled on me like some fairground sideshow. Why the hell would I want to spend time with him out of choice?'

'Bella, please.'

'No, Lucerne. I won't do it. I've no desire to spend time with him in London or anywhere else, and I'm sure he feels the same. If you must invite him, do so yourself, because I won't.'

Lucerne got to his feet, so that he towered over her. 'If that's your attitude, I think you'd better stay behind.' His expression had hardened so that his high cheekbones stood out and his blue eyes had turned to ice. She'd never seen him look so angry or cold, but his reaction didn't chill her own fury. There was no way she was backing down. It was bad enough sharing Lucerne here at Lauwine; it was unthinkable to expect her to do it in public.

'Fine!' she shouted. 'I'll leave you and Ganymede to your perverted love. I hope you both hang for it.'

Bella slammed the drawing room door closed behind her and fled across the courtyard. Her footsteps crushed the crisp, frosted grass, leaving a clear trail, but she was barely aware of it. Her own angry tears blinded her to everything. One stupid argument and it was all over between her and Lucerne. Blast! She hadn't even told him the truth, but she was damned if she was going to stand there like an idiot while Vaughan told her they'd all rot in hell before he'd share Lucerne again.

'I didn't mean it,' she said to the empty air. A tear splashed on the cracked paving stones at her feet. Stubbornly, she wiped her eyes and then threw her back against a quiet, leafless tree.

'Annabella!' Vaughan dodged between the trees to reach her, while his coat tails flapped in the wind behind him.

'Not now,' she muttered under her breath, but it didn't stop him. He slowed to a walk a few yards from her. She realised that he must have been next door to them in the billiards room and had probably overheard them shouting. Bella held her head up straight and faced him defiantly. 'Have you come to gloat?' she spat.

'Hardly. You just threw Lucerne over. Why?'

Bella looked into his eyes. She expected to see mockery or triumph, but neither was particularly evident in his expression. He grasped her arm and she tried to shake him off, while the sharp prickle of tears throbbed at the corners of her eyes. She blinked very slowly, determined that he wouldn't see her cry.

'Why?'

'Let go of me!'

'Not until you explain. I can't believe you're just going to give up. Where is all your fury?'

Bella couldn't answer; all at once, her throat was as dry as a riverbed in a drought. Vaughan studied her carefully. He tilted her face up with the edge of his index finger and looked at her as though the secret of her actions was written on her face. 'Won't you talk to me?' he asked more gently.

Bella held his gaze for a moment and then looked away. She turned her back on him and walked down to the stream alone.

Bella locked herself in the yellow morning room, out of sight and, she hoped, out of mind of everyone. Since her argument with Lucerne, life at Lauwine Hall had turned sour. In the end she had not immediately quit the hall as she had first intended, but had agreed to stay and keep Louisa company until the wedding. It had made life very hard. This was the last day before the wedding; she had spent three hours alone in her room, packing her trunk as the endless minutes ticked by, and she tried to summon enough courage to propel herself through the rest of the day. She was terrified of seeing Lucerne. They had not exchanged a single word or masochistic glance since he'd told her it was over, and she feared that if she saw him now she would cause a scene.

The sound of a key turning in the lock broke into her thoughts. She turned towards it in resignation. Vaughan entered without waiting for her invitation, closed the door and locked it behind him. 'I had a suspicion that I might find you here,' he said.

Bella turned her back to him and stared at the window. The outside world was completely obscured by ivy, so she watched a spider scuttle along the ledge. She heard Vaughan's soft footfalls, and pictured him drawing his jewelled fingers through the locks of his hair as he moved towards her. His scent ran through the musty air, herbal with a musky base. She stiffened as she felt his presence immediately behind her.

'Who exactly are you hiding from?' he asked.

'Who's hiding?'

'You are.' He exhaled forcefully, and took another step towards her. She watched him as he watched her in the dark glass. 'I think you owe me an explanation and Lucerne an apology.'

'Is that right,' she snapped, the hairs rising on the back of her neck. 'What for, precisely? Letting you win?'

Instead of rising to the argument, Vaughan sighed wearily and rested his hands upon her shoulders, but his touch was too disturbing to Bella and she quickly shrugged him off.

'If you must put it like that, yes,' he said. 'Why did you refuse his request?'

'Perhaps I outgrew my infatuation of him.'

Vaughan shook his head of dark locks. 'Infatuation? I think not. That would be Louisa's province, well, at one time, anyway. Why don't you tell me the real reason?'

'Go to hell.' Bella stepped away from him. She didn't want the reminders of his scent and heat addling her thoughts. She noticed him turn to watch her as she fidgeted with the front lacing of her dress. 'Just leave me alone,' she pleaded in a much softer voice.

'As you wish.'

Too easy, she thought, as he turned towards the locked door. He paused and held her gaze.

'You did it because of me,' he guessed.

'My arse. I did it for me.'

'I said because of me, not for me, Bella.' He reached

out then and gripped her firmly about the arm. Bella struggled and tried to pull away, but his grip was steely. She kicked him, but he still didn't let go.

'Stop it!'

Bella continued to struggle and kicked him again. This time he released her, and like a cat she lashed at his face with her nails. The scratches drew blood.

'Hellion!'

Vaughan caught her hands and pinned them to her sides, then walked her back three paces to the wall, where he forced their bodies into contact from hip to shin. 'Just this once, will you listen to me?'

Bella opened her mouth to scream, but before the cry left her mouth, his lips were against hers, and his body pressed against her laced bodice and imprisoned breasts. She panted. Her heart beat wildly as she met his eyes. He bent to kiss her again, pausing just before their lips met. 'Why?'

'He wanted you in London with us. I was to invite you.'

'So?'

'You'd have laughed in my face.'

'Not true. I would have been offended, but I might have come round to the idea.'

Bella shook her head. 'You bet on me like a horse. You made it clear that you were unwilling to share Lucerne.'

Vaughan sighed. He brushed a loose curl back from her face. 'Perhaps I was equally unwilling to share you.' As if to confirm this he pressed his solid erection against her. Bella wasn't fooled. She knew he was lying, but she didn't want to reject the gesture, although if she denied him he'd probably take what he wanted anyway. She turned her face to the side.

'Damn it all, Bella! Don't be so bloody obstinate.' His lips met hers and she felt the nip of his teeth. She gave in, clasped his buttocks as he pulled up her skirts, and wrenched open his breeches.

Vaughan lifted her against the wall, and lowered her onto his shaft. As he slid easily into her, she gasped and struggled to get him deeper, then she twined her calves around his thighs and clawed his back, while he dug his fingers into her bottom. This might be my last chance, she realised, as Vaughan snarled his passion. She twisted his hair around her fingers and pulled to stop him biting her lips. In response, he drove her powerfully and repeatedly against the wall until they gasped and sobbed out their orgasms. As they came down, Bella buried her face in his rosemary-scented hair and clung to him as tightly as she could.

She never wanted to let go.

Bella lay in a daze, contented providing she didn't think too hard, happy for the moment just to lie in Vaughan's arms and be warmed by his body. Vaughan lay with his head on her stomach with one arm circling her thigh, while his fingers lightly combed through her pubic hair. 'Behave, Vaughan,' she said half-heartedly, before attempting to swat him away. 'It's cruel.'

'I know.' And he did it some more.

'Behave, you'll drive me wild.'

'That is the plan.' He drew a pattern on her belly with a fingertip, and seemed greatly pleased with himself when her body arched upwards in response.

'Vaughan,' she gasped. He kissed her navel and sat up to straddle her hips. 'Oh!' She saw his renewed erection rear above her stomach as he pinned her down. A jewel of pre-come glistened at the tip. Vaughan smeared it over the head of his cock then, taking himself in hand, he pressed his glans to her body and began to move it slowly across her skin, leaving behind a silvery trail.

'What are you doing?' she asked, deeply suspicious.

'Writing your name. W . . . H . . . O . . . R . . .'

'No!' she shrieked in outrage, and tried to wipe it off. The glistening trail smeared over her skin. 'Urgh, you've made me all sticky,' she protested, and wrinkled her nose.

Vaughan shuffled up her body until his cock stood poised above her bosom. 'Bella, I've barely begun.' To her indignation, he lifted one breast in each hand and moulded her cleavage around himself. Then he began to slide his prick back and forth within the soft prison.

'Vaughan!'

The head was visible with every thrust, pointed directly at her neck and face.

'Hmmm? I'm fine, thank you.'

She sighed in vexation. Helpless, she had no alternative but to shut her eyes and turn her face away. A few moments later he gave a drawn-out cry and a thick jet of semen splashed across her cheek. The rest pooled on her neck and breasts, leaving her slick and soiled.

Vaughan sighed in contentment and wiped his cock on her belly. 'Thank you so very much,' he said with a grin.

Bella pushed him away. She sat up, incensed, and tried to slap him, but he easily evaded her clumsy swing. Her skin was shiny with come that glistened like mother-of-pearl. She scooped up some of the sticky mess and flung it at him. Vaughan laughed, even when it hit him, and easily pinned her down. When she struggled he leaned in and licked her face clean. 'Hush,' he said before he kissed her.

Afterwards they sat outside on the stone steps together, talking. Bella smoothed out the crushed satin of her gown and gazed up at him, somewhat dazed. Vaughan sat with his knees folded up before him, his cheek pressed against his knee, and his long hair tumbling in a reckless cascade over his face.

'He'll forgive you,' he said, but Bella shook her head.

'Not after what I said.'

'Nothing you might say could make it that bad. Hell, I'll admit he's rather hurt at the moment and it may take him some time to come around, but that's because he loves you and it's always worse coming from those you love.'

He watched her drawn expression, and Bella felt his concern. When her own frown didn't break up, he matched it with a slightly worried look of his own. 'What did you say to him?' he asked.

'That I'd leave you two to your perverted love and that I hoped you'd both hang for it.'

'Vicious! Anything more?'

'Nothing. Oh, I called you Ganymede.'

Vaughan frowned then suddenly his mood broke and he laughed. 'Ganymede!' He almost choked on his own mirth. 'I've never seen myself as a cup-bearer. Don't worry, Bella.' He put his arm around her. 'I'm sure we'll get him to see the funny side.'

She hoped he was right.

# 16

The morning of the wedding came like salvation day, but Bella remained unsure of how she would be judged. She rose late to give herself just enough time to dress before breakfast. Lucerne still hadn't spoken to her and, if Vaughan had conveyed her feelings to him, the marquis hadn't reported that to her. She packed her last belongings into a large cloth bag and then descended the stairs. After arriving at Lauwine with little she was destined to leave with less, since now her hopes were gone. If Vaughan hadn't worked a miracle by now, it was too late: she was returning to the Grange, while they were leaving to spend the rest of the winter in the more civilised south. Lucerne, it seemed, had finally realised that winter in the country was only for the truly hardy. Bella was more or less resigned to a life full of the worn-out joys of Wyndfell Grange.

Louisa was waiting for her in the hall; she looked truly radiant in her cream satin dress. 'I'm really nervous,' she confessed as she linked arms with Bella, and they walked into the dining room. Lucerne wasn't present; instead Vaughan sat at the head of the table. He was already eating. Bella took one look at the poached kippers and lost her appetite.

'Not hungry?' he said to her. His gaze flicked over her face, but his expression was unreadable. Bella shook her head, and prayed he'd give her some good news.

'It'll be a long day. You should eat.'

Her heart dropped into her stomach.

Shortly after twelve, they set off in the carriage for the little Norman church where the service was to be held. Reverend Hindes, the ancient parish priest who had christened both Bella and Joshua, lisped his way through the vows in the same deadpan style that served him equally well for all occasions. The congregation emerged stiffly an hour later to find a white blanket of fresh snow laid across the green, and snowflakes still swirling in the air.

Bella managed an outward smile for the small party of guests who retired to the Grange for refreshments. In the comfort of her childhood home, she could pretend that she'd never been away, and that the last few months hadn't happened. People mulled around her and tried to draw her attention with small talk. However, even complaints that she'd been neglecting them didn't gain them more than a brief, semi-apologetic, 'Sorry'.

Louisa caught up with Bella after lunch on her tour of the guests. 'I've just had a letter from Mr Pryce,' she said. 'It was all a hoax. The poor man was locked in the bell tower of St Mary's and wasn't rescued until the vicar went to investigate the strange noises. He's only just recovered.'

'So you're not destitute any more.'

'No, I suppose not. I haven't told Frederick yet. I thought I'd save it for later.'

Bella nodded. 'Probably wise. Mind you, it's a bit late for him to change his mind now.'

'Thank God,' said Louisa. 'I've also heard from Charles. Just a quick note, delivered by his estate manager, to say congratulations and an apology for his absence. Apparently, he's in final negotiations with his publisher.'

'Nothing to do with a debt to Vaughan,' Bella remarked dryly. 'I don't suppose there was a return address.'

'Now you mention it, no, there wasn't.'

Bella looked up as Louisa moved on, to find Lucerne observing her, and her half-smile faded. His attention made her wince. She tried to ignore him but with Vaughan also at his side that was impossible. They were beautiful together, darkness and light, and hers weren't the only eyes in the room directed towards them. Beside her, Mrs Castleton was speculating on who would capture Lucerne, but even this notorious matchmaker seemed wary of discussing Vaughan. Bella sighed. She might love them both, but she was sure she'd ruined her chances with either.

Frederick found her to say goodbye as the guests crowded onto the lawn. They left the house together, their footprints leaving indents in the already crushed snow. Neither of them spoke much. The brief moment they'd once shared together remained safely in the past. Bella gave him a kiss then turned to Louisa, while he withdrew several discreet paces.

'Will you . . .'

'Can you . . .'

They stopped. Louisa's wide blue eyes clouded over briefly.

'I'll be fine,' Bella said. 'If you'll be happy.'

'I'll do my best. Frederick's received orders to join his regiment in India,' Louisa responded doubtfully. 'We might be there for years. Promise you'll write.'

'I promise. Good luck.' They held each other for several moments.

Bella waited with Vaughan while the couple boarded their carriage. She sensed that he had something to say, and that it was almost certainly goodbye. Unwilling to face the inevitable, she stubbornly looked at her own feet. The snow had melted around her shoes, staining the green satin with water marks. His solid leather boots were far more suitable to the season. Helplessly, she let her gaze drift upwards, to take in the line of charcoal-grey fabric that lay against the black satin. From there, she glanced across his skirted coat, admiring the sparkling beads. He looked like a priceless treasure, and she realised now just how much she wanted to keep him. There was a tightening in her chest as her vision reached the ends of his black ringlets. A few fleeting glances across his face, and she found herself looking into his glittering eyes.

Bella shivered under his scrutiny, half aroused and half-afraid. It felt as if it had taken a lifetime to look over the length of his body, though in truth it had been little over ten seconds.

'Well, are you coming or not?' he said, and pointed to the crested carriage that dominated the driveway.

Bella stared at him, totally confused and unsure of his meaning. To where, exactly? London? Behind him, she saw Lucerne climb the step into the interior. Suitably enigmatic, Vaughan extended his arm for her to take.

'What about Lucerne?' she asked.

'Lucerne be damned. I'm asking you.'

'But . . .'

She looked back at the stony façade of Wyndfell Grange then across at the carriage. There was no choice to make; Joshua would understand. She accepted Vaughan's arm.

With his assistance, she climbed aboard into the cold, leather-scented interior. A warm hand touched her own, and she knew it was Lucerne. Behind her, Vaughan rapped his knuckles against the roof. 'Drive on,' he called, and the carriage jolted forwards.

Bella reached out blindly; Lucerne's arms snaked around her waist and pulled her into the seat beside him. He kissed her forehead, and then her cheek. 'I'm glad you came. I feared you wouldn't, that you'd still be too cross . . .'

'I'm an idiot, I always wanted to come,' she confessed. 'I'm just too stubborn.'

Vaughan, who had sat down opposite, was nodding his head in agreement, but now that he had their attention he reached into an inner pocket and pulled out several large pieces of official-looking paper. He glanced over them; the debt bonds were enough to make a man modestly wealthy.

'What are those?' Bella asked.

Vaughan smiled, the same unguarded smile he'd given her back at the start of November when he'd invited her to share his joke in the yellow morning room. 'An Italian carnival tradition,' he said, and he tore them into several small squares then cast the pieces out of the window. '*Confetti.*'

# LOOK OUT FOR THE ALL-NEW BLACK LACE BOOKS – AVAILABLE NOW!

*All books priced £7.99 in the UK. Please note publication dates apply to the UK only. For other territories, please contact your retailer.*

**THE SILVER CAGE**
***Mathilde Madden***
ISBN 978 0 352 34165 5

Iris and Alfie have been driven apart by the strongest forces in the werewolf world – the powerful thrall of the Divine Wolf – the mother of them all. Now Iris needs to win Alfie back, not just for herself, but because the fate of the world could depend upon it.

But the only way to free Alfie from the power of the Divine Wolf is to kill her. Something that could end the lives of all werewolves. Including Alfie himself – Iris' true love.

**POSSESSION**

***Mathilde Madden, Madelynne Ellis, Anne Tourney***

ISBN 978 0 352 34164 8

Falling Dancer: Kelda has two jobs: full-time bartender, part-time exorcist. She meets vengeful spirits and misguided demons wherever she goes. She wishes the spirit world would leave her alone so she could have a relationship that lasted longer than twenty-four hours, but when she's contacted by a sexy musician who wants her to solve the mystery of his girlfriend's disappearance, she can't help getting involved . . .

The Silver Chains: Alfie Friday is a werewolf. For 7 years he has controlled his curse carefully by locking himself in a cage every full moon. But now he's changing when it isn't full moon. His girlfriend Misty travels to South America to try and find a way of controlling Alfie's changes, but discovers the key to the problem lies in Oxford. The place it all began for Alfie and the place he has vowed never to return to.

Broken Angel: After stealing a copy of an ancient manuscript, Blaze Makaresh finds himself being hunted down by a gang of youkai – demons who infiltrate human society in order to satisfy their hunger for sex and flesh. When the Talon, an elitist society of demon-hunters, come to his aid, he's soon enmeshed with the beautiful Asha, and the dawning of an age-old prophecy.

To be published in March 2008

**CASSANDRA'S CONFLICT**
*Fredrica Alleyn*
ISBN 978 0 352 34186 0

A house in Hampstead. Present-day. Behind a façade of cultured respectability lies a world of decadent indulgence and dark eroticism. Cassandra's sheltered life is transformed when she gets employed as governess to the Baron's children. He draws her into games where lust can feed on the erotic charge of submission. Games where only he knows the rules and where unusual pleasures can flourish.

**PHANTASMAGORIA**
***Madelynne Ellis***
ISBN 978 0 352 34168 6

1800 – Three years after escaping to London with her bisexual lovers, Bella Rushdale wakes one morning to find their delicate ménage-a-trois on the verge of shattering. Vaughan, Marquis of Pennerley has left abruptly and without any explanation. Determined to reclaim him and preserve their relationship, Bella pursues the errant Marquis to his family seat on the Welsh Borders where she finds herself embroiled in his preparations for a diabolical gothic celebration on All Hallows Eve – a phantasmagoria! Among the shadows and phantoms Bella and her lovers will peel away the deceits and desires of the past and future.

## To be published in April 2008

**GOTHIC HEAT**
*Portia Da Costa*
ISBN 978 0 352 34170 9

Paula Beckett has a problem. The spirit of the wicked and voluptuous sorceress Isidora Katori is trying to possess her body and Paula finds herself driven by dark desires and a delicious wanton recklessness. Rafe Hathaway is irresistibly drawn to both women. But who will he finally choose – feisty and sexy Paula, who is fighting impossible odds to hang on to her very existence, or sultry and ruthless Isidora, who offers him the key to immortality?

**GEMINI HEAT**
*Portia Da Costa*
ISBN 978 0 352 34187 7

As the metropolis sizzles in the freak early summer temperatures, identical twin sisters Deana and Delia Ferraro are cooking up a heat wave of their own. Surrounded by an atmosphere of relentless humidity, Deanna and Delia find themselves rivals for the attentions of Jackson de Guile, an exotic, wealthy entrepreneur and master of power dynamics who draws them both into a web of luxurious debauchery. The erotic encounters become increasingly bizarre as the twins vie for the rewards that pleasuring him brings them – tainted rewards which only serve to confuse their perceptions of the limits of sexual experience.

**THE NEW BLACK LACE BOOK OF WOMEN'S SEXUAL FANTASIES**

***Edited and compiled by Mitzi Szereto***

ISBN 978 0 352 34172 3

The second anthology of detailed sexual fantasies contributed by women from all over the world. The book is a result of a year's research by an expert on erotic writing and gives a fascinating insight into the rich diversity of the female sexual imagination.

# Black Lace Booklist

Information is correct at time of printing. To avoid disappointment, check availability before ordering. Go to www.black-lace-books.com. All books are priced £7.99 unless another price is given.

**BLACK LACE BOOKS WITH A CONTEMPORARY SETTING**

- ❑ ALWAYS THE BRIDEGROOM Tesni Morgan ISBN 978 0 352 33855 6 £6.99
- ❑ THE ANGELS' SHARE Maya Hess ISBN 978 0 352 34043 6
- ❑ ASKING FOR TROUBLE Kristina Lloyd ISBN 978 0 352 33362 9
- ❑ BLACK LIPSTICK KISSES Monica Belle ISBN 978 0 352 33885 3 £6.99
- ❑ THE BLUE GUIDE Carrie Williams ISBN 978 0 352 34132 7
- ❑ THE BOSS Monica Belle ISBN 978 0 352 34088 7
- ❑ BOUND IN BLUE Monica Belle ISBN 978 0 352 34012 2
- ❑ CAMPAIGN HEAT Gabrielle Marcola ISBN 978 0 352 33941 6
- ❑ CAT SCRATCH FEVER Sophie Mouette ISBN 978 0 352 34021 4
- ❑ CIRCUS EXCITE Nikki Magennis ISBN 978 0 352 34033 7
- ❑ CLUB CRÈME Primula Bond ISBN 978 0 352 33907 2 £6.99
- ❑ COMING ROUND THE MOUNTAIN Tabitha Flyte ISBN 978 0 352 33873 0 £6.99
- ❑ CONFESSIONAL Judith Roycroft ISBN 978 0 352 33421 3
- ❑ CONTINUUM Portia Da Costa ISBN 978 0 352 33120 5
- ❑ DANGEROUS CONSEQUENCES Pamela Rochford ISBN 978 0 352 33185 4
- ❑ DARK DESIGNS Madelynne Ellis ISBN 978 0 352 34075 7
- ❑ THE DEVIL INSIDE Portia Da Costa ISBN 978 0 352 32993 6
- ❑ EDEN'S FLESH Robyn Russell ISBN 978 0 352 33923 2 £6.99
- ❑ EQUAL OPPORTUNITIES Mathilde Madden ISBN 978 0 352 34070 2
- ❑ FIRE AND ICE Laura Hamilton ISBN 978 0 352 33486 2
- ❑ GOING DEEP Kimberly Dean ISBN 978 0 352 33876 1 £6.99
- ❑ GONE WILD Maria Eppie ISBN 978 0 352 33670 5
- ❑ HOTBED Portia Da Costa ISBN 978 0 352 33614 9
- ❑ IN PURSUIT OF ANNA Natasha Rostova ISBN 978 0 352 34060 3
- ❑ IN THE FLESH Emma Holly ISBN 978 0 352 34117 4
- ❑ LEARNING TO LOVE IT Alison Tyler ISBN 978 0 352 33535 7

- ❑ MAD ABOUT THE BOY Mathilde Madden ISBN 978 0 352 34001 6
- ❑ MAKE YOU A MAN Anna Clare ISBN 978 0 352 34006 1
- ❑ MAN HUNT Cathleen Ross ISBN 978 0 352 33583 8
- ❑ THE MASTER OF SHILDEN Lucinda Carrington ISBN 978 0 352 33140 3
- ❑ MIXED DOUBLES Zoe le Verdier ISBN 978 0 352 33312 4 £6.99
- ❑ MIXED SIGNALS Anna Clare ISBN 978 0 352 33889 1 £6.99
- ❑ MS BEHAVIOUR Mini Lee ISBN 978 0 352 33962 1
- ❑ PACKING HEAT Karina Moore ISBN 978 0 352 33356 8 £6.99
- ❑ PAGAN HEAT Monica Belle ISBN 978 0 352 33974 4
- ❑ PEEP SHOW Mathilde Madden ISBN 978 0 352 33924 9
- ❑ THE POWER GAME Carrera Devonshire ISBN 978 0 352 33990 4
- ❑ THE PRIVATE UNDOING OF A PUBLIC SERVANT Leonie Martel ISBN 978 0 352 34066 5
- ❑ RELEASE ME Suki Cunningham ISBN 978 0 352 33671 2 £6.99
- ❑ RUDE AWAKENING Pamela Kyle ISBN 978 0 352 33036 9
- ❑ SAUCE FOR THE GOOSE Mary Rose Maxwell ISBN 978 0 352 33492 3
- ❑ SLAVE TO SUCCESS Kimberley Raines ISBN 978 0 352 33687 3 £6.99
- ❑ STELLA DOES HOLLYWOOD Stella Black ISBN 978 0 352 33588 3
- ❑ THE STRANGER Portia Da Costa ISBN 978 0 352 33211 0
- ❑ SUITE SEVENTEEN Portia Da Costa ISBN 978 0 352 34109 9
- ❑ SWITCHING HANDS Alaine Hood ISBN 978 0 352 33896 9 £6.99
- ❑ TONGUE IN CHEEK Tabitha Flyte ISBN 978 0 352 33484 8
- ❑ THE TOP OF HER GAME Emma Holly ISBN 978 0 352 34116 7
- ❑ TWO WEEKS IN TANGIER Annabel Lee ISBN 978 0 352 33599 9 £6.99
- ❑ UNNATURAL SELECTION Alaine Hood ISBN 978 0 352 33963 8
- ❑ VELVET GLOVE Emma Holly ISBN 978 0 352 34115 0
- ❑ VILLAGE OF SECRETS Mercedes Kelly ISBN 978 0 352 33344 5
- ❑ WILD BY NATURE Monica Belle ISBN 978 0 352 33915 7 £6.99
- ❑ WILD CARD Madeline Moore ISBN 978 0 352 34038 2
- ❑ WING OF MADNESS Mae Nixon ISBN 978 0 352 34099 3

**BLACK LACE BOOKS WITH AN HISTORICAL SETTING**

- ❑ THE AMULET Lisette Allen ISBN 978 0 352 33019 2 £6.99
- ❑ THE BARBARIAN GEISHA Charlotte Royal ISBN 978 0 352 33267 7
- ❑ BARBARIAN PRIZE Deanna Ashford ISBN 978 0 352 34017 7
- ❑ THE CAPTIVATION Natasha Rostova ISBN 978 0 352 33234 9

- ❑ DARKER THAN LOVE Kristina Lloyd ISBN 978 0 352 33279 0
- ❑ FRENCH MANNERS Olivia Christie ISBN 978 0 352 33214 1
- ❑ LORD WRAXALL'S FANCY Anna Lieff Saxby ISBN 978 0 352 33080 2
- ❑ NICOLE'S REVENGE Lisette Allen ISBN 978 0 352 32984 4
- ❑ THE SENSES BEJEWELLED Cleo Cordell ISBN 978 0 352 32904 2 £6.99
- ❑ THE SOCIETY OF SIN Sian Lacey Taylder ISBN 978 0 352 34080 1
- ❑ TEMPLAR PRIZE Deanna Ashford ISBN 978 0 352 34137 2
- ❑ UNDRESSING THE DEVIL Angel Strand ISBN 978 0 352 33938 6

**BLACK LACE BOOKS WITH A PARANORMAL THEME**

- ❑ BRIGHT FIRE Maya Hess ISBN 978 0 352 34104 4
- ❑ BURNING BRIGHT Janine Ashbless ISBN 978 0 352 34085 6
- ❑ CRUEL ENCHANTMENT Janine Ashbless ISBN 978 0 352 33483 1
- ❑ DIVINE TORMENT Janine Ashbless ISBN 978 0 352 33719 1
- ❑ FLOOD Anna Clare ISBN 978 0 352 34094 8
- ❑ GOTHIC BLUE Portia Da Costa ISBN 978 0 352 33075 8
- ❑ THE PRIDE Edie Bingham ISBN 978 0 352 33997 3
- ❑ THE SILVER COLLAR Mathilde Madden ISBN 978 0 352 34141 9
- ❑ THE TEN VISIONS Olivia Knight ISBN 978 0 352 34119 8

**BLACK LACE ANTHOLOGIES**

- ❑ BLACK LACE QUICKIES 1 Various ISBN 978 0 352 34126 6 £2.99
- ❑ BLACK LACE QUICKIES 2 Various ISBN 978 0 352 34127 3 £2.99
- ❑ BLACK LACE QUICKIES 3 Various ISBN 978 0 352 34128 0 £2.99
- ❑ BLACK LACE QUICKIES 4 Various ISBN 978 0 352 34129 7 £2.99
- ❑ BLACK LACE QUICKIES 5 Various ISBN 978 0 352 34130 3 £2.99
- ❑ BLACK LACE QUICKIES 6 Various ISBN 978 0 352 34133 4 £2.99
- ❑ BLACK LACE QUICKIES 7 Various ISBN 978 0 352 34146 4 £2.99
- ❑ BLACK LACE QUICKIES 8 Various ISBN 978 0 352 34147 1 £2.99
- ❑ MORE WICKED WORDS Various ISBN 978 0 352 33487 9 £6.99
- ❑ WICKED WORDS 3 Various ISBN 978 0 352 33522 7 £6.99
- ❑ WICKED WORDS 4 Various ISBN 978 0 352 33603 3 £6.99
- ❑ WICKED WORDS 5 Various ISBN 978 0 352 33642 2 £6.99
- ❑ WICKED WORDS 6 Various ISBN 978 0 352 33690 3 £6.99
- ❑ WICKED WORDS 7 Various ISBN 978 0 352 33743 6 £6.99
- ❑ WICKED WORDS 8 Various ISBN 978 0 352 33787 0 £6.99

❑ WICKED WORDS 9 Various ISBN 978 0 352 33860 0
❑ WICKED WORDS 10 Various ISBN 978 0 352 33893 8
❑ THE BEST OF BLACK LACE 2 Various ISBN 978 0 352 33718 4
❑ WICKED WORDS: SEX IN THE OFFICE Various ISBN 978 0 352 33944 7
❑ WICKED WORDS: SEX AT THE SPORTS CLUB Various ISBN 978 0 352 33991 1
❑ WICKED WORDS: SEX ON HOLIDAY Various ISBN 978 0 352 33961 4
❑ WICKED WORDS: SEX IN UNIFORM Various ISBN 978 0 352 34002 3
❑ WICKED WORDS: SEX IN THE KITCHEN Various ISBN 978 0 352 34018 4
❑ WICKED WORDS: SEX ON THE MOVE Various ISBN 978 0 352 34034 4
❑ WICKED WORDS: SEX AND MUSIC Various ISBN 978 0 352 34061 0
❑ WICKED WORDS: SEX AND SHOPPING Various ISBN 978 0 352 34076 4
❑ SEX IN PUBLIC Various ISBN 978 0 352 34089 4
❑ SEX WITH STRANGERS Various ISBN 978 0 352 34105 1
❑ LOVE ON THE DARK SIDE Various ISBN 978 0 352 34132 7

**BLACK LACE NON-FICTION**

❑ THE BLACK LACE BOOK OF WOMEN'S SEXUAL FANTASIES Edited by Kerri Sharp ISBN 978 0 352 33793 1 £6.99

To find out the latest information about Black Lace titles, check out the website: www.black-lace-books.com or send for a booklist with complete synopses by writing to:

Black Lace Booklist, Virgin Books Ltd
Thames Wharf Studios
Rainville Road
London W6 9HA

Please include an SAE of decent size. Please note only British stamps are valid.

Our privacy policy
We will not disclose information you supply us to any other parties. We will not disclose any information which identifies you personally to any person without your express consent.

From time to time we may send out information about Black Lace books and special offers. Please tick here if you do not wish to receive Black Lace information. ❑